Since the Riots

MELISSA JANE KNIGHT

ACKNOWLEDGMENTS

To the young people, especially in Lewisham, Southwark, Greenwich and Lambeth. Thank you for giving more than you can ever know. It's been an honour to watch so many of you grow.

To my immigrant mother, single parent, who helped me become who I am today. To the boys I fancied, and all the pen-pen pals in Y.O.I. To the girls I hung with until it all fell apart. To my own youth workers – Lianna, Nick, Steve, Mark – introducing teenage me to words like community inclusion, equal opportunities, social justice. To GYPC.

To Stephen Lawrence RIP; your murder hung over our heads at Blackheath Bluecoats and helped ensure we were one of the first schools to receive black history education.

To Goldsmiths & the LSE for teaching me more than transatlantic slavery.

To my husband Thaddäus, our children and my entire patchwork global family, especially my siblings: writer, Julia Knight-Williams for your expertise, Andrei for your guidance, and James for always fixing my laptop.

Thanks to proof readers: Dorian Lovett, Vidula Kotian, Angus Hanton, Thaddäus Knight, Kara Towers, Danielle Smith, and Tony Laverty, and members of the Alt-Stralau Writers Group: Deborah Ben Nun, Ummul Kadir Chodhury, Elizabeth Jacyshyn-Owen, Jenny Feuerpeil, Emma Maar, Alejandro Sánchez, Patricia Ann Crossen and Stéphanie Dussault.

To Roslyn Edwards at FillyaBelly for checking my patois.

Thanks to Dwayne Clarke and Kris Webb for managing the book launch.

To Clemens Majunke for the promotional film and all the young people who took part in the book trailer: www.clemensmajunke.com.

Finally, and most importantly, the staff at Kita Weserwichtel in Berlin. This paperback novel has been made possible thanks to your childcare.

DEDICATION

This book is dedicated to Boris Johnson. You were mayor of London at the time of the riots. A decade later, the prime minister.

INTRODUCTION

In August 2011, riots erupted across England. Big cities like London, Manchester, and Birmingham blazed as shops and cars were looted and set alight.

The public were shocked. Outraged, we judged and scapegoated sub-groups and communities: the young, the black, the poor, the uneducated.

Our anger may have stemmed from a response mechanism, helping us to come to terms with the destruction, to understand the chaos. How anyone could do so much damage on their own streets, harm to their own shopkeepers, their own neighbours?

When the riots erupted, I had been a youth worker in Lewisham for nine years. Nine years working with a whole spectrum of young people: posh, poor, abused, cushioned, gifted, struggling, you name it. From teenagers seemingly throwing their education down the drain to those handed learning difficulties from foetal alcohol syndrome still battling the battering of alcoholic parents. Boys grappling with life after their dads were found dead in police cells or rough sleeping. Girls groomed for sexual exploitation, performing line-ups, that is, forced to suck several dicks in a row or else be beaten up, then silenced by the threat of being exposed online.

I worked at a motorbike project, delivering life skills workshops and at a Pupil Referral Unit, running sex education programmes and one-to-one guidance. I also ran several youth theatre groups. There were good days, taking boys destined for prison to the top executives in the apex of Canary Wharf's Barclays Bank, telling them, 'This could be you one day' and I meant it. Taking girls with reports that said they can't sit still and concentrate for even a minute and watching them carefully make pasta from scratch in Jamie Oliver's Fifteen kitchen in London's Old Street. Watching proud as RBS handed out certificates to an all-black group of young entrepreneurs who spent their evenings in workshops with me listening to professionals teach them about communication, advertising, elevator pitches: 'If you do what you love, you'll never work a day in your life!' That was eight years ago and some still haven't found a decent job.

Work regularly brought tears to my eyes, both good and bad. I've pulled knives from various socks and got between fist fights while carrying a baby in my belly. But I'm no hero. And this isn't about me.

I wasn't surprised many of the young people I worked with rioted. I was surprised by the response from adults. Our current Prime Minister, Boris Johnson, who was London's Mayor at the time, called for tanks laden with water cannons; he even bought them as if pushing someone away hard enough ever stopped them coming back. Especially those with little to lose.

When stories emerged of the rich looting and posh kids breaking shop fronts, those young people were met with disgust, as if having money means a problem-free life; that wealth, somehow, shelters us from being damaged and wanting to tear up our home. Actually being wealthy often prevents kids from entering social services, because we still believe, on the whole, that if someone's rich, they've got nothing to complain about.

I was already thinking of writing this book. To try to open up a dialogue, to explore the nuances in youth culture, the sub-cultures, the judgements, the misunderstandings.

When my blog post on the riots went viral, I realised most of us want to know about these young people. We want to hear their voices. We want to grasp the complexities. We want to know how to solve this.

Since the Riots is a window into the world of British youth culture, particularly from inner-city London, and a lot of what's in here is based on many of the teenagers I have worked with as well as my own school life and adolescence.

*

You may be a mum or dad, with your children hitting puberty. Or a teacher, looking for clues. You may be training to be a social worker or youth worker. Or better still, you're a police officer or policy maker. Hopefully, you're an elected politician.

This book is for them, our young people, and for you, their protectors, mentors, carers and sometimes, unfortunately their enemies.

MELISSA JANE KNIGHT, AUGUST 2021

CHAPTER 1

AUGUST 2010 – A YEAR BEFORE THE RIOTS…

'Issy!' Carol calls from the downstairs, 'Hayley's down 'ere.'

The bedroom door belonging to the fifteen year old slams shut, muffling Kiss FM radio, playing *LDN* by Lilly Allen.

'Is-o-bel,' Carol yells louder starting a coughing fit.

'You need to give up those fags, Carol,' Hayley says sarcastically, her hand out to imply she'll help by taking them off her.

'Get out of it,' Carol says between coughs.

Hayley grins as she dodges Carol's playful whack. Leaning on the wall between the living room doorway and the corridor of Carol and Issy's two-bedroom flat, Hayley takes off one of her Nike Air Max trainers, skinny blue jeans turned up to avoid the ends scuffing against the floor. Her white and pink trainers match her tight vest top and her purple laces match the ribbons in her hair. Both Issy and Hayley wear the same size shoe and have this trend of wearing one foot of each other's trainers. It's like their thing.

'Just go up and get 'er,' Carol says.

'I don't wanna get sucked in,' Hayley replies. 'That room's like the twilight zone.' But Hayley belts up the creaky stairs towards her friend.

'And tell 'er to turn that racket down,' Carol calls after the thuds.

'The crap they listen to,' Carol mutters, wrapping her pale blue towelling dressing gown around her waist, returning to her sofa. It's Carol's day off, which routinely includes catch-up television over a pack of pink wafers, forty cigarettes, and a fresh pot of Tetley.

'You deaf?' Hayley says, bursting into Issy's room and jumping on her single bed. Each spring felt dearly, as she lies back.

Issy turns down the music. 'What?'

'Half of London's been calling you.'

'Ain't you supposed to be with your mentor?' Issy asks.

'Can't be arsed. It's well hot out there.'

Issy frowns.

Hayley ignores her: 'You look shit.'

'Do I?' Issy inspects herself in the mirror.

'Joking. You alright?'

'I'm knackered.'

'Chatting to Jerome?' Hayley asks, having a nose around Issy's bedside table.

'Obviously.'

'What the fuck do you two talk about? Don't think I've ever been on the phone to Dwayne for more than a minute, bruv.'

'Stuff,' Issy blushes, carefully putting down the hair straighteners so they don't burn the plastic cover painted with fruit to protect the already battered dresser.

'Look what he gave me,' Issy hands Hayley a passport photo of Jerome, one eyebrow up, holding his chin, pouting like a rap star.

Hayley bursts out laughing, 'Is that it?' Hayley starts digging around her gold necklaces, 'Dwayne got me this yesterday,' tugging the chain with a clown attached.

Issy leans over and inspects "the gift".

'Blatantly stolen.'

'No, it ain't!' Hayley pulls the chain away. She pauses, before asking: 'How d'you know?'

'Well, if you look closely, there's dirt in the cracks. Meaning it's not brand new.'

Hayley tucks the clown back into her vest top, like a mother protecting their child from ridicule. 'He probably got it from a pawn shop.'

'He's probably robbed it from some younger. Give it back.'

'I don't care if you're teefed,' Hayley coos, pulling the chain back out again and kissing the clown.

'Yeah, we know,' Issy mutters taking out another section of hair, she continues with her straighteners.

'What's that supposed to mean?'

Instead, Issy focuses on making her highlighted hair as straight and neat as possible before meeting the boys.

'Shops don't mean nothing,' Hayley says after some silence, defending her honour. 'Ronnie told me, they have insurance for teefing. I'm actually doing them a favour.'

'Really now?' Issy looks over at Hayley's raised eyebrows as if stealing cosmetics from the pound shop is a charitable deed.

'They get out of paying tax, or some shit. I dunno, ask Ronnie.'

'Yeah give me his prison number and I'll send a postcard!'

'Funny. Not.' Hayley fidgets, the mattress keeps digging into her ribs.

Issy smiles, thinking of Jerome's smile, the way he licks his lips before winking.

'Oh yeah,' Issy turns sharply, pointing her hair straighteners Hayley's way, 'when we go Savers from now on, you better not steal around me After what Steve said about Joint Enterprise.'

Feeling Issy's glare, Hayley keeps her eyes down, inspecting the passport photo and mumbles something indistinguishable.

'And please get your trainer off my bed sheets; Mum only changed them yesterday!'

'Dwayne's much better looking,' Hayley says, casually throwing Jerome to the floor.

'Oi!' Issy scoops the photo up, stroking and kissing it, before tacking Jerome back onto her mirror, thumb pressed firmly into his forehead.

'Argh, come on!!! It's well nice outside and you've straightened the same bit of hair about five million times!'

'How's it look at the back?'

'Good,' Hayley replies without paying too much attention.

'No bumps?' Issy asks, this time looking over to see Hayley's doing her job.

'None! Now can we get the fuck out of here?'

'Don't carry on like I'm the hair freak!' Issy laughs.

Hayley laughs looking at her own hair, pulled up tightly in a bun; the baby hairs above her forehead intricately gelled into swirled patterns. Hayley's hair is the main reason she's late to school. She loses her temper if it goes wrong and sometimes bunks off altogether.

Issy unplugs her straighteners and smooths any evidence of Hayley's body from her crumpled bed sheets.

'So can we go then m'lady?' Hayley says, opening Issy's bedroom door, bowing like a butler, arm extended, holding out her trainer.

'Oh yes, we may!' Issy grabs the shoe, handing Hayley one of hers.

They both laugh and run down the stairs.

'Fucking hell, wanna break my flat?' Carol shouts from the living room.

'What's wrong?' Issy asks, going into her mum.

'You two. Coming down like two elephants.' Smoke releases through Carol's teeth as she speaks in her weird sort-of Scottish sort-of Cockney accent. She's sitting down with feet up to one side of the faux-leather sofa.

'It ain't our fault this shithole's made of cardboard,' Hayley says.

Issy and Carol both look at her.

'What?' Hayley asks, 'It *is* a shithole.'

'My flat ain't a shithole, thank you,' Carol snaps, pressing the cigarette into the glass ashtray resting between the cracks of the sofa arm.

'It ain't personal or nothing. I live here too, you know. I didn't mean *your* flat in particular.'

'Mum, can I have some money?' Issy asks.

'For what?' Carol asks, already reaching for her handbag.

'Sex and drugs and sausage rolls,' Hayley chuckles.

'Don't be cheeky!' Carol points a finger Hayley's way. 'You lot make me die. I would never dare said that at your age!'

Hayley pokes her tongue out and grins. 'They didn't have Greggs in the Stone Age.'

Carol chuckles. 'Think I've got a few quid.'

Hayley watches Carol hand Issy a fiver from her battered blue leather purse. Hayley looks away, as if the moment is intimate.

Issy grabs the money out her mother's hand, kissing Carol on the cheek. Hayley pretends to puke.

'That's nearly an hour's wages you know,' Carol says.

'Yeah I know, Mum. Love you!'

And the girls run out the flat before Carol asks to see any change.

They hurry down the iron steps of Issy's block. There's never any time pressure, but they're always in a rush, making the older neighbours worry. No one likes to see a teenager running. But most teenagers never think about that.

As London council estates go, it's not the worst but it's in need of repair. Unless you lived there, you wouldn't know its name. Most letters have fallen off all the signs. The usual 'NO Ball Games' signs have the 'NO' scratched off, one replaced with 'suck my Balls.'

The Council recently painted the outside walls cream, but the feel of prison remains – harsh lines of concrete slab floors, steps and corridors. There's a few plants on the green. They dug a massive oval patch of mud that's supposed to be the community garden. Someone sporadically planted rose bushes a few years back but they hardly bloom.

After a short bus ride, listening to rap on loud speaker from Hayley's mobile, Hayley and Issy jump off and head to Lewisham Shopping Centre. They walk arm in arm, left foot, then right foot and every now and then they do this skip-shuffle from a rap video everyone's now rating on YouTube.

'I'm getting fags,' Issy says, 'I'll get them while you–' Issy puts her fingers in quotation position, '"buy" hair gel.'

'Stay with me. What if Teena and them are on road?'

'Hayley, don't wanna go on but you ain't teefing with me.'

'Issy, man, I told you I wouldn't.'

'Fine, come shop.'

Arm in arm they march into Mr Patel's.

'10 Mayfair please?' Issy asks in her most grown up voice.

'ID please?' replies Mr Patel, looking down at his paper.

'What?' Hayley says.

'ID please? Government law changed. You have to be 18 or over and I can't sell cigarettes now without ID.'

They stand there for a while, the two of them, staring at their shopkeeper, Mr Patel seeming uncomfortable with the silence.

'This is fucking stupid,' Hayley shouts, 'You know we're old enough. You always sell us fags.'

'Calm down, Hays,' Issy gently nudges her friend, before switching tactics. 'Mr Patel, we don't have ID today. Can you let us off this one time, please and we'll bring ID next time.'

'Sorry, not my rules. You could be working for the police.'

'Working for police!' Hayley screeches. Issy swallows down the little jump in her chest, 'Do you know what my family think of police?'

Mr Patel, not realising the loaded sentence, tries to soften the rising temper of his little customer, 'Look, last week my cousin was fined five hundred pounds because two young girls – working with police – bought 10 Benson and Hedges without ID.' He sighs heavily, 'No offence, but I can't risk that sort of fine.'

Mr Patel's explanation fails epically.

'Are you thick?' Hayley shouts back. 'We hate police.'

'We don't hate police,' Issy says. 'But we wouldn't do that to you. We always come here.'

'Sorry but I can't risk this,' Mr Patel's voice goes up to a squeak. 'Please, these are not my rules,' he says.

Disgruntled with the wait, the man behind shouts, 'Oi, come on kids. This ice-cream's gonna melt.'

'Who are you calling kids?' Hayley turns to face a mid-thirties stocky man with a shaved head, 'Don't fucking talk to me like that!' Hayley shakes her head violently his way.

Unfazed, the man croaks in his deep cockney tone, 'Well you ain't adults are ya? Behaving like this. I wouldn't serve you two a lollypop.'

'Hayley leave it,' Issy pleads, worried things will escalate. Raising her eyebrows, Issy gently whispers, 'Let's go.'

'No, let's not fucking go,' Hayley stomps her feet in protest. 'Let's buy our fags. Here. Like we always do.'

Two old ladies standing well back, decide to leave the shop.

'Please? I'm losing customers.' Mr Patel curls his spine and places his hands in the prayer position, 'These are not my rules.'

'Fucking little chavs.' The man pushes past Hayley, slamming down coins on the counter. 'Keep the change, mate.'

As he turns, Hayley shouts at the top of her lungs, 'Who are YOU calling a CHAV?!' Grabbing a handful of bubble gums from the counter, she chucks them full pelt at the man's back. 'Fucking prick.'

He turns to face Issy and Hayley, Mr Patel's worried face in the background. The man gives Hayley a dirty look, 'You fucking kidding me?' he spits a series of profanities her way. His white t-shirt tightens over his chest as his anger rises. Issy looks at his well-built upper arms; one with the crest of Arsenal football club peeping through one sleeve, the other a tattoo of a bulldog. His coarsely shaven jaw cracks. He looks Hayley up and down, stretching his fingers then clenching one hand into a tight fist.

'What you gonna do, hit me?' Hayley says in her usual sarcastic tone. Issy stands by her friend, taking deep breaths, hoping this will end without another police arrest or trip to A&E.

They both hold their stares then the man yells: 'Get out the shop.'

Hayley refuses. 'Gonna make me? You ain't my dad.'

He grabs Hayley by the arm. Hayley punches and kicks in all directions as the man grips hold of her, pulling her away from the till area. Issy tries to pull Hayley away from him but he's way too strong.

Mr Patel, a pacifist, stands back in shock. Hayley's like a wild animal. She scratches the man's cheek as he drags Hayley towards the shop's front door. But Hayley resists, her feet kicking over crisps and packets of biscuits.

Just then, the shop bell rings and a little girl clasping a small puppy pops her blonde plaited head in, 'Dad, got my ice cream?'

Hayley falls to the floor. She blinks up to see the cute little girl about seven years old wearing a pretty summer dress and matching sandals with crisp white frilly socks wrapped around tiny ankles. The man notices Hayley's reaction to his daughter's squeaky voice. He kneels down, getting his mouth right near Hayley's ear and in a chilling voice, whispers, 'Your dad must be really proud of you.'

The words pierce through her like a stream of bullets, 'Yeah, yeah, yeah, he, he is, actually,' Hayley mumbles, not understanding fully how and why her anger dissipated. She feels exposed, like she's naked or something.

But the man wasn't interested in any reply. He picks up the ice-cream that got dropped along the kerfuffle and gives it to his daughter: 'Here you go princess. He only had strawberry.'

'Daddy, what was you saying to that lady?' the little girl asks as they leave the shop.

'Lady?' he laughs, 'That ain't no...' his voice fades out into the hot summer sunshine.

The door closes. The bell stops ringing. Mr Patel stands there shocked, not knowing what to do with this teenager. Hayley, crumbled and speechless, hasn't gotten off the floor. The man's words still ringing in her ears. Issy stares at the bubble gum splayed over the shop floor.

'Here, take them,' shouts Mr Patel, slamming a pale blue packet on the counter, picking up the crumpled five-pound-note Carol gave Issy earlier and chucking it in the till, 'But don't come back to my shop again!' he nods firmly to Issy handing her the change.

Issy nods back, 'Sorry for all this,' she says, taking the cigarettes, not checking the change. 'I'll pick all the stuff up,' she adds.

'No. No, please. Just go – please?'

Issy lifts her friend to her feet.

As they leave the shop, Hayley turns to see the man with his daughter in his arms talking to some men outside the pub. He gently strokes a wisp of hair away from the pink-coloured ice-cream on her chin. Meeting Hayley's eyes, he kisses his daughter on her forehead. Hayley looks away. Frustrated, she kicks a nearby bin, 'If his daughta wasn't there, I would've knocked him spark out, bruv.'

CHAPTER 2
THE MUGGING

'I know!' Hayley says, 'Let's text the boys and whoever texts back first is gonna marry us and have our babies.'

Issy smiles, imagining her and Jerome's baby with its cute mixed-race skin and afro curls.

'can't w8 2 suck ur dick l8r,' Hayley says as she types.

'Hold it down!' Issy says, 'We're on a bus!'

'I'm joking, man. Just put something like, 'Hi babes, still wanna meet up? Kiss. Kiss.'

The pair type their messages.

'Ready yet?' asks Hayley.

'One sec.'

'Make sure we send it exactly the same time!' Hayley adds while pressing SEND.

'Okay, ready.'

'GO!'

'Time it too,' Hayley insists, '4.37pm on my phone, what does yours say?'

Hayley's phone beeps.

'You and Dwayne!' Issy squeals.

'Nah, run out of credit. Bollocks. This tune comes on when Dwayne texts…'

Hayley puts the volume up as the beats scramble through the speakers of her brother's old phone.

'I love that tune,' Issy agrees.

As they start singing the chorus, a woman turns with a disapproving growl. Hayley gives her a dirty look followed by her middle finger.

Weighing it up, the lady turns back, shaking her head.

'Yeah shake your head. Stupid bitch,' Hayley mutters loud enough for the lady to flinch her shoulders.

'Do you always have to do that?' Issy whispers.

Beats echoes from Issy's phone.

'Jerome!'

'Nah, it's Tameika.'

'Crazy Christian Tameika?'

'Yeah.'

'Why's she got your number?'

'Some project she's doing at school.'

'Dat girl's always on a Jesus flex.'

'Nah, it's that Duke of Edinburgh thing. She's sending Inspirational Messages to Empower Women.' As she says it aloud, Issy wishes she'd signed up too, but felt like the gang would've taken the piss out of her.

Hayley's stopped listening anyway. Instead, she scans the streets, hoping to see a familiar face.

'Quote: Be the change you want to see in the world, Gandhi.'

Who's Gandhi?' asks Issy.

Hayley turns back, 'That dude from Lord of the Rings.'

'Ah, never seen it.'

Issy's phone beats again, this time making her jump.

'Ha that got you shook!' Hayley laughs.

Issy reads the text: Hi babes, yeh I'm gud. Cum 2 da Endz. Wer gonna go park l8r. Wot u doin 2nite. Can I cum ovr? Jx

'What should I text back?'

'Ask him if Dwayne's there?'

'Dwayne's always there.'

'Ask him,' Hayley begins, 'If Dwayne loves Hayley.'

'Like Dwayne talks to Jerome like me and you talk.'

'Ask him...if they've got weed?'

'He wants to come over. You know… My mum's going pub tonight… get me?'

Issy looks to Hayley to read between the lines but Hayley's eyes are back surveying pavements, 'Oi FRANKIE!!!' Hayley jumps on the bus seat to shout out the small window: 'FRANKIE!!!' A teenager looks up but the bus moves too fast to recognise Hayley's thumb in the air.

'Yeah, so...you know,' Issy pulls Hayley back down. 'I'm not chatting my business to the bus, Hays. Should he come round?'

Hayley makes porno noises towards the annoyed lady's direction.

The two girls jump off the bus and head up to meet the boys.

'Why do they call this a road when it's blatantly a hill?' Hayley puffs, as they climb the hill to the park. 'Spark up and twos me?'

There's two blocks on the estate where the teens live. Issy lives in the first and Hayley the second. They walk arm in arm, turning into Jerningham Court estate. The pair can hear laughter echoing from a stairwell. Jerome and his older brother Dwayne live in the other block of flats on the other side of the street but they choose to hang around this side of the road to avoid troubling their grandmother.

Following the laughter, the girls head to Hayley's block to find their gang on the steps smoking.

Most adults living between New Cross Gate and Brockley have never heard of the Graff Gang, but if you're a teenager, Dwayne Madaki and Jerome Campbell are a well-known duo. More than half-brothers; they're best friends. When their mother left for the last time, Dwayne made a promise to Jerome that no matter what happens, he will never let his little brother out of his sight.

Jerome catches Issy approaching in the corner of his eye, 'Babes!' he cries, his voice going up slightly before deepening with the onset of adulthood.

'Ahhh! Swag!' shout the boys, laughing at their friend jogging up the stairs to meet his girlfriend.

'You alright?' Jerome asks kissing Issy on the cheek and putting his arm around her shoulders.

'I'm fine fanks, darling,' Hayley utters sarcastically, pulling Issy tighter towards her.

Jerome laughs, 'Sorry Hays. You alright though?' he gives Hayley his flagship little wink and smile.

'Datz, little miss to you!' Hayley snips as the trio join the rest.

The name Graff derives from Telegraph Hill, where they all live, though they pronounce it 'graff' as in graffiti. If you look around the estate, you can see the gang's logo scribed on bricks, stairwells, and bins. Issy thought it up.

Dwayne is sitting on the steps with his back towards them. Hayley decides to creep up on him. Putting her hands over his eyes, she shouts 'Guess who?'

'Watch, man!' Dwayne snorts, shrugging Hayley off at the same time she tries to kiss his cheek. 'Can't you see I'm building?'

'Sorry,' Hayley replies, quietly, 'Didn't see.'

The boys laugh. Hayley scowls at them before sitting a couple of steps down from Dwayne, looking up at him, waiting for a smile. For all her big mouth and rudeness, Hayley's forgiving of her boyfriend's aggression, something Issy finds highly annoying. The others continue to laugh, because that's what they do all day: catch jokes.

They head to the basketball court but it's full of university students from

Goldsmiths playing football. As they approach the royal blue painted fencing, Dwayne sizes it up. Graff usually hang out and smoke weed by the benches inside the court, but instead their spot's taken by a few girls with rollers in their hair and high-waist floral shorts sipping cans of cider. His friends watch Dwayne to see what he's thinking. Dwayne looks up at the light blue sky, then back at the students.

'Come we go top park,' he says, not wanting a fight. Everyone follows, relieved. They walk past the students as their football bounces over into the bushes in front of Dwayne.

'Kick it over, lads?' shouts one of them. Dwayne shoots the skinny pale guy his usual screwed-up face and continues walking. Issy, embarrassed, runs to get the ball out from the bush. Jerome takes it and kicks it back into the court.

'Nice one, bro,' the student says, raising his thumb to Jerome. Jerome nods back.

'He ain't your bro,' Dwayne snorts.

The student, unfazed, shakes the indie cut from his eyes to tackle his friend before securing a goal. Issy smiles at Jerome and hangs back to hold his hand.

The group cross the road and head to the highest point of Telegraph Hill Park. The Upper Park doesn't have the swings, slides, pretty ponds or basketball court. There's a tennis court though, and a large grassy bank. Inside, couples are playing tennis while owners walk their various sized dogs and a group of middle-aged women look tortured by a personal trainer. Get to the top and there's this amazing view of London. Just go there one sundown and see for yourself.

Today's perfect. The sky's clear. The evening sun still warm with a soft breeze tickling the skin. Everyone's still wearing their t-shirts and vests and not a goose-pimple in sight. The gang settle on the grassy bank for the evening, laughing and joking, as they do, at the expense of each other.

'Barry, Barry, Barry.' Andre repeats, still laughing, 'if you keep saying it, it just sounds more and more nutz, bruv.'

'Barry. Barry. Barry. Barry. Barry!' They all join in.

Barry's parents knew a Barry who was really kind to them when they moved here. How were they to know calling a black boy living in London, Barry – and one trying to be gangsta – was not a good move? They thought an English-sounding name would stand their son in good stead for the future.

'A future stacking shelves,' Anton laughs.

'Nah!' cries Dwayne, 'You mean brushing toilets, bruv.'

'Nah man,' Barry sits upright, 'I'm just gonna get it changed when I'm eighteen. Done.'

'Bahhh haaaah…' they continue laughing, Issy producing tears and belly cramps.

'Yeah, it ain't funny though,' Barry watches everyone hugging their torsos at his expense. 'And why you laughing you little prick?' Barry turns to Anton, 'Go phone Beyoncé, nah!'

So Anton's extremely gullible: Dwayne, Jerome and Barry once made up a fake profile and downloaded pictures of Beyoncé then added Anton and convinced him she was a girl from Brixton who wanted to 'suck his dick' begging photos of his cock. They then photo-shopped his naked arse and texted to everyone round school.

'Where d'you think the word doppelganger comes from,' Anton shouts, 'you fucking dickheads…'

'Bahhhhh-rahhhh-haaah.'

'Ask your mum what she's eating tonight?' Anton tells Hayley. Although since Hayley and Dwayne started sexing she gets less flack. Hayley's weakness is her chaotic family. Her dad's in and out of prison and the Graff boys joke about how poor Hayley is. She's lost it a couple of times when failing to see the funny side.

Hayley punches Anton in the arm.

'What man? not even a full-sized bucket; your mum'll suck my dick for a half-eaten fried chicken leg.'

She swings again.

'Alright man, allow her,' Dwayne says, rolling another spliff.

Top boys in this crew are Dwayne, Jerome and Andre. These three don't receive the same level of humiliation, but they do get cussed: Andre for his big lips, Dwayne for his dark skin, and Jerome for being a pretty boy and a soft touch, both qualities exaggerated since he got with Issy.

Every day, the seven of them hang out, smoking weed in the park or watching music videos when someone's got a free yard. Weekends, they drink rum and juice when they put their money together. But their passion is music, and whenever open, they play their self-made beats on the Karaoke machine at the youth club and spit bars to the youngers.

Lastly, Issy. The gang rip her for being a neek. She doesn't like breaking the law, she enjoys school, likes police and never shoplifts. She's no square though, believing some things, like underage smoking, drinking and sex should be the responsibility and choice of the individual, not the politicians.

So that's them. It's late August. Soon the summer holiday will be over and their final year of school starts, except Dwayne who's two years older but dropped out of college to 'do man's own ting.'

One by one, the lights of London pop up as darkness descends over the summer twilight, 'I love this bit,' Issy says inhaling her spliff, 'Makes me tingly.'

Andre chuckles.

'Can't you feel it, Jerome?' Issy asks, looking up to him, with her head on his chest.

'Feel what, babes?'

'I dunno, feels like... like magic in the air.'

'Yeah,' Jerome says, slightly uncomfortable, feeling Dwayne's eyes on him.

'Whatever, bruv,' Dwayne snorts.

Jerome looks at his brother scowling and then back down to his girlfriend and smiles.

The group sit in silence until Andre's phone rings.

'Hello,' Andre says, in command, with a deep voice like some army general. Everyone poised to see who it is. His tone lifts: 'Yes Mum, on that. Soon come, soon come.' Andre turns to the group, 'Curried goat.'

'Yes, G,' Anton jumps up assuming an invitation.

'What the fuck?' Barry tosses his phone on the grass. He turns to Andre, 'Bruv I'm coming with you. I can't get fed up proper in that house of mine. Woman tinks she can cook up nutin' on a Saturday.'

'What, your mum ain't cooked nothing?' asks Hayley.

'Woman's texting about some fish finger sandwich.'

'I love fish fingers,' Issy says.

Anton starts laughing. 'She thinks if she feeds you up white people's shit, one day you're gonna wake up white.'

They all join in as Barry pans his friends the middle finger.

'Try skin lighting cream,' says Dwayne. 'Works better than mayonnaise!'

'You can't talk, you blick prick,' Barry replies.

'Bahhahhhahaa!'

They're so loud, nearby couples start to empty prosecco bottles, pack up their picnic blankets and leave the park.

'What you two on?' Anton asks Dwayne and Jerome.

'Dem mans is eatin something else, bruv,' Andre points at Issy then Hayley.

Anton doesn't get it.

Andre clips Anton over the head, 'You sooo dumb. Some next level fish fingers, get me?' Andre jabs his forefinger and middle finger together up and down in the air.

'Ah yeah yeah,' Anton laughs, bumping fists with Andre. Still not getting it.

'Excuse me, I am here you know,' Issy says. 'Jerome?'

Jerome looks at the boys, 'Allow it, man.'

They knock fists several times then Andre, Anton and Barry head back down the hill, leaving the brothers with their respective partners.

'Actually, fooood,' Hayley groans, once the trio are out of sight. 'I ain't eaten since breakfast. Want some chips, D?'

'You got money?' Dwayne snorts his question, looking at Hayley in a manner Issy detests.

Hayley digs in her pocket and pulls out the same pound coins from this morning. Issy looks at her, then at the hair gel in the plastic bag.

Issy snatches the bag.

'What you doing man!' Hayley shouts, attempting to snatch it back. On closer inspection the bag is crumpled and discoloured at the handles.

'Just looking at the gel you bought,' Issy says, pulling out a receipt which doesn't match the label on the bag. Before she can read the receipt properly, Hayley swings for the bag again, this time managing to grab it.

'What's your problem?' Hayley demands, dusting cigarette ash off her jeans, 'Look what you made me do?'

Issy decides to leave it. She's lean from the weed and can't be bothered.

'Come we go shop, then,' Dwayne says jumping up from the grass. He walks off, not noticing Hayley holding up her hands to be assisted. Hayley whimpers like a neglected puppy. He turns to see her arms outstretched, 'What man? My belly's rumbling,' he huffs back, pulling Hayley up. She's immediately happy, putting her arm around his waist, forcing Dwayne to reluctantly place his arm over her shoulder.

Jerome and Issy snuggle up. Cheeky bitch, Issy thinks to herself watching Hayley and Dwayne disappear out the park. Fake receipt and everything. She should take acting classes.

'You alright babes?' Jerome asks.

'Yeah? Just wish she wouldn't teef round me. It proper pisses me off. I feel like not hanging with her when she blatantly lies to me, know what I mean? She promised.'

'Yeah, I know. I rate you, you know that, innit?'

'Yeah. I really rate you, too.' Issy kisses Jerome's hand.

'Babe, you gotta stop them boys making sex jokes about me. It's getting too much these days and we ain't even done it yet.'

'I know, I know,' Jerome agrees. 'I'll tell them. Promise.'

Jerome strokes Issy's hair as they watch London glittering with traffic down below. Issy notices a train weave in and out the tall buildings. The window lights run across the city, it looks like a thief stealing a string of sparkling diamonds.

'Babe, I've been thinking, yeah, and I don't want you to feel a way, but...' Jerome mumbles, 'You don't have to... Nah... So... Fuck it.'

Jerome sits up a little, and starts again. 'Basically,' he takes Issy's hands, 'You know I've done tings with other girls before us?'

'Urm, yeah,' Issy uneasily sits up straight to face him, unsure if she wants to hear what is about to come.

Sensing her unease, Jerome adds, 'Nah, nah, nah, it ain't nothing bad. What I'm saying is… I've done stuff, even with you, but like... you know…'

'What you trying to say?'

'What I wanna say sounds fucked up in my head, so I don't wanna say it that way.'

'Try,' Issy assures. 'You can tell me anything. You know that.'

'Basically, I've been, bashing. A lot. Over you.'

Issy starts giggling.

'What's funny?' Jerome feels a rush of awkwardness through his body, annoyed Issy is laughing, but he pushes his negative feelings away, as he always does.

'Is that it? You wank over me?' Issy asks, still giggling.

'Dat's a hard ting to say ya nah,' Jerome defends himself in a Jamaican accent, placing his hands down his chest as if flattening out a creased shirt.

'I do too,' Issy gulps, 'When I think of you I mean. I look at your profile pictures on my phone.'

'Do you do it loads?' A cheeky smile spreads over Jerome's face. 'Describe your technique.'

'No!'

His eyebrows lift a couple of times cheekily, 'Can I watch one time? You can give me some tips!' He tickles her ribs and they both start giggling.

He's so funny, she thinks. Her heart beating loud in her chest. His skin is soft and picture perfect. His teeth so white and sparkly and his lips are like two perfectly plump silk cushions. But the things Issy loves the most, are the two jewels below those cheeky eyebrows. Jerome has incredible brown eyes that are adorned with long thick black eyelashes. He reminds Issy of an Egyptian prince from back in the day. Jerome is, quite literally, beautiful. Inside and out.

Issy's also beautiful, but her best features are hidden away. She has freckles, which Jerome and her mum find sweet but she hates. They're always covered up with cheap foundation that doesn't match her skin tone. To match the freckles, Issy has greenish-blue eyes. They seem to change colour depending on her mood. Issy's wavy auburn hair, which is naturally wavy, is dyed with awful blonde highlights and brown lowlights and is straightened daily. Sometimes she has her hair corn rolled at the front and, like Hayley, puts different coloured hair bands in depending on what she is wearing. Her breasts are small and though her hips are widening, her body isn't that of a fully developed woman. She's a girly fifteen. She bites her nails, worse still, the skin around the nails, often resulting in two or three scabby cuticles most days of the year. Her skin has a dullness to it because she rarely eats vegetables. She only likes apples and bananas and refuses to eat most food unless it's been cooked by her mum, usually burgers, baked beans, chips. Though Issy has started trying Jerome's grandmother's food.

She loves her barbecue chicken with rice and peas.

As they lie on the grass, Jerome can't shake the image of his girlfriend touching herself. Licking his lips, he asks, 'So *can* I watch, then? Educational purposes innit.'

'Yeah, obviously. You're my man, innit. Just say when,' Issy replies, calling his bluff.

'Issy, I'm a virgin, innit,' Jerome finally blurts out, as if it were his last breath. He looks at her to note her reaction, 'I've never told no-one before. I know I go on like I ain't, but anyway…'

Jerome relights his spliff, 'Every night he's on about this girl he's beating, that girl he's got on lock. I don't lie, you get me. He just assumes like I've done it too.'

'You mean Dwayne?'

'Yeah, all dem mans.' Jerome looks at Issy then down at the grass, 'I was thinking… you know… if you are, you know…'

He looks up. She doesn't make it easier by not speaking.

'It don't matter if you ain't,' Jerome quickly adds, 'I still rate you. I thought about it a lot. Obviously it's better if you are, but at the end of the day, I won't feel a way about it.'

'I won't tell no-one your business or nuttin,' he adds, remembering things he Googled about how to speak about sex for the first time with your partner. One thing was to promise confidentiality. He feels happy he remembered that one. But Issy just sits there. Jerome feeling his anxiety convert to paranoia, 'Shit I'm chatting too much.'

Issy thinks of the black and white film she watched the other day with her mum. In it, the actress had a long cigarette holder and sultry eyes. Her character never gave much away and the men were all crazy for her. Issy takes Jerome's spliff and slowly inhales. Mimicking the style of the film, she asks in a cool, calm manner, 'Are you asking me if I've done stuff with other boys?'

'Not stuff. Obviously we've all done stuff at the end of the day,' Jerome now feels the paranoia meet a hint of jealousy. He shakes away images of Issy with others.

'Yes,' Issy tells him.

'Like I said, it's no ting.' Jerome clears the lie from his throat.

Issy drops the act, 'I'm still a virgin, Jerome.'

Jerome sighs in relief. 'You're not just saying that? Like to make man feel better or some shit?'

'Jerome, come on, I'm fifteen. How many boys you seen me with?'

'Five. Since you moved to Jerningham.'

'What? I ain't had five.'

'White Barry, James, John, that boy Russell and some boy last year.'

White Barry and James were in primary school, so that don't count. John was in Year 7 and we only kissed a few times. Russel, well we didn't have sex.'

'What about that other white boy?'

'Who?'

'He stayed in your bedroom last summer.'

'Urgh, man, Bradley? I didn't want him there! He was into some shit computer game he was playing with some Chinese boys. In China. It was well weird. He got addicted in the end. Mum says he never leaves his room and gets these like anxiety attacks if he misses one day gaming. Urgh, and he bites his toe nails.'

A silence falls between them. The purple sky now charcoal grey, forcing the surrounding bushes, trees and grass to become shrouded in darkness.

'Am I your first black boyfriend?' Jerome pulls a daisy from the grass.

'Yeah, you know you are.'

'Does it bother you?'

'What? That you're black?'

'Yeah,' Jerome looks up and out towards the city lights.

'No. Does it bother you I'm white?'

'Not really.'

'Then how come you asked?'

Jerome looks uncomfortable again, 'I'm probably talking like this because I'm mash up but I'm feeling like chatting tonight.'

'You can tell me anything, Jay,' Issy moves closer towards him.

'Issy, you know my dad's mixed, that's why I'm lighter than Dwayne innit?'

'Yeah.'

'Well, one thing my dad kept saying is on my mind since me and you started...' Jerome trails off again. 'Basically, yeah, he said..., basically... to never to get with a white chick.'

'Why?' Issy asks, carefully.

'Basically, his mum, my other gran, said white people don't marry black people. They grow up and realise life's tough for black people and leave them for another white person.'

Jerome flicks the daisy away and looks out again towards the city. 'Apparently my granddad ended up treating her badly for being black, which is nutz when you think about it because he made a baby with her then he married some white woman and forgot my dad ever existed. Never paid nuttin', not even a five-minute phone call.'

Issy sits for a few moments thinking about what Jerome just said, 'The thing is Jerome, in those days it probably was bad to be in a white and black couple. I know my London nan was pretty racist. But things are different now. I never even thought about it being anything.'

'I was just thinking that all your boyfriends were white.'

Issy straddles Jerome's lap. She gently pushes him back onto the grass. Sitting up, she relights the last bit of spliff then leans into Jerome, exhaling the smoke into his mouth. He returns the gesture as they kiss.

Looking to see who is around – dog walkers, tennis players, joggers dispersed – Issy begins to grind her pelvis into Jerome hips. He gets hard and she feels it underneath her. 'I'd love to lose my virginity to you,' she whispers in his ear.

Jerome sits up and wraps his arms around her, 'Yeah, but not here though babes.' He looks at Issy, 'I want it to be special. Some Barry White red wine flex.'

Issy laughs.

'Serious now, I'm a one woman man, babes. So it's gonna be special, ya get me? If it's our first time, like for me and you, then I'm gonna make it the perfect night. Get a hotel room, bottle of champs, chocolates. The other thing is—'

Issy's phone interrupts them, 'It's my mum.'

'Okay, Mum, bye.'

'Everything cool?'

'Yeah. Just letting me know she won't be back till late. She's in the pub with Karen. Sounds pissed already.' Issy's noticed Carol drinking more alcohol recently. Last weekend Issy got woken up by the sound of vomiting. She blinks back to now, 'anyway, do you wanna come over and watch a film? Got Chinese in the oven.'

'Gonna check my Gran first. See if she's okay.'

The two make their way down towards the estate. In the summer, the huge trees that line Jerningham Road block out most of the dim yellow light the street lamps provide. Halfway down the hill, Issy and Jerome see a group of boys surrounding someone.

'That looks dodgy,' Issy says, holding onto Jerome's arm.

As they get closer, Jerome and Issy can see a girl around their age clutching a small bag. One of the boys is trying to grab it but the girl refuses to let the strap go.

'Please, please, take anything but this,' they hear the girl plead as they approach. 'It has all my schoolwork on it.'

'Oi!' Jerome shouts in as deep a voice as possible. One boy immediately runs. The other goes but hesitates because the third remains.

Unfazed by Jerome, the third shouts 'What?'

'What you manz doing merking up my Endz?'

Jerome keeps his voice deep and his tone aggressive.

'Is dis your Endz?' the masked face replies.

'Dis is Graff, skeen. I know all Graff manz,' Jerome says, 'and you ain't one.'

'Is it?' The boy asks sarcastically, 'Who you know from Graff?'

'He is Graff,' Issy interjects, annoyed at the boy's lack of respect. Adrenaline pumping, she adds, 'His brother's Double G.'

'Is it?' the boy replies. Jerome isn't happy Issy just exposed him, but continues to stand his ground.

The timid girl is hunched in the middle, terrified yet looking relieved another girl has showed up. Issy stares at the girl briefly before staring back at the boys with her serious face. She wants to smile and reassure her but first she has to look tough.

'Where you manz from?' Jerome asks, chest puffed out, standing tall.

'Don't watch that, innit,' says the second boy with his face covered by a headscarf.

Jerome looks at him, keeping his voice deep, he shouts, 'Don't think I can't see you're a pussyhole. I saw you about to run out on your bro. So what, you don't back it for your man dem?' Jerome's eyes go back to the ringleader holding the bag. 'Now a few tingz can run from here,' he continues. 'You either give the bitch back her bag and disappear, or I can make a few phone calls and we can settle tingz different.'

The ringleader stands firm staring at Jerome, bag still in his gloved hand, strap still over the girl's shoulder.

'See man like me don't shit on my own doorstep and you can appreciate I don't like other breddars shitting here neither. Feds come and this bitch tells them a few niggas robbed her. You manz know all feds see is one black face! I don't want no feds getting inna my business, my flat gettin' raided up and for what?' Jerome snatches the bag from the boy's hand, pulling the girl with it. He undertakes a mock inspection, 'A shitty camera?' Jerome looks at the girl. 'Is dat all datz in there?'

'Yes,' the terrified girl stutters, tears streaming down her face. 'My, my brother g-gave it to me.'

'No phone. No money.' Jerome looks at the ringleader, 'I seen dis ting in Cash Converters for a tenner, bruv. Same make and everything. It ain't worth rucking Graff, trust.'

Jerome aggressively pushes the camera back into the girl's chest before grabbing her arm. The girl lets out a whimper as he pushes her into Issy. 'Take her to your yard,' Jerome commands Issy. 'Now!' he yells, pushing both of them towards home. Issy instantly obeys, knowing Jerome is putting it all on to scare the boys, which he is. He never speaks to her like that in real life.

Spitting violently on the floor he turns to the boys, 'Now if you manz want real dough, I'm gonna reveal a few tingz about Graff business. Come we go.'

The boys, slightly baffled, find themselves walking down towards the main road with Jerome.

As soon as they reach the stairwell across the street and are out of sight, the girl begins to shake uncontrollably, thick hot tears streaming down her snotty face. Issy manages to convince the girl she's safe. Issy gets her inside and sit her on the sofa in the living room. She's the same height as Issy but looks a lot smaller. She's skinny and dresses like those uni students Issy always sees in the park – floral and frilly. Vintage.

With a cup of sweet tea and two custard creams, the girl eventually calms down.

'I was so petrified.' She holds her camera close to her like a baby. 'Thank you so, so much.'

Issy isn't sure how to respond when the girl squeezes Issy's hand. Instinctively she pulls it away though inside feels glad to have helped but she's also worried for Jerome. Those boys could beat him up. The one that ran off could come back with a knife or more boys. Issy reluctantly decides to text Dwayne what just happened.

CHAPTER 3

Having slept with her mobile directly under her pillowcase, Issy wakes and immediately checks her phone. Relief.

Morning shorty, Soz, fone bttry died. tingz went fine wid dem breddas. Hope u wernt too shook from it. Nxt time leave Dwayne out tingz. He went mad. Lucky I was bak home den. How was da girl? Uokay? Jxx

Issy puts on her baby pink towelling dressing gown and bunny slippers she got for Easter. Still tired, she walks down the creaky stairs to the kitchen at the front of the flat to put the kettle on.

At the end of the hallway floor lying by the front door is an envelope ornately decorated with flowers and exotic birds. The prettiest envelope Issy's ever seen. In the most magnificent handwriting the card is sort-of addressed to her. She flips it over to read the back, **Emily Sutton, 55 Pepys Road, Telegraph Hill.**

A rush of excitement replaces her sleepy head. Issy doesn't get anything posted to her directly except school truancy reports and junkmail. Stuffing her mobile in her dressing gown pocket, she sits at the small kitchen table.

Dear Isabelle,

Thank you so much for helping me out yesterday. You and your friend risked your own safety for a stranger, and this fills me with immense joy. I am both overwhelmed and humbled by your good deed. I don't know how things would have ended had you not come and rescued me. Looking back, I should never have put up a fight, but my camera is a precious gift that means more to me than anything else.

I told my mother what happened and she would like to invite you and your mother over for tea and cake, this afternoon, if you're both free? If this is not convenient for you, then let us rearrange another time that suits. If this is convenient, then I would be grateful if you could let us know so that we can begin baking you the best thank-you cake in the world.

My kindest regards,
Emily Sutton
Then written in grey pencil: P.S. Remember what we said xx

Issy looks up at the clock as she fills the kettle with water. It is just after eleven. Perhaps Mum wants one, she thinks. Better not shout; probably hung over.

Issy walks back up the creaky stairs, gently knocking her mother's bedroom door, 'Cup of tea?' she whispers, gently pushing the door open, popping her head inside. No sign of Carol Richards. The bed's still made with several rejected outfits spread over along with an empty bottle of rosé. Dread instantly replaces the excitement of Emily's card as Issy calls her mum's mobile. She hears the ringtone faintly coming from downstairs. She goes back down to the living room. Carol's lying on the floor. There's puke on the carpet.

Issy kneels down, resting her ear near her mother's mouth. Her eyes sharply focusing on Carol's chest. She's breathing. Issy sits up, looking at the rip down Carol's black tights. She strokes the greasy strands of hair away from Carol's face. Mascara smudged down her cheeks. She's been crying again.

'You smell homeless,' Issy whispers before noticing the picture frame on the floor. She reaches over her mother's body to reveal the image of her father. Issy recognises the photo but not the frame. Any anger towards her mother's drinking dissipates as Issy lets out a huge sigh. 'He's never coming back.'

Somebody starts banging on the front door. 'What now?' Issy mutters to herself, putting a blanket over Carol, still passed out on the carpet.

'You alright?' Hayley asks, sidestepping straight from the front door into the kitchen.

'Sort of,' Issy replies, following her friend. Third time lucky, she'll make that cup of tea. 'Why you banging up my door?'

'What's the matter?'

'Where d'you want me to start?'

Hayley follows Issy around the kitchen.

'Mum's passed out. Got pissed out her brain. Again. I ain't had no sleep. Last night after you and Dwayne left, me and Jerome—'

'Oh my god! You fucked him!'

'Shhh. Keep your voice down, Hays. Mum's only in the living room. Ain't you spoke to Dwayne?'

'About what?'

'Oh my days, so me and Jerome was walking to mine, all cosy and everything, then these boys were merking up some girl, like proper merking her up. She was so shook, Hay. Crying ain't the word. Me and Jerome run over to stop it.'

'What – did Jerome ruck with dem?'

'Nah. He was chatting to them for ages. Then took them back down the hill.'

'Did they beef with him?'

'That's the worst part. His phone was going to answerphone and I was stuck with this girl.'

'What time was this?' Hayley asks wide-eyed.

'Like nine or ten.'

'Naaaah, that ain't on. Where they from?' Hayley asks, her voice becoming increasingly incensed.

'Don't know.'

'Did they know you was Graff?'

'Yeah I told them. But the main one didn't give a-'

'Shi-t,' Hayley remarks, 'Nah, this is madness.'

Hayley shakes her head, 'Jerome okay?'

'Yeah, I got a text this morning, but I couldn't sleep all night, Hay. I was crying my eyes out. I wanted to go his house but I couldn't knock on the door and wake his nan up. But anything could've happened. Everyone's getting stabbed up these days. You got ten year olds not scared to stab a grown man.'

'I know. That's why my brother said he's gonna get me a strap.'

'What?' Issy turns sharply to see if Hayley's serious.

'Yeah. I said no, obviously, but now I think I should say yes. That way if they come back, I'll do more than knock 'em out.' Hayley picks up a takeaway chopstick from last night's Chinese and jerks it in the air.

'Hayley, what are you on about?' Issy looks at her best friend, 'You're talking about killing... a person!'

Issy pours milk into her friend's tea.

'D'you think if someone pulls a knife out, I'm gonna just have it?' Hayley pours in three sugars from the sachets Carol always takes home from Wendy's. 'No way, bruv. They're getting a gun pulled out. Done.'

'Hayley, you're talking madness. And, if not, then make sure you and your gun stay right away from me. Joint enterprise, remember. If police – oh yeah and that reminds me, I ain't happy with you.'

'Fucking hell, I just walked in the door!'

'You know what I'm on about. You stole that hair gel yesterday.'

'No I didn't. Oh yeah,' Hayley switches things back on Issy shaking her head from side to side, 'I should be angry with you, getting fag burns in my new jeans, but you're lucky I saw you was being paranoid. Don't smoke weed if you can't handle it.'

Issy takes the chopsticks from her friend and theatrically places them against Hayley's chin, 'Swear on your nan's life you didn't steal anything yesterday.'

'I swear on my mum's life.'

Issy looks Hayley square in the face, 'I said your nan's life.'

'You was outside smoking so if anything happened you wouldn't-'

'I don't care where I was! I'm serious. What if police stop you an hour later? These days, I'll get done too. Joint enterprise.'

'What you keep saying joint enterprise for?'

'Because police don't see it that way. You do know what it is, if you steal shit when I'm there, I get done just for being with you.'

'Alright, man! I come here to get away from all this argy-bargy,' grabbing one chopstick back, Hayley uses it to stir in the sugar deposited at the bottom of the cup, 'So who was this girl they was robbing?'

Distraction successful.

'Some girl who lives in one of those massive houses on Pepys Road,' Issy replies, sitting down at the table,

'Did you take her home, then?' Hayley asks.

'Yeah but I brought her here first though. She was a proper mess. All shaking and crying.'

'Did you call her mum?'

'She didn't wanna tell her mum. Said it would tip her over the edge or something.'

'Did she sleep here?'

'Nah, she just washed her face and we chatted. Proper well spoken.'

'Old? Young?'

'Same year as us but already doing A-Level stuff, kept saying prep-work,' Issy remembers, impressed, having not met anyone who does coursework on time let alone anything before the school year begins.

Hayley gets up to raid Carol's biscuit tin. 'What a boffin!'

'She says she'd been doing it all summer. Got Art GCSE in Year 10. A-Star.'

'Megatron boffin,' Hayley dips a chocolate biscuit into her tea. She takes three more biscuits before pushing the tin Issy's way.

'Make sure you eat the whole thing, don't just lick out the chocolate!'

'Alright man! Why you so moany? What was they robbing her for?'

'Her camera, but she wouldn't let go of it,' Issy says, picking out a custard cream. 'Jerome was well good though, he pretended like it was some cheap shit to stop them taking it. But it's like eight hundred pounds.'

'Eight hundred! You should've robbed it! Did they teef anything else?' Hayley pulls the tin back to her end of the table, taking two more bourbons.

'Nah, she only had that on her, and her door keys. Gonna meet up with her today. Oh yeah, that reminds me, what's the time? I have to ring and say yes.' Issy briefly flashes Hayley the card.

Hayley snatches the card back once Issy dials Emily's home phone number. She starts to mimic a posh English accent, 'I am both over...whelmed and hum-bled by your good deed. Blo-ody hell,' Hayley exclaims, 'did you save the Queen?'

Issy grabs the card back and notions to Hayley to be quiet while she waits for someone to pick up. Meanwhile Hayley sneaks the biscuit bits of the bourbons back to the tin.

'Erm, hello. Is Emily there? This is Isobel Richards. Yeah, from last night.'

'This is Isobel Richards,' Hayley mimics.

Without pausing between sentences, a voice that really does sound like the Queen, says: 'Oh what an amazing child you are, Isabelle. Emily told me all about it. I'm Janie, Emily's mum. You received Emily's card I gather? Are you both able to make it today?'

'Erm, I can, but...' she pauses to think of an excuse, 'my mum is a bit sick.'

'Pissed as a fart!' Hayley shouts. Issy, already stressed out trying to pronounce each word properly, silently mouths to Hayley to shut-the-fuck-up.

'She, she, has an upset stomach,' Issy continues. Deciding to remove herself from the kitchen, opening the front door.

'...AND SO I TOLD THAT CUNT, RIGHT...' Issy slams the front door on her neighbour's conversation and walks past the kitchen down the hallway.

'Oh poor her,' replies Janie, in an overdone way. 'Do send your mummy our kindest regards. She must be very proud to have such an honest daughter.'

Watching her passed out drunk of a mother from the crack of the living room door, Issy replies, 'Yeah, she is.'

Carol stirs. Issy gasps, rushing up the stairs and into her room.

'Okey-cokey, Isabelle. We shall expect you at teatime,' Emily's mum says with a little sing.

'Erm. So, what time?' Issy asks.

'Well, teatime...'

Silence...

'...So four o'clock.'

'Oh. Okay. See you then. Bye.'

Issy flips her mobile phone shut and falls back onto her bed, exhausted from the mental concentration of having to speak to a posh person.

Back at Pepys Road, Janie puts down the phone and chuckles to herself, 'I forget some children are not educated in the same way as you, dear. I mean, the girl doesn't even know when teatime is. It's a British institution.'

'Oh Mum,' Emily groans, 'you haven't made her feel self-conscious have you?'

'Would I do that?' Janie softly tuts. 'Just an observation, that's all.' Janie begins to collect her keys and jacket to go shopping. 'Where exactly does this girl live?'

Emily smiles at herself in the huge silver framed mirror in the hall, 'Ommaney Road.'

Emily glides her hands over the wooden panelling, following her mother, now in the kitchen digging out the reusable bags, 'Mum, this will be so cool.'

Janie peers into the kitchen cupboard. She resurfaces, popping two squares of folded-up cotton shopping bags into her leather handbag before turning to her daughter, 'So I'm doing something cool for once?' She smiles, thinking this may be the first time her teenager has used that adjective about her.

'Of course you are. I really feel like we clicked. It felt like meeting an old friend.'

'Well, Emily dear, before you fill that pretty head of yours with dreams, can Mummy give you some advice?'

Emily shrugs, all set to mentally block what is about to come from Mrs Sutton's lips.

'It is right and proper to thank someone for a good deed. This tea will be just that. As far as friendship goes, darling, well, I cannot see it.'

'But Mum!'

'Now, you have just about convinced me to invite a stranger into our home and I do want you to make new friends, even local ones, but do let me be clear: This is a one-off. I just heard the way that girl speaks and, well, your father most certainly-'

'Mum, you haven't even met Isabelle yet; how presumptuous and unchristian. And she's not a bad person. Look what she did?' Emily points to her camera sat on the mantelpiece.

'I know. Mummy does understand. Heaven knows, had I foolishly left my camera on a wall, even back in South Ken, I'd not expect to see it returned to me. You're very lucky but this really does not mean you need to become friends,' Janie pauses to gather up all her emotions over the issue, 'Perhaps I have made an error of judgement here. I should have consulted your father before inviting–'

'No!' Emily intercepts her mother's growing angst. 'Really, you're quite equipped to make your own well-judged decisions, without Mr Sutton getting involved.' Emily pushes her chin in towards her neck, deepening her voice, she frowns, mimicking her father's choice phrases.

'That's very naughty,' Janie giggles. 'But you shouldn't mock your father. Or keep calling him Mr Sutton.' Emily's mum heads towards the front door, grabbing her car keys on the way, 'I'm off to Lordship Lane. You know what you have to do now,' Janie points at the piano.

Emily salutes: 'Concerto number three in D minor, Ma'am.'

Janie does a terrible impression of an army general, but plays along, 'Piano exam in three weeks, soldier. Off you pop!'

Once Emily sees her mother drive off, she picks up the phone and presses the redial digits to retrieve Issy's number.

'Hello, can I speak to Isabelle please?'

'Speaking,' Issy rushes out the kitchen. After a few minutes, she returns with a grin.

'So what did posh girl want?' Hayley says, narky.

'Her name is Emily.' Issy gives Hayley a sarcastic look. 'And she just called to ask me not to say nothing about the mugging to her parents. They'd make her go hospital for a full examination, then police to record the crime, then lock her in the house for the rest of her life.'

'What happened, love?' Carol asks, back in the land of the living, lighting a fag hanging between her lips.

'Can I have one please, Carol?' Hayley asks ever so sweetly.

'No,' Carol replies bluntly. 'Buy your own.'

Hayley pokes her chocolate-soiled tongue out at Carol, breaking another bourbon biscuit up.

'So last night some girl got mugged and me and Jerome stopped it.' Issy hands her mum the card, 'She posted this today, wants me to go over.'

'Oh that's nice.' Carol stirs instant coffee granules into a cup of hot water. 'What a lovely wee card.'

Issy grabs the card back before Carol reads the bit inviting her along. Not noticing this urgency, Carol takes out her purple-coloured gel eye mask from the fridge, 'Well I'm proud. Now excuse me but I need a dark place. Have fun. I'll cook a roast later.'

Carol kisses Issy's forehead then drags her hangover upstairs. After a final lick, Hayley puts the biscuit halves back into the tin.

3.59pm Isobel Richards stands outside 55 Pepys Road wearing her nicest top and jeans, some black flat pumps with a matching handbag. 4pm she rings the doorbell.

5.30pm and Issy is back at home, a slightly changed person. She opens the door to her and Carol's little flat, floats upstairs to her room, falls back onto her lumpy bed, and stares at the crack in the ceiling.

Marx and Engels, Emily thinks, looking at her mother. No, start again. Think. Think of someone. Eliza Doolittle!

'Perhaps we should watch *My Fair Lady* while we wait for Mr Sutton?' Emily suggests, biting her upper lip.

Janie cuts Emily a knowing look.

'But who says rich and poor can't be friends?'

'Emily, don't put words into my mouth. I mentioned nothing about money. I am more concerned about your education. This is a big year for you and I don't want you polluting your environment with distraction.'

'Mum, I want the same things. This is all linked to my education,' Emily forms a Shakespearean theatrical pose.

'Really'

'A rich ethnographic study. From which I'll derive the highest possible A Level grade the art department's ever seen. Imagine the critical acclaim!' Emily now takes her bow.

Janie's picks up a cake crumb missed by the broom. Emily watches her mother. Antique pearl earrings an everyday occurrence, as is the modest necklace with a small ruby pendant and her thin gold bracelet. Janie's wedding and engagement rings sparkle as she fluffs her hair in the hallway mirror. For her fifty-two years, and at five foot six, Janie looks deceptively normal, in her finely pressed polo shirt and navy trousers. On the face of it, her mother looks like other upper- or middleclass women except she's not. Not at all.

'And when I'm living in Paris,' Emily continues, 'you can read about me in the Times supplement: Emily Sutton: artist or social visionary? You can say to yourself, I helped my daughter meet her muse.'

Janie mutters something to herself, putting on her navy cotton cardigan. She stares at her daughter theatrically fluttering an invisible paintbrush around an invisible easel. 'I don't know where all this comes from. Neither from my side of the family, nor your father's. Let's prepare supper and forget this little event ever happened. Your father will be home from the golf tournament in…' Janie's dainty fingers inspect Emily's watch, 'precisely one hour and Daddy shall be expecting food on the table.'

Emily pokes her tongue out behind her mother's back, vowing to God she'll *never* be in a marriage like this. Like ever. And with every intention of making Isabelle Richards her new best friend, Emily follows her mother reluctantly to the kitchen.

CHAPTER 4

Emily Sutton rushes to the front door, 'Issy! Poor you, come in, quick!'

Issy cleans her feet on the doormat before stepping into Emily's home.

'So glad you could make it, come through, come through and I'll make us some tea.'

The girls walk along the long corridor leading to the kitchen at the back of the house. Issy gets the same twinkling sensations she got yesterday from the polished oak panelling and Victorian tiled floors. Dwarfed by the high ceilings, they enter the large modern kitchen, Victorian painted floor tiles replaced by large slabs of light grey granite. Emily offers Issy a seat at the cherry oak table. Issy nestles into one of the magnificent chairs opposite the garden and starts fingering the fruit carvings on the chair next to hers. She imagines Hayley face: *Blooody Hell, You did save the Queen!*

Emily busies herself around the kitchen, 'I was simply bursting to talk more with you. So sorry you couldn't stay longer. My father was returning from a weekend of golf and we usually, well I say usually, always, we always have supper at 6.30pm. Hope my mum didn't offend you. She often gets antsy around five o'clock.'

'Didn't really notice. Seemed nice to me.'

'Oh she is,' Emily adds, not wanting to sound too negative about Janie Sutton. 'Mum's very nice.'

'Where is she?'

'Who Mum? Erm, she's gone to visit my uncle and aunt. I managed to get out of it because I have a piano exam coming up. I told a little fib that I needed to perfect my reach in order to play Beethoven's, well…' Emily finds herself mumbling. 'Great pianist. And did you know he was deaf?' Emily watches Issy gazing at the French doors and into the garden. 'Erm, oh well, anyway, I'm blabbing,' Emily pours water from the kettle into a porcelain teapot. 'So tell me more about you?'

'Erm,' Issy looks unsure of what to say, 'Well, I'm fifteen, well you know that. Erm... Dunno. What you wanna know?'

'What options have you taken for your GCSEs?'

'P.E., erm, English.'

'Do you get to choose English?' Emily asks enthusiastically, 'It's compulsory at my school.'

Issy scratches her head, 'Yeah, it is in ours, actually. I mean Music, and... History.'

Emily sits down with the teapot. 'Cool, I'm taking History too. How about Art? Are you taking Art?'

'Nah. Can't draw. You really love art don't ya?'

'Oh yes.' Emily places a hand over her chest and sighs a breath, 'More than anything. I think it's the best form of communication.'

Communication? Issy doesn't get it. She's still wondering why Emily mentioned Beethoven's penis.

'You know when you're in a gallery and see these astonishing paintings that tell a magnificent story?'

Issy can't remember the last time she was in a gallery. Maybe primary school trip.

'Look at these teacups,' Emily holds one to the light. 'Can you see the geisha?'

Issy nods, as Emily points to the outline of a Japanese bust.

'Even in those days, art was becoming interesting and different. The geisha full of beauty and yet in some way trapped. I love how art tells the human story.'

'So what's your story?' Issy asks, 'in your art, I mean,' deciding asking questions is easier than answering them.

Emily leans forward, 'Do you really want to know?'

Issy nods, uneasily.

'It's my desire to be an artist, as a job. I admire people like Tracey Emin, do you know her? She created the famous work My Bed. Wait there!' Emily exclaims scuttling off upstairs.

Issy leans back on the wooden chair. The arms have dark red velvet patches, no stains or holes. She fingers the cold bronze studs along the sides. Looks like a throne. Feels as special as it does intimidating. Issy looks up at the painting hanging on the wall by the table: Sir James Sutton, the inscription says. His beady brown eyes spook Issy and she looks away to the glass cabinet, full of beautiful crystal wine glasses. What an amazing place to live. What a life.

Emily rushes back to the kitchen arming a huge portfolio.

Several quick page turns, 'This is My Bed.'

Issy looks at it, 'It's a bed.'

'It's art.'

'Really?'

'Worth hundreds of thousands of pounds.'

'What?'

'Look more closely, it tells you an intimate story, Isabelle. The story of a troubled life.'

Emin engages the viewer by inviting them to see an intimate portrayal of her life, known as confessional art, 'My Bed' forces us into a space that is extremely private. We are that fly on the wall of Emin's life, as much as life is intruding into the artist's space. The world of the artist and the world of the viewer mesh to become one inextricably linked continuum.

'Did you write that?' Issy asks, looking up from the text.

Emily nods. 'It's for my current project,' she explains. 'I want to complete my A Level Art this year so I can prepare for Art School as soon as possible.'

Issy carefully turns each page of Emily's portfolio. There are dozens of colour samples: painted, crayoned, pencilled, chalked. Pages of crisscrossed squares patch-worked together, with notes attached. *Warm. Sensual. Inviting. Cool. Tepid. Retracting. Retreat. Honest. Trusting. Exploiting.* Issy has never seen such an amount of work.

'All this for *one* subject?' Issy can't believe what she's seeing. 'And is this English coursework?' Issy flicks through pages and pages of writing inside the portfolio.

'That's the theory part, we have to write several essays to accompany our works, as well as research everything we're working on. All artists must critique the socio-economic and political forces that surround their stuff.' Emily sees she's confusing her new friend. 'I mean, in other words, work out why things are the way they are. Oh and that's a journal of our artistic journey to show the examiner we have engaged in our work from the very start right through to final exhibition.'

'Wow, glad I didn't choose Art. Was gonna but I love Music more.'

'Can you play an instrument?'

'Erm,' Issy pauses to think about telling Emily she once played the recorder in primary school, then too embarrassed, decides not to. 'No, not anymore. I rap and sing, sometimes.'

'Do you get to compose your own songs at your school?'

'Erm, don't really know. To be honest, I got kicked out last year because I was mucking about with one boy and I hit him with the thing you whack the big drums with. It was the soft ball at the end, not the hard one.'

'Oh,' Emily looks shocked on hearing this violent episode, 'Do you get into fights often?' she asks slowly, worried she may have misjudged Issy as a nice girl.

'Usually stop them, but he said something about… my dad and I flipped.'

'What did he say? If you don't mind me asking?' Emily briefly inspects her hands, wondering if she could ever hit anyone.

Issy looks at her own hands, nails bitten down, two cuticles with dark blooded scabs attached. 'I'd rather not. Still pisses me off.'

'You should hear what the girls say about each other at my school.'

Emily gets up after an awkward silence falls between the two teens.

'Do you want a cupcake, or a biscuit?'

'Who are them boys?' Issy asks.

Emily returns to the table, 'These? These are photos. For a new set of paintings. For my A Level,' Emily reveals a little sheepishly.

'These those boys from the other night?'

Emily looks at the floor. 'They were doing street art so I thought I would take photos. They didn't see me.' Emily looks at Issy to gauge her reaction, 'Street art is part of the wider theme I am looking at.'

'No wonder they wanted to rob you,' Issy exclaims, talking over Emily's explanation, 'You can't go around snapping yutes you don't know,' Issy continues to turn the pages. She sees photos of her estate, and the surrounding houses, 'That's my front door!'

'Yes, erm…' Emily thinks how she can explain the subject matter without being patronising, 'Isabelle, I'm looking at the complexities of contemporary British society, with a focus on the concept of' – Emily motions the quotation marks with both index fingers – '"the estate".'

Issy looks at Emily and tries to unpick what she just said, 'So you're studying us.'

'So I want to show an intimate portrayal, like My Bed, but using the estate, including your estate, where you live, as an example, and juxtapose that with the concept of 'the estate' as owned by,' Emily searches for the right word, *don't say posh, don't say rich, DON'T say better off or privileged,* 'by people who have mansions and gardens and land, horses, fine wine, things like that.' Emily turns the page to reveal a series of photographs of a manor house with manicured grounds. 'I'm trying to see if inequality is at the heart of social unrest.'

'So you want to basically show the difference between posh and poor.'

'Exactly. What do you think about the idea?' Emily asks sheepishly, her eyes squinting.

'Yeah, it's good.'

Issy turns the page to reveal a slight man on a horse and lots of people with horses in the background.

'That's dragging.'

Issy sees the same young man standing in front of a huge house, and another of the same young man with a small woman holding a puppy at some kind of party.

'That's my brother, James,'

Issy can't believe the size of the house. 'I always imagine living back in a house.' Issy turns to the next page that shows a photo of Emily and James together. James is wearing those square hats they always throw up in the air in American movies.

'That's James once he finished his degree at university.'

'Yeah, uni's the best way to buy a house according to what Mrs Salmon says but Mum says electricians and builders earn more these days.'

'Well people with degrees still tend to earn much more money than people who don't have them.' Emily looks down at Issy, still standing over her shoulder. 'Especially if you go to places like Oxford or Cambridge.'

Emily sits down at the table, deciding to postpone the cupcake extravaganza.

'So my brother got an Oxford degree. So did Dad. And so did his dad! Even Mum's brother went there. That's how Dad met Mum, through my uncle.'

'So will you go Oxford then? It's the best. Our Head is always banging on about it after Manpreet got in last year.'

'No way! I want to wear scruffy jumpers and have messy hair and talk French in downtown Paris.' Emily scruffs her hair and hugs herself. 'Does your mother want you to go to university?'

'Not sure,' Issy replies, not knowing if Carol Richards even knows what a university does. 'Never asked her.'

'Do you want to go?'

'Oh my god, I'd love to, but…' Issy trails off. 'I'm not posh enough, especially for Oxford.'

'Nonsense, loads of people from all over the world go there. You just need the grades.'

'I don't have them either.'

'There's still time. You just need to–'

'Why's this photo ripped?' Issy asks, changing the subject.

Emily breathes in, then pauses, looking torn herself as she exhales, 'Long story but essentially my dad. He can be…' Emily changes the subject, 'Want a tour? I'll show you my bedroom.'

'Er, yeah,' Issy gets up. She fixes her hair in the mirror next to the creepy man painting while Emily tidies her portfolio away. The cupcakes left untouched.

'We'll start at the top and work our way down!'

The girls run upstairs.

They spend the rest of the afternoon on Emily's bed. Issy exciting Emily with stories of how she got with Jerome and his dreams to be a famous music producer and buy her a sports car and live in one of those houses with automatic gates and roses growing everywhere. Emily tells Issy about her dream to go to Paris and live in a tiny crooked flat in the top of a crumbling mansion, living cheaply on bread and cheese and making art and organising exhibitions. It feels like they've known each other for years.

The girls each promise they will help the other. Emily takes out a pen and two squares of rose-coloured note paper:

~~Isabelle's~~ Isobel's and Emily's three big dreams:

Emily: Live in Paris. Win the Turner Prize. Be an Artist.

Issy: Read at Oxford. Buy a big house with a garden. Marry Jerome.

The rain's stopped by the time Issy leaves, though the thick cloud hangs over London like a soggy grey blanket. Issy looks around. It's as if she's wearing fresh eyes. All the houses up Pepys Road are as big as Emily's and as she turns into Ommaney Road, they become slightly smaller, but still three floors up and one down. Some have shabby net curtains and several doorbells stuck to the front like acne. Others only have one neat doorbell and nicer curtains. Some polished brass knockers. Some houses have no net curtains and Issy can see right into their living rooms. She hadn't realised how many people own pianos. You couldn't get one up the stairwell, let alone fit it through the door of her flat.

At the end of Ommaney Road is where the houses turn to flats, her flats. As Issy arrives at the steps into Jerningham Court, she can see her bedroom from the road. The living room balcony is nothing compared to Emily's huge garden, but at least they've got a few flower baskets. Looking at the place from here, Issy can understand why her mum was so grateful when the windows got painted by the Council. The estate is a shithole.

Entering her home feels surreal for Issy. The outside of the front door looks filthy. Paint cracks everywhere. She turns the key in the lock. No carpet in the hallway, just stuck-on lino floor tiles from the pound shop. They looked nice when they were brand new on but the two by the front door keep coming unstuck. Issy kicks them back into place. She'll buy some glue tomorrow.

CHAPTER 5

Issy's bare feet rush down the hall into the kitchen. Grabbing a roll of bin liners, she rushes back upstairs to her bedroom.

'Shit!' Issy stomps back down the stairs almost catching the hook of her dressing gown with the broken door handle. She sifts through the kitchen drawers, let's out another frustrated 'ahhh' grabbing her mobile phone: **Mum! We got tape? Txt bk asap!**

Why didn't she do this yesterday? Issy fumes with herself. The mobile phone lets out a song, 'What's it doing there?'

Issy dashes back upstairs to the toilet, grabbing the roll of masking tape hanging on the inside doorknob. Glimpsing the sweat patches forming under her arms in the bathroom mirror, she peels off the red polyester dress then presses the hair dryer plug firmly into the socket. She links her phone with the stereo, loading the playlist she's made. Then she dries the wet patches with the hairdryer before laying the dress on the bed. She sees Jerome leaving his grandmother's flat as she sticks a black bin liner over the window, one bag's enough to block out the hazy September light trying to pretend it's still summer. Issy draws the pale pink curtains her dad made her when she was six, switches on the electric tea light candles she bought from the pound shop, and puts her red dress back on. Just as the doorbell rings, she spritzes body spray around the room and presses play on Track One.

Track Fifteen plays. Jerome holds Issy close. They lie on her single bed, gazing into each other's eyes. Jerome strokes her hair and kisses her forehead gently. Issy lies there feeling completely protected and warm. It feels surreal that he can't take his eyes off her.

'Was that how you wanted it?' she asks.

'More, babe,' Jerome replies, smiling. 'It was amazing.'

'Was you nervous?'

Jerome looks worried, 'Did it show?'

'Nah,' Issy says, though Jerome's arms were shaking as he got on top of her.

'Was it how you thought it was gonna be?' he asks, thinking of the sick feeling, a fear of making a mistake, losing his erection, making Issy bleed, hurting her, busting early... He nearly had to stop.

She kisses his soft lips, 'I'm glad you was my first.'

'Did I hurt you or anything?'

'Nah, you was gentle. Really nice.'

'I dunno how I'm gonna be able to sleep now. I just wanna be in your bed, all the time.'

'I know. It's gonna feel nuts... but I reckon my mum would let you sleep over, when we're sixteen.'

'Gran would flip though.' Jerome mimics an old Jamaican lady's accent, '"Lawd Jesus, we have a sinner!"'

They both laugh.

'Speaking of Gran,' Jerome says. 'What time is it? Barbecue chicken tonight. Wanna come over?'

'Mum's out with Karen again, so yeah, love to.'

Issy leans over the side of the bed to pick her clothes from the floor. She starts putting on her knickers and bra, trying her best to be discreet. Jerome laughs as he watches Isobel wriggling about under the covers. 'I just seen...'

She blushes as Jerome candidly stands in front of her completely naked. He puts the playlist back a few tracks before pulling on his boxer shorts. She feels high, tingly. Like the world is different, or she's changed. Still her, but older? Wiser? She can't put the right words to it. What she does know is that it feels good and she has no regrets.

They head, hand in hand, to Jerome's flat to feast Mabel Clarke's Caribbean cuisine. Issy is eating there more these days, if her mum does the late shift at the supermarket or is out drinking. Issy had never eaten fresh mango before Jerome - or homemade coleslaw.

Jerome opens the door to his council flat. That familiar smell of cinnamon and nutmeg. There's something constantly bubbling on Mabel's stove, curried goat or oxtail, always rice and peas. Mabel calls it, 'the smell of love.' She often makes barbecue chicken for Issy, knowing Issy can't take the hot jerk spice or Scotch bonnet peppers.

Jerome's block is directly opposite Hayley's block. That's how they met. Issy was visiting Hayley and they bumped into each other. Jerome fancied

Issy the first time he saw her. She would always avoid the steps leading to Hayley's when Jerome and Dwayne were there with all the boys. To her, they were a bunch of scary black boys. She didn't know any "coloured people" before she moved to Lewisham. Now, she feels ashamed she was ever afraid of them because of the colour of their skin. Jerome, on the other hand, would stare, wide-eyed at Issy sitting with Hayley, and would be jealous when Hayley's older brother Ronnie would chase her and pretend to grab her plaits.

The tiny kitchen is steaming away with the window ajar, mixing London city breeze with hot island spices. Jerome's grandmother is by the stove, listening to old reggae love songs on the local radio station, swaying while she cooks. The radio reception flowing in and out, makes the music seem to mirror the steam clouds escaping every now and then from the rice pot and out of the window. For a woman in her seventies, she can still move to the beat.

When Issy and Jerome first got together, she wondered if his grandmother would accept them. She grew up with a family who called black people "coloureds". They lived in the East End and never thought it proper for black and white people to mix in that way. Bad enough that Issy's mum was Scottish, 'How far north you wanna go, son?' is what her grandparents would say to her dad. 'Northerners,' was the response whenever Carol did anything not to their taste, even though Carol had been living in East London since she was sixteen. But when Jerome introduced Issy for the first time, Mabel grabbed her with both arms and locked eyes. She felt scared until Mabel relaxed her grip and smiled sweetly, 'Yes, you're a good child,' she had soothed in her soft Jamaican accent, later telling Jerome, 'So long as dem eyes kind.'

In the time that Jerome and Issy have been together, Issy's also fallen for Mabel Clarke. Fascinated by how much love the old lady has in her heart, bringing up her grandsons, leaving her own life in Jamaica. And to Granny Mabel, Issy is the perfect potential granddaughter, always polite, always thankful.

'Jerome, fix some plates from the cabinet.'

Jerome goes into the living room and takes out the family's best plates.

'Granny Mabel, you don't have to use them for me,' Issy says every time.

Mabel lifts one eyebrow, 'Why not, dear?' she asks, giving Issy an overdone-confused face. 'Come, let me see you?' Mabel takes Issy's arm, 'I can see love in these eyes today. Yes, Lawd.'

Issy's cheeks burn with paranoia – the loss of her virginity stamped across her forehead. Mabel turns up the radio and demands she dance. Jerome comes in with the plates and chuckles. He's never felt so happy to be alive. Granny Mabel stops to take the plates from Jerome. She gently pushes the two teens together.

'Yes, Lawd. This is real music, mmm mmm…' Mabel chuckles as she turns the radio down again. They stop dancing, feeling awkward, embarrassed.

'You two remind me of when I met Earl. He was standing at me father's garage. Tall and strong. He said to me, "Beauty, can I fix your car?"' Jerome looks at Issy. They've heard this a million times.

'I said, "I have no car, Sir. I'm only sixteen year old."' Mabel opens her mouth to mimic a gasp, placing both hands on her chest, '"This is my daddy's garage".'

Mabel throws back her head, raising her arms in the air, and laughs, 'Him look shocked. Thought I would tell Daddy and him lose his job. I jus' smile and say, "Thank you for the compliment. Enjoy your day."'

Mabel adjusts the heat on the stove. 'And from that day, him told me, "I'll wait for you, Mabel Johnson. I'll wait for you to become a lady." I say, "Earl, I am a lady." Him reply, "A lady-woman".'

She turns back, the reggae station fires up a new song but the reception keeps cutting in and out. 'Since that day, he always called me, "lady-woman". Never wife, never woman, never jus' a lady… always—'

'Lady-Woman,' Jerome and Issy both join in.

Mabel turns to the teenagers. 'Do I tell it too much?'

Jerome and Issy laugh, nodding. 'Yes.'

Mabel throws up her hands, 'Oh well, never mind. Come, sit pon di table and let me feed you into strong people.'

After dinner, Jerome and Issy head to the upper park again to relax above London's skyline.

Issy sits inside Jerome's legs, much to the disapproval of a local dog walker. Oblivious, they continue to kiss and share cigarettes.

'Can I tell you something?' she asks, leaning her head on his chest.

'Course babes.'

'Think I'm gonna do A-Levels, you know, after my GCSEs.'

'That's cool,' Jerome strokes her hair.

'So I can go uni. If I go university, I have more chances to get a proper job, you know.'

'That's great, babe.'

Issy wriggles around to face Jerome, 'Honestly?'

'Yeah, babes. I've been thinking now we're back at school and ting, I wanna go college too, study music production. Stuff with the pirate radio proper kicked off over summer. Been producing all these tracks and started talking to Steve at the youth club and he was saying about starting a record label. Spoke to Dwayne and the boys were like: Let's start our own label and selling tracks from now.'

'Serious?' Issy kisses Jerome. 'That's amazing!'

'We're thinking Graff start linking with other man dem and having MC battles and setting up raves. Selling bare tickets and downloads, get me. Us and dem war.'

'Ain't that a bit dangerous? You know... battles.'

'Nah, nah, nah,' Jerome stands up, animated with this talk of the future. 'We don't want, like, real beef. Both sides on it, to make papers. Dwayne was telling me about how that's how all dem man dem run. You get all these little yutes on a hype ting, but really, everyone's sitting down like businessmen.'

'Ah, yeah, I get it. That's really clever, actually.'

'Makes nuff money trust. Plus it's legit.' Jerome pulls out his rolling papers and sits back down. He licks the seal of a cigarette then peels off the paper and empties the tobacco into the Rizla. 'I'm nearly sixteen. Can't keep selling weed. Couple of years, I'll be in big man's prison. Dwayne's eighteen next year. No joke. No way is my batty getting raped by some fifty-year-old, trust.' Jerome hunts round his pockets for the weed to roll a spliff.

'Babe, if I make just one Number One track then tings will be amazing for me and you.' He pans his arm across London's skyline, 'We can buy a fat house anywhere you like, trust. I just got a feeling.'

Issy watches the twinkles from the city reflect in her boyfriend's eyes. 'With a garden?'

Jerome gives up searching his pockets, 'Shit, lost my weed.'

'To be honest, I'm not feeling like getting mashed,' she says. 'I'm proper happy.'

Jerome smiles. 'You know what, me too, babe.'

Stuffing the rolling papers into his pocket, he takes stock of London at twilight. 'Best day of my life, trust. Man dem hotting up hoes just to get their tings wet up, but me, I done it right. Just like Steve was saying.'

'Steve from youth club?'

'Yeah, with them nasty photos of warts and shit, remember? But the ting what shocked me wasn't even the photos. Remember he was saying how like ninety per cent regret their first time. How that girl went and said that the bredder forced it on her and he's like, all I said was 'come on, you'll like it.' I'm like yeah, cool: prison for smoking weed but no way is some dutty side chick try call me a rapist. I was like, nah man, this needs to be proper. One woman. No nasty diseases. Just pure love. Straight up.'

'I don't know any boy who cares like that,' Issy says, proud Jerome is her boyfriend. She can't deny how good it feels to lose her virginity to a good guy.

Jerome wraps his arms tight around Issy. 'If they had someone like you, they would, trust.' He kisses her softly.

'So dis uni flex,' Jerome asks, putting a cigarette to his lips, 'is it because of what Mr Robbins was saying in assembly?'

'Sort of. But more since we met that girl.'

'What's her face? Emily?' Jerome pulls out his yellow lighter.

'Yeah. She's well nice. I know, a bit posh for our crew, but I rate her. So she goes private school with a sixth form. She was saying not all the kids have to pay though. Some have, what's it? Erm…'

'Scholarship.' Jerome lights his cigarette, letting out two donut-shaped puffs of smoke.

'Yeah, scholarship.' Issy takes Jerome's cigarette and inhales. 'She got me the application. Mum's gotta fill it in, ASAP basically…'

Issy looks at Jerome, handing him back the lit cigarette. He looks famous, park-light reflecting from his smooth skin. 'So you don't mind if I try get in this private school? Means we won't be at the same place after GCSEs?'

Jerome sees she's worried. 'Put it this way, I know you love me, innit, and I definitely love you so no matter what we'll be together. We're a team, babes.'

Issy's eyes well up.

He kisses her cheek to seal the pact, then pulls away, 'Wait. Is it mixed?'

'Girls only.'

'Good, otherwise, I'd have to think twice,' he winks along with that cheeky grin.

'So you're not scared I'm gonna make loads of rich friends and change? Hayley said I will.'

'Fuck Hayley.' Jerome sucks his cigarette harshly, the glow lighting up his jawline. 'Posh people are just people at the end of the day. You ain't the type to change. Plus, d'ya wanna end up like Hayley's family? No disrespect, but I'd rather be posh than be some hoodrat fucking up their kids.'

'That's a bit raw.'

'Issy, she's a big woman. The way she treats Hayley is raw.' He brings her back between his legs and wraps his arms around her waist. 'Boy it's getting cold right about now. Summer's done.'

'Yeah, we better go.' Issy springs to her feet. 'Got school tomorrow.'

'Boffin!' Jerome jibes. 'Hey, I was joking, babes!' He takes her in his arms and lifts her up and he swings Issy around. 'My girlfriend's going uni. That's good. I like that, still.'

Walking out the gates of the park, two policemen approach. 'Evening kids. I'm afraid I am going to have to stop you both to ask some questions.'

Jerome squeezes Issy's hand. The second officer notes this and gives his colleague the eye.

'What have you been up to this evening?' the second officer asks.

Tempted to say 'Fucking my wifey,' Jerome stops himself, remembering sex under sixteen is illegal. 'We were at my girlfriend's until about six. Then we went to my gran's to eat, then we come to the park and now we're going home to get ready for school.'

'What time would you say you left your grandmother's house to go to the park?' the first policeman asks, his eyes seeming kinder.

Issy looks at Jerome, 'About seven-thirty,' she replies. 'We come here a lot to watch the sunset.'

'How romantic,' the second policemen remarks dryly.

The first police officer, ignoring his colleague, continues, 'I'm afraid that I am going to have to perform a stop and search on you, sir. Are you aware of the procedure?'

Jerome drops his gaze to stare at the ground.

'Have you been stopped and searched before?' asks the second police officer.

Jerome, disliking the second officer more and more, answers sarcastically, 'What do you think?'

'It's okay babe, you ain't done nothing.' Issy squeezes his hand reassuringly.

'That's my point,' Jerome says, breaking the embrace, frustrated his perfect day is ending on a stop and search.

'Unfortunately, I'm just doing my job. I'm not sure what you mean by your comment.'

The first officer sees the stalemate coming. 'We've received two reports of theft this evening in the Telegraph Hill area, and the young men in question fit your description,' he says calmly.

'So, black? Yeah? Black?' Jerome spits on the floor. 'Congratulations on your investigation.'

The second officer stares at Jerome, 'Perhaps if so many of the crimes around here were not made by people of your colour, we wouldn't have to search you. Had the victim told us the criminal in question is white, we wouldn't be stopping you, would we? Now shut up or we'll do this down at the station. Your choice.'

Issy links Jerome's arms. She gets why he is annoyed but being rude to police always spells trouble.

Jerome bites his lip as he spreads his legs. His face flushes with the humiliation as the policeman's hands move closer to his groin, while the second officer fills out the slip, taking down Jerome's details. Jerome shakes his head, 'Today was special and you feds have to go and fucking spoil it.'

'Right, enough backchat,' the second officer grabs Jerome by the clothing around his chest, 'You're under arrest.' He nods to his colleague.

'For what? For what, though?!' Jerome protests, his adolescent pitch rising and falling.

41

The first officer doesn't look happy with his colleague, but begins the spiel as handcuffs are put around the boy's wrists.

'You don't have to arrest him. He didn't do anything wrong!' Issy re-attaches herself to Jerome's cuffed hand. Just moments before they were in a haze of blissful love, 'Please, it's our anniversary,' she fibs.

The police ignore Issy and radio the station to prepare for Jerome's arrival. Jerome sighs heavily. Anger turns to acceptance as the policeman empties his pockets. The second one calling a car to come.

'Please?' Issy asks again, tears forming in her eyes. 'He hasn't done anything wrong.'

Jerome sits in the cell, tears filling his eyes. He punches the wall. Four bare walls and a silver toilet bowl with a camera pointing right at him. His fingerprints taken on both hands. His saliva swabbed for DNA records. All before any solicitor or his grandmother has been spoken to.

After four hours, and finally a call to Granny Mabel, the policemen, satisfied Jerome is not who they're looking for, let him go, not without making a comment about hanging around the park at night with king-size rolling papers in back pockets and a big mouth.

Jerome finds his weed back home in the left foot of yesterday's sports sock, relieved they didn't find it, but he's devastated still. Losing his virginity will always be tarnished with being wrongfully arrested and thrown inside a police cell.

Issy lies in bed, waiting to hear from Jerome. She wonders if the same people what tried to rob Emily are back again. Dwayne texts her: 'Graff is protecting the Endz and me and da man dem will sort it.' His text doesn't help. She'll ask Graff to be careful. Crazy Christian Tameika told her Peckham yutes carry knives.

CHAPTER 6
NINE MONTHS BEFORE THE RIOTS…

Cant 2nite mum promised 2 do skool form, Issy presses send. The scholarship application has been stuck to the fridge for weeks.

boffin! :P

'Whatever,' Issy whispers to herself. It's now November and Issy feels the sting of cold weather hitting in the air as she jumps off the bus. Her fingers stiffen and she takes out her phone to read Emily's text.

Hi Issy! The absolute deadline for the application is December 10. So in one way you have plenty of time, though the school look favourably on early applicants. Good Luck, Emily xx

Issy arrives home looking forward to changing out of her school uniform. As she enters the flat, something can be heard from the living room. She opens the door to a smoky room with Carol and Karen inside, holding microphones. There's a half empty bottle of rose wine and their karaoke games sprayed across the floor.

'What are you doing!' Issy shouts.

'Let me introduce you to Karen Fitzgerald - also known as Cher - my best friend!'

Carol laughs flinging her right arm over her friend's shoulders, almost singeing Karen's ginger frizzy curls with her cigarette.

'We're supposed to be doing the application, remember?' Issy slumps down on the sofa, not wanting to be angry in front of Karen,

'I ain't forgotten. Why d'you think I got Karen to schlep over? She's used to all this.' Carol sits next to Issy and strokes her hair. 'What do I know about uni forms?'

'Then why you drinking?' Issy sulks. 'And it's not uni, it's A Levels to get to uni.'

'Right! Karen, Turn it off!' Carol leaps up and switches the games console off.

'Let me get the wee paperwork.' Issy's mum fumbles down the hallway to retrieve the form.

'Cheer up, love,' Karen says, her Irish accent gets thicker the more she drinks. She leans over and pats Issy on the shoulder. 'We've only had one.'

Issy half-smiles, sceptical. Instead of pens and reading glasses, she had to walk in and find both of them singing if they believe in life after love. Plus they pretended to be quiet when they heard Issy come in. Proper immature.

'Please do it proper.'

Karen looks at Issy, 'I will make sure this application is the best I've ever done.' Karen crosses her heart with her two fingers, 'I'm the queen of form filling, Issy. I work inside a palace of bureaucracy!'

Carol hands Karen the form.

'If you want this school, you get it,' Karen continues. 'Just don't end up a Tory.'

'Aye, you'll have Grandfather turn in his grave,' adds Carol, waving her cigarette like a magic wand.

'Promise.' Issy crosses her fingers, now feeling excited.

The three of them sit down in the living room and get to work on finishing the six sided form. After their hard graft, the trio leave the house to celebrate, popping the A4 envelope in the post as they head down to the pub.

'An Irish woman, a Scottish woman and a London teen walk into a bar... What happens next?' Karen asks the bar tender, opening her purse.

He looks warily at Karen and shrugs, 'They drink?'

'Two double vodka and tonics and a large lemonade.' Karen pulls a face when he turns to make the drinks, 'Boring.'

Karen and Carol are great to be with. They love their bingo, nights out, ladies' nights in. For all Issy worries about her mum's drinking, at least Carol has Karen by her side.

Tonight's karaoke night and aside from two older men singing Irish folk songs, the trio have full use of the machine.

'Come on with ya, sweetheart?' one man calls to Karen, holding the microphone up, 'The stage is cold.'

'Well we can't have that now, can we?' Karen gets to her feet.

Karen gives Issy a sneaky vodka in with her lemonades. 'Shhh, don't tell yer mam,' she winks.

Carol later sneaks a vodka Issy's way, whispering 'Don't show Karen.'

Three hours later, the all-singing, all-wobbling threesome stagger back onto the estate, only to find a frantic Jerome racing towards them.

'Issy!' he calls out, sweat pouring down his face. Jerome grabs Issy's shoulders, looks her over then holds her close. He pulls back to face her, 'I've been calling all night, man. Where you been?'

'Been with Mum and–'

'You wanna watch men like that, Issy,' Karen jibes.

'Man like what?' Jerome snaps without thinking.

'Hey, don't talk to Karen like that,' Issy tells him. Her cheeks burning part-vodka, part-shame. 'She's only joking.'

Jerome lets go of Issy and walks in a circle with his head in his hands. 'Aarggh!' he shouts. 'Them boys are gonna get it!' He punches the nearest tree.

Issy, Carol and Karen watch him rest his forehead on the bark.

'Jerome, what's wrong, love?' Carol walks over and gives his shoulder a reassuring squeeze.

Her smile calms him. 'Sorry, Carol. Sorry, Karen. Issy, I'm proper sorry. I just, I thought... I got told...' Jerome trails off.

'What? What's wrong?' Issy asks.

'Nothing. It's fine.' He shakes his head, rubbing his eyes. 'Boy,' he exhales, with some relief. 'Man got shook.'

'Jerome have you been smoking the wacky-backy again?' Carol laughs as she lightly knocks him on the head.

'Yeah, something like that,' Jerome forces a chuckle. 'Come, I'll walk you ladies home.'

Karen grabs Carol's arm to let the lovers walk ahead. As soon as she's out of ear shot, Karen whispers, 'You not worried about that?'

'About what?' Carol asks putting a cigarette to her mouth.

'Issy, being with that...?' Karen whispers back, looking up, checking they can't hear.

Carol takes the cigarette from her mouth, 'He's a good kid, Karen.'

'They can be violent, those... boys.'

'Karen! I never took you to be racist,' Carol snorts.

'Be Jesus, how can I be racist?' Karen chuckles awkwardly, 'I'm part of the holy trinity meself, so I am: No Dogs, No Blacks, No Irish. I'm just saying, looks like he's got a temper, that's all.'

Issy and Jerome walk back to her flat. They don't say much and in the silence, Issy takes comfort in being held tighter than usual. She feels more than safe. She feels like he's exactly the person she wants to be with, so lucky to have him.

Issy leans into Jerome once they get out of Carol and Karen's sight. 'Kiss me?'

'I can't,' he says, pulling away.

She thinks it's because she stinks like her mum does after a night in the pub.

He follows her up to her room. They sit on Issy's bed, still wearing their coats, Issy with her matching pink hat and scarf and Jerome with his woolly hat in the shape of a baseball cap.

She picks up her mobile which she left charging and switches it on. Jerome grabs it as it starts beeping with unread messages.

'What you doing?'

'I don't want you to see what's on there,' Jerome says. Jerome strokes Issy's hair and takes off her scarf. 'I've fucked up, babe.'

Jerome goes silent and she thinks the worst: he's cheated. Said he was different but gassed her up like all boys do. Acted nice to take her virginity and now he's gonna dump her. Tears well in Issy's eyes.

'First it was all cush, get me. Us and Brockley crew making tracks. We're thinking one track per week. Ours comes out Tuesday, theirs Thursday. All the little yutes on it. Then these next bredders from Peckham endz wanna in on it. They're making tracks saying they're at war with us. But these next breddars don't know this war's a hype ting for us, get me. Well, then Andre starts gassing up this girl from Peckham endz. Now she's some bredder called F-Manz's little sister. Little sister.' Jerome repeats, as if Andre could be so stupid. 'Like underage, get me. And boy, I don't know if he got set up or what, but now the girl's trying to say it was rape.'

Issy looks at the notifications on her phone. Missed calls from Jerome, and a series of messages from an unknown number:

Bitch.

Bitch? Were u @ Bitch

Im watchin u

I no were u live

Redy to b rapped bitch?

Gonna rape u 2nite

Issy looks at Jerome, 'Is this some joke?'

'I got a call from Tee-z saying F-Manz is gonna rape our block's girls starting with you. I don't fucking know this F-Manz. Some snake gave these bredders your number, sending Andre screen shots. I got some prank call saying you're being raped and if I wanna go see you, you're tied up on Peckham Rye. I got shook when you didn't pick up. Me and Andre and dem manz been looking all over. Dwayne's got some chick's car now so he could ride round Peckham. No joke. That's why I was in a mess when I saw you. I was on my way to tell your mum we gotta call feds.'

Issy sips from the plastic cup of squash by her bed from this morning. Tastes disgusting.

'I wound myself up more and more when I kept getting your answerphone. I was so shook these breddas weren't gassing.'

Issy's eyes widen, 'D'ya think… they'd…?'

Jerome turns to Issy, 'I don't know, babe,' he whispers. He holds Issy's hand. 'I was proper shook tonight. Never felt like this before.'

They sit in silence, staring at each other until Issy starts to laugh.

'It ain't funny, man. I was going nuts.'

'I know, I know, but I feel stupid now.'

'Boy trust me. What was I gonna tell your mum? How we gonna cope with you being…? That shit can mess you up, trust.' Jerome's eyes prick tears as he thinks of his childhood.

Certain she's more relieved than scared, Issy feels strangely happy knowing he wanted to protect her.

Carol knocks on the door. 'Issy love, it's nearly midnight…' She opens the door ajar but doesn't poke her head in, 'Best turn off that music.'

'It's okay, Mum, you can come in.'

Carol enters. She turns down the stereo and kisses her daughter's forehead. 'Goodnight, darling. Jerome, time to get going, my lovely.'

Jerome immediately acting on Carol's words, gets up from the bed.

After Carol leaves, Jerome turns back to give Issy a kiss on the cheek. 'I'm so sorry, babe,' he whispers.

'I'm fine, Jay. I thought you was gonna tell me you'd cheated.'

'I'd never cheat, babe,' Jerome smiles his gorgeous smile. 'You're my only One. My first, my last. So you're not shook up about dem texts?'

'It's fine: delete, delete, delete.'

'Gonna pick you up and walk you to school from now on, yeah?'

'Okay.'

One good thing about the winter, when the leaves have fallen away, Issy can see through the branches to Jerome's block. She watches from her bedroom window, kneeling on her bed, as he crosses the road and jumps over the stairwell gate then bops down the corridor. He turns and blows her a kiss then opens his door and is gone.

That night, Issy's phone beeps several times. The messages name her, name Jerome, their school and tell her she'll be raped before Christmas.

Much as she wants to delete them, remove them from her life, she keeps them as evidence, just in case.

Lying in bed, her mind spins, thinking about all the possible scenarios. Someone forcing them into her. Hitting her. More than one guy. Grabbing her from the street and dragging her down an alleyway. Pulling her into a car. Trying to scream but no sound coming, her voice frozen…

How she fell asleep she couldn't say, but her night was full of nightmares.

CHAPTER 7

Before they moved into the flat, an alcoholic had recently died there. The housing officer informed Carol she had to wait two extra weeks before moving in. Council staff discovered the carpet under the bed caked in urine and faeces, and so the clear out took longer than expected. That was the worst time and yet Issy's mum just accepted it.

Issy couldn't understand why she had to move from her old house in the first place. It was pretty and full of colourful wall paper with flowers and stripy borders. The houses were all wonderful and her favourite neighbours, an elderly couple, Ethel and Brian, always let Issy play on their grandson's swing. It wasn't Carol's fault that she couldn't afford the house payments.

Issy even wrote a letter to Queen Elizabeth II. As Carol read the uneven words and back-to-front letters, tears filled her eyes. Her six year-old daughter asked the Queen if she would sell her crown so they can use the gold coins to keep the house. That her mummy is a kind woman and would be very happy if the Queen did this. Carol kissed Issy for being such a sweet little girl. She then was taken next door to watch *Beauty and the Beast* with Ethel whilst Carol 'took a long hot bath.'

Carol broke down before she could make it back to her own front step. She was uncontrollable, her stomach churning with grief and no way to comfort it. All she wanted, needed, was to feel her husband's arms around her, to be kissed and told he was back and would sort everything. Issy ended up spending the night. Brian gave Carol a hug and a few glasses of his finest scotch until she felt a little better. The smell of whiskey reminded Carol of her own father; her idyllic childhood in the Highlands before it all went wrong. She thought about how he would wear the family kilt on every occasion, how he would put her on his knee, have all the children round the bonfire; his stubby fingers and thick neck animated, telling scary tales of local Highland mysteries. The torch momentarily lighting the whites of his eyes before his beard seeped them into darkness.

It was Brian and Ethel who paid to store their furniture, though most of it had to be sold because of the size of their new flat. Many more pieces later went as things got tight for Carol and Issy. Lovely pieces of furniture sold in Lewisham for next to nothing. Things Carol's mum had given her. Things she had wanted some day to pass to Issy. Gone. Forever. Traded for school shoes. Sometimes toilet paper and shampoo. Horrendously after years of quitting, Carol even sold earrings for cigarettes. What did she care? Bill never smoked a single day of his life and yet who was in that coffin?

'Karen helped us with the housing stuff. That's how we moved here. Then Mum got a job, and things got slightly better. She got a bit of her confidence back. Made friends. You know…'

'I'm so, so sorry,' Emily says, tears streaming down her face. 'Can I possibly give you a big hug?'

Issy notices Emily's eyes. The skin so thin and pale and what with the crying, they've become sore-looking. Anyone would think it was Emily's dad who'd died.

Emily flings her arms around Issy. Feeling awkward, Issy stiffens up and Emily stops hugging her and sits up. 'Then what happened?'

While they waited for the stench to clear, Carol and Issy found themselves in temporary accommodation about two miles away in a place called Lee. There they witnessed some awful stuff. Issy had a handful of good sleeps on nights when police were not knocking the door arresting prostitute mothers, escorting distressed children away with social workers, kicking and screaming. When ex-lovers didn't arrive on crack to smash windows. Kids with black teeth, mothers with no teeth; both covered in stained clothes and bruises. Carol came out of there thankful for life. The women's hostel was the best thing that could have happened to her. She walked away realising that there were many more rock bottoms, hundreds and thousands of them, deeper and darker. The worst thing her husband had ever done to her was to die young. And even that he fought tooth and nail against it.

For hours, he would watch Issy sleeping, just to know in his soul, he had spent more time with his daughter in her lifetime than his father had in his. He would read stories long after she'd fallen to sleep. He would sit in silence as Carol came home from the shops with a new box of tampons. Peering into the bathroom bin, then down at his own body, emasculated; desperate to give Issy the gift of a brother or sister before things would become impossible. He would collapse in his wife's arms, a giant compared to her tiny frame, devastated to be leaving her alone in the world. Carol would only cry when he would plead with her to love again. That he loved her so much, and someone so special doesn't deserve to be alone in the world. Issy needs a father. She needs a husband. Carol would slam doors and hit him to stop talking. As if anything could be so replaceable, her arms shaking frantically jolting from the pain in her chest.

He would get angry he never saved more as a young man, that his father drank their money away and passed him on damaged genes. But most nights they cuddled on the sofa. Every moment precious. Every day, every second noted it had slipped past and was never to return. And slowly, the cancer spread until he could fight no more. His muscles wasted. His skin discoloured and loosened around his bones. The brown eyes than won him his wife, paled. His breath stank like death days before Issy's father eventually lost organ function and died. The strong six foot man reduced to a curved heap of weakened diseased flesh.

'You don't have to talk about your past,' Emily wipes the tears from her soggy cheeks, 'if it's too upsetting.'

'No, no, I don't mind,' Issy replies, trying to piece together how they got from cupcakes to cancer.

Issy wonders why she couldn't like the cuddle. It felt weird. Too much. She slumps onto the wall by her bed, hiding part of the wallpaper that's ripped away, 'What about your parents?'

'My dad? Total nightmare,' Emily snorts, 'He's angry, pompous. Controls my mum.'

'Your poor mum,' Issy whispers. 'She's so nice.'

'Sometimes I hear her crying. Often I catch her staring out the window, dreaming of the possibilities, her potential futures if she just gathered up enough courage to pack her bags.'

'Then what happens?'

'She gets up and cooks supper. She has to have everything ready bang on time.'

'Doesn't your dad see your mum's sad?'

'Hmm,' Emily frowns, 'Dad can only see what's in his mind. A construction of family. He's rational to the point of ridiculous.'

Issy doesn't understand what Emily means by that. 'Why doesn't your mum tell him to change?'

'Don't know.' Emily finds herself fiddling with the rip in Issy's duvet cover. 'Too weak, I suppose.'

'Why don't you tell him?' Issy asks, watching Emily play with the feathering around the tear, sad it's there but there's nothing she can do about it. Her other bedsheets are in the wash.

'Don't know how to. I'd rock a boat I don't want to rock. I mean if they split up, all the attention would be on me. To be honest, I just want out of there as soon as possible,'

Emily flings her arms in the air. 'I just want to live in a pokey little flat on top of a hill somewhere in Paris, where all the walls are wonky and the plates don't match.' Her eyes light up whenever she talks Paris.

'I don't know a single person who's got a decent dad,' Issy says as way of consolation. 'Or step dads or real dads with other kids to care about. It's all fucked up. Like Hayley, her dad treats her so shit, but everyone loves him down the pub. He hasn't given Hayley a single penny for new school uniform this year but he'll buy randoms drinks all day long. And if she or her mum goes in there without his permission, he won't think twice before lashing out when they're back at home. Andre's dad's in prison for robbery. Ronnie, Hayley's brother, supposedly has a kid on the way but he's in prison for stabbing someone over nothing. Some bloke accidently rode into a pothole and crashed his bike into Ronnie's moped. It was a bicycle. One tiny scratch and he went mental. This girl at school's dad buys her everything because he touches her up…'

Issy looks at Emily. 'When I met your mum, I thought you were perfect. Your house is amazing. It's like my dream to have a massive garden. Double bed…'

'It's not that simple,' Emily cuts in then, letting out a huge sigh. 'Who knows what it takes to get a happy family?'

'Love.'

'We love each other,' Emily finds herself taken aback.

'Sorry, didn't mean you didn't.' Issy's cheeks burn with shame. She often worries she's offended Emily, that she'll get it wrong; that she's not good enough.

Emily backtracks, 'Sorry I snapped. I guess, I'm embarrassed.'

'Don't be. We're friends.'

'Friends for life!' Emily sits up, crossing her legs to face Issy. 'Please, if you're my true friend, promise we'll never be unhappy. Promise we'll never marry awful men. Promise?'

Emily holds out her little finger.

'Promise.' Issy says, holding out her little finger.

'I mean it,' Emily stares wide-eyed before committing to the finger shake. 'We have to look out for each other. Because we see the truth in things. It's an artist's gift. To search and portray truth. Let's lead the revolution of love!'

The two girls lock fingers.

Later that afternoon, Issy carefully brings up a plastic Forever Friends tray with a pot of tea and biscuits on. One of Jerome's music tracks is playing while Emily stirs in one sugar.

'So what's been happening with Jerome and those Peckham threats.

Sounds like it's old hat now?' Emily kicks herself. Her father says that, 'Old news, I mean.'

'Erm, well, yeah it is. Turns out the girlfriend only said it was rape to stop being dumped and beaten up by her boyfriend who she cheated on with Tee-z.'

'Is Tee-z, Andre?'

'Yeah, Jerome's best friend. Then her dad got involved, demanded she go police and that's when she confessed he never raped her and squashed the beef.'

'Squashed the beef,' Emily scribbles the term in her sketchbook, 'that's...'

'End the madness, you know, stop the trouble. Solve the problem. Whatever. So, since the girl never got raped, the revenge wasn't needed so I never got raped. Then neither of the boys wanted her and she was left with no-one. Plus her dad beat her for having sex at fifteen. Oh and check this out,' Issy leaps off the bed towards her wonky computer desk. Logging on to her social media profile, she clicks to Andre Tee-z's page and finds the girl's profile. 'Three weeks ago she had like six-hundred friends,' Issy says, eyes fixed to the screen, 'now she's got sixty-two!'

Emily's fascinated by this story as the two girls scroll the friends list. 'I can't believe she's been shunned by so many people.'

'But you can't say you was raped.'

'Were raped.'

'What?'

'You can't say that you were raped or you can't say that you had been raped; you can't say you was raped. That's bad grammar.'

'Oh yeah, were not was.'

'You still want me to correct you?' Emily asks, tentatively.

'Yeah. I want all As in my GCSEs.'

'What an extraordinary story. Poor you. To be involved in such a saga,' Emily gives Issy a puppy-like expression, big eyes, sympathy. Issy doesn't know how to accept it. She doesn't need sympathy. This kind of 'madness' happens all the time on estates.

'Were you frightened?'

'Actually it turned out good,' Issy insists, 'I didn't have to move with Hayley, wasting time sitting on streets, freezing my tits off. I did all my English and History coursework.'

Emily laughs, "freezing my tits off' - Can I write that, too?'

'Sure,' Issy dunks a chocolate biscuit in her tea. 'I mean it. I've had this break from everyone and it's amazing how much work you can do if you don't hang out all night every night. It's like I got headspace. And I really like studying. More than I thought.'

Emily opens her large notebook and scribbles, 'This is such good stimulus.'

'Wow! Where is that?' Issy remarks, looking at photographs of a mansion set within acres of manicured gardens.

'It belongs to a family friend of my father's. Their French chateau.'

'Have you ever been to a place like that?' Issy can't imagine knowing people who live in such a magnificent place, it's like MTV Cribs with taste.

'We visit often. They invite us to stay every summer.'

'Wow, you go away every summer.'

'It's just France.'

'Never been anywhere apart from Butlin's,' Issy says, 'Don't have a passport.'

'You've never been abroad? But it's so cheap nowadays.'

'How did your dad meet a French person?'

'The Sparlings are British. It's their holiday home. They went to the same boarding school then both read law at Oxford at the same college. When you go to Oxford, you'll meet hundreds of people from all over the world. My brother has friends in Japan, Australia, New York, and in Mexico. He's always flying off to someone's wedding.'

'That sounds amazing,' Issy sighs, holding the teacup against her cheek, to feel its warmth. 'Imagine living somewhere hot or near a beach? My life would never look like that. I watch that show where people wanna move, to like Spain or Australia.'

'Seriously Issy, you need to have a passport. I have so many friends who have holiday homes abroad. We'll have the best time of our lives once we're eighteen! I'll start introducing you to my circle. It's who you know in this world, you know that? The whole system is rigged to the rich. Read about it anywhere…'

Issy listens to Emily telling tales of who her friends are, their rich and famous parents and relatives; her eyes wide with curiosity; her mind full of Ibiza yachts and secluded Caribbean beaches, just like in magazines.

Emily talks about Issy spending summers with her in Paris. She'd teach Issy French. Issy would use all the spaces on the balcony to grow flowers, while Emily paints them.

Emily stops and turns her head.

'What's wrong?' Issy asks.

'You hear that?'

Issy sits up. She looks out the window.

'No, not outside. This music, why do you listen to it?' Emily asks.

'Jerome makes it.'

'He does?' Emily frowns. 'Does he write the lyrics?'

'Why? Don't you like it?'

Emily tilts her head, 'Issy, they're really violent. The lyrics, I mean.'

'Yeah but it's not real…' and Issy explains the façade behind the lyrical battles.

'But don't you think it's slightly irresponsible to make songs like this?'

'All rappers rap about violence and stuff.'

'No they don't,' Emily insists.

'How would you know?' Issy feels defensive. 'You don't have black friends.'

'I do!' Emily retorts. 'In fact, I'm going to a black boy's party next weekend.'

'Really?' Issy looks surprised.

'Like he eats and breathes and talks like a real boy?'

'Join me, if you don't believe me.' Emily playfully pokes her tongue at Issy. 'I am not ignorant, you know.'

'Is he posh?' Issy screws up her nose. 'One posh friend's enough for now!' Issy smirks.

Emily grins. 'Well, he's a bit posh.'

'He must be if your mum's letting you go out at night.'

'Actually I met him through my dad.'

'Would you ever kiss a black boy?' Issy teases.

'Of course I would! I have, this boy George.'

'Boy George!'

'George used to have a crush on me,' Emily continues not getting the reference. 'D'you want to come?'

When is it?'

'Next Friday.'

'Can I bring Jerome? Love him to see Boy George.'

'You can't make fun of him. He is a really, really nice person.'

Issy offers her little finger. 'Promise.'

'Okay, I'll call George just to make sure it's okay to bring friends.'

'Will this George play good music?'

'Yes he will, but not this. Seriously Issy, if you do one thing before bed, it's listen to it properly.' Emily is stern. 'I think a thoughtful reflection about this music will unlock some answers as to why all these gangs keep bashing each other up. I mean, somebody threatened to rape you and you've been more or less under house arrest. It's no joke.'

Emily, for the first time, sounds less lofty artist and more like a concerned teacher. Her tone is sombre and as Issy meets Emily's eyes, she feels the icy chill of honesty. She never took any of this into consideration after Jerome convinced her the battles are fake. And besides, Jerome's calm. He never wants to fight. He's the master of keeping out of trouble. He's the artful dodger of detentions, suspensions and 'meet-me-at-the-school-gate tensions. But after Emily rushes to her piano lesson, Issy listens to Graff's latest tune, but this time she really listens. Some lyrics are worse than others: spitting on people, slapping up bitches, kidnapping rival gang's family members. Jerome and her are usually mash-up laughing at the insults but she did think at the beginning things could get dangerous. And Jerome once tried to bring it up but Dwayne just looked at him, and said 'Bring it, then.'

As each track fires the opposing gang with insults, Issy wonders if Emily has a point. Only this week on the school bus she overheard little Year 7s and 8s talking about the gang war between Graff and EndzUpCrew.

'I heard Tee-z tied up f-Man's sister then pushed her off London Bridge,' one boy cried out on the back of the bus.

'I heard if anyone from Brockley goes New Cross, they get stabbed up,' replied his podgy freckled-faced friend.

'Who do you think's harder, Double G or f-Manz?' asks one of them, 'I think f-Manz.'

'I think Double G!'

Issy pauses the music. It might be a business deal between Telegraph Hill and Brockley, but it is real to Emily and their listeners.

Emily rushes through the gate at 55 Pepys Road, but before she gets to the front door, Janie Sutton opens it. Once out of view of any neighbours, Janie whispers in Emily's ear, 'You're thirteen minutes late!'

'Sorry I was at Merle's and lost track of time.'

Janie narrows her eyes at Emily then ushers her daughter into the drawing room towards the warm smile of her piano teacher.

Janie lifts the tone of her voice to sound jolly. 'Mr Appleby has been sat here patiently…'

Mr Appleby smiles at Emily, setting the delicate china teacup down rather clumsily before hoisting himself up from the armchair.

After the lesson ends, Janie sends Mr Appleby off with a jar of homemade plum chutney. Closing the door, she summons a retiring Emily to the kitchen.

'I rang Merle's mother. She said you were not there. In fact, Emily Sutton, you have not been at Merle's house half as much as you say you have.' Janie folds her arms and leans back on the granite counter, 'so Missy, where have you been?'

Emily looks at her mother. How to explain? Perhaps she should confess her secret friendship. Perhaps, with the right words, Janie Sutton could relax those folded arms and let the union continue out in the open.

'Emily, I do not want you with that girl, do you hear?' cries Janie's angry pitch, that annoying grade of shrieking.

'Yes, Mum.'

'And if I find you've been wasting any more time on her, I will be extremely cross and will have no choice but to explain all this to your father!'

'Mum!' Emily outcries, 'She's helping me with my Art A Level!'

Janie scowls at Emily. 'Do you think Isabelle is some kind of pet?'

'No.'

'Or something you can consume?'

'No!'

'Well, it certainly sounds that way.'

'I genuinely like her.'

Janie notices her own hands start to tremble. She pours a glass of elderflower squash and sits at the kitchen table, and takes stock of the situation.

'Emily, darling, I frequently drive past Ommaney Road. I have seen your 'friend' with her friends. They smoke and gawd knows what else…' The thin and aging skin across her brow creases.

'But I don't smo–'

'And they spit on the pavement.'

'She doesn't spit,' Emily insists, 'Unless you're being street and mean rapping?'

Janie doesn't get it. Emily slumps down at the kitchen table, burying her head in her arms.

'The children on that estate are always terrorising locals in the park. Such is the scale of the graffiti problem that the matter took up an hour at the residents' assembly last Tuesday.'

Emily lifts her head up to look at her mother. She is so annoyingly perfect. Nicely blow-dried hair. Antique pearl earrings. Neatly ironed pale blue shirt and navy trousers. A maroon V-neck cashmere jumper she's had for years, with her stupid machine that clips the fluff ensuring its bobble-free. Her mother sits straight as an arrow. Thin as a pancake. Touch of rouge on each cheek. Just enough lipstick to look peachy, but not too much to avoid appearing bold. Two strokes of mascara on each upper eyelashes, one stroke on the lower ones. Never black, always light brown so people wonder if she is wearing any at all. Picture perfect. Prim and proper: Emily's worst nightmare. Why can't she be more avant-garde? More edgy like Hendrike's mum? Emily imagines Janie Sutton with tussled rock-chick hair, skinny faded-black jeans, converse pumps and a baggy Adidas jumper she's had since the eighties. Up pop a pair of headphones plugged into her new iPod playing Blondie and The Smiths.

'Are you listening?'

Emily stares at her mother's pearl earrings. Radio 4 analysing war poetry in the background.

'Mum, I know you might not believe me but the people doing the graffiti are not from here. Besides, graffiti is not a crime. It's an artistic form of expression.'

'Not when it's on private property!'

Emily rolls her eyes.

'I see you won't listen,' Janie says, arms still folded tightly, 'so let's make things extremely clear. You will now be grounded for two weeks.'

'But I'll miss George's party!'

'Well then, you should have thought about this before lying to your parents. Honestly, you are going to be sixteen. In less than two years, supposed to be fit to live alone on campus, yet you trick me more now than when you were six! Perhaps we'll choose a London college so that we can keep an eye on–'

'What!?' Emily stands up. 'You can't do this! Yes, I am sixteen-years-old I can enter the army at sixteen. I can work legally paying taxes with my National Insurance number. I can even have sex! But somehow I can't choose my own friends because you are a snob!'

'How dare you speak to me like this?' Janie stands up to her daughter, pointing an unsteady index finger towards the hall. 'You will go to your room, immediately.'

Emily stomps up the stairs, slamming her bedroom door shut in tears. Who does her mother think she is? She can be friends with who she wants and can study where she wants. She doesn't need her parents constantly on her back, hawking her every move. She doesn't need anyone oppressing her. Emily punches her pillow red-faced and firmly defiant. Janie Sutton may have won this battle, but she most certainly won't ever win the war.

A worried mother sits down at the table. Janie isn't cut out for conflict. The elderflower is replaced by pinot noir. How to explain there are wrong sorts in the world? That these people disproportionately come from... This is certainly not her being awkward or pushy... or controlling. Since puberty kicked in, Emily has been much more of a handful. Shaving her legs, wearing tight clothes, sneaking out. Janie looks up at the oil painting of Sir James Sutton. 'You always knew what to do.'

Sir James Sutton's beady brown eyes often scare people, yet she only ever sees the kindness. She often talks to the painting.

'I should tell your grandson, surely? He'll be cross, but he does handles these sorts all the time.'

And with that, Janie takes her wine glass through to the living room and makes a call to her husband's chambers.

CHAPTER 8
BOY GEORGE

Sometimes, life's easy. Issy's bus comes straightaway, there's space to get on, even a seat. The driver's friendly and it's not too cold out considering it's only February, so she opens her window, freshening the upper deck so it isn't steaming with over excited schoolkids and their chicken and chips.

In tutor group time this morning, Issy got a certificate of achievement for completing her GCSE English and History coursework targets. Hayley laughed, shouting 'Boffin!' and the boys made fake fart noises but Issy was too delighted to care. She smiles at the reflection of her face in the bus window. A proper certificate, not a merit mark or smiley face. In a wooden frame with real glass, real ink signatures from the Head Teacher. It felt good. Still feels good. She can't wait to show Emily.

As Issy walks home from the bus stop, holding the frame to her chest, she's excited about tonight. She even finds a rolled up ten pound note on the stairwell. Result!

She runs upstairs to her room and carefully places the certificate on her dresser before laying out various options to wear for. The radio plays as she rushes from the bathroom to the mirror in her room, to her mum's room to borrow black tights and search for some jewellery.

Meanwhile over the road, a different beat is thumping Mabel Clark's flat. The dark, gritty grime Jerome is producing is booming from the speaker Dwayne forever borrowed from some girl.

Dwayne and Jerome have single beds adjacent to one another. Unlike the baby pink bedroom inhabited by his girlfriend, pinned to grey walls are posters of muscle-clad rappers holding guns and platinum medallions covered in diamonds with large-chested women bending over red convertible cars in drawstring bikinis the colours of the Jamaican flag, which their grandmother constantly reminds them represent nothing Jamaica.

Jerome tidies his hairline with an electric razor. It takes twice as long because he keeps dancing to his music and scribbling down studio instructions along with time codes before heading back towards the long mirror glued to the wall on his side of the bedroom.

He creams his body with shea butter then waits for it to dry before putting on his boxers. When he comes back from the bathroom, he finds Dwayne lying on his bed.

Dwayne eyes Jerome suspiciously. 'You on this, then?' he asks, with attitude.

'Yeah.'

Dwayne stares at Jerome, narrowing his eyes, 'You know Fridays are big for business.'

'It's one night, D,' Jerome says, taking out his best jeans.

'We need to be out shottin, ya get me? Not pussying around some neek's yard.'

Jerome looks over at his older brother. 'I'm taking tings with me. There'll be nuff rich kids gonna want weed.'

Dwayne looks up at the ceiling.

This is the first time Jerome is going to a party without inviting Dwayne. Guilt is soon replaced with excitement as Jerome looks in the mirror. Proper buff. He's happy to be doing something different for a change.

Dwayne looks back to his brother: best jeans, designer belt, church shirt.

'Why you going looking like a batty boy?'

Jerome screws up his face.

'Just because dis bredder's rich, don't mean you have to g'wan like someone you ain't. One invitation and you're dressing like some next coconut.'

'Don't!' Jerome raises his voice, before lowering it again, 'call me that.'

Dwayne jumps from the bed to face his brother, 'Why you getting vex?'

Jerome holds Dwayne's stare.

'Bredda's black,' Jerome says before kissing his teeth.

Dwayne walks out. Jerome hears the front door click. He peers out the kitchen window to see Dwayne jogging over to Hayley's block. He hardly kisses his teeth at Dwayne but his brother went there.

Back in his room, Jerome takes another look in the mirror. He opens his closet and pulls out his Nike t-shirt and matching light grey hooded jumper. He looks at the poster stuck inside his wardrobe door, then at his own thick gold chain hanging on the bedpost. He changes out of his clothes, places the chain over his head and puts on his matching gold bracelet. He then puts both his diamanté earrings back in, laces up his brand new trainers, puts his hood up, shuts off the music, and rocks out the door.

An excited Emily is putting the finishes touches to her outfit. She turns and poses for a proud mother to take a photo.

'You look absolutely gorgeous. So pretty.'

'Thank you,' Emily replies as they walk down the staircase to await the taxi.

'Your father will be picking you up at midnight,' Janie says as she fiddles with Emily's hair then brings her coat from the coat stand. 'Now, you have the card from us. I'll pay for the taxi this end, and there's the hamper for George's parents. Be sure not to drink more than one glass of any sort of alcohol, though I'm sure William will be there to supervise and certainly won't have purchased anything other than a celebratory bottle or two. Perhaps I should call ahead and find out?'

Don't do that, Emily thinks, though actually, yes, if she calls now then…

'That's a good idea.'

Janie looks suspiciously at her daughter. 'Are you tricking me? Saying yes, so I won't make the call?'

Janie walks into the kitchen to call George's parents, meanwhile Emily texts Issy – who is now saved as Merle in her phone – to get ready to jump into the car.

Issy sees Jerome and gasps. 'I thought you were gonna wear your nice shirt.'

'Changed my mind.'

'You look like a hoodie!'

'I am one,' Jerome snaps, then immediately feels bad. 'You got one on.'

'It's on my coat,' Issy snaps back, unzipping her faux-fur trim hooded coat to reveal a black party dress.

'You look nice though, still,' Jerome licks his lips but this time a miffed Issy ignores him. She wraps her coat around her, arms folded, to avoid both the wintery chill and Jerome's advances.

'Excuse me, can we stop here and pick up these two?' Emily says to the taxi man.

'I was told one stop only love, at Mayfair.'

'That's my ditsy mother for you,' Emily chuckles, 'It's probably because she knew we have to go through this road because of the one-way system. Those are my friends, standing just there.'

The driver pulls over reluctantly to pick up the two hooded teenagers.

'Hi guys!' Emily squeals.

'Wow, never been in a black cab before!' Issy squeals back. 'It's like

61

EastEnders.'

Emily's mouth remains open as Issy reveals she's rarely been through Central London at all, 'I've never been West.'

'Don't you ever go to see museums, restaurants or musicals?'

Issy shakes her head, embarrassed.

Emily sticks out her little finger, 'I promise to take you to a museum. They're free to get in, you know.'

Hayley, actively excluded from the invite, is seen walking up the hill as the taxi drives down towards New Cross Road.

'Look there's Hays!' Jerome points out.

Before Issy can tell him to stop, Jerome winds down the window and shouts out her name. Fortunately, the car drives too fast for Hayley to recognise his face.

'Oi mate!' the disgruntled driver shouts over his shoulder. 'Can you not do that in my cab?'

'Yeah, sorry mate,' Jerome replies in his thickest South East London accent. 'She looked down,' Jerome tells Issy.

Issy looks angry.

'What's up?' Jerome asks, 'I thought she's your best friend?'

'She looks like a prostitute when she dresses up,' Issy snaps, still peeved Jerome's wearing a hoodie to the party. 'Anyway, she wasn't invited.'

'She could have come,' Emily says.

'And we can't do everything together,' Issy adds.

Tension hangs in the air as they cross Bermondsey towards Tower Bridge.

'So, looking forward to the party?' Emily asks, trying to make conversation, wondering if having them come was a bad idea.

'What kind of party is it?' Jerome asks, leaning over Issy.

'I told you, a house party,' Issy snaps, before Emily can reply.

'How we getting back?' Jerome looks out of the window, 'I don't wanna be left in no mad endz after dark.'

Emily leans over Issy and places her hand on Jerome's knee, 'I assure you this neighbourhood is far from mad. The only hoodies you'll see are marathon runners!'

Emily chuckles at her own joke. Issy smiles awkwardly. Jerome doesn't quite jump on board.

Noting Jerome's hood and Issy's hooded coat, Emily clears her throat, 'I guess the night bus or taxi.'

Jerome looks at the numbers click from thirteen pounds to fourteen pounds. Every blink the meter adds twenty pence.

'I would bring you home but my dad is picking me up and he wants to stop off via a friend's house to pick up golf clubs,' Emily lies. Who picks up golf clubs at midnight? The truth is, she hasn't told Issy she's banned from being friends with them, or that the reason her dad is picking her up is because Emily is actually grounded and had to beg George in tears to plead for her attendance.

Jerome is now feeling more trapped than excited. He has no idea what to expect and his brother's attitude towards going out has put him in a shit mood: 'So what music is this bredder gonna play?'

'All sorts,' assures Emily.

'Like what?' he continues, 'Best not be any boybands or nuttin, get me,' Jerome lets out a forced humph through his nose. He feels Issy's elbow in his side as Emily's mobile rings.

'Merle,' Emily says nervously, definitely starting to wonder if the benefits of taking them to George's party will outweigh the risks.

While Emily is on the phone, Issy whispers, 'If you're gonna be a prick, why bother coming?'

'So what, that's how you're moving now?'

Issy sighs. 'Sorry, I didn't mean it like that,' she strokes the outside of Jerome's right hand. 'But what's up with you? You were all on this party and now you're acting proper moody.'

Jerome looks at Issy. She looks really pretty with her pink lip gloss and eyelashes painted black. Her eye shadow has glitter bits that catch the city lights as they cross Parliament Square past the Houses of Parliament.

Taking a deep breath, he decides to chill.

'Yeah, I am on this. Dwayne was being a prick, vexed me up. Sorry, I'm gonna stop.' He takes Issy's hand and kisses it, 'You look really nice.'

Emily comes off the phone relieved to find the pair have made up. 'That was my friend Merle. She can't make it tonight, which is a shame as she was my cover.'

'Your cover?' asks Issy, intrigued. 'For what?'

Emily goes extremely red having slipped up. She asked Merle to come via train and tube because Merle's mum is far cooler than Emily's and will let her daughter go off about London all she likes. Merle takes herself to Tate Modern and to the V&A exhibitions all the time and certainly knows how to get to Mayfair. Merle would have been the friend pick-up story in case the cab driver told Emily's mum he had to do an extra stop and wanted more money. Merle lives on Jerningham Road, and the direct way to her house is via Ommaney Road where Issy and Jerome live. Perfectly thought-out alibi.

'Oh nothing,' Emily sighs, fiddling with her phone. 'Just something for school. We needed to get a story straight... Merle and I wanted to... meet some boys this evening,' Emily, again, lies painfully.

'Wow, have you got a crush on someone?' Issy asks.

'Crush?' Jerome notices Issy talks differently when Emily is around. And speaks in a weird fake posh accent.

'Kind of. My mum is a total control freak, as you know, and I, well,' Emily really doesn't want to lie anymore. Ping! A slice of truth helps her out, 'I kind of fancy this guy from George's school.'

'Oooo, you haven't mentioned this before. What's his name?'

Jerome rolls his eyes. Trapped in girly gossip for the rest of the journey.

The black taxi pulls up at the corner of a large square. Out get Issy, Jerome and Emily.

'Wow Emily, that's a – pretty original dress,' Issy remarks, as Emily reveals the knee-length navy blue dress with velvet trim and a deep purple ribbon running through the waist.

'Really? I worry I look a bit middle-aged. Mum picked it and I really wasn't up for an argument.'

'It's nice, ain't it, Jay?'

Jerome lifts his eyebrows; it's the kind of dress African girls wear to church in Deptford.

'Shame, we forgot drink!' he exclaims.

'No, I've got wine,' Issy tells him.

'What am I gonna drink?' asks Jerome. 'Need to hit a shop before we roll in.'

'I'm sure that there'll be lots to choose from,' Emily assures them. 'Shall we rather go in? It's chilly.'

'Man can't rock up empty-handed.'

'Man can,' Emily says climbing the wide white stone steps.

Jerome and Issy follow her.

'What flat number is it?' Issy asks.

'This is it.'

'What? This whole thing?' Issy stares at the property.

'Afraid so,' Emily says as she rings the doorbell. 'Seven-bedrooms, five-bathrooms, one swimming pool, a library, billiard room, cinema...'

'Nah man, I really can't rock up to man's yard empty-handed,' Jerome says, putting his hood down.

Issy feels like a tiny ant crossing a huge meadow. She's not sure she can go in. It feels harder than she expected.

The large front door opens. George's father, William, appears smiling, 'Emily! Great to see you. Come on in.'

'Sorry we're late. Some traffic–'

'You're bang on time!'

'Mr Addy,' Emily says awkwardly, she thought George would have his parents out for the evening.

'Come on, you kids are young adults now, call me William.'

Issy stares at Mr Addy as if he's a robot or piece of art. A very dark-skinned black man with an accent sounding like Prince Charles, dressed from head to toe in African dress, a tunic and trousers with gold, purple and green swirl print.

'Do come in, come on in.'

Jerome is also taken aback by the accent. 'It's like a hundred times posher than Emily's,' he whispers to Issy as they walk in.

'This is Issy Richards and this is Jerome–'

Mr Addy shakes Jerome's hand reassuringly while giving him a pat on the shoulder.

'Campbell,' Jerome finishes his own name.

As William shakes Issy's hand, she does a curtsey.

He chuckles. Sensing Issy is overwhelmed, he says, 'We'll have none of that formal stuff here. You guys are adults now. Official.'

William tries to put them at ease as he ushers the teenagers into the kitchen towards his wife.

'Emily, look at you!' Petra Addy exclaims, smile a little forced, as she opens her arms.

She is the most beautiful woman Issy has ever seen in real life in her gold floor-length Ghanaian dress wrapped around her slender body with a matching traditional head piece. She stands like a film star at the Oscars, moves like royalty. Her arm extends, gold painted neatly manicured hands takes Issy's and she air kisses each cheek, 'Call me Petra, please.'

'You look like a queen,' Issy says, searching for something to say.

The Addys laugh.

Emily goes bright red.

'I can assure you I am no queen!' Petra says.

'Drama queen, perhaps?' William winks at Jerome. 'He knows what I'm talking about.'

Issy suddenly can't breathe, trying a few times to swallow the lump in her throat.

Emily is also impressed. The kitchen has been refurbished since she was last here, now covered in cream marble with black onyx trimmings. The high ceilings with crystal chandeliers give off a flattering light. There are scented candles and fresh flowers everywhere, adorning the place with a deeper sense of elegance.

The kitchen alone is the size of Jerome's entire flat. This is next level luxury living. Jerome and Issy often watch those television shows where you get to see inside footballers' homes, but this, this is different. This feels… it feels… Jerome's speechless, even in his own head.

'This is from Mum– and Dad,' Emily says.

'Oh how precious,' Petra receives the basket, embellished with ribbons, 'your mother remembered! Darling, look, Janie made that chutney we loved.'

'Wonderful.'

'The wine is from the Dubois chateau. Dad said it's ready now and best with pheasant or wood pigeon,' Emily says, looking up, trying to recall if she forgot anything.

Issy pulls out her bottle from a blue plastic bag. 'And this is from my mum.' She holds it out, then adds, hastily, 'I know you don't know her, but she says thanks for having me, us, me and Jerome.'

Jerome smiles. Petra smiles too, taking the litre bottle of Lambrini from Issy, price tag still attached. 'Be sure to let your mum know I said thank you very much indeed.'

'Petra, may I call home to say I arrived safely?' Emily asks. 'My mobile just died.'

'Of course, sweetie. I'll come with, to thank her for this adorable hamper. Oooh I could eat you up, you're such a darling,' Petra takes Emily's hand and leads her into the lounge.

Issy feels a tinge of jealously not to have Petra's hand on her. She looks down at her bitten cuticles and vows to stop biting her nails.

'So, we spoke to Janie earlier and she allowed us to treat you all to a little birthday tipple. One glass on arrival, and one with the cake. Sound good?' William asks, taking three champagne flutes from those lined up on the kitchen side, 'I mean, would your parents approve a little sip of alcohol?'

Issy and Jerome smirk at each other.

'Erm, yeah,' Issy nods.

'Yeah, please.' Jerome emphasises the please, glancing at Issy.

'Please,' Issy adds.

'So I gather you both live nearby Emily?' William asks taking a bottle of Moet from the fridge.

Issy nods, wishing she wouldn't become so mute in front of posh people.

'Telegraph Hill,' Jerome says, knowing that sounds posher than New Cross.

'Thanks for travelling all this way. It is quite a journey. That river seems to divide us more than it should.'

'Cabby was a bit of a—,' Jerome starts then stops.

Issy's cheeks burn with shame, relieved when William Addy hands her a glass of champagne topped with peach juice.

'So are you the same age as George?'

'Who's George?' asks Jerome.

'The host. My son. This is his birthday party.' William winks in jest.

'Oh, yeah, yeah, sorry. To be honest, I'm just Issy's boyfriend. I ain't actually met him, yet.'

'Have you met George, Issy?'

Issy shakes her head, and takes another sip of champagne. This is awful. She's a busted gate crasher.

'Oh, I see.'

They stand in awkward silence for a moment before William smiles, 'Well, not to worry. You're both extremely welcome here and once Emily returns, I'll take you to the action. Cheers!'

'Cheers!' Jerome holds up his glass to George's father's. He then looks at Issy to join them.

'Cheers,' she mumbles timidly.

The journey to the party area is like walking through a palace exhibition. The hallway they are told, has paneling dating back to the seventeenth century. The thick silver wallpaper, are embossed with hand-painted peacocks. Massive paintings of ships in stormy seas and wood sculptures of African-looking heads. With each step, Issy's feet sink into the thick, bouncy - and very clean - carpet.

'In Ghana you see nothing but peacocks strolling around the King's palace,' William tells Issy as they walk down the solid oak staircase.

'Is that where you're from?' Issy asks, as she slides her hands down the polished bannister.

'Where my forefathers originate; however my family have been here since the 1800s.'

'Was this house theirs then?' Emily asks.

'Unfortunately not,' William chuckles. 'I've had to work extremely hard to be here.' He stops and looks at Jerome, 'Nobody tells you that a wife with a pretty face comes with expensive habits, so you better watch this one!' he says, nodding at Issy.

George appears at the bottom of the staircase.

'Did he just call me a gold digger?' Issy whispers to Emily

'No!' Emily whispers back, giggling, 'Meant you're pretty.'

'Here he is!' William proudly puts his arm around his son, 'Man of the match!'

George winces within his father's clutch, 'Hi guys. Hey Mimi.'

Emily smiles, 'Hi George, Happy Birthday!'

'Happy Birthday,' Issy repeats.

'Happy Birthday, man.' Jerome offers George an American rapper style handshake.

'I can do that,' Mr Addy playfully joins in, to George's discomfort, turning his forearms up and down, elbows awkwardly poking out in all directions.

'Come on, my brother!' William persists, knowing full well he's getting it wrong.

'Seriously, Dad? This is more than embarrassing.'

Luckily for George, William is called away as the doorbell rings.

'I told them, there's no need to be here. People can just wander straight down from the street. But no, "Guests must have a proper welcomed entrance!"' George mimics his parents, looking the whole time at Emily. He turns to Issy and Jerome, 'Don't worry, they are banned from my room.'

'It's fine,' smiles Emily, feeling a whole lot more relaxed after speaking to her mother. Doesn't sound like the cab driver mentioned the extra pickup. 'Look, we have champs!' she adds, lifting her flute to the air. 'From your parents!'

'I know, funny isn't it? You'd think my dad's won an Olympic medal or something.'

'Of course he has, George,' Emily theatrically pulls out her bottom lip to show disappointment at George's lack of sentiment. 'His only son, turning into a proper grownup,'

'Mimi, please don't say it like that. You sound just like those aliens upstairs.'

George pulls a face as he opens the door, 'Who wants to grow up?' he says, raising his shoulders to a shrug before extending his arm out: 'Shall we?'

CHAPTER 9
THE PARTY

Jerome is stunned to see what looks like a whole recording studio in one corner, guitars hanging on the wall, a keyboard, flute and saxophone on stands, and DJ equipment – both digital and vinyl.

At the decks, two teenage boys are searching a laptop for songs, both in hooded jumpers, but scruffy and faded unlike Jerome's crisp ironed one. One boy looks like a typical grunger, the other more skater-like with a large afro. Jerome nudges Issy, giving her his cheeky smile, raising one eyebrow. Issy smiles back, apologising again for being harsh.

George's bedroom is T-shaped. To the left, a huge bed, leading out to the terrace with what looks like a covered up hot tub. Towards the widest part of the room is a lounge area with white leather sofas and a glass coffee table the size of Issy's mattress back home. A flat screen television showing flames of fire, is mounted on the wall, above a real fireplace that's not lit but the room is warm enough.

Sitting in the lounge area sipping champagne are three teenage girls. All of them super over-dressed, one in particular wearing a skimpy black number and huge high heels with gold chains running across her ankles down to her toes. Her long hair is dead straight, peroxide blonde. She could be mistaken for Hayley from behind. The middle girl is darker haired and has the rock chick look, whilst the third looks like she asked for a 20s look at the hair salon, with flapper girl waves in a blonde bob. All three have huge amounts of make-up on and now Issy feels under-dressed.

'Mimi, come over and introduce us to your friends,' shouts one of them, waving her arm, while Peroxide giggles something into the blonde bob's ear.

'Meet Issy and Jerome,' Emily says, quickly adding, 'Issy's boyfriend,' noticing Hendrike's eyes already sizing him up.

'Jerome, Issy, meet Hendrike, Helena and Sophie.'

They clink their glasses like proper adults and sit down.

'Do you want me to refill your glass?' Hendrike asks Jerome in a sultry voice.

Issy looks up to the ceiling and takes a breath, thankful that Hayley isn't here to see her doppelganger make a move for Jerome right in front of Issy's eyes. She could bet her rolled up tenner, Hayley would have ripped Hendrike's extensions out before midnight.

'Yes, please that would be lovely,' Issy pipes up, handing a surprised Hendrike her empty glass. She may be mute in front of the parents, but there's no way she'll be losing face in front of Jerome to someone her own age.

'Yeah, go on then, love,' Jerome also hands his champagne flute to Hendrike.

Issy shoots a look at Jerome, Don't call her love! spread across her face.

Hendrike swans out to the terrace, where the champagne bottles are nestled, 'Come and help, Mimi.'

Emily runs after her. The two remaining girls start giggling.

'Good one!' Sophie tells Issy, giving her a high five, 'That's how you have to manage that one.'

'So how do you know them?' Hendrike asks Emily pouring two Bellinis.

'She's the one I told you about. Who stopped my camera being stolen.'

'Who's that guy she's with?'

'Again, her boyfriend.'

'Shame.'

'I know, all the best boys are taken.'

'No. Shame the best girls take them away,' Hendrike's look fills Emily with dread. That familiar smirk her friend does when she's going to be badly behaved.

Hendrike flounces back to the sofas. 'I think Mimi has yours,' she tells Issy firmly.

Hendrike leans over Issy to hand Jerome the other glass. Issy watches Hendrike's cleavage and Jerome's eyes to make sure they don't meet.

'How do you'se know each other?' Issy asks the group, leaning forward to force Hendrike back.

'We grew up not far from here,' begins Sophie, playing with one of her blond bobbed curls.

'South Ken,' adds Hendrike, smug.

'Then George's dad bought this place, and Mimi moved to New Cross,' continues the softly spoken Sophie. 'But we keep in touch. Our parents remain friends.'

'Some,' adds Helena. Sophie gives Helena a serious look. Helena raises her eyebrows then looks away.

Jerome, noticing tension, starts to look around the room. 'I can't believe a bredder wearing African threads lives here,' he says, mainly to himself.

'Jerome, are you from New Cross?' Hendrike asks, moving to sit the other side of him, 'I hear it can get rough south of the river,' she adds, leaning into his personal space.

'It's fine,' Issy interjects, placing her hand on Jerome's thigh. 'Really lovely, ain't it, babe?'

Issy looks at Jerome, then Hendrike, then Sophie, 'We're right near a park with the whole view of London.'

'Telegraph Hill?' Sophie asks, the friendliest of the three, 'Haven't we been there for a picnic once, Mimi?'

'Yes, that's the one,' Emily replies, meanwhile trying to eye Hendrike to sit beside her, enlarging her eyes as subtly as possible.

'Half the size of my garden!' Hendrike laughs, flicking her hair back.

'Hen babe, you don't have a garden,' Sophie jests.

Issy tries to hide her smirk by taking a sip of champagne.

'Well no, unfortunately I don't have a garden at my London home, unless you count the lawns in the square. But fortunately, I have both a seaside cottage and country residence. Oh and there is that bit of green nearby, what's it called, Hels?'

'Don't fucking bring me into this!' Helena says, cigarette in mouth, searching inside her bag for a lighter.

'Oh, that's it: Hyde Park!' Hendrike smiles straight at Issy.

Emily looks on in distress, giving Helena the eye to intercept.

'Well now,' Helena laughs nervously, 'Let's be real, none of it is ours per se. It belongs to our fucking parents, doesn't it? The fuckers! We'll be lucky to see any of it the rate they're living. Fuck them!' Helena raises her glass. They all follow. 'And fuck Hyde Park, too. The Queen owns it anyway!'

Hendrike gives Issy a wry smile, Issy smiles back, stroking the back of Jerome's neck. She sees that even Hendrike's friends think she's a cunt.

'Are they both drunk on one glass?' Emily whispers to Sophie, wondering why Hendrike has taken such a stance against poor Issy.

'Unfortunately not. That's her third or fourth and there are a couple more cases keeping cool outside. And yes, Helena's dad bought everything.'

'He's so naughty,' Emily gasps.

'Keeping her sweet, what with the divorce,' Sophie whispers back, before offering Helena a lighter.

'This is going to get messy, Mimi,' Helena says, leaning over Emily to take the lighter.

'You keep your eye on Issy and I'll try and tame Bratcula,' Sophie says, watching Hendrike eyes on Jerome.

Jerome, eager to leave, jumps from the sofa as George comes through with another guest. He heads over to the skater boy with the afro and the grungy one to check out George's mixing table.

'You alright?' Jerome says.

They both nod.

'I'm Toby.'

'And I'm Max.'

'Jerome.'

The boys knock fists.

George sets the room lights to blue-violet. Aside from his huge bed, gadgets and sentimental tokens lying around like seashells and comic-books, you could easily mistake the place for a swanky club.

By ten o'clock the party's in full swing. Toby and Max have persuaded Jerome to plug a microphone into the mixer to start spitting bars. Turns out Toby likes grime beats and the crowd love Jerome's rapping. The girls start winding towards the floor and rubbing their bodies against each other while the boys, not sure how to get involved, continually sip their drinks feeling awkward and self-conscious given Jerome keeps flashing his six-pack.

Emily lifts one eyebrow at Issy. Issy thinks she understands the gesture – Jerome's lyrics are dirty, littered with violence and sex. Yet looking around, Emily seems the only one who cares. Nobody is listening to the words spouting from Jerome's lips. They are staring in wonderment- he is so cool, so street, so now. They're cheering, responding to Jerome's, 'Put your hands up for the birthday man!' and, 'Let me hear some noise London Town!'

A group of boys arrive in the middle of Jerome's set. Issy notices Emily's reaction and swoops over to her, 'So which one is he?' remembering the conversation in the black cab.

Emily looks at the floor.

'Oh come on, Mimi – I'm gonna call you Mimi from now on.' Issy slurs her words playful, the bubbles from the fourth Bellini popping inside her head.

'How do you know he's one of them?'

'Because you went that pretty pink colour you're going,' Issy giggles as she pokes one of Emily's dimples. 'Okay let me guess. Oooh, it's that one isn't it? He's the fittest.'

Issy's eyes gesture to a tall well-built young man with a gorgeous smile and handsome brown eyes. 'He looks like one of them magazine models with that Ralph shirt on.'

Issy admires the neatly ironed but loosely worn baby blue shirt. Then the colour flashes to her own cheeks as he meets her stare. Worse still, a rush of butterflies flows from her stomach up through her spine, as their eyes lock and he smiles at her. The first time that has happened with another boy since she got with Jerome. The handsome stranger immediately heads over. Issy finds herself stuck to the carpet with no means to flee.

'Mimi!' he kisses Emily on the cheek. 'Sophie!' he kisses Sophie on the cheek. 'And you must be?' he takes Issy's hand.

'Issy, Richard. This is Issy. Issy Richards in fact,' Emily says bluntly.

'Issy Richards... Well I'm Richie, Richie Saunders. Very pleased to meet you. So, how are you ladies? Looking like total babes.'

Emily rolls her eyes. But Issy doesn't see it. Richie's full lips and chiselled jawline move in to kiss Issy's cheek. He really is the best looking sixteen year old Issy has seen in real life. Richie scouts the room, 'What's that about?' he asks nodding to Jerome rapping.

'That's Jerome,' Emily answers. 'Issy's boyfriend, in fact.'

'I see.' Richie looks at Issy. Issy feels his disappointment then hates herself for feeling disappointed too. She shouldn't be thinking of other boys.

'George has a great turnout,' Emily remarks, making other conversation. But Richie makes a swift exit.

Issy pulls Emily close, 'Is that him?'

'No, and I don't know why he keeps acting like that.'

'Like what?'

'That fake charm.' Emily tucks her hair behind both ears.

'Perhaps he's finally maturing?' Sophie suggests.

'I need to use the loo. Excuse me.' Emily chooses to ignore the en suite and leaves the room.

'Is she okay?' Issy shouts into Sophie's ear over the music.

'Come have a smoke,' Sophie suggests, making a smoking sign with her hands.

Issy follows Sophie to George's private patio. There are small Chinese paper lanterns lighting the place and multi-coloured fairy lights wrapped around the wood beams above them. Issy sees the clipped vines and can imagine what it looks like in the summer.

Sophie lights a cigarette from the outdoor heater, 'It's much quieter away from that speaker.'

Issy admires the way Sophie holds the slender all-white cigarette. She waves it Jerome's way.

'Your boyfriend is great by the way. Look, they love him. Does he want to be a musician?'

'Yeah, but a producer, not a rapper.'

'Clever,' Sophie says. 'More money in producing. Do you smoke?'

'Erm yeah, but in Jerome's pocket.' Issy turns to go inside, but Sophie gently takes her arm.

'Don't be silly. Have one of these,' she says, handing Issy the packet. 'So you see that boy over there? The tallest one that walked in with Richie. With the floppy blonde hair?'

Issy eyes a puffy-faced, rosy-cheeked, blue-eyed, well-fed, rugby-playing sort epitomising all Issy's stereotypes of Posh. She switches to Jerome who has taken off his hoodie and tucked his t-shirt over his head to reveal his six-pack. The party are waving their hands in the air and making gun shapes with their fingers.

'Henry's his name,' Sophie continues, 'The one Emily loves. Liked him for years. Off and on. Hopeless case.'

'Why?' Issy asks, noticing Sophie's dark eyebrows and lashes against her blonde hair. Her skin is porcelain white and she's lucky enough to have a real Marilyn Monroe mole, set against red lips that haven't rubbed off since she arrived. They're not big lips, or even plump, Issy thinks to herself, but they are beautiful, thin but not too thin, perfect for Sophie's face. If Issy were drunk enough, she'd probably like to kiss them.

'When she likes him, he ignores her. When she ignores him, he'll call to say hi or take her out to the cinema.'

'One of them ones,' Issy says, finishing the last drops of her fifth cocktail, before lighting her cigarette from Sophie's.

'Indeed,' Sophie agrees. 'Pathetic.'

Helena spots them.

'Do you think we can smoke out here?' Helena asks closing the French doors behind her.

'We are.' Sophie's matching red finger tips hold the thin white cigarette to her lips, 'Besides, your dad knows you smoke.' Sophie turns to Issy, 'Her dad bought us the champs.'

Issy smiles at Helena. She feels outnumbered and muted again. The beautiful fingers of Sophie coupled with the sheer confidence of Helena force Issy into inadequacy. She looks down at her podgy fingers holding the super slender cigarette with the letters YSL entangled. She didn't manage to stop biting her nails, even though she vowed to for the party.

'It's a nice house,' Issy pipes up.

'Isn't it. Lucky fucker!' Helena exclaims. 'I wish I had my own swimming pool.'

'Do you live in a house like this?' Issy asks Sophie.

'I wish. No, no, my father is no billionaire. You?' Sophie immediately grimaces knowingly.

Issy finds herself stumped for an answer. She can't think how to describe her home.

'Well anyway, I'm glad Emily has a friend like you,' Helena remarks, filling the gap.

'Like me?' Issy looks at Helena for clarification.

'Someone nice. Who lives nearby,' Sophie chips in, remembering Emily telling them how poor Issy is. 'I often feel sorry for her because we still live in South Ken while her father's way more strict so we don't get to see her much, unless her cousin agrees to have her stay over or we go-'

'Which Rosie hardly does because she's out every weekend on coke thinking we don't know.'

'Helena!'

'It's true!' Helena leans across and sucks Sophie's cigarette, 'She thinks we give a shit. We just want to see Mimi more. Oh I fucking love this tune! Right, back to the dancefloor,' Helena stubs a hardly smoked cigarette out to Issy's surprise and throws it in a plant pot. 'Your boyfriend rocks by the way. Is he famous?'

Issy shakes her head.

'Not yet!' Sophie cries after Helena.

'I didn't know what it was gonna be like tonight,' Issy confides, exhaling; her feelings of self-consciousness and inadequacy coming in waves.

'I hope you're having a nice time. Hendrike can be a dick by the way, but just ignore her. If you knock about with us a bit more, you'll see she's not without her issues, but who hasn't got issues, right?'

Jerome looks up at the clock. It's nearly midnight. The cake has been done, fireworks displayed and George's parents have gone up to bed. George sees some friends out before returning to the boys. Jerome slouches on George's bed with Max and Toby and a few new friends who shook his hand post-performance, all eagerly waiting to buy weed. They're still praising him for his skills. Jerome laughs, taking out his weed.

'This party's nutz blood,' he tells Toby and Max, building a spliff. 'I never knew there was bredders out there like this.'

'Yeah man, we exist!' replies Toby handing Jerome a twenty pound note.

'Yeah but this is some next level, get me. You lot are like proper dons.'

'Depends on what you notion a don,' replies the returning birthday boy, watching the transaction. 'Some of these people won't string a sentence together before it benefits them.'

'George is a man of the world,' Max sighs, taking ten pounds out his pocket and passing it to Jerome.

'I see that. I see that,' replies Jerome. 'I mean, bruv, look at your threads.' Jerome takes some time to assess the African tunic, the same gold, green and purple swirls his father had on.

'Wow. That is something, bruv. Did your parents make you wear that?' Jerome's eyes follow the jeans down to George's leather shoes, the type of shoes he only sees the Africans in Peckham wear. Max and Toby try to suppress their rising giggles. Jerome looks across at the duo trying not to laugh.

'No,' George replies rather bluntly.

'I don't mean it in a bad way or nothing,' Jerome adds hoping he hasn't offended his host. 'It's just that I thought man like you would bust some garms, ya get me? I bet you got some nice labels in your wardrobe?'

'I'm not offended. I like straight talking. So you'll appreciate when I say that unlike the jumpers you all are wearing – which sport different labels that I suspect are produced in the same cramped sweatshop paying women and children a pittance to work a twelve-hour day, in dangerous conditions – this fabric has been handmade by well-fed, well-loved women and men from the village of my ancestors. This pattern depicts the roots of tribes-people who fought for their customs and traditions against not just other tribes, but the British, the Portuguese, the Dutch...'

Toby and Max exchange knowing glances as George continues in his painfully plummy English tones.

'This pattern has survived war, hunger, famine, disease, denial, and yet people my age refuse to wear it with pride because they fear ridicule. Even in their own village, they would rather wear a logo that is actually the mark of exploitation than this, a mark of survival. I would feel more ridiculous wearing that symbol of criminality,' pointing to the swoosh on Jerome's hoodie.

'George!' Emily calls, walking towards the bed. 'I have to go now. Dad's picking me up.'

'Excuse me. We shall continue in one moment.'

'Bye Jerome,' Emily says, waving over her shoulder.

Jerome gives Emily the thumbs up.

George sees Emily to the door.

'What the fuck was that about? Have I got him pissed?' Jerome asks Toby.

'Dude, that's George. Look around you,' Max points to the large framed photographs that hang on the wall either side of his bed.

'Martin Luther King I know that one. And I know them bredders from the Olympics.'

'Black Panthers' adds Toby, licking to secure his joint.

'Datz the one. So he's one of dem ones. That's cool. My bro said he'd be some coconut.'

Max and Toby stare at Jerome in surprise.

'I don't mean nuttin by it. It's a good ting. He's into black power, his roots and shit. So who's this one?' Jerome points to a slight man wearing small round glasses, in white cloth with his legs crossed.

'That's Gandhi,' replies Max. He looks around for confirmation.

'Yeah, Gandhi,' adds the boy buying a bag from Jerome.

'See they don't teach us none of this in school,' Jerome says, scrolling down his mobile. He reads out the text he got from Tameika just as George returns, 'Be the change you want to see in the world, Gandhi.'

'One of my favourites,' George says, clearly relieved not to have let a total cretin into his personal space.

'Look, bruv, I didn't mean no offence about your top, you know that, innit?'

'I know,' George assures. 'I'm not offended. What does offend me slightly is... Actually, forget it.'

'Go on,' Jerome insists.

'Perhaps this is not the time or place. We've only just met.'

'Bruv, it can't be more your time or your place, get me. This is your house, your shubs.' Jerome looks down at the long white papers between his fingers, 'Shit, is it the weed?'

George can see Jerome is a good person and he completely understands what Emily sees in Issy. But how to explain the long and complex history of black migration, slavery, commonwealth, empire, exclusion, police brutality, positive discrimination, under-funding mental health services, over-subscription to prison, disproportionate school expulsions and arrests? How to explain the wider issues of poverty, inequality of opportunity, hidden curriculum? As George's mind thinks things through, he meets Jerome's eyes, 'Well, we can come to that in a moment. If you must know, it's your lyrical wax?'

'My what?'

'Your spitz,' Max tells Jerome.

'Shit man, did I take over your shubs?'

'The spitting was good George, what you on about?' Toby defends in an increasingly faux-South London accent.

'I'm not saying that the rapping, sorry spitting, wasn't good. Talent-wise, you are brilliant. Good timing, good flow. I liked it.'

Jerome nods his head to take George's praise. 'But?'

George takes a deep breath, 'Okay, how do I say this without offending you?'

'You won't offend, trust. Can I smoke inside?'

George looks at the boys. This was inevitable. Soon playing computer games or camping with organic steaks on the fire would slowly morph into slouching on beds and sofas in a semi-conscious daze on illegal substances. George opens the window above his bed with a remote control, the cool February air chills the back of Jerome's neck.

'Yes,' George agrees, 'but exhale that way, if you can. My parents won't come down, but Maggie might say something if she smells it.'

Jerome takes a few deep pulls then passes it to Max.

George puts the heated air conditioning up via his phone app. He sits on the corner of the bed, opposite Jerome. 'Issy is your girlfriend– is that correct?' George asks, his lips pursing with each crisp syllable.

'That is correct,' Jerome replies taking a sip from the crystal champagne flute given to him by William Addy some hours ago, now full of rum.

'My one and only,' Jerome raises a personal toast, looking over at Issy in a deep and meaningful with Sophie and Helena – Hendrike slumped on the adjacent sofa talking to Richie and Emily's crush, Henry.

'May I be blunt as to ask whether you've cheated on Issy?' George keeps a straight face.

'Well boy, that's a personal, personal kinda question on day one, but I ain't, still. She's one in six billion.'

'Exactly,' George moves swiftly to his next point, 'Now may I ask, do you own a knife, or a gun?'

Jerome sits up, not sure where this is going.

'Do you own a knife, or a gun?' George repeats the question, completely still, his expression calm, blank; his voice, polite: clear, yet cutting.

'No, well I've obviously got knives I eat with at home and shit.'

'Have you ever shot or stabbed anybody? I'm assuming you haven't, though I promise you I will not call the police if you happen to say yes.'

Jerome searches Toby and Max for clarification, but they both shrug.

'What I am getting at, is this. As a black male I feel it is my responsibility to conduct myself in a certain way so as not to fall foul of the laws of this nation, whilst taking care not to disregard my heritage.' George presses his forefinger into his chin, 'History may well be the collective of stories we have interwoven to create a patchwork narrative of how we arrived from the past to our present–'

'George, man, no offence but, really?' asks Max.

'Or at least speak English, dude!' adds Toby.

George looks at the trio. One dressed like a skater, the other in grunge, and Jerome the gangsta: smoking weed in unison, numb to the truth.

'I'm talking about the history of... Not just stories but collective accounts of truth: The roots of narrative.'

'Jerome,' George continues, kicking off his leather sandals and sitting down, crossed-legged upon his bed. 'Hip-hop, rap, spitting, whatever you call it, has roots in a higher more spiritual place than what you just did. They have a history as words of resistance: of oppression, of lack of opportunity, of inequality, injustice. What you're doing by saying all this stuff is bastardising the movement, and for what, when you don't – and thankfully so – carry out these threats or actions? What I'm saying is why rap words that aren't real for you or to you?'

Jerome looks at this young man opposite him, a real life son of a billionaire. A black man speaking the Queen's English, inside his own mansion, wearing African garms telling Jerome not to rap the stuff he raps. Jerome can't be angry. Why should he be angry with George? He already admitted it wasn't real life. As the weed sinks into his brain, Jerome leans back on the bed. I'll merk that black face to a red face, so don't step in my Endz bruv, it's ain't a nice place. 'Yeah, it's pretty violent, still,' Jerome admits.

'And sexist.' George senses he's losing as the marijuana depletes any possibility of debate.

'Don't simply listen to what I'm saying,' George says, sitting up. 'Let the music tell you.'

George jumps from the bed pointing his finger at the boys, 'You, my friends, are going to hear the history of hip-hop, right here, right now.'

George puts his headphones on and plays a series of politically charged tracks, with penetrating lyrics and infectious beats. He uses the microphone to introduce each song and the events that inspired them. Lyrics fill the room with conditions of working weeks, of poverty and police injustice.

'BBC Radio 4,' Toby whispers to Max, 'presented by Tupac.'

'Sir Trevor McDonald does pirate radio,' Max sniggers back.

While Toby and Max catch jokes, Jerome allows the weed to lead him into the philosophical world of words. The sound system George owns makes every beat distinct, every word as clear as if the rapper were saying it in his ear. Jerome imagines the lyrics flowing through cities and forests, from mouths into doorways that lead into rivers and mountains; words that cut through gold chains and melt knives and guns. He looks around at the posters of all the black political and social figures, the rows of books that fill one of the huge walls. He looks at George, and the remaining guests; the girls get up and dance some more, waving their hands and swaying as they did before. But these lyrics are strong. Purer than his. Jerome gets it. And they're scary, for some reason. They mean something, he realises.

Jerome looks at Issy dancing with the posh girls. Their bodies swaying from side to side, their waists moving in seductive circles - with the speakers isolating every word, delaying them, as if each sentence had to be inscribed into Jerome's mind forever. The thick dirty bass pounding his bloodstream, fusing with the rum.

Jerome inhales his spliff and listens to George's set. Anger denouncing the degradation of females by other rappers, 'For the ladies, the queens, never bitches.'

That's nice to hear, Jerome thinks. Issy looks over and smiles. Jerome smiles back and blows her a kiss. Not breaking eye contact, Issy catches the kiss and rubs it onto her heart. A jealous Hendrike notices this exchange, as does an intrigued Richie.

Jerome passes the spliff to Max.

'Take no notice of George, man,' Max says, 'Your bars are tight.'

Toby agrees, 'At the end of the day, people get tired of listening to political shit.'

'Yeah,' Max says, 'No-one gets sick of money or sex.'

'Plus violence,' adds Toby. 'Basically, money, sex, and violence are the biggest turn-ons.'

'Add some fried chicken to that list,' Jerome says with a cheeky smile.

'Yes!' Toby knocks fists with Jerome.

'Violence or power?' Max asks.

'Both, well, nah, violent power,' Toby replies. 'When you get all Foucault and shit, that's when you lose people.'

'So what did you think of it, babe?' Issy asks, taking Jerome's arm in hers as they turn the corner from the house. 'Shame Emily had to leave early.'

'It weren't what I was expecting. Dem boys were proper,' Jerome kisses Issy on the cheek. 'Thanks for inviting me.'

Issy kisses the arm of Jerome's jacket. 'The girls were nice too, except that one bitch.'

'Funny you was worried 'bout Hayley, but some of dem were rocking batty riders dancehall queens would be like, Rah, dats some nasty girl dem outfit!'

Issy laughs as she watches Jerome poke out his hip, pretending to be feminine.

'I feel bad. She text me to come over but I said I was at a party the other side of London. She didn't text back.'

'So what's happening with you two? Serious ting?'

Despite being a little embarrassed about her negative thoughts, she decides to spill the beans, 'Lately, I kinda gone off her. I mean, Jay, every day there's a drama, innit? Always an argument, a fight. If it ain't her starting, then it's her brother or mum, or dad.' Her worried eyes search Jerome's for any sign of judgment as she looks to Jerome for reassurance. 'I don't know, I just think, this can't go on. I see her mum and it's like, Hays is just gonna end up like that. And do I want that for my life? In my life? I know it sounds selfish but I wanna get away from drama. Does that sound bad?'

'Try living with Dwayne.' Jerome replies. 'He thinks he's running some mafia ring, when it ain't like that.'

Issy peers around as they walk towards the bus stop. They're engulfed by six-story town houses and detached mansions.

Jerome follows Issy's eyes taking in the surroundings, 'For real, though, we're never gonna be billionaires. We ain't from round here.'

'I don't want billions, babe. Honest. Look at that girl tonight. She's rich yeah, but she dressed and acted cheaper than the drunks in Deptford.'

'That 'cos it's not about the money, babes,' Jerome does a funny walk down the street. 'It's the swagger!'

Issy laughs. Jerome's cute when he's drunk.

'I was shocked the boys aren't wearing the latest trainers,' Issy says, taking Jerome's arm again. 'Proper scrufftafarians.'

'I rate that boy George for wearing his tribe's threads. He's gonna send me playlists from back in the day. Gonna do some old skool roots sessions with it.'

'Amazing,' Issy says. 'Yeah and I owe you an apology.'

'For what, babe?'

'Being moody earlier, about you wearing a hoodie.'

'Already forgotten, and anyway, I should say sorry for being moody. Dwayne proper pissed me off. It's like, yeah we're brothers but at the end of the day, I'm my own man too, get me?'

'That's how I feel about Hayley.'

'They're both as bad as each other.'

'Quick! That bus goes London Bridge!'

The N343 from London Bridge to New Cross Gate takes ages. Jerome and Issy doze at the back of the top deck and miss their stop. The driver pulls in at New Cross Gate bus garage and climbs the stairs to wake them.

They're almost home, walking tiredly up the hill, when screaming sirens shock them awake. Jerome takes the remaining weed from his sock. 'Shall I put it in my bra?' Issy asks.

'Never do that for anyone, babe. Promise?'

Jerome quickly hides the weed under some leaves by a nearby tree but hands Issy his money.

A police car pulls over, lights flashing in the dark. As they approach the estate entrance, more police officers are questioning a frantic Dwayne.

They walk towards Dwayne, Jerome's heart pounding. His first thought, Where's his gran? Is she safe? Has their flat being raided?

Dwayne shouts over, 'Where were you, bruv? Yeah! See what? Where were you, ya get me?'

They get closer and see his face swollen and bloody.

Police usher Dwayne away from his approaching brother.

'What you touching me for?!' Dwayne shouts at the policewoman. 'No-one wants you here!'

Granny Mabel is there, holding on to the iron bars at the bottom of the stairwell. Jerome jogs over to her.

'Lawd Jesus, you safe,' she tells a wide-eyed Jerome. 'I been calling, worried sick.'

'Sorry, Gran. What's happened?'

'Me nah know!'

'Are you okay? Did anybody touch you?' Issy asks Mabel softly, holding her arm, wanting to support her without being patronising.

'I'm fine. All I know is him left the house, some children come pass and jump.'

Mabel makes grabbing moves with her hands, fear written into her eyes.

'Issy your mother is worried fe you. Better go show you safe.'

After making sure, Dwayne isn't going to do anything stupid, Jerome walks Issy to her door. 'So much for our end to the night.'

'It's okay, we can do it another time.'

Issy kisses Jerome on the lips.

'Shall I try sneak over afterwards?'

'Nah, stay and calm your nan down. I feel bad now we ignored her calls.'

'I know. I'll come round tomorrow, yeah. Say hi to your mum from me, and tell her sorry for making her worry.'

A paramedic applies two butterfly stitches on the spot, happy to avoid A&E with this angry teenager. After another round of answerless questioning and the police go home. Dwayne refuses to press charges or seek an investigation.

Back inside the flat, an exhausted Mabel pleas, 'Police can't help, if you nah tell them nuttin,' her hands clasped in prayer position.

'Police don't help, Gran,' Dwayne protests. 'They bang man like me up.'

Jerome wearily looks up to the plastic cuckoo clock in the kitchen - chiming four o'clock.

'So will you tell me and your brother di truth?' Mabel asks, staring at her grandson's swollen face.

'What's there to tell, innit?' Dwayne snaps, swirling a nearby tea towel around and whacking it at the door. 'My bro wasn't there to back it.' Dwayne shoots a cool look Jerome's way.

'Who did this? Why?' Mabel lifts herself from the tiny kitchen table to inspect Dwayne's face but he pushes her hand away.

'Leave it!'

'D, don't shout at her like that, okay?' Jerome puts his arm around his grandmother and ushers her to sit back down at the table.

'Well, she don't get how it is for yutes these days!' Dwayne storms to their bedroom, slamming the door.

Mabel rests her forearms on the small kitchen table. 'What won't I get?' Mabel turns to Jerome, 'Me nearly seventy year old.'

Jerome sits at the table and takes his grandmother's hands, 'To be honest yeah, I don't get it, but I'll chat to him and find out.'

'Jerome, I can't have any more trouble 'pon me door. I had too, too much with your mother. Me nah want this for my grandsons.' Mabel forces her hands into fists and knocks them on the table, letting out a weak thud.

Jerome sits opposite, unable to say anything in return, fearing it will be a lie or give her false hope. Instead he bows his head.

After a pause, Mabel lifts Jerome's chin, 'I need you to be better people.' A tear trickling down her soft wrinkled cheek, 'Or I come back fe what?'

Jerome has never witnessed his grandmother's tears before. His guts churn with anguish and shame; she of all people doesn't deserve this.

One tear is enough for Mabel. She mops up her show of weakness and stands up. Jerome sees she is getting older, more frail, more tired; and yet she still wants to remain the strong head of this household. Anguish turns to anger as he blames this all on his brother. He excuses himself from the table.

Jerome eases the bathroom door open. Dwayne in there, examining his injuries.

'Police can't do nothing. Can't be trusted. What feds gonna do? They don't care, you get me?'

Jerome watches his brother ranting at himself in the mirror.

'She carries on as if it ain't a racist world out there, bruv. Like I can just rock up and don a nice suit and man will give me a nice job. No. It don't work like that.'

'What happened?' Jerome asks in a calm, low voice, trying to defuse his brother's temper, or at least stop it escalating.

Dwayne looks back at Jerome, 'Nothing too tough yet.' He takes a deep breath, 'but it's hotting up, trust.'

'I don't get it,' says Jerome.

Dwayne stands upright, flexing his muscles in the mirror. He turns to face Jerome – 'It's time to step up, bruv. To make money we need to sell more drugs to more areas, and these boys don't like it.'

'What boys? What drugs?' Jerome tries to keep cool, to remain calm but that dreaded feeling in his gut isn't going away.

'Anyone can shot weed, blood, but the money's in coke, bruv.'

Jerome stares at Dwayne, worried for what's next.

Dwayne peers down the hallway, then in a low voice says, 'And we're gonna.'

Jerome follows Dwayne into their bedroom and shuts the door.

'We're gonna sell white, harder, faster; make more money than dem pricks can imagine.'

Dwayne sits on Jerome's bed; Jerome sits uneasily on Dwayne's.

'I've got a business plan. Man like me is gonna take over. I'm getting foot soldiers out everywhere. I've got all these youngers knowing I'm boss -

dem little yutes will love a bit of extra cash. Need to get a car, some fresh garms… Time to man up. Execute some next level business.'

'This why your face all mash-up?' Jerome shakes his head. The alcohol and weed has worn off to reveal the sobering mess of his life.

Staring back at him, topless, pumped with adrenaline, Dwayne leans in, 'They've tried it with you, saying they're gonna rape your bitz. If we don't sort it, it's only a matter of time before one of dem boyz actually gets her.'

'That was a hype ting.'

Dwayne gets up to wipe the dripping blood with some toilet roll. He blots inside his nose, then waves the bloody paper at Jerome, 'Is this a hype ting?'

'But what about Gran? She can't take no more madness.'

'If we don't rise, don't step up, we're gonna be here 'til we're her age. Fuck that. Fuck that shit, plus I've got a kid on the way now–' Dwayne pauses to enjoy Jerome's shock. 'Yeah, I have to think about my family now, you get me?'

'What? Baby?'

'Yeah, Hayley stupid ho forgot to take her pill, so now man like me has to think about my future. That's why I ain't about to be taken for a pussy. And these boys think they can try it?' Dwayne punches the creaking bedroom door shut. 'I'm a bigger man to them.'

Jerome struggles to take it all in. Meanwhile Dwayne continues to wind himself up, his hot breath snorting into the cold February night like a bull about to be released into the ring.

'See this nose, bruv. This is the last time someone makes this nose bleed, and for this one nosebleed, man like me's gonna bust a hundred.'

Dwayne switches on his laptop. While it loads, he grabs his mobile, frantically typing messages, sending them out to all his boys and music fans. He posts notices all over the net. In a trance-like state, immerses himself in the replies: Tell all man dem war starts tonight Graff V 'Nam. He laughs as his fans write back.

shoot dem up…RIP Peckham…Every bredda best strap up 4 da wintar!

Jerome decides to keep his phone switched off, avoiding any part of Telegraph Hill versus Peckham. Instead, he collapses onto his own bed watching Dwayne sat at the small desk they found on the street. His head spinning with the weight of the evening, Jerome stares at the poster opposite, imagining Gandhi's head on top of the oiled muscles of the rap star then imagines the rapper's head sat on Gandhi's skinny body sat cross-legged.

Jerome compares his tiny room to the huge space he was in just a few hours ago. George's party seems so far away from anything right now it feels fake, like it never happened. Despite Jerome knowing he physically walked into George's mansion, that house is out of bounds, the welcome expired, the party over. This is Jerome. This room. This brother. This life. He can hear George's voice, 'Do you own a knife, or a gun?'

Jerome thinks about the words he rapped at the party while his older brother makes plans for Graff's revenge. He closes his eyes hoping Dwayne will stop shouting out ideas, worrying how to explain all of this to Issy in the morning. He loves her too much. She'll be devastated. And what about his grandmother? "Spoke to Dwayne, Gran, and basically he's started a turf war with Peckham."

Jerome finds himself praying the hype calms down and some sort of normality returns. It usually does. He thinks how Issy has it right, wanting to escape. Who really wants to live like this? He looks at Dwayne, still online, the screen-light spotlighting the blob of blood clotting under his nose. Jerome turns to face the wall, so tired but restless and panicked, he eventually falls to sleep.

CHAPTER 10

The next day, Jerome visits Issy. He'll be careful not to tell her everything, hoping most of his brother's rant about starting a drugs war was his overactive imagination.

Issy bursts into tears as soon as she sees him. Jerome sits on the sofa and hugs her while she splutters into his jacket. Carol comes in with a mug of tea and some Wagon Wheels. Jerome looks at Carol ashamed he is putting Issy through this. Part of him thinks she doesn't deserve this but then again, he doesn't deserve to lose his girlfriend because his brother wants to be London's next Top Boy.

'I'm proper sorry,' Jerome tells Carol. Issy's head buried in his jumper.

'Don't worry, lovely,' Carol kisses Jerome's forehead. 'It's that girl's fault for getting her wee hopes up.' Carol nudges her daughter to take the mug.

'It's not Emily's fault!' Issy's puffy face resurfaces. 'She was trying to help! It's your fault for being pissed when you wrote it.'

'Emily?' Jerome is confused.

'Came today.' Carol shows Jerome the letter. He opens the thick cream envelope, a red waxed stamp showing a swirled pattern.

'Don't be upset,' Carol says. 'Them places ain't all that.'

Issy wipes the smudged mascara from her eyes.

'I'm proper sorry, babe.' Jerome says as he reads the long and winding prose that ultimately says a big fat no to Issy's chances of going to Emily's school for A Levels. 'I know how much you was on this.'

Carol's heart melts seeing Jerome be so kind. 'You'd be bullied anyway,' she adds.

'Come Lewisham College with me. Won't be millionaires but I'm priceless,' Jerome squeezes Issy's hand, forcing her to smile at his joke.

'There you go,' Carol pats Jerome on the shoulder leaving the teenage lovebirds to it.

'I don't wanna go Lewisham College.' Issy falls back onto the sofa. 'I don't wanna go anywhere!'

'Told Emily?' Jerome asks.

'Yeah, I text her.'

Jerome puts his arms around Issy, 'I'll cheer you up, babes.'

Mozart's Sonata in C Major plays joyfully from the radio to a silent audience at 55 Pepys Road. Emily sits at the table, watching her father read the weekend papers. Janie Sutton flusters around the kitchen in her nervous manner. There is little light from the dull grey sky, but Mr Sutton refuses to put lights on during the day. He looks above the Financial Times to see his daughter staring at him. 'Go help your mother.'

Emily heads towards the AGA. Each footstep feels rigid and unnatural. Her home, the environment she should be most relaxed in, is a maze of invisible hoops and tests. Words. Actions. Beliefs. Wants. Dreams. Everything is under surveillance; everything policed.

'No. No need, Emily,' Janie Sutton pinches her words. 'Everything's done.'

Mr Sutton checks his watch against the kitchen clock.

Janie Sutton turns to her husband, 'Darling, would you like tea or coffee?'

He pauses, looks at his wife, 'Tea please.'

Eyes return to China's rise in economic hegemony, 'We should be teaching our children Mandarin.'

'You can,' Emily pipes up, as she sits back down at the kitchen table, hoping to break the frosty atmosphere. 'At our school, Mr Jiang, the Maths teacher started an afterschool club and it's so popular they're looking at making it part of the timetable so students can take GCSEs and A-Levels. Only problem is, Mr Jiang doesn't want to be a language teacher and the kids really like him. Not sure they'd go otherwise. He's from Manchester and we all love his accent.'

Mr Sutton ignores his daughter's response. 'British schoolchildren shrink under the achievements of Asian schoolchildren, especially the sciences.'

'Apparently there are more Chinese living in America than anywhere in the world,' Emily offers with a smile.

'China has the world's largest population, therefore the most Chinese in the world.'

Mr Sutton glares at his daughter facing down at the tablemat in front of her.

'Perhaps Mr Jiang should transfer to the languages department.' He turns a large pink page to climate change; not only real but unstoppable.

'Honestly Janie, why do I pay for this girl's schooling? Utterly pointless.'

Emily presses her cold fingertips to her burning cheeks to ease the redness. She meant outside of China, obviously.

Janie puts a full English breakfast in front of her husband. 'Mustard?'

'Why on earth would I want mustard for breakfast?' He checks his watch against the clock again.

Now Janie's cheeks flush. She laughs nervously, 'Well, the butcher, he recommended this particular mustard, for these sausages, a new sort.'

Mr Sutton looks unimpressed. He plops a blob on the side of his plate.

After a few moments of tense chewing, the radio's jumpy Mozart turns to the peaceful sound of the Stuttgart Chamber Orchestra playing Pachelbel's Cannon, one of Mr Sutton's favourites though the youngsters keep ruining it with awful renditions while walking down the aisle to be married. Still, his mood shifts. He slurps his tea.

'Lovely tea,' he remarks, hoping his wife will see he is annoyed with Emily, and not her. 'Thank you for breakfast.'

Janie smiles at her husband, exhaling relief as she sits down. She doesn't eat much in the way of fried food. Her yogi recommends fresh fruit and yoghurt followed by two hardboiled egg whites, though Janie has to make an exception on the weekend in order to keep things traditional, and family-oriented. Otherwise described by Emily as: What Dad dictates.

'Awful weather,' Janie remarks. 'I doubt there'll be many at the golf club this evening.'

Emily turns to watch the rain splashing down the French patio doors. The large drops pound the flowers in the pots outside. Domestic violence – the one form of abuse not to enter 55 Pepys Road.

'Dad,' Emily looks at her father, unable to eat while fraught with anxiety.

'What now, Emily?' Mr Sutton replies, enjoying his three fried eggs, two sausages, bacon, tomato, and mushrooms served with a fried slice.

'I'm sorry. For lying,' she says quietly, looking at her plate. Emily has one fried egg, one sausage, one slice of bacon and the other half of the beef tomato sat on her father's plate. She doesn't like mushrooms. Or fried bread.

'You are a silly child, who cannot be trusted with responsibility.'

'Eat please,' Janie nods at Emily, her eyes encouraging her daughter to replace talking with eating.

Emily pierces the fried egg with her fork, watching the thick yellow yolk drain onto the greasy bacon rind.

'It's just that…' She starts again. 'I really like this girl…'

Nothing.

Her eyes remain down. 'She's genuine, honest, and trustworthy. All the things you expect in a friend–'

'Enough Emily!' Her mother's tone is stern. 'Your father is more than equipped to know what's best.'

Emily ignores her mother, and continues, 'I can't understand why I can't be trusted to make a good judgment. People trust your judgments all the time.'

Mr Sutton puts his fork and knife down. He breathes into his large belly and adjusts his belt two notches out. He looks at his daughter as he exhales. Emily can't gauge where this is going. Mr Sutton could actually be calm, but more likely he will start calm, then get angry as he usually does.

Janie especially doesn't want an angry husband. Not every weekend. It's exhausting. Mr Sutton is like a pressure cooker. He slowly builds his argument, telling people his views with no recourse and if anyone challenges him, he becomes a hot-blooded bully who storms the house shouting 'Silly unthinking simpletons I have the misfortune to live with!'

'While I was out getting the papers, I bumped into Merle's father, Mr Bradley. He informed me that late last night, his bedroom was awash with blue light. In and out this light swirled his ceiling, until he was compelled to go and see what the fuss was about. Lo and behold, the same girl Merle's parents have seen you with, is there with her gang friends, shouting, shouting at police! There had been some sort of fight. Blood everywhere.'

'That can't be,' Emily pipes up.

'The police suspect it's linked to drug dealing between various postcodes,' Mr Sutton continues.

'Well I can prove it wasn't them.'

'Emily, stop arguing with your father!'

'Don't get involved, please,' Mr Sutton sternly commands his wife. His eyes fixed upon Emily. 'You were tucked up in bed before the commotion took place.'

She knows this is a trap but she must save Issy's reputation, or else their friendship is doomed. Emily takes a gulp of her sweet tea and with all her courage says, 'because I invited them to George's birthday party. They were both in Mayfair.'

'You did what!' exclaims Janie, slamming her serviette down.

'They were there long after I left. George told me.'

Mr Sutton looks at his daughter. Emily herself can't quite believe what she just did. Courageous. Brave!

Mr Sutton brow furrows. Lips pressed together.

Janie nervously looks at both daughter and husband; her eyes move from one side of the table to the next, back and forth, like a Wimbledon final, yet nothing is said by Mr Sutton. The red fades from his cheeks as he lets out a cough. Eyes down, he continues his breakfast.

'Emily—' Janie begins. Her husband shoots Janie a cool look commanding everyone to finish their breakfast.

The family eat in silence for what feels like eternity to Emily. Even the radio has gone quiet, just a mumbling presenter, with nothing to say.

Back in Jerningham Court, Carol is wrapped in her favourite baby blue dressing gown, curlers in her hair, painting her daughter's toenails lilac. Issy sits slouched on the sofa, head to toe in pink pyjamas, and a fluffy cow patterned dressing gown. Jerome is perched on the opposite armchair looking uncomfortably at a young Travolta gyrating Grease Lightning on the television.

Jerome didn't sleep much, worried about Dwayne's online tirade about Peckham. His phone has been on silent all morning. So far, missed calls from Andre, Barry, Anton and loads from Dwayne, plus texts asking him to go studio for one o'clock. It's now twelve-thirty. Everyone's meeting there.

A sinking feeling hits him every time he looks at Carol's plastic cuckoo clock, the same one Issy bought for his grandmother at Christmas. Mabel loves it.

Carol finishes the final toenail. 'Right, I'll get the toasties,' she says closing the nail polish and shuffling off to the kitchen.

While Carol makes lunch, Jerome moves to the sofa, 'Babe, is it okay if I head off?'

'But you promised to stay with me all day.' Issy gives him the big sad eyes.

'After Grease, we're gonna watch The Sound of Music.'

Jerome looks at her and then at the television, then at the cotton wool between her glamorous toes.

Carol bustles back in and plonks a plate on Jerome's lap. He looks down at the sandwich. Cheap white bread, margarine, plastic cheese melted over watery ham pumped with sugar and salt.

'Want a wee bit ketchup?' she asks with a smile.

Jerome looks up at Carol, 'No thanks, Carol. This is perfect.'

As Carol leaves to do Issy's toastie, Jerome pleads, 'Babe I love you, but, you know, I'm black.'

He winces at the plate on his lap, then licks his lips at the thought of his gran's chicken, rice and peas. He takes Issy's hand and smiles, 'Come with me to Gran's?'

Issy looks at Jerome's toasted sandwich, 'Why didn't you say no when she asked you?'

'I dunno. What am I gonna say?'

Jerome takes a bite, chewing like he's eating sand. He washes the dry bread down with squash that tastes like the plastic cup it's in.

'I wanna see how she's doing, after what happened with Dwayne.'

'He alright?'

'He's fine, face-wise. Don't know 'bout his mind, though.'

'Mind if I stay here? Fancy being home today...' as in does not fancy seeing Dwayne today, or tomorrow, or ever again, if being honest.

'Yeah, no, course babes. Stay with your mum. It'll be nice for you both,' Jerome looks back to the skipping Pink Ladies on the screen. He gets up to mimic their dance moves. Issy laughs.

'Say hi from me,' Issy says then her mobile beeps. 'Hayley.'

Jerome suddenly remembers Dwayne saying Hayley is pregnant and not to tell no one, not even Issy.

Issy glances the text. 'Babe?'

'Yeah,' Jerome says, nervous. He assumes Hayley has seen Dwayne's comments online, or Dwayne has asked her to text Issy to see if Jerome is with her.

'Are you going studio?'

Jerome looks at Issy. He can keep some things from her, but somehow if she asks him to his face, he can't lie, 'Yeah, probably, later on, maybe.'

Issy tosses her phone and looks at Jerome, 'Can you talk to your brother and the others about changing the music to more friendly lyrics, like we said? Same beat, different vibe?'

'Yeah, course I will, babe.'

Jerome's head is confused with all the revelations. He remembers the walk home from George's party, promising Issy he would try and convince Graff to stop the hype and make nicer lyrics.

'Promise?' Issy looks at him serious.

Jerome looks at Issy, then at the clock. 'Promise.'

He opens the window and throws his toasted sandwich down to the bulldog on the green then up at the incoming rain.

'Tell your mum I said thanks for lunch. Delicious!' He winks at Issy before kissing her on the lips. 'Thanks for being my girl. You're the best, no matter what. I'm lucky to have you.'

Jerome does call in on his grandmother and not just for some rice and peas. Mabel seems to be okay, considering. So, unable to resist the call, Jerome heads to the flat in Brockley they call their music studio. The beats are blaring as he walks in and the lyrics, far from cleaning up, are the hardest the gang have written yet.

Inspired by last night's fight, Dwayne calls an all-out war on Peckham vocally, and the EndzUp crew are up for it. Jerome sits uneasily among his friends. He tries to laugh along at the cusses and insults, but knows it's wrong and Issy will be upset about what he's been doing. Being the producer, it's his job to think of beats and rhythms to go with their lyrics. But today, Jerome's not up for it. His head is full of Issy in tears and George at last night's party, then coming home to police sirens and a hectic punched-up Dwayne, then finding out Hayley is pregnant. He sits in a daze, in the crackhead's flat wishing he was producing with the equipment inside George's mansion.

'Oi, what's up with you?' Dwayne demands.

The rest of the boys fall silent.

Jerome looks up. Should he tell his boys the truth? This ain't a war he wants? Or should he go with the flow? Business as usual?

'Listen, fam, Issy is not feeling this lyrical war ting. First rape threats. Now manz coming to the Endz. She thinks it's gonna end with one of us stabbed up, or worse, get me.'

Dwayne answers first, 'She's a chick, bruv. She's gonna carry on flaky.'

'What happened last night?' Jerome asks. 'This shit is supposed to be a hype ting.'

'And?' Dwayne spits out his manifesto: 'If these yutes wanna fight big manz, see what happens.'

These are the moments teachers and youth workers tell you to listen to your gut feeling but Jerome can't find the strength. Peer pressure topped with family loyalty is an unstoppable combination. He picks up his headphones. Issy can shut her phone off to Hayley but Jerome has to sleep opposite Dwayne.

Everyone goes back to laughing and joking. None of them seem worried about their lives. The incident last night has provided endless excitement with something to get heated about. Andre shares stories of school fights, Anton talks about other gang wars, Dwayne tells everyone what battles he wants. Jerome remembers what youth worker Steve says: if the hours spent chitchatting about nonsense fighting were translated into a serious hobby or sport, most of you would be playing for England.

The headphones take Jerome out of the exchange. Beats penetrating his body act like a soothing antidote. He watches his friends and brother and something switches inside. He feels like an outsider. These friends, strangers. The room, surreal, as if he is a secret visitor inside his own body.

Here couldn't be more different from the party last night. Eight teenagers packed in the dirty living room of a tiny council flat. All the wallpaper ripped off, walls covered in tag names and graffiti of girls sucking cock, of money and gold chains. Crisp packets and rolling papers littering the floor. No curtains. No heating. The toilet stained brown and reeks of piss. The rancid carpet sticks to Jerome's trainers, it like even the dirt's trying to escape.

Feeling claustrophobic, Jerome gets up.

'Where you going?' Dwayne demands.

'Going shop.'

Andre follows Jerome out the flat, 'You alright?'

'Dwayne,' Jerome says, keeping his eyes firmly on the pavement, 'was on a proper hype ting last night.'

'I know, bruv,' Andre chuckles, 'My phone was non-stop.'

'It ain't funny, though,' Jerome snaps in a sober tone. 'Saying Peckham yutes are gonna get it, putting it online, telling all manz to get ready to war.'

Andre turns to Jerome, but Jerome won't make eye contact. Lately he feels a distance between him and Andre. It was always them two together, but since Dwayne got kicked out of college, Andre started bunking his GCSE year to hang with Dwayne.

'What's his problem?' Jerome continues, 'This ting was a hype ting. I'm not about to start busting up mans' noses. For what?'

Jerome stops in his tracks and stares at his friend. Maybe if he tells Andre how he really feels, it will get back to Dwayne and his brother might see where Jerome is coming from. 'I got Issy already been threatened rape by some yutes. I got Gran shitting herself we're gonna end up like her son and daughter. I've got Dwayne keeping me up all night, telling all of London he's the next don. What the fuck?' Jerome takes out a box of cigarettes and lights one up. 'Man's life ain't about this shit.' He inhales the smoke aggressively, 'I'm a bigger man than this, trust.'

Andre remains silent. They sit on a wall overlooking Crofton Park Cemetery. The weather is bleak. A black bin-liner blows out of a nearby rubbish bin. Sweet wrappers and bits of paper scatter over the road. A cyclist avoids a rolling beer can. The car behind beeps. Jerome and Andre put their hoods up to avoid the cold wind slicing into their necks as their eyes wash over the gravestones.

Emily's older cousin Rosie has arrived at 55 Pepys Road. She has been given strict instructions: Emily is not allowed out of the house, grounded for lying to her mother and taking up an unsuitable friendship with an unsightly girl who smokes, drinks alcohol in the park, vandalises the area with graffiti and spits on the floor. This girl also has a boyfriend engaged in gang violence, and they can only speculate what the two underage youths are getting up to elsewhere. If it were not such an important engagement for both the husbands and the wives of the Redbridge Golf Club this evening, then Janie would stay home herself.

With her blouse buttoned right up, a pleated white skirt that falls below the knee, grey woolly tights and a matching grey woollen cardigan, Emily's cousin Rosie understands completely. 'I shall have a good chat with Emily to explain the importance of keeping good company,' she assures her aunt and uncle.

'Rosie is doing so well academically and has friends in very high places,' Janie tells Emily. 'Listen to her.'

Rosie smiles at Emily then at her uncle and aunt.

Relieved to have such a sensible niece, the Suttons leave for their engagement.

Once Emily's parents are well on their way to the countryside, an equally relieved Emily confesses exactly what's been happening. She tells her cousin the complete truth – from the mugging to the secret meetings with Issy, the arrangement for Issy to apply to her private school to do A-Levels (and not being accepted), to last night at George's birthday party.

'They're not listening to me and won't give me any respect or trust. I really like Issy and I'm missing out on a great friendship.'

'Come here,' Rosie gives Emily a cuddle. 'You must learn to play your parents at their own game. They are old fashioned conservatives, so behave that way in front of them. Do as they want you to do and when you are packed off to university, behave how you like.'

Rosie unbuttons her blouse to reveal a tattoo of a dragon wrapped in flowers along her chest and rib cage. She looks at Emily's gaping mouth with a wry smile, 'You have to be smart about things, Mimi. I wouldn't be caught dead wearing this outfit to a bar, but this is how to behave in front of Mummy and Daddy.'

The two giggle as Rosie takes out her phone and shows photographs of last summer in Ibiza – tight bikini tops and hot pants showing off all her tattoos and belly button ring. Rosie points out her fellow Oxford students dancing on top of enormous podiums waving glow sticks.

'You see, I do have friends in high places!' she grins, kicking off her ballerina pumps and nestling into the sofa.

'Now go hang out with Issy while your hungover cousin gets some much-needed beauty sleep. I didn't get to bed 'til four this morning.' Rosie hands an elated Emily the door keys.

Issy's phone rings.

'I'm really sorry you didn't get in to my school.'

'Who's this?' Issy asks suspiciously.

'Emily. Mimi. Sorry, on my cousin's phone. My parents confiscated mine. I'm free. What you up to?'

'Wearing PJs, watching films. Just finished Grease. About to put on Sound of Music, interested?' It makes her cringe hearing her accent become posher. She hates that she does it, but it's become automatic.

'Yay! I'd love that. Are we doing snacks because my cousin baked these amazing flapjacks with butter churned from a farm near her flat in Hackney. The cows probably smoke weed!' Emily laughs at her own joke.

'You're such a neek, Mimi.' Issy giggles at Emily's attempt to be street. When Emily tried to smoke, she choked her guts up.

The phone vibrates again, a call-waiting alert from Hayley. Issy ignores it. 'So yeah,' she continues, 'come over and bring your slippers.'

'You seen the latest about how Dwayne is gonna get revenge on every man in Peckham…' For the first time ever, Issy deletes Hayley's message half-way through. No longer interested. Especially not today. Besides, Jerome promised no more violent songs and he's the producer.

The deleted second half of her message went on to say, 'I ain't seen you for ages. Whatever I've done, I'm gonna change. I know I'm gonna change because something's happened.'

Hayley looks out her bedroom window to see the thick cloud darkening her already miserable view. Fifteen and pregnant. Her boyfriend never around. Her brother in prison. Her mum busy plaiting her little sister's hair. No way can she talk to her dad, and anyway, he's already down the pub.

She didnt get in2 dat posh school. Shes @ home wid Carol watchin films. Go der. Jxx

So Issy isn't ignoring her. Hayley was being paranoid. She pulls on her jumper and trainers. She won't say she got upset over ignored calls and message or that she needs her friend back. Forgetting her own problems, Hayley decides to cheer Issy up like old days; watching films on a rainy day is something they always do.

Hayley hunts for her fluffy animal socks and stuffs them and her pyjamas into her tiny rucksack. She grabs an unopened packet of biscuits from her kitchen cupboard. Who cares if she gets hit for nicking them? Custard creams are Issy's favourite.

As she closes the front door, Hayley sees Emily walking past holding a pair of slippers under her umbrella. Hayley's stomach churns. She watches Emily walk across the courtyard and into Issy's block. Hayley runs down the concrete steps and round the back to see Issy's front door. The door opens and Emily gets hugged from a happy, smiling Issy.

Issy pretends not to see Hayley watching from the carpark. She closes the door, leaning against it with a guilty heart. She feels bad about blanking her but as Emily puts on her slippers and starts bouncing around in them, Issy feels better. She doesn't have to spend all her time with just one friend. She has Emily now and can't always be by Hayley's side.

Hayley stands in the middle of Jerningham Court with icy rain spitting in her face. Lost and alone, she catches her reflection in the window of a parked car. She looks at herself with disgust. Her jeans are grubby and her coat is last year's. Soon she'll be fat and even uglier. No wonder Issy doesn't want to hang with her. She wouldn't if she had the choice.

The rain falls heavier, dripping stolen hair gel into her sore eyes. She smudges her makeup across her face wiping away the sticky hair gel with her coat sleeve. With nowhere to go, the park wet and the youth centre closed on weekends, Hayley reluctantly heads back home.

Inside, the walls are filthy from the dog's tail painting mud down the hall. Hayley's mum, slim from too much alcohol and not enough vegetables, dressing half her age in Hayley's opinion, has finished Kaya's hair and they're sat watching Matilda.

'Look at the state of it!' Sandra screeches, watching Hayley slump into the arm chair opposite. 'What's the matter?'

Hayley looks at her mum's hair scraped up into a high ponytail, her face wearing too much makeup for this time of day. Her slippers are filthy from going to the shops in them. Her black knee-length leggings have a hole between the thighs but her lacy black top is new.

Sandra wraps her acrylic cardigan around her waist and dusts off cigarette ash from one arm. Her skin looks fucked after years of cheap booze, expensive cigarettes and sunbeds.

'You gonna tell me or what?' – Her voice, harsh; she lights another cigarette with the one she's about to put out.

Perhaps Hayley should tell Sandra how she's feeling. Plucking up the courage, she says, 'Issy don't wanna hang with me no more.'

But before Hayley can finish, 'What you done now?' Sandra replies. 'Been nicking again? Stupid cow, I told ya…' Sandra continues, oblivious to the pain in her daughter's voice, eyes on the television, stroking her youngest daughter's braids.

Hayley silently sobs. Sandra looks up.

'What you crying for?'

She gets up and pushes Hayley's head as if to wake her from her tears, 'Stupid cow, stop it. Tell her to fuck off, she ain't worth it.'

Kaya, starts laughing at her big sister's tears.

'Stop fucking laughing, you little bitch!' Hayley shouts.

Kaya cuts the sound, but continues silently mocking her sister behind Sandra's back. Hayley goes for Kaya, intent on thumping her one. Kaya screams loudly before Hayley comes close.

'Oi!' Sandra yells, dropping the remote to grip Hayley firmly at the jaw.

Hayley lets out a yelp as Sandra grabs Hayley's hair twisting it in her fingers forcing Hayley back onto the armchair.

'I'm sick of ya,' Sandra screams. 'Every day, you have to start.'

'She fucking started it!' Hayley protests, rubbing her scalp.

'You're older ain't ya? Set an example. Fuck's sake!'

The dog starts barking madly. Kaya starts to cry.

'Stop pretending!' Hayley yells at her little sister, 'I didn't even touch ya!'

'She's scaring me,' Kaya says to Sandra.

The pressure is all too much for Sandra. She slaps Hayley across her face. Then slaps her again, harder. And again. Deep down a part of her knows she's exploiting her daughter to make herself feel better but the dog keeps barking on top of Kaya's crying.

'Shut that fucking dog up!' Sandra presses her cigarette into the dog's back leg, and he yelps out of the living room. Sandra slams the door shut. Out of breath, she walks over to Hayley curled in a ball, protecting her face. Sandra digs out Hayley's head and pushes it into the back of the armchair. 'We've been happy all morning 'til you started.'

Sandra takes her burning cigarette from the concrete floor. She sits on the sofa and cuddles Kaya to stop her crying. Kaya gives Hayley a secret smile, showing Hayley firmly who is boss. Sandra roughly wipes Kaya's tears with her hands.

'Mummy, I'm not big enough to win a fight with her,' Kaya says, putting on a few more tears.

'That's what I'm here for.'

Hayley watches her mum cuddling her sister.

'No wonder you ain't got no mates,' Sandra says, 'Now fuck off out my sight.'

Hayley thuds up the stairs in tears, slamming her bedroom door, then she kicks it, then punches it and punches it again and again until the skin around her knuckles starts bleeding. She kicks her bin, throws her clothes around until she catches her reflection in the broken mirror mounted on the wall opposite. She pulls at her own hair and punches herself in the stomach over and over, hoping the baby will die. She leaps at the mirror and head-butts it so hard she falls backwards onto her bed, tears sinking into the pillow.

CHAPTER 11
THE COUNTRY PILE

With glowing weather forecasts, the Sparlings have invited the Suttons for a relaxing bank holiday weekend at their home near Bath. Emily, sitting in the back of the car, is soaking up the May sun. Charles Sparling is Mr Sutton's favourite golfing partner, which means her father will be in a jolly mood all weekend. The hosts are also the parents to Henry Sparling, Emily's long-standing crush. She sits in the car feeling excited to get time alone together with Henry. Emily checks for the condoms Helena gave her. She fingers the ridge foil edges inside her dress pocket. She uncrosses her legs, imagining Henry's lips moving down her…

As the Suttons move off the motorway and onto country lanes, Emily winds down her window to smell the freshly cut verges. She lists what she likes about Henry, his stature, his confidence, his belief in success, his drive to do anything he puts his mind to… Rivers chase the car along its path as they drive past cows and sheep grazing in roughly hewn fields. The river flitters out into lesser streams and ditches. Emily sticks her face out the window and breathes in. She can see why artists retire to the countryside. It owes us nothing, yet gives us everything.

Emily receives an extra special rush of delight as they enter her favourite lane where trees stand tall on either side meeting together overhead. She looks through Mr Sutton's open sunroof, the different shaped leaves dancing like a kaleidoscope against the clear sky, sunshine bouncing off different shades of green, adorning each leaf momentarily with shimmering gold.

Sighing happily, Emily revisits how her crush began. It was a day much like today. She was taken with her older brother to this very house. There, a boy her age stood with some of his friends. The family moving back home after ten years in South Africa. He had thick gold hair and a funny accent. He turned and gave her a lovely smile.

They spent the afternoon in his garden playing rounders. Emily guessed she liked Henry after feeling extremely hurt when he didn't pick her for his team. Being the only girl wishing to play, Emily was forced to watch the boys running around, bottom lip stuck out in a sulk.

Emily's hurt soon melted when Henry ran over and said 'I only passed you up because I didn't want to spoil your pretty dress.' He hoped she wasn't upset. He didn't mean any harm. Henry ran the fastest. He was bigger than all the other children, even the older ones. Tall or small, they all seemed to look up to him anyway. Henry Sparling is my darling, Henry Sparling is my darling, Emily would rhyme in her head.

He has this energy about him which commands respect. Even Mr Sutton was impressed the last time Henry came back from boarding school. He patted Charles on the shoulder and remarked 'If Emily ever brought home a man like Henry, I would be extremely proud.'

Charles Sparling shook Mr Sutton's hand, and smiled, replying similarly his regard for Emily. It annoyed Emily to see two men barter their children like some Jane Austin novel. She didn't want to say it out loud, but Daddy liking Henry made him more appealing. Mr Sutton is so hard to please it must mean there is something special to Henry Sparling.

The Suttons pull up to the front gates. The descendant of a very successful family of Victorian merchants, Charles, whilst having made a few business deals himself, largely inherited his late father's wealth – including the manor house.

The estate is jaw-droppingly grand. Emily takes her things from the car, as always, a little intimidated by the cultivated beauty. It appears even more amazing than the last time they visited. The grey stone walls adorned with ivy and wisteria in full bloom; the front courtyard with its marble fountain, water lilies and brightly coloured goldfish swimming happily below the emerald green surface. Whatever Emily's position on poverty and inequality, she can't help but feel drawn in; happy beautiful places like this exist.

The front doors open as Charles and Elizabeth Sparling arrive to welcome their guests. After cheerful hellos and handshakes and air kisses from the women, they wander in.

Inside the entrance hall, one can immediately feel the vastness of the house. They are given a tour of the new renovations and interior design: seven large bedrooms, four bathrooms, two dining rooms, a drawing room, a morning room, a sewing room and a spacious kitchen with alfresco dining area facing the lawns. There are manicured gardens, with trees and bushes chiselled into pyramids and swirls, set against a riot of colourful flowers. Elizabeth shows them how she recently converted part of the old servant quarters into an exercise studio and yoga retreat. Emily can see her mother's envy as the thick sunshine pours over the exercise balls and kettle bells.

'Dreamy, isn't it?' Elizabeth beams.

Back inside the house, Emily slides a hand along the polished oak banister and panelling. The carpets are thick and bouncy under her feet. Nothing is overdone, nothing tasteless or tacky. There are antique ornaments on every corner table: bronze statues of boys holding water buckets and horses in gallop. Despite its age, the furniture stands firm, much of it, apparently, from the travels of Charles's great-grandfather Edgar.

'Shame such quality is so rare these days,' Elizabeth Sparling laments, after Emily's mother expresses her admiration for the cabriole leg side table in walnut wood. 'This country had such craftsmanship.'

Emily smiles to herself. Elizabeth's table is clearly French.

As Elizabeth shows the Suttons to their rooms, a disappointed Emily finds out Henry isn't home. 'He's away as part of an Army training weekend.'

Alone in her room, Emily drops her weekend bag and reclines onto the bed's cushioned headboard. There's a matching padded footboard, both in pea green velvet with silver trim. The pelmet attached to the wall above her gives the bed grandeur, framing it with curtains that match those at the window. She fingers the hand embroidered pattern on the bedspread. Opposite the bed is a dresser laden with hand-carved grapes. An oval-shaped mirror above it, beautiful despite a small chip and blackened corners.

Emily levers herself from the bed and goes to it. She looks at her reflection. She has a frame much like her mother, who was once a ballet dancer. She looks closer at her facial features. Her cheeks are popping up with freckles. Today her eyes look greener than grey and her hair is already looking lighter from the sun. Today is a pretty day.

She wanders around the room, touching walls and windows and furniture; this could be hers one day. Henry is the Sparling's only son and they are frightfully traditional. She imagines what it would be like to live here. To paint and sew while Henry works. Having large dinner parties in the evening then later dancing in the library. The yoga area would be an art studio, with fellow artists from all over the world coming to retreat. What fun, she thinks, fluttering around the room. They could camp on the lawns.

Mrs Sparling has placed a set of towels at the foot of the bed, along with some bath bombs and a vanity set of shampoos and body lotions, *Welcome Emily*, reads the note.

Emily takes the face cloth to the en suite. The bath immediately becomes her new favourite thing. It has cast iron feet with pipes coming up from the floor over the side of the tub, so one can just sink in without feet or head having to wrestle with either hot or cold taps. Genius, and sexy. A bath tub for two, Henry; me and you, Henry!

The walls are white and royal blue with hand-painted bathroom tiles that chart the affair of two young lovers. First boy sees girl. Girl notes boy watching her. There is a bit of courtship, a bit of denial, a bit of swinging from a willow tree by a pond. The boy wearing silk breeches entices the girl (in a court dress) over with an apple, before kneeling by her feet. Emily gazes at each tile in delight, imagining she could hop into each scene like Mary Poppins, back to seventeenth century England. Emily swinging from the apple tree, her hair in ringlets bouncing behind her, Henry beckoning her to dismount with a packet of hobnobs...

'Emily?' Janie Sutton knocks on the door, before peeking in. 'What are you up to?'

'Daydreaming.'

'Well, enough of that. The Sparlings are waiting to serve tea!'

Janie marches Emily downstairs.

'Oh no, Mum!' Emily stops in her tracks. 'Look!'

'What?' Janie turns around, worried. 'What is it?'

'It's only half past two,' Emily points to her watch. 'We can't possibly entertain afternoon tea at this time. What shall we do?'

Janie Sutton tuts. 'Impertinent child.'

The kitchen has painted plates mounted along the back wall. 'Each one worth around five hundred pounds. But I would never sell them,' Elizabeth is saying as they walk in.

Janie rolls her eyes.

Emily is escorted through the kitchen to the conservatory. White and yellow cheesecloth curtains hang from the windows, with yellow ribbons tying each back. First thing to go, Emily thinks as she sits down.

The table is spread with tiers of cake and fruit scones, sandwiches and savoury bites. The gentlemen have already turned to a sneaky brandy, and are talking golf.

Elizabeth pours Emily a cup of Lady Grey. Emily takes a cucumber sandwich. Janie Sutton gives her a frown.

'Napkin,' Janie lets out a nervy laugh, to hide her chagrin. 'Must I constantly remind you of such basic manners?'

'We rarely bother with Henry,' Elizabeth Sparling says. 'I'm sure you do so at home.'

'Oh, I assure you she does,' Janie replies, placing the napkin over Emily's lap.

'Must be the holiday spirit...' Emily says sarcastically. How was she born to such people; so stringent, so stifling?

'He's a hopeless case,' Elizabeth continues.

Conversation throughout tea remains light. The ladies talk about bread baking, yoga poses and gardening, specifically in vogue vegetables. Emily is having a simultaneous conversation inside her head: So Liz, darling, any chance of me fucking your son on this very table? At some point the conversation turns to the differences between London and the countryside...

'London must be a completely changed experience since you moved south of the river?'

'Well Telegraph Hill is different to South Ken, yes,' Janie replies, graciously accepting more tea.

'I'm sure,' Elizabeth says, while pouring. 'I don't know many who could take that leap.'

'Thank you,' Janie says looking into her cup, hoping to change topics.

'Well, I like it,' Emily pipes up, annoyed at Mrs Sparling's snob-like manner. 'There's a mix from all walks of life, people you simply won't find in the countryside.'

Janie Sutton's cheeks flush pink at her daughter's outburst.

'So I hear from Henry,' Elizabeth says sweetly. 'You've made some rather interesting friends.'

Janie stops fidgeting.

Elizabeth smiles.

'He mentioned Emily having brought two "hoodies" from the local council estate to George's party.' Elizabeth's expression remains fixed. 'His words not mine. He mentioned they live just at the end of your street, Janie.'

Janie becomes flustered. Unsure of Elizabeth's motive for bringing this up, she doesn't know how to respond.

'They're not hoodies,' Emily giggles, trying to smooth over her mother's obvious neurosis, 'and I shall tease Henry when I see him for being so naughty.'

Mr Sutton and Charles' conversation ebbs.

'Emily made an unfortunate friendship, but we dealt with it,' Mr Sutton grunts catching the tail end of things.

Elizabeth changes subject seamlessly as the men join the conversation.

Back in London, Issy's front door jolts from a fist banging it. A hungover Carol stumbles down the hall mumbling. As she swings the door open, Jerome has Hayley in his arms. She's shaking uncontrollably, pleading to be put down and left alone. Carol makes way for Jerome to usher Hayley inside.

'What's happening?' Issy calls out rushing downstairs.

Leaving Hayley curled up on the sofa, Jerome takes Issy aside, 'Sandra and Ray just beat the shit out of her.'

'What the fuck? Issy's heart sinks. 'Why?'

'For having Dwayne's kid.'

'Pregnant? How far is she?'

'Four or five months.'

'What?' Issy's eyes well with tears. She's avoided being with Hayley at all costs. 'Why didn't you tell me?'

'I promised Dwayne, in case she didn't keep it.'

'I've been a shit friend.'

'Well you can make it up to her now, can't you?' he says, leading Issy back to the living room.

Hayley refuses to uncurl herself as Jerome and Issy walk in. Issy's phone starts ringing. She looks at her mum, 'It's Sandra.'

Carol picks it up as Sandra yells down the phone demanding Hayley 'Get here and pack her stuff!'

'Sandra, it's Carol. Calm down, love. What's happened?'

Sandra's screaming, 'them fucking niggers across the road!'

Carol gulps her embarrassment. Jerome can hear the words echo clearly from Issy's mobile. He shakes his head as he sits down and puts one arm around Hayley.

'Sandra. Sandra? Sandra!' Carol can't get a word in. After several attempts, she hangs up.

'Issy love, go get Hayley your wee dressing gown.'

Issy runs upstairs.

Jerome tries to get Hayley to uncurl herself, but she resists.

'Do you think we should call the police?' Jerome asks, as he follows Carol to the kitchen.

'Social services need to sort this.' Carol offers Jerome a cigarette. She lights hers, furiously blowing the smoke out. 'She can't keep getting hit. Especially if she's pregnant.'

Bringing the pink fluffy gown, Issy shuts the living room door, 'Hays, it's just me and you now. You okay?'

Hayley refuses to say anything, or lift her head. She remains tightly compact, shaking. Issy wraps her pink fluffy dressing gown around her friend and rubs her back. Hayley flinches, shaking off Issy's arm. Sad and guilty at Hayley's rejection, Issy sits on the floor beside her, feeling powerless.

The ladies are in the Sparling's rose garden. Janie Sutton has gotten to a raunchy bit of her novel, happy to hide with her sunhat and big sunglasses, feeling the sunshine warm the crotch of her swimming costume.

Emily is painting with Elizabeth, who is talking loudly about how she loves watercolour and the time she spends painting her flowers.

'Apparently, just twenty hours of solid practice and anyone can acquire a skill...' Emily says.

'I simply lose myself in this garden. I become so captivated, I forget to eat,' Elizabeth pats her flat stomach and smiles at Emily. 'It's rather useful having helpers, otherwise I'd simply starve when the weather's like this. Look at the blues and purples of the irises. The delphinium has come out so well this year. If only I could capture it with my brush...'

Emily cuts her mother a look as Elizabeth retreats to the house, 'for a comfort break'.

Both Suttons are tired of her pretensions.

'She's getting worse with age,' Janie Sutton whispers, as her daughter comes to join her.

Emily wonders if the majority of adults inevitably decline into artificiality. These are the teenagers of the eighties, Bowie and Blondie for god's sake.

'Why does she keep using Latin words?'

'Not sure, but it's getting up my Centaurea Cyanus.' Janie Sutton lifts up her sunglasses to theatrically wink.

'Mother!'

'What? The simple cornflower to the likes of you and me,' Janie Sutton says, settling back into a chair and returning to her novel, happy to have made her daughter laugh.

'Do calm down, dear,' she adds, sunglasses back on. 'The Antirrhineae returns.'

Emily looks quizzically but Janie keeps that definition to herself.

The gentlemen are inside one of Charles Sparling's outhouses, deep in conversation. Sabs keep coming onto his land, attempting to stop hunts. 'Nobody in the countryside is following the ban, so why have it?' Charles says. 'All it does is give scruffs the ammunition to pick a fight with good and decent people...'

Mr Sutton listens intently. As a judge, his job is to uphold the laws of the land, though he is also an enormous believer in tradition and conserving values.

'It makes absolutely no sense, Butty. This country can imprison me for upholding a sport that's been in my family hundreds of years. I mean, why on earth do we have all these equal opportunity laws when my own cultural heritage isn't being preserved?'

Charles wipes the sweat from his brow and flicks his dyed brown hair from his eyes. 'I have chickens and geese and ducks to think of. And get this, you'll love this, Chief Sab, a woman called Sally Gordon, always on Facespace or whatever it is, seven o'clock, she has all these rubber clog wearing fools pouring oil everywhere to confuse the hounds. Where is she midday? In Ed Browne's butcher buying my meat for her Sunday's roast. I mean, come on.'

Mr Sutton's bushy eyebrows frown in sympathy as they carefully handle Charles's guns.

'And want to know something else? Sally takes disability allowance. Fat as anything, yet able to organise sabbings. And people wonder why half these good folk are registered citizens in Switzerland, Jersey, Luxumbourg – you name it. My taxes propping up the likes of Sally – the middle class sort of thorn in your side.'

'We have awful issues with travellers too...' Charles continues, caressing the polished wood barrel in his hands. 'Steal anything they can get their hands on. Heather Thorpe's field – completely ransacked by those filthy buggers. And little she can do about it. They target elderly landowners, scour the stables and outhouses, sell petrol drained from tractors, take anything – horse feed, gardening tools – you name it, they take the lot. It makes me furious. You must see it every day.'

'Oh, I do,' Mr Sutton replies, carefully placing the musket back on the display wall, 'day in, day out.'

'They are, quite frankly, the dregs of society.'

'Some sit in my courtroom carving their names on wood that existed before their great-grandfathers were born. Assuming they're British, that is. Most from the colonies. They care little for this country. They care nothing for our services, our values, I mean we give these people free education...'

Mr Sutton breathes deeply into his round belly then loosens his belt; Elizabeth provided a generous spread.

'People think they have a right to behave any way they please,' Charles says. 'Human Rights gone mad.'

'The financial costs to the legal system is staggering,' Mr Sutton sighs. 'I see no answers, no solutions.'

'Here's the answer, Butty,' Charles aims his shotgun at the window. 'Pow, pow! Shoot the lot of them.'

'Ah, as if it were that simple.'

Charles and Mr Sutton chuckle.

'Speaking of, what's with these kids at William Addy's party?'

Mr Sutton breathes in again, adjusting his belt another notch.

'Emily, the silly fool, has romanticised a friendship with one of the girls from a nearby block of flats.'

Charles sympathises with Butty – Mr Sutton's nickname for being an insolent pupil and by far the most strapped boy at their boarding school.

'The girl is just a child,' Mr Sutton continues, 'she has no idea the problems these people bring. I do. I see it on a daily basis in court. There really is no room for these sorts of friendships. If I thought her mother could handle the loss, I would have packed Emily off to board somewhere years ago.'

'Ah, but then you have your wife rattling around the house. Trust me on this one, it's best when they can fuss over a child. I rather wish Lizzy had more children to fuss over.' Might also stop her fucking the gardener.

'The matter is dealt with now.' Mr Sutton fingers the trigger of the French Flintlock. 'Emily is under strict supervision. She's not to see this girl, under any circumstance. Janie is supervising her, and instructed the school on days we can't be home early she is not to leave before six o'clock.'

'What about these summer holidays? I worry Henry will be up to all sorts, what with no ties to his old school and not yet having started the new one.'

'My niece is back and forth to London. I trust her to look after Emily, if needed.'

'Ah yes, Rosie,' Charles looks at his friend for a moment, 'She's a good girl.' Charles places the final musket back into the display cabinet and firmly locks it. 'Perhaps the answer to our social ills will come from these clever folk.'

'If only Emily had something of Rosemary in her.' Mr Sutton polishes the last of his fingerprints from the gun.

'She will, Butty,' Charles pats his old friend firmly on the shoulder. 'She will.'

'Hays. I've been shit,' Issy says, guilty. 'I know I ain't been there and I'm really sorry.'

The girls sit in silence. Hayley still curled into herself and Issy by her side.

'I heard you're pregnant,' Issy says softly.

Hayley stirs, starts to unravel.

Issy gasps at Hayley's distorted face: both eyes puffy and bruised, top lip fat and bloodied.

'Hayley,' Issy whispers in shock, 'you need to go hospital.'

'I ain't.'

'You seen your face?'

'Don't care!' Hayley shouts.

'The baby? Don't you wanna know if it's safe?'

'Don't give a shit about the baby. Hope it's dead.'

Hayley's swollen eyes well up with tears, 'Where were you, yeah?

Where?'

Issy looks down, unable to answer. She picks at a cigarette burn in the carpet.

'You dumped me for that rich bitch and her mates.'

'No, I didn't,' Issy says. 'I hardly see Emily. I just wanna study.'

'Why ignore my texts? We don't go school together. Nothing.'

'You stopped going,' Issy snaps, feeling the weight of Hayley's tone.

'Because you stopped going with me.'

Issy searches for ways to defend herself but can't. Hayley is right. Issy has been avoiding her. She's been getting to school early and leaving late to work on coursework.

'I'm shook. I don't wanna end up here my whole life.' Issy signs. 'Hate this shit flat. Hate this shit area. I hate all the trouble the boys are starting with their shit music.'

'Yeah, you think I'm shit too. You think I'm a piece of shit on the floor.'

'I don't.'

'She made you hate us.'

'It's not her. This whole thing started before...' Issy wants to go on, to tell Hayley that watching Hayley, Dwayne, Anton and Andre constantly on a grind, stealing, shoplifting, robbing friends of friends, makes her feel sick to her stomach. Like who are you people? Supposed to be my best friends? Issy has been brought up to work for what she wants. The missing piece of information was that education is the best thing to work on, not working in the supermarket barely keeping rent and bills paid, eating reduced food every night to keep booze on the table. She's had enough of Hayley picking fights with teachers, school kids, store detectives and police. Emily's life hasn't produced Hayley's life. Emily's family being rich and well-mannered hasn't made Hayley's family violent and criminal.

'You're gonna get good grades and leave me behind,' Hayley says, staring at the photograph of Issy's father on the mantelpiece. The frame is different.

Issy can't find words to reply. What Hayley says is true.

Angela Pompton is joining the Suttons and the Sparlings for supper. Angela happens to work as timetable coordinator and PA to the Principal of Emily's school. Emily cannot bear her. Mrs Pompton's mother lives in the neighbouring village – and coincidently – is visiting the same weekend as the Suttons. Small world, and all.

'I'm not surprised the teachers were flabbergasted,' Angela explains. 'They never saw so many grammatical errors in one application. Their there's from their they're. Your and you're. At one point, we wondered if the whole thing was a practical joke made by one of our students.'

The table joke as they pass around the photocopy, personal details blacked out.

'How will your child cope with the challenges of adapting to the demands of private school workloads?' reads out Charles. 'Watching television relaxes her!'

The whole table roar with laughter, everyone except Emily, who sits in painful discomfort. Angela Pompton is talking about Issy's application, Emily knows it. She prays she doesn't mention the girl's name and address.

'Oh, deary me, that is funny,' Janie remarks, patting the corners of her mouth with a napkin. 'Where do these people get such ideas?'

Emily notices Mrs Pompton shoot a glance at Elizabeth. Both ladies share a dry smile.

'Actually, she comes from London: SE14. I'm assuming that's not that far from you?'

'May I be excused?' Emily asks.

'No,' her mother flatly refuses, understanding what's happening.

The table goes quiet. Emily's face turns red. She pretends to examine the intricate patterns on the tablemat.

'Was the girl's name 'Isabella' by any chance?' a sober Mr Sutton asks.

'Well, now you mention that name, yes, yes. I think it was. Though the Scottish spelling Is-o-bel. Yes the name has come to me now. Isobel.'

Angela glances again at her host, then sideways at Emily's mother, who also has her head facedown towards her lap, taking time to smooth out the creases in her napkin. 'Do you know of her?' Angela continues.

'Emily decided to take on her very own Eliza Doolittle,' Charles says, trying to keep it fun.

'Really?' Angela replies. 'How interesting. So tell–'

'Butty has things sorted,' Charles continues.

'The matter's closed,' Mr Sutton adds firmly, to pipe down the ladies.

'Emily, you may be excused – father permitting – to freshen up.' Charles looks to Mr Sutton for agreement.

'Yes, go upstairs, wash your face and return for pudding.'

Emily leaves the table, tears forming in her eyes, trembling with anger at their belittlement of her friend.

'Don't be too hard on her,' Elizabeth insists. 'She's such a sweet girl, really.'

Janie keeps her head bowed, teeth digging her bottom lip, mortified at Elizabeth Sparling's insincerity.

Ed Bradley is walking up Jerningham Road with his daughter, Merle. They often have father and daughter time together, and spent today in town. Firstly they had a walk along the South Bank, from London Bridge to see Donna Aqua's Tate Modern exhibition. Finally they hopped on a bus to Chinatown for noodle soup and steamed buns. Now they're headed back to

Telegraph Hill to watch a film at home.

Mum text to say she's making toffee popcorn,' Ed says, reading the text.

'Yummy.' Merle's favourite.

As they near the entrance to their four bed, semi-detached house, they cross Issy's estate. A woman runs out in obvious distress. A man follows her holding a baseball bat,

'WHERE IS HE? WHERE'S THAT FUCKING BLACK CUNT?'

Net curtains rustle as some neighbours peek at what the fuss is about. The couple stand in the middle of the road screaming up towards Mabel Clarke's block. The man slams his baseball bat on the road in defiance to a car beeping to pass.

'They're after someone,' Ed says.

'I'M GONNA CHOP HIS COCK OFF AND MAKE HIM EAT IT!'

Across the courtyard, in another flat, Hayley stirs from her friend's lap, 'That's my dad. I can hear him' she says, as the shouting comes in through the open window. 'He's gonna kill Dwayne, I know it.'

'Gran!' Jerome jumps up and rushes out the flat.

Issy runs after him. Hayley begins to move but she's stiff and sore.

'Hays, stay here,' Carol insists, 'You can't take another hit.'

Hayley listens for once and eases back on the sofa. She puts a hand on her belly and wonders if the baby survived.

Outside, Issy screams as Hayley's dad swings the bat at Jerome.

'What the fuck, man!' Jerome shouts at Ray's angry face; red and puffy from years of drinking and doing white.

Hayley's dad is short and stocky. His love of fried food and cocaine and beer have led to him being less than agile. Jerome easily dodges another swing of the baseball bat.

Ray's body is slow and awkward, he moves like a block of lard. 'Where's your fucking brother!'

Carol arrives at Jerome's side.

'Why you getting involved?'

'The wee lad's never said a cross word to you, Ray, and you know it,' Carol replies.

'Who you talking to?!' Sandra screams, moving in to go for Carol. Ray uses his baseball bat as a barrier. Sandra can easily push the bat out of the way but she stands behind it like a schoolchild in the playground.

Carol pushes up the sleeves of her top. Mess with a Scotswoman at your peril.

'You're both lucky I didnae call social services,' Carol says, struggling not to slap Sandra. Carol points at her flat, 'Her face looks like she done ten rounds with Tyson.'

Sandra glares but says nothing.

'What you looking at?' Ray shouts over to Ed Bradley and Merle.

Ed clutches his daughter as they cross the road to their house.

'Those are the same ones Emily made friends with, aren't they?' Ed asks Merle, drawing her close.

'Afraid so, Dad. I think Emily thinks they're nice people.'

'Well, some people can see the good in everyone,' Ed strokes Merle's hair, 'even the likes of Hitler and Jack the Ripper had friends – Yes, good evening, the police please... and possibly an ambulance.'

'She set me up,' Janie whispers to her husband as they retire to their bedroom for the night.

'Nonsense,' he replies.

'Do you believe it was a coincidence Angela happens to be in Bath and happens to have the application on her, and happens to embarrass me in front of Charles? This is going to be the talk of Redbridge. That silly, stupid, child. The one time I allow her to venture out after dark. This was never about photography–'

'Will you pipe down?'

'Emily is trying to ruin me. She hates me, I know it.'

'Enough!' Mr Sutton grabs Janie's arm. Janie freezes. He releases his hold, 'I'm very sorry for that, but you will work yourself up.'

Janie rubs her arm. She storms into the bathroom, closing the door.

Mr Sutton sits his heavy bones on the bed and rubs his eyes. Yes, they called him Butty. Hit so many times he still has whip marks across his back. He vowed never to lift a finger to his own family, well, who can honestly say they never broke a vow?

He hates how stern he is, how his temperament worsens with each year. His father's recent death is certainly playing a role, there is no denying. The problems with his own son and his late father's estate. Then the cases he presides over. The sick things humans do to one another on a daily basis when really people should treat each other with decency and respect. That's what school had been trying to beat into him.

Mr Sutton gently taps the bathroom door. Silence. He slowly opens it to reveal his tearful wife sat on the dressing chair.

He kneels beside her. A very rare moment of tenderness occurs as the grizzly man Janie battles with daily takes her hand and kisses the wedding ring.

'I'm enormously lucky to have you.' He means it. He knows how good she is. How patient and kind.

Janie looks at her husband. He's never kissed her wedding ring before.

'You're completely right, those women are silly fools. Emily has her

110

youth and inexperience to blame for an honest mistake. Charles snuffed the conversation because he knows Elizabeth. You acted, as always, in the most polite manner. I was very proud of you. I am proud of you...'

Mr Sutton takes his wife by the hand and lifts her from the chair, then escorts her back to the bed.

Janie kicks herself that she forgives this rude and cantankerous man so easily. He kisses her under her upset eyes then her lips, neck...

Janie feels relief as she receives these tender gifts.

He slips her nightgown to one side and kisses her bare shoulder. 'You looked very beautiful this evening, darling.' His eyes look watery, pale, tired.

Janie sighs as her husband floods back to her. He takes off her nightdress and strokes between her legs. Janie is limp and willing, it's been months since they indulged in anything resembling sex.

She gasps into his neck. Mr Sutton's body might be fat and old, but Janie still sees the young man behind the blue of his eyes.

One floor below, Charles Sparling knocks on Emily's bedroom door then opens it to find her in her nightdress, rooting in her bag for her bedtime novella.

She turns, shocked to see him.

'I want to apologise for this evening,' Charles says, closing the bedroom door behind him. He sits on Emily's bed, placing his scotch on the bedside table.

'It's fine,' Emily says stiff, awkward. She expected one of her parents.

'I hope you weren't too upset,' Charles continues, as he glances Emily's small, firm-looking breasts. He crosses his legs.

'I'm fine, thank you,' Emily replies, feeling his eyes where they shouldn't be.

'Good.' Charles takes another gulp of the scotch. 'Let's tuck you in.'

He pulls the duvet off and places it on the floor. 'Probably too warm for this.'

Emily climbs uneasily into bed, her novella pressed to her chest. Charles takes the book out of her hands and puts it next to his scotch.

'I often wished I still had little girls,' he tells her, as he smooths her nightdress with his hands and pulls the summer sheets over her body.

'I'm probably a little old for this now,' Emily affirms, worried he's drunk.

Charles looks at Emily and strokes her hair from her face.

'Yes, yes, I suppose you are. Forgive me...' he pauses, not leaving. 'I mentioned to your father I would have a word with you about your newfound friendships.'

Emily's bites the inside of her cheeks, feeling the pain behind her eyes spread to her temples.

111

'Emily, you are clearly a sweet, innocent girl,' Charles Sparling continues, sipping his scotch, 'It's unfortunate you should hear such cruel words, but as your father's best friend I have taken it upon myself to relay some facts of life.'

'You see, Emily,' Charles says, returning the tumbler to the coaster, 'we live in a society that is shaped rather like an isosceles triangle.' He uses his middle finger to draw a triangle shape on the sheets resting over Emily's stomach.

Charles takes Emily's arm. Her body stiffens as he strokes it then rests his hand on top of her hand. Is he being a pervert or just over tactile? She doesn't want to but can't help thinking he has an erection, though it might be the shape of his trousers.

'If you cut lines across the triangle,' Charles goes on, continuing to use his fingers to aide his analogy, 'one could say certain people in our society are attributed to certain areas of that triangle. Those in the bottom section are mostly poor and uneducated, often criminals and immigrants at the very baseline. In the middle section, here, are more respectable people, those who work for a living, perhaps builders at the bottom middle section, here, rising up to teachers in the middle, here, then those who, dare I say it, work for the government, and here bankers and businessmen. Then you have the apex…' He fingers the circumference of his make-believe isosceles triangle. 'This section is for those who not only have done exceedingly well for themselves, but have what's called breeding. We all have our place in society. If we were all the same, life simply would not work. A bin man can never become king, he has nothing in the way of qualifications, of cultural capital, understanding. Do you follow?' Charles asks. He tucks the fallen piece of hair back behind Emily's ear.

Emily nods hoping that will get rid of him.

'Your great-great-grandfather owned that magnificent house on Telegraph Hill, where you now live. You come from a family of successful shipping merchants who made a fortune using their hard work and skills. Unfortunately, time passes; life modernises. Council estates go up around the homes our ancestors worked so hard to acquire.' Charles's shoulders slouch after he takes the last sip of scotch. 'Think about your father and all he's done for you. He pays your school fees so you can be around equally fortunate children. Why?' Charles leans in close, so close she can smell the alcohol on his breath.

Emily's gulps.

'So you can move in the right circles.'

To her relief, he reclines again.

'He cares for you, and that's why he fears these sorts of friendships. These people have no concern for civil society. They're dangerous.' Charles says, staring into Emily's eyes. He can see she is uncomfortable and would like nothing more than to climb on top of her and fuck her senseless. That fresh, innocent skin. The flavour of her virginity. He takes a deep breath then exhales to compose himself. 'I am well aware that a certain Henry Sparling has his eye on you.'

Emily looks up then.

He tries to take another gulp of single malt but the glass is empty. 'I'll just visit your bathroom,' he says, kissing Emily on the forehead.

Emily watches Charles go into the adjoining bathroom. She lies completely still, ears pricked like a hunted animal. She thinks she hears him groaning. When the toilet flushes, nobody comes out. Eventually Charles darts out the bathroom and exits her room without a word. What just happened?

Elizabeth peers through the banisters as she spies Charles leaving Emily's room.

'What were you doing in there?' she whispers walking up the stairs holding a carafe of water with slices of lemon inside.

'Emily saw a spider and asked me to deal with it. Hence this,' Charles looks into his scotch glass. 'Oh, where's he gone?'

Elizabeth looks at her husband with suspicion, 'You should have called her father. A grown man visiting to a young girl at night looks rather odd.'

'Why?' Charles stares innocently at his wife.

'Why?' Elizabeth frowns, the sharp line between her eyes deepening. 'You know it's not the done thing to do?'

'I'm not sure what you're insinuating Lizzy, but I don't like the tone of it!'

Elizabeth stops. Perhaps her imagination is working overtime since the new gardener began attending to more than her lawns.

'That's the problem with today,' Charles chuckles, 'One cannot chuck a spider out the window without suspicion.'

'I thought you said you'd captured it in that glass?'

'Come on woman, allow me to escort you to your room.' Charles puts out his arm. 'Though I can't claim to act as innocently with you,' he whispers with hot boozy breath deep into her ear.

'Charlie,' Elizabeth jests, 'you're incorrigible!'

Next morning, Emily wakes to a loud rap at her door. Awake most of the night, worried Charles might return, she placed the dressing chair under the doorknob.

'Open this door at once,' Janie demands.

'What is wrong with you?' she says as Emily removes the chair jarring the door. 'Those are antique!'

Emily looks at her mother; her skin looks peachy, fresh.

'Everyone's ready for breakfast and here you are still in your bedclothes. Come on, let's get dressed.' Janie takes the cotton nightdress in her hands but Emily steps back.

'I would like to get dressed alone, please,' Emily tells her mother, eyes bloodshot and tired. 'In private.'

Emily's mind has been spinning: although Charles was touchy feely, nothing really happened, nothing reportable and he is her father's closest friend. Remembering Rosie's advice, she decides to keep his visit a secret. Get through the day. Mr Sutton doesn't like to be home late on Sundays anyway so no doubt she and her mother will be packed up and in the car soon after breakfast.

'Your father and I spoke last night…' Janie's tone prickles Emily's skin, 'and we'll talk at home about this nonsense with Eliza, I mean Issy. There was no need to barricade yourself in.'

Janie opens the bedroom window, taking in the fresh May air.

Emily folds her arms awkwardly. The breeze that invigorated her the morning before now intrudes her privacy. She pushes past her mother and closes the window. Any beauty outside has disappeared.

Janie stares at Emily in amazement. 'I know I was your age once, but I can't remember being quite so odd.'

'Do you remember being quite so submissive?'

Janie pinches her lips together and swallows her upset: that she gives in to her husband, attends to his temper. But if Emily didn't exist, she wouldn't have to constantly question her role as housewife, mother, woman, individual. 'As you wish. Please be down in ten minutes.'

Emily slumps on the bed, angry and conflicted. She just used her mother as a punch bag, a panacea for her own weaknesses. Hendrike would have punched Charles in the nuts at the first sign of something dodgy. Issy's friend Hayley would have grabbed his scotch and glassed him in the face with it. Imagining this makes Emily laugh.

She stares at the bathroom tiles as she packs her toothbrush and comb in her makeup bag on top of the unused condoms. Visions of Henry beckoning her with an apple replaced by a dirty old man making shapes over her breasts. Who has it in them to touch others like that? But she never said stop. She never said no. She never said anything. He muted her.

She looks down at her slender hands. Elizabeth had given her a French manicure before supper. Emily thought the Sparlings were darling perfect. Even if Charles's actions were not meant to be sexual, how can Emily be with someone like Henry when he's been raised an elitist? Emily thinks about using triangles in her art. Perhaps that will help, to channel all of this into her A Level project.

As she dresses, Emily decides there shall be no more being infatuated with Henry Sparling. Forget boys. Forget Charles. Manage her parents.

Take her power back.

Mabel Clarke is with her two grandsons. She feels tired, weakened by yesterday's events. Mabel tries to take Dwayne's hand but he refuses, tucking both tightly under his armpits.

'So this true?' Mabel pleads in her soft Jamaican accent.

Dwayne refuses to speak.

'Jerome?'

Jerome looks at his brother, 'Shall I tell?'

'Tell her what you like, bruv,' Dwayne snaps. Arms still folded, his pectorals tensing behind the yellow string vest.

Jerome takes his grandmother's hand. 'Yes, Gran, it's true. Hayley and Dwayne are together.'

'I'm not talking courtship. I'm talking lickkle pickney. A child being pregnant wid a child.'

Jerome looks at Dwayne.

'Don't watch me, bruv,' Dwayne spits at Jerome.

Mabel's wrinkles glisten as the sunshine streams into the kitchen onto her freshly moisturised face, 'Dwayne, please, please, in Lawd Jesus's name, speak like a gentlemen inna yuh home.'

'Home?' Dwayne snorts again. 'Is dis home? This area is one piece of shit.'

Jerome gently squeezes Mabel's hand, knowing how painful it is to see her grandson speak at her so violently, 'D, come on now, have some respect.'

'Respect? Like them Nazis, yeah?' Dwayne looks straight at his grandmother, 'Wanna talk respect when they're calling your grandkids niggers in the street. Police don't arrest them for discrimination, do they? And you sit here thinking some Lord Jesus is gonna mend this shit?'

'D, man,' Jerome starts.

'That shit's been brainwashing black people from day. How many Johns and Marks you know chilling in Jerusalem, bruv? Middle East Matthew.'

'Dwayne, stop!' Jerome's shoots a harsh look at his brother.

'Stop why? Because this family's fucked!'

Mabel bows her head through Dwayne's tirade.

'Fucked from the get go. Mother's a crackhead, probably sucking some man's dick as we speak. Fuck knows where my father is. Somewhere with his tenth girlfriend living on some housing estate. And yours – fucking off to Jamaica. Can't even send you five pound for your birthday yet all over the internet with his gold teeth and garms. And then there's us, yeah, sharing a fucking bedroom. Man can't take a bash in peace.'

Mabel gets up from the kitchen table, walks across the narrow hall to her bedroom and closes the door. Her fingers search inside the bedside drawer for her rosary beads. She feels the cool of the silver cross and the smoothness of the marble beads. Her reward for finishing high school and one of the few links – along with her Bible – to her childhood in Jamaica.

Mabel chants the Hail Mary – gently rocking forwards and backwards while sat on her bed. Visions of Jamaica flood to her. Her father working as a mechanic for the rich people. Her going to Ocho Rios to be by the lapping waves of the sea. She would have picnics in the lush tropical countryside of Lower Trelawney. Of course there was poverty, and slums. Most people too poor to buy a round of ginger beer. Yet life was good, better than this. With the sun on your face, among your people, you feel good. Why she left her daddy for England? Her husband thought he could do well here. The status of being in England with the Queen and the police with funny shaped hats. No-one ever predicted dem police with their batons beating her children. Dem riots in Brixton. Her daughter and son listening to rap music. She hated it but she also knew in her core that it was their war-cry, the youth dem finding dem voice like rhythm and blues was born through the pains of slavery. Her grandsons think she doesn't know. She knows. Mabel's no fool.

But this world has meanings on a bigger scale. First a baby need a guardian: parents best, then blood kin, but so long as dey love dem children, dat di base. From that love comes respect for others. Since secondary school, her grandsons change. They lost the fear of authority. They are braver than she or her husband could ever dare to be. But somehow that bravery isn't powerful. They powerless, and she knows it.

For power, you need love: love for thy self; love for thy neighbour, no matter our differences. Jesus preached love. Right now, there's no love in Dwayne. Him cold, harsh like The Devil. Mabel wipes her eyes, trying to push those thoughts and fears away, if Dwayne was repeatedly raped and molested by the sinners her daughter allowed in, high on substance, trying to forget her own hurts. Mabel tries to think back, send her thoughts back to the coastline of Jamaica, when a young man asked a young woman's daddy if he was allowed to talk with her. When holding hands was enough. Cracking coconuts on the beach. Watching the sunset. That soothing warm from the last rays of the day on her shoulders. She kneels down and clasps her hands together and prays for Dwayne.

Jerome looks at his brother, 'Tell me why I don't punch you in your face?'

'Because you know I'm talking Truth. Datz why.'

The boys sit in silence.

'Whatever happens,' Jerome says, 'you're gonna be a dad. So if you're so angry with your life, what you gonna do to change things?'

Dwayne looks at Jerome, 'What am I gonna do? I'll tell you what I'm gonna do. From now until Carnival, I'm gonna be out on road shotting weed, coke, anything my man gives me. I'm gonna save it all. Then I'm gonna buy a whip and drive the fuck away from all of this.'

Dwayne slams his fist on the table, spilling some drink from his glass. 'And take my baby with me.'

'So that's it? That what you're offering Hayley and your baby, yeah? Daddy's a drug dealer with a car. Don't you think she deserves more?'

'Hayley what? D'you think I love her or some shit? Hayley's just one of many on the grind, bruv. She ain't nuttin to me. She ain't coming with me. It's me and my yute. Fuck Hayley.'

Jerome stares at his brother, disgusted. 'She took beatings for you,' Jerome says. 'Bare beatings from her whole family, for you, and won't have an abortion, and dis is how you repay her?' Jerome puts his head in his hands.

Dwayne often took beats to save Jerome's skin and more. He knows what it's like to take abuse to protect others from pain. He quickly pushes those memories away. 'She okay?' Dwayne asks, softer now.

Jerome looks up. 'No bruv, she ain't okay. Face like she's been hit by a truck. And my girl still defends you.'

Jerome stands up. Kicking back his chair, he walks out the kitchen. He stops at Mabel's bedroom opposite, he gently taps the door. 'You okay, Gran?'

Mabel comes to open the door. Jerome would never go in without permission, 'I'm praying,' she says.

'Yeah. We need it.'

Jerome kisses his grandmother's cheek and whispers apologies in her ear. He turns back to the kitchen, 'If you wanna see your grind, she's with Issy... my girlfriend Isobel, yeah. My queen.'

Dwayne kisses his teeth.

Jerome opens the front door which faces Issy's block. Police still parked outside.

Jerome sits on the grassy bank of Telegraph Hill's upper park. He tries to work out how all the shit in his life can get resolved. Dwayne's set on being a gangsta. Hayley will always be connected to him now she's having his brother's kid. That means Jerome's mixed-race nephew's always gonna be connected to Hayley's racist family. Issy wants out. She doesn't want to study in London and stay home. If Issy goes to a faraway uni, Jerome can't see how he can follow. He can't leave his gran. He can't afford to take Gran with him. Or maybe he can? Maybe Jerome can make enough money to get them all out of London. Issy's right, there's something about the city that drags people like them down. Imagining himself living by the sea, somewhere calm, like Brighton, brings a smile to his face and he forgets for a while, the chaos back home.

CHAPTER 12
AUGUST 8TH 2011 – THE LONDON RIOTS

Three months later and Jerome is in the same spot, no closer to his plans, sitting on the grassy bank reading *The Sun* newspaper. The past few days London has been nutz. Police shot dead a bredder in Tottenham. Now people rioting all over, mashing up the place. Jerome turns the page: pictures of broken shop fronts and people stealing anything they can get their hands on. So it's not just his family or his friends. It's happening all over the country. People are sick of police killing black people. And tell me why Duggan's a road man? Because he's black? Nah. Because he's poor? Nah. Too many of us poor meanwhile the rich man cheats tax and politicians cheat expenses; Jerome thinks about the MPs who used their allowance to buy a second home and that white MP who bought a moat for his ducks. Meanwhile police on Jerome's back, stopping and searching him for one bag of weed, when bankers crash the economy and getting bailed out billions. Jerome knows, he ain't dumb.

Jerome scrunches up the newspaper and chucks it in the bushes. This thinking don't help. Being negative keeps him down. He knows that, too. Got to be business minded. Have a plan.

He rolls a joint, thinking about how to raise enough to pay for Issy to go university and get a deposit on a home. He takes out his notebook and pencil and sketches out a few sums:

50 CDs @ £5 each per month = £3k = one year's uni fees

50 bags of weed x 12 @ £10 = £6k a year

Year 2 the same = £9k = 3 x £3k uni fees, plus extra for living costs, etc.

In September, depending on their GCSE grades, he'll start college and Issy will start her A-Levels. In two years, Jerome would have his music qualifications and can find a proper job near Issy's uni. By the time she finishes, Jerome will have saved enough to put a deposit down on a flat. Between the music and the weed, he can save enough to pay her fees and rent, maybe start with a bedsit and work their way up to the house with a garden Issy dreams of.

Lots of ifs in his future, still, he thinks pulling out his lighter. He looks around before lighting the joint. The trees are green and everything in the park looks healthy. Feeling the breeze against his cheeks, he gets a rush of excitement about this 'get-away' plan. If he got a job producing music and Issy got a job with her degree, they can get a mortgage with their joint income. Everything legit. They could get a three-bedroom house with a garden and Carol and his grandmother can live with them. Then upgrade to a five-bed when they have kids.

Jerome knocks his fists together. 'That's what I'm gonna do.'

He lies back and plucks a daisy. Smiling to himself, he closes his eyes, daydreaming the near future. He'll continue making music, do some solo, sell his tracks, go raves and DJ sets, do a bit of pirate… He won't sell cocaine or crack, nothing like that. Just weed and music. Jah Rastafari. The grass feels soft and the breeze caresses his face when he's jolted awake by frenzied beeping from his phone:

Cum now bruv - Dwayne

Manz raiding Currys - Anton

Riots in NX - Dwayne

Ery1 taking bare – Anton

Get me hair stretners – Hayley

Staff gone – Andre

And a fone – Hayley

Cum urself, bare girls on it – Andre

Jay, wer u @ - Dwayne

Nutz blood – Anton

Brockley Manz on it – Andre

Barry, wer u @ - Dwayne

A sinking feeling hits him as he pictures what his boys are getting up to at the bottom of the hill.

Issy calls. 'Babe?'

'Babe, you safe?' Jerome asks.

'Yeah, you? Hayley just text. Everyone's teefing down Currys.'

Jerome sighs.

'You there?' Issy asks.

'In the park.'

'Who with?'

'No-one.'

'Don't go down there, Jay.'

'I ain't.'

'It's all over the news, saying CCTV will be watched, everyone caught is going prison. Guilty. No joke. Getting extra judges in.'

Jerome exhales, his phone vibrating group text messages throughout the call.

'People fighting. Hayley's family down there she said. I feel sick, Jay. What's happening?'

'Where are you?'

'At home. Mum's worried in case people start raiding the Co-op. Come here.'

Currys is unrecognisable. People are piling in, grabbing everything that isn't locked up, smashing open what is. They're looting the store cupboards, running out with whatever they can carry in their arms. Filling car boots and going back for more. There's so many people inside, with more cars pulling in, to pick up bounty that can't be carried: computers, vacuums, printers. Kids running out with cameras, headphones; one boy juggling a sound system. People are euphoric, laughing, shouting, chanting. Onlookers panicked as fighting erupts over who gets what. Pushing and snatching like toddlers over toys. A black woman with her hair in tied rags and black leggins starts screaming, 'Dutty teefs! Dutty teefs!!' at two men carrying a 30 inch flat screen television into a van.

Andre stuffs two USB video cameras in his rucksack wishing it was bigger: teacher's voice in his head telling him there's no space for books or learning in that tiny one he uses.

Anton is happy pushing things over and generally ransacking. He feels free, like this is his five minutes of fame to show the world he doesn't give a fuck what anyone thinks.

Dwayne calls a girl he knows has a car, trying to convince her to come load up her boot.

'Dutty teefs, this ain't no protest,' the same woman shouts at them from outside. She looks at Anton, 'You think you're bad man; you a teef?'

Anton, in his frenzy, runs up to her and claps her around the head. She drops to the floor to protect herself, and he kicks her then others jump in. Some men in Ghanaian dress pull Anton away and point to the CCTV camera outside. Anton puts his middle finger up at it then runs off, trying to keep all the boxed mobiles he's nicked from falling out his zipped up hoodie.

The girl from Dwayne's request arrives. They fill the trunk and back seats with two televisions, a toaster and some random music equipment.

Feds on it – Jerome's message to the group, relieved Issy hasn't got a BlackBerry like everyone else.

Dwayne is covering his face with a plastic shopping bag. Andre uses his t-shirt to cover his face, but his chest tattoos give him away. More and more people arrive to take what they want.

Peckham riots on news – Jerome messages again.

Dwayne and Andre don't want it to end. The vibe is electric. It's like the power cables have come down and the pavement is a live wire. Dwayne runs to the petrol station opposite, empties the water bucket used for cleaning windscreens and fills it up. He runs into the car park and pours the petrol all over a sports car then sparks up his lighter and throws a lit Currys leaflet onto the roof. The car explodes into flames. It's so hot, it heats the plastic on Dwayne's face and he quickly backs off.

Police sirens come from all directions. His ride yells at him: 'Get the fuck in my car!' One of the rare incidents he lets a female shout at him but he rushes to the open door, Andre already in. They drive away with a car full of stolen goods just before meat wagons come and block the entrance and exit to the car park.

As Jerome arrives at Issy's block, he sees several kids scurrying up Jerningham Road carrying loot. He's not gonna lie, there's a part of him that feels sad to miss out on the madness. He's not bothered about big companies losing stock. But he also knows the part of him who wants to steal stuff is a part of him that needs to be kept in check. He doesn't like himself getting that taste for greed, or feeling jealous not to be involved in the hype. He has to remind himself: prison is real, especially for black yutes. Steve told his youth session last night that police officers are 28 times more likely to use stop and search on black people rather than white people.

Jerome hopes Dwayne ain't up to anything too stupid. He knows his grandmother won't have anything stolen in the flat. He also knows Dwayne lies and is getting out of hand with his rudeness.

Issy opens the front door and pulls him in to see the news. The car firebombed in the car park, the rioters stealing from Currys...

Jerome, shaking his head, looks down at his buzzing phone to see footage of Anton slapping a woman. Andre filmed it.

'Let me see?' Issy asks.

Reluctant, Jerome gives over his phone.

'Jay, I am not being funny,' Issy shouts, scrolling through the messages, 'but that's it for me. I'm not Graff. It's over, I'm done.'

'You see this,' she points to Carol's TV, 'This is lowest of the low. Ruining businesses, scaring normal people. Mum's shitting it at work.'

'They should close.'

'Yeah but how long? What's it now, like three days?'

Issy watches as the news show scenes across London of people smashing windows, throwing bricks, taking what they want. Small businesses robbed, small corner shops smashed in. People in tears. Neighbours injured. Police backing away overwhelmed.

'WHAT'S WRONG WITH YOU ALL!?' Issy shouts at the television. 'My country looks like the third world,' she mutters, watching a building in Croydon blazing. Police cars firebombed. Teenagers with balaclavas chucking cans at police on horses. 'Anyone would think it's a warzone. I feel sick knowing MY friends are out there doing this to their own country.'

'People are angry,' Jerome offers.

'So this is how to deal with anger, yeah?'

'I'm not saying it's right,' Jerome replies, 'but it's a way to protest against shit.'

'Dwayne and Andre and Anton are protesting right now, yeah? Is that what you're telling me?'

'In their own way, yeah.'

'Against what? That toasters are too expensive?'

'Against police just shooting up people! Against the fact that population-wise bredders have a better chance going prison than uni.'

'That's bullshit, Jerome, and you know it,' Issy shouts back. 'It's not rocket science. You just have to sit and read.'

'Read what, though? Henry the Eighth? Empire? Do you know how warped that is to a man like me?' Jerome breathes slowly to keep his anger in check. 'Babe, going round the world stealing shit and killing people and slaving them up then inviting them over on British passports with one foot on their heads, do you even get what I'm saying? Not a day goes by when I don't think, am I getting put in a cell today? Even when I'm weed-free and helping old ladies cross the street, I'm thinking, who watching is gonna try say I'm on a job.'

'I don't get how that changes anything.'

And in that moment, in that very moment, something shifts. Jerome sees Issy differently. Someone opposite to him. Complicit.

'What I mean,' Issy corrects herself, 'What I'm saying, is why does that mean black people have to loot shops and rob and sell weed in the first place.'

'It's the box we've been shoved in.'

'That's a copout. Your two legs walk to studio, walk to pirate radio, walk to that crackhead flat in Brockley to carve up buds Anton's dad gets you to sell. So why can't you use those two feet to walk to the library? Or sit here with me and study?'

'It's summer holidays...' Jerome trails off. He looks away, unsettled. It's like Issy doesn't get him at all, doesn't see the black struggle. He's not using slavery or empire as an excuse. It's deeper than that. It's a collective grief, a historical wound remaining over them, continually reopened by tales of black aggression, black criminality, black benefit cheats, black immigrants taking jobs, black boys not willing to work, study, obey the system, raping up girls…

'Your brother ain't gonna change if you excuse his actions,' Issy says in the silence.

'It's not an excuse!' Jerome snaps. 'It's an explanation.'

Issy stops. She's not in the mood for a fight. She'd hoped Jerome was safe and he is. She wanted him with her and he's here. She switches the channel, scenes of fire, and switches again, American comedy *Friends*, but neither of them are in the mood.

Jerome looks at the screen: six white friends living in New York and not a black actor in sight, coming from a land where the real natives were slain and the rest pushed onto reserves. Foundations of displacement and conquest and yet somehow his people are the monsters? Yes, he's reading the books George gave him. Books that ain't in his school library.

He gets to his feet. Issy looks up.

'Don't go,' she says.

'I feel like… My mind…' Jerome stops, sick of explaining. It's not just black people looting, bare people are down there. The media keep saying black. Always black people blamed. Hayley's whole family are down there.

'I'm sorry,' Issy says. 'I didn't mean it to sound harsh.'

'It's true. People, any colour, shouldn't be teefing up the place.'

'Stay.'

'I can't.' He feels the rift widen, stepping back, keeping his distance. 'I need to check Gran. She's probably seen this.'

'I'll come.'

'Issy, man!' Jerome takes a deep breath. 'Wait here for your mum.'

Issy nods. She looks sad. He feels bad but he needs to be alone.

She walks Jerome to the door and watches him cross the street. First time he's left without kissing her goodbye.

Carol finishes her shift just after ten o'clock. She walks down the road and into the local graveyard. Two people meet her and hand over two shopping bags. She gives them twenty pounds.

On the bus home, Carol is paranoid about being stopped. But she is a middle-aged mum in Coop uniform. Police in riot gear are taping up the area around the petrol station by New Cross Gate train station. Her heart is thumping as she makes eye contact with an officer. He looks down at her shaking hands carrying the plastic bags cutting in to her fingers, then nods his head. Carol nods back. 'Get home safe,' he says.

Carol quietly opens the front door. With any luck, Issy is out or watching telly and not interested in seeing her. She opens the cupboard under the kitchen sink and stashes the vodka and gin bottles behind the bleach and pack of 20 sponges. Then tiptoes upstairs to change out of her shop clothes.

Carol peers in the bathroom mirror. Dark circles under her eyes. White as a ghost. What has she done? She didn't loot. Those bottles could have come from anywhere. A mate's leftover wedding stock, the guy said. She knows that was a lie. The Indian family next to the Coop had their off licence ransacked. Still, could be wedding stock.

Issy knocks on the door.

'Jesus!' Carol cries.

'Mum?'

Carol starts washing her hands.

'You okay?' she asks from outside the bathroom door.

'Yes, love.'

'Did anyone loot your shop?'

'No love, they didn't.'

The next six days, the city blazed. Issy watches as her friends become strangers to her. She hates every one of them. The news showing broken glass after broken glass. Shopkeepers crying their eyes out. Jobs lost. People being attacked by mobs gone mad in the frenzy of supposedly taking their power back. Five people dead. Hundreds of citizens trashing up their own streets.

Issy doesn't hear a peep from Hayley, who goes out with Teena and Ronnie to see what she can steal. Every. Single. Day. Then comes this moment, it feels so big but it happens just sitting on her sofa. It's like someone has picked her up and put her back but on a different path. A switch in her mind. She's doesn't know what to do to describe what's going on. But she feels like she had a life before the riots and now a new life since the riots.

Across the street, Jerome also feels a division; he's not with Issy on this. The fact she won't accept these riots ain't just about smashing stuff up, and that's all people on the news and in the Houses of Parliament care about, and it's pissing him off. He feels like no one has his back, will speak up for him. And now Issy is going on like she's never speaking to Andre or Anton, his two best friends, ever again. How does that work? Six days of ruckus but what about whole lives stuck in cramped damp flats; stuck unemployed; stuck suffering racism? Every. Single. Day. How you gonna help people when most jobs don't pay better than housing benefit? He feels sick at how people care more about Primark being busted than an unarmed black man getting killed.

CHAPTER 13
TWO WEEKS LATER

Issy looks up at the Black History Month mural behind the teacher who ticks her off the list. Hand trembling, Issy signs her name next to the words, Received 25 AUG 2011 at 11:32AM. There is a steady flow of parents and students in and out the assembly hall, screams going off in all directions. Issy didn't want to bring her mum and Carol looked so disappointed it made Issy feel sad the entire bus ride to school.

Her palms are clammy and she feels sick. She doesn't want to open the envelope here, not in front of all the teachers, smiling at her with eager anticipation. The Head Teacher really got behind her "tremendous turnaround" as her interview for the school newsletter read: "Two years ago I didn't know what a university did, now I want the chance to go to Oxford."

'Happy results day!' exclaims her tutor. Issy smiles back but inside, she is disappointed in Jerome. Why would anyone so bright throw away their education? At least sit the exams. He's so smart; such a waste. Out of Graff, only Barry did all his GCSEs.

She looks around for a friendly face, regretting telling Carol not to come. Some parents smile Issy's way, 'We saw you in the school newsletter,' one lets her know. Funny, most families here are from the children she and Hayley used to laugh at and look down on. It's true what her tutor always says: Those geeks and neeks will be your bosses one day.

'You gonna open it, then?' her tutor asks.

Issy presses the brown envelope to her chest. She wants to know in private. Why should anyone take this from her? This is something she did.

Worked hard for. She wrote the answers. Sitting in her bedroom for ten months, resisting temptations to give it all up and cotch in the sunshine, smoking weed with Jerome, giggling about nonsense. Angry, again. She regrets wasting so much time with Graff. She could have done her Duke of Edinburgh Award like Tameika. Finding it hard to breathe, Issy brushes past all the smiling faces holding their plastic cups filled with orange juice and rushes out the assembly hall.

Issy pokes her head inside Mrs Salmon's English classroom; it's empty. She sits on the table where she usually sits, facing the sunlight flooding in from the windows - fading part of the Macbeth display on the adjacent wall. Pearls of sweat gather on her brow. The heat intensifies Issy's clammy hands as she tears the envelope open.

A fear grips her. She slams down the envelope. What if she failed? What if there isn't a single A, B or C grade? What happens then? She paces the classroom. She can handle boys who threaten her with knives or rape, but this?

She knows she's feeding the monster. She leans back on the wall and cools her back. The only thing holding us back is ourselves, is what Mrs Salmon says. Issy sits at her desk and takes the results out the envelope:

English Language	C
English Literature	B
History	C
Religious Studies	C
Science	DD
Mathematics	D
French	D
Spanish	D
Music	U

Five D grades. Five! Three C grades. The B sticks out like a sore thumb, special guest at a party of fails. Issy slides off the chair and slumps to the floor. The base of her spine hits the concrete. Fucked. Everything's fucked. Hours spent revising. For what? Tears fall as she calls herself dumb, thick, fake, a wannabe wanting more than who she is.

She sobs violently into her knees. The thought of going back downstairs to her classmates, their parents, and all the teachers' expectations. She cringes at herself in the school newsletter sat on Mrs Salmon's desk: "I'd love to buy me and Mum a big house with a garden." The Head Teacher wants to speak to her.

Every time Issy stops crying, she starts again. The thought of telling her mum, showing Emily and Jerome. Mabel's baked a cake. Karen wants to celebrate with a Chinese...

Though Emily has walked this so many times the past year, the corridors seem so far bigger, so hostile and intimidating. She catches her reflection in the large black-framed windows, filled with anxiety, she looks out to the neat lawns the same moment the sun beams from behind a moving cloud.

Usually filled with several hundred schoolgirls, all that can be heard are the echoes of Mr Sutton's court shoes clacking. Wearing one of his finest suits, her father walks on, oblivious to his daughter's nerves. Janie Sutton has her arm inside her husband's, cheerful in a pale blue chiffon dress that falls just under the knee, cut perfectly in at the waist.

The thick glass doors lead to the school's central courtyard. The Suttons head to the chapel to hear the service. Emily's nerves ease seeing friends from her class looking equally fraught. She puts on her choir gown in the changing rooms, relieved to have some personal space away from her parents.

After mass, Principal Evans gives a speech then teachers usher everyone to the Great Hall where parents are met with a champagne reception. Emily slips off as her parents mingle, skipping over to friends. The riots mentioned briefly as the girls exchange parts of the exams they liked, bits they didn't understand, which grades they think they've got...

Tutors herd parents and students to various tables to receive their results. Around the hall, the oak dining tables are decorated with thick white table cloths and large bouquets of flowers. Each white envelope has the red waxed stamp used on Issy's rejection letter. Behind each table are free-standing displays of work and achievements throughout the year, plus a preview of what to expect at sixth form level. There were several expeditions: Costa Rica with a focus on preserving wildlife and biodiversity; walks and camping in Scotland; coasteering in Wales; marine watching in Belize; exchanges in France and Germany and trips to see shows on Broadway.

Mr Sutton expresses surprise at seeing girls in service uniforms. Janie admires aloud the costume drama and dance performance photographs, particularly Swan Lake.

'Mr and Mrs Sutton!' comes a call from across the room. Catching sight of Emily with her parents, Mr Elliott rushes towards them.

Mr Sutton looks blankly at his wife.

'Mr Elliott,' Janie whispers, 'Emily's art tutor.'

'Mr Elliott,' Mr Sutton says as he arrives.

'So wonderful to finally meet you!' Mr Elliott shakes Mr Sutton's hand with a sweaty loose grip, 'And how are you, Jane? Have you collected your daughter's examination results, yet?' he asks, bubbling with excitement.

'Here in my pocket,' Mr Sutton says curtly.

'We shall open them at home,' Janie says, trying to add some sweetness to the conversation.

'Well, may I make one tiny revelation?' Mr Elliott says. He stands lopsided, tall and bony, eyes frightfully wide. His stubble offends Mr Sutton, as well as his scruffy shoes and dog-eared laces.

As Mr Elliott talks about his finest pupil, Mr Sutton continues to examine the rest of the art teacher's pathetic excuse for smart dress: baggy camel-coloured corduroy trousers and a faded shirt, also far too big, and clearly not been ironed.

'Darling?' Janie Sutton squeezes her husband's arm, breaking his train of thought.

'Would we like to see Emily's AS-Level Art?'

'The school left the works up,' Mr Elliott says, swaying back and forth from the balls of his feet to his toes, 'for those parents who missed exhibition night.'

'No, it's fine, sir, really,' Emily swallows her nerves to pipe up, 'I doubt my parents have time to walk to the art block.'

'Of course we do,' says Janie.

'This man's a buffoon,' Mr Sutton whispers in his wife's ear, as he reluctantly follows Mr Elliott's swallow-like sway.

Janie shoots her husband a look before following Mr Elliott who is already walking off with Emily.

'I wasn't made aware of the exhibition night,' Janie remarks as the Suttons enter the Art Department.

'That's odd.' Several confused lines appear across the thin skin above Mr Elliott's sweaty brow. 'Actually, I did wonder where you were since Emily's work has been highly commended.'

Mr Sutton stops to admire a series of paintings of the sea, 'I know this chap's father.'

'Adam Dubanowski. Hugely gifted artist.'

'But this is a girl's school,' Mr Sutton remarks.

'Yes, but our Sixth Form is twinned.'

Mr Sutton looks at the two oil paintings, 'I'm impressed.'

'Adam is a big fan of Turner.'

'Yes, one can see that clearly,' Mr Sutton replies, watching Mr Elliott use his shirt sleeve to mop his forehead.

'See,' Emily turns to her father, 'you do like art.'

'Who couldn't love a fresh take on the classics?' Mr Elliott dramatically waves his arms.

Janie Sutton smiles, finding Mr Elliott quite the entertainment. Emily finishing secondary school and about to start A-Levels is a real milestone. Soon she'll be at university and Janie will have fewer worries and more time, quality time, with her husband. Perhaps some travel abroad.

'Where are your paintings, Emily?' Janie asks.

Emily's face drops.

'Here!' Mr Elliott almost bows at the series of collages and prints, 'Some of the finest displays of mixed media this school has seen.'

Emily's parents stand back, shocked, as they behold their daughter's works. The main piece shows a chicken and chips takeaway box with various cut-out images bursting from inside.

'What I love most is the word play. Emily has taken *The Estate* and juxtaposed the imagery of council estates against English manor houses, as you see here with the graffiti and how Emily has used it to write home sweet home over this remarkable building.'

'That's Grandfather's house!' Mr Sutton exclaims.

'Yes,' Mr Elliott continues excitedly, 'Real images to Emily's life that now have a dialogue preserved in art. Our term topic was Confessional Art. I shouldn't be biased of course, but I have to say, I love it. Absolutely love all of it! So raw and honest and brave!'

Emily's cheeks burn. Her parents say nothing. Mr Sutton remains tight lipped as he stares at the images of Jerome and Dwayne smoking weed in string vests and low hanging jeans and tracksuit bottoms showing most of their underwear collaged over the lawns of his own childhood home which his son was left in his father's will. Images of teenage boys with hoods up spraying graffiti over Charles Sparling's bathroom tiles. Items within their own home: clocks, chairs, their sofa on Pepys Road. Rays of sunshine burst from the dark edges of the chicken and chips box, the chip paper inside the box has real headlines of gang violence, benefit cuts, abuse of politician expenses. Across a building in what looks like Canary Wharf are stop and search figures of black and minority teens cleverly disguised as FTSE 100 forecasting. Another image shows chips and tomato sauce splashed over their own antique French dining table.

'What do you think?' Mr Elliott asks, becoming slightly less ebullient as his audience remain silent. 'There's lots to take in,' Mr Elliott mumbles, unconvincingly.

'Yes, very interesting indeed,' Janie Sutton pipes up, noting her daughter's increasing discomfort, and her husband's face reddening.

'Is this art?' Mr Sutton asks.

Mr Elliott is taken by surprise, 'I beg your pardon?'

'Isn't this... child's play? A collage... of nonsense.'

'Well, erm...' Mr Elliott clears his throat. He shoots a look at Emily whose expression speaks volumes. He thought she was being shy or humble when in fact, she was terrified. 'It's modern, contemporary art.'

Mr Sutton's bewilderment turns to anger, 'Is this what I pay for?' he faces Emily, tearing open the envelope.

Janie Sutton winces.

'Well, this perhaps may not look like a complex piece but I can assure you,' Mr Elliott splutters, watching Mr Sutton taking out Emily's examination results, 'Your daughter has deeply researched her subject matter. This is a multifarious story that is both current and timeless. Of poverty, life chances, luck. The accompanying essay is truly remarkable.' Mr Elliott's crumpled blue shirt dampens at the armpits. 'You'll see the examiner has praised her considerably–'

'Thank you, I've heard enough.' Mr Sutton glares at his daughter, 'Emily, you failed Mathematics and your sciences.'

Emily bows her head.

'Not here, darling,' Janie whispers with a smile, touching his arm. 'Thank you for your time, Mr Elliott.'

'Yes, yes, of course,' Mr Elliott makes his excuses and exits but Mr Sutton stands in the exhibition hall like a stubborn bull in the road.

'Let's go to the pub, as planned,' Janie says, singing voice on.

'I won't let this lie, Jane,' Mr Sutton glares at his wife. 'The school assured me Emily is capable of beginning A-Level Art without this affecting other grades. Complete nonsense.' He shakes Emily's GCSE results, 'Look at this!'

'Darling, this is neither the time, nor place.' Janie begins to walk back towards the main hall.

'This is certainly the time, and I find this the appropriate place, don't you?'

Janie Sutton walks back to her husband, 'With all due respect,' she sternly whispers, 'I will not be known as the hot-headed awkward parents. By all means, put your concerns to the Principal, ask for a rebate, whatever, but please...' Janie takes a breath, realising she is being rather aggressive and unladylike, 'write a letter or book an appointment.'

Janie points her finger towards the double doors that lead back to the champagne reception and with desperation in her voice, continues, 'Out there is not the place. Today is about parents celebrating the achievements of their children.'

'Wipe those tears and lift your chin,' Janie tells Emily, 'I won't give Angela Pompton or anyone more ammunition against me.'

'You are absolutely right, darling,' Mr Sutton says, getting a hold of himself. 'Emily?'

Emily, whose nerves meant she hasn't eaten all day, collapses to the floor. Janie Sutton shrieks as her husband rushes to attend to his daughter.

Issy is still sat inside her English classroom, jumps up when she hears a key turning in the lock. The movement causes Mrs Salmon to unlock the classroom door and enter.

'What are you doing here?' Mrs Salmon asks. The brightness of summer bounces from her favourite teacher's white blouse. 'Everything okay?'

'I've blown it,' Issy says, slumping back on the floor.

'Blown what?'

Mrs Salmon rests her colourful handbag on the table and joins Issy on the dirty school floor. Her nails are clean; not one bitten, blooded cuticle among them.

'Everything. My whole life. Fucked it.'

Mrs Salmon looks at the open envelope by Issy's side, 'Your results?'

Issy nods, a tear slips from her eye. 'Sorry, Miss, for swearing.'

'May I?'

Issy nods as the teacher leans over and pinches the sheets from the floor.

'Told everyone I wanted to go Oxford, now I can't. I wanted to go to this private college on a scholarship thing but they said no. Then my friend said sometimes if you get good grades, you can go to ones last minute, once you post them your GCSEs...' Issy stops. 'I thought I got rejected because my mum wrote the worst application ever, but actually I'm too thick to get in.'

'Issy, you're not too thick and it's not too late. There's lots of ways you can get to Oxford University if that's what you want.'

'Really?' Issy looks up at her teacher, 'Like how?'

'You can still do AS Levels with these grades. Haven't you been told about your post-16 options? We posted all this home.'

'Mum's so dumb, probably put it straight in the bin.'

'What do you want to do at Oxford?'

'Don't know.'

Mrs Salmon looks at Issy, 'Well, why do you want to go there then?'

'To get away, get a good job, get us off the estate. It's getting worse, Miss. Two boys from Brockley gang which is like our ally gang got stabbed. I'm getting threatened, and my boyfriend's brother is a prick and got Jerome involved in his stupid gang shit, selling tracks with bare fighting lyrics and last week Jerome got beaten up and now he's gonna get a scar down his face, for life. Hayley got her head kicked in by her mum and dad, like proper kicked in and is now in care. The riots...The whole summer was just one big madness. I cant even...'

'Hayley Briton from this school?'

'Yeah, Miss. She's pregnant by my boyfriend's older brother. Her family's terrible. Proper racist between you and me.'

'The same brother starting fights with everyone.'

'Yeah, Dwayne, getting little kids to sell weed. She was supposed to come with me today but she doesn't even care what she gets, didn't finish them properly anyway. She doesn't want a job, so she don't even care about her grades. All she cares about is getting a flat so Dwayne, who don't even love her, can move in. He's using her now for a place to store drugs. Don't tell anyone I told you though–'

Mrs Salmon shakes her head, 'Don't want my head kicked in, do I?' She clears her throat. 'Joking.'

'I just want a different life, Miss. I met this girl last year and she's posh and showed me photos of Oxford but I've fucked it with my grades. Should just get a job in Co-op like my mum.'

Mrs Salmon looks across the room, at the afternoon sunlight.

'You probably don't want to hear this right now,' Mrs Salmon says, 'but there are loads of people earning mega bucks who have never stepped foot inside an Oxford college.'

'Did you go uni, Miss?'

'I went to a uni called Manchester Met, near where I'm from in Stockport. Then I did a teaching qualification at Goldsmiths. I lived in a place near your flat on Telegraph Hill for about two years.' She takes her mobile from her back pocket.

'That's Hayley's block,' Issy says, looking at Mrs Salmon's photos on her phone. 'No way! How comes I never saw ya?'

'Was years ago.'

'I bet you hated it. It's a dump, ain't it, Miss?'

'No way. Neighbours were lovely and I could see the whole of London from my bedroom; shared with an eccentric French artist called Pierre. He'd play Bach and Chopin on his electric piano with headphones throughout the night.'

'Didn't that piss you off? Living with people you don't know? Mum says it will.'

'That's the fun of university, for me anyway. Reminded me of when I had a hamster. The clacks of Pierre's piano keys sounded like Hamish the hamster's feet clocking miles on his wheel.' Mrs Salmon sighs with the rush of nostalgia. 'We didn't move far. My husband and I bought a place in Deptford.'

'You bought a house there, Miss? It's full of druggies. Don't mean to be rude, though.'

'Deptford? It's brilliant. The whole area is steeped in history. My husband is from one of the oldest living black families in London. He has heritage right back to the slave trade. We live on a road called Friendly Street – nice sounding, isn't it?' Mrs Salmon rubs a sapphire stone silver ring with her thumb. 'This is my wedding ring.'

'Ain't you supposed to get a diamond when you get engaged? Be honest,' Issy says with a cheeky smile. 'Was he being cheap, Miss?'

Mrs Salmon laughs.

'Jacob proposed to me while we were standing by a stall selling silver at Greenwich Market. I said yes and as we hugged the light from this ring shot right into my eye. It felt like a bolt of magic. It wasn't expensive and as it turns out, it's perfect.'

Mrs Salmon looks at her watch, 'So, you starting to feel better?'

'I feel shit, if I'm being honest. Don't really know what to do next. Like, I proper studied, Miss. Every night, practically. And I only got Cs and Ds. Doesn't that say something?'

'Do you want some friendly advice? I mean, I know I haven't worked here long.'

'Miss, you're one of the safest teachers here. Everyone rates you, and that's not easy, trust me.'

Issy's comment throws her. She swallows her emotion and continues, 'Why not stay here, at the school's sixth form. Looking at your grades, you could take English, History, Religious Studies and maybe something like Sociology.'

'Sociology?

'The study of society. Looks at things like poverty, gender inequality, racial tensions. Sociology tries to work out the answers.'

Issy sits up, the base of her spine feeling sore sitting too long on concrete.

'It's a new subject and I'll be teaching it. You only get to do it at AS and A-Level, and at university.'

Issy's smile disappears, 'Can't believe I didn't get one single A.'

'I never got a single A grade,' Mrs Salmon reassures. 'I only got Bs and Cs at GCSE but look at me now? I'm a teacher. I've got A-Levels, a degree, and a teaching degree.'

'Has your house got a garden?'

'My house has got a garden,' she laughs. 'Not a big one, mind...'

'You know Issy, there is always more than one way to get to the beach and there's always more than one beach you can choose to get to, know what I mean?'

'Sort of.'

'Well, before I told you this was my engagement ring, would you say it looks like an engagement ring?'

'Not really, no offence though.'

'None taken. But now I told you the story behind the ring if I asked you what this ring means to me, how would you answer?'

'It means a lot because it's from your engagement.'

'Would you say my ring is not as nice as someone else's because it's not a gold ring with a massive white diamond?'

'No, Miss, honestly, I wouldn't.'

'Precisely. So imagine Oxford University is the gold diamond ring. If you were looking for a ring and the shop only had one, you would probably want it because that is your only option, right? But this shop has lots rings. Do you like gold?'

'Prefer silver. Or platinum.'

'So already Oxford isn't quite what you're after. You want something else, something different.'

'Miss, I think I get what you're saying. Like if all As at GCSE was money then I would have enough to buy Oxford as a diamond ring, but because I only have mostly Cs and Ds which is like fivers and tenners, I can only afford a silver ring like yours?'

Mrs Salmon weighs it up, 'Yes, kind of, though I think you're underselling yourself a bit. Oxford may be a diamond, but what's a diamond that nobody wants or can afford? You, Issy, can reject the diamond, not the other way around. You can choose your university yourself. Don't rely on someone else's ideas on life. That's their family's traditions or decisions. You can look on the internet and see what else is out there. Manchester, Goldsmiths, Brighton, Bath, Lincoln, Nottingham, Greenwich... They're all out there. You decide. It's your life.'

Issy's mind fills with possibility. 'I'm still in the uni game?'

'You are and this time you can decide it all for yourself.'

'Which is probably a good thing,' Issy says, since that uncomfortable feeling she has when she's with Emily's friends does put her off going to Oxford. She cringes, remembering saying in the school newsletter she wanted to go Oxford and deflates.

Noticing the change, Mrs Salmon asks, 'Now what's wrong?'

'What am I gonna tell the Head? About my grades?'

'Well, you have five A to C grades. That's a pass. You passed.'

Mrs Salmon gets to her feet.

Issy looks up at Mrs Salmon holding out her hands.

'Miss, I don't wanna see anyone,' she says, taking both her teacher's hands and pulling herself to her feet.

'Well you can't stay here, my lovely. I've got to lock up.' Mrs Salmon pauses. 'I do know a secret way out but you must promise not to show any kids, especially if you do come back for sixth form. It's where teachers go for a quiet break. Not even the Head knows.'

Mrs Salmon holds out her little finger.

'Promise, Miss.'

They lock little fingers.

'Turn left here.'

They climb down the fire escape steps along the back of the Humanities block. Issy's trainers crunch crisp packets and cigarette ends. She smirks at the empty prosecco bottles and lager cans neatly lined up alongside a wall decorated with graffiti saying **school sucks** and **when the fuck's half term?**

CHAPTER 14
FRESH STARTS

It's September.

Now that Jerome has left secondary school, Dwayne has a few younger boys interested in making him money there. Dwayne's been reading this book his key worker gave him about gangs in Brixton. Instead of putting him on the right track, as intended, Dwayne is impressed by the gang leader's business model. Dwayne immediately sketches out a model to earn thousands by Christmas through building up a team of younger "sendouts". Next step in Dwayne's plan - getting inside more schools.

The best business is term time because parents give their children lunch money. Dwayne sends each boy out with mini bags of weed that cost three pounds each, enough for a couple of blunts. Everything is noted down and if one of the boys is even a penny short, Dwayne takes him round the back of the flats and punches him up. He knows first-hand that fear is what controls people. Nothing else works.

Anton and Andre are still in prison for their part in the riots, so Dwayne is dealing directly with Anton's father who supplies the large quantities of marijuana. Anton's father earns the biggest cut so Dwayne has started pre-rolling the joints, adding less weed and combining the weed with cheap knock-off tobacco. This way, Dwayne can control how much weed he is distributing and make more of a profit. Dwayne makes the first batch strong so that they get proper mash up and come back for more.

Dwayne sees Tameika walking towards their block of flats holding her younger brother's hand. He's turning eleven and starting at Issy's school. With Graff finished there, Dwayne needs younger heads lined up to continue business. As Tameika enters the block, she passes Dwayne on the stairs.

'You alright, T?' Dwayne asks, feeling particularly pleased with himself today.

Tameika looks Dwayne up and down, 'I don't do criminals.'

'Babes,' Dwayne smiles, licking his lips, 'I ain't got no record.'

'In the eyes of the Lord God Jesus Christ, you do. Come, Emmanuel.' Tameika pushes past Dwayne chuckling to himself.

'Wanna come work for me, little man?' Dwayne calls up the stairwell, looking up Tameika's skirt.

Tameika stops, then stomps back down, getting in Dwayne's face, 'If you even tink 'bout corrupting me lickkle pickney, see what a'gwaan!' She points to the sky, 'God's watching.'

Dwayne stares into Tameika's eyes, adorned with thick fake lashes. Her eyebrows are neatly threaded with a thin line of makeup highlighting each arch.

'You sexy when you vex.'

Tameika kisses her teeth.

'Giving man a boner, get me.'

'Getting youngers to do Devil's work.'

Tameika's younger brother watches from the steps above.

'Come check me any time, bruv,' Dwayne calls out to him.

Tameika kisses her teeth again. She stomps up the stairs, grabbing her brother's arm, telling Emmanuel, 'See when dem pickney get arrested: No job. No education. No rights. Done. Yuh feds property. Dem sendouts think it's good money, yeah, some twenty pound here, twenty pound there... den when they older and want a nice flat or a car, no bank won't give no credit with some criminal record, yuh hear?'

'Yeah.'

'Yuh hear me?'

'Yes!' Emmanuel repeats.

'Best stay away or I'm gonna lick you up proper, Mummy and Daddy lick you, Uncle Micah, Aunty Rochelle; whole family beatings, trust.'

Issy took Mrs Salmon's advice and signed up to the school sixth form. It isn't the fresh start she wanted, the same walls, same little children running through corridors, spitting toilet paper at each other through straws from McDonalds. But there are some exciting new changes. She gets to sit in the sixth form common room, where only older kids can go. It's clean and has a kitchen area where she can make cups of tea plus a vending machine in the corner and a shelf with free condoms. She takes out her new notebooks and writes on each: Sociology, English, History, Geography and Religious Studies, plus, after listening to Emily's advice, she's retaking Maths.

Emily is back studying in West London. Her father took the decision to change schools after her C grade in Mathematics though Emily has a sneaking suspicion the South-East London private school was too diverse for Mr Sutton's hidden prejudices. The new timetable makes it impossible for Emily to complete her A2 Level Art, but her parents have assured her if she passes GCSE Maths with grade A* or A Emily will complete her Art A-Level next academic year along with her other A2 Level exams. What her father omitted to tell her is that he has no intention whatsoever of sending Emily to any art college in Paris, or indeed letting her pursue Art at all. She will be reading Classics or English, and she shall be going to Oxford where Rosie can keep an eye on her. Mr Sutton can contribute to Rosie's allowance, which should make his miserly brother-in-law happy.

Mr Sutton is also pleased with himself because Emily will be spending much of the week with her aunt. Janie's sister has the brains of the family, while Janie was apportioned the looks. Although this option is nearly a third more expensive in terms of travel costs and school fees, Mr Sutton feels it money well spent – to have Emily back mixing with the right sort of peers. Henry Sparling will attend this school, along with her former neighbours, George Addy, Hendrike Spark, Sophie Little, and Helena Black.

But Janie Sutton commits twice a week to yoga. Without fail. And by the time she's stretched her body, emptied her mind, then filled it up again with gossip post-class, Emily has enjoyed three hours parent-free which she earmarks now as sacred Issy time, who also has Friday afternoons free from class.

It's another Friday together. Lying on Emily's bed, legs up the wall, Issy is feeling guilty. She didn't tell Emily her real GCSE grades, feeling embarrassed since Emily went to so much trouble to try and get her into the posh girls' school in Sydenham. Unbeknown to Issy, Emily feels equally awful. Choosing to remain quiet about the horrible jokes Angela Pompton and the admin department made of Issy's application, or the real reason she is now in a new school – that her father is a power crazy maniac who hates Issy and Jerome.

In the end, it's Issy feeling so wrapped up in her own inadequacy that her head feels like a pressure cooker about to explode. 'I need to tell you something.' Issy sits up.

'Sure,' Emily replies, smiling reassuringly.

'So, still wanna be friends?' Issy asks nervously after confessing her grades. 'I didn't mean to lie. It was more that you went to all that trouble.'

'Oh Issy,' Emily flings her arms around Issy's neck. 'I would never judge you like that!'

Issy stiffens in Emily's hold. She peers around Emily's room. The furniture is so different to hers and there are so many books everywhere. She has nothing compared to Emily. Issy's eyes rest on a photograph of Emily with her brother at his graduation.

'It's not so bad actually,' Issy continues, pulling away from the hug. 'My teacher told me there's loads of other unis, you know, other than Oxford.'

Emily folds her arms.

'To be honest, I didn't think I'd get in, anyway' Issy sighs. 'Deep down.'

'Me neither,' Emily looks seriously at Issy before breaking into a huge grin. 'I'm definitely, definitely moving to France.'

'Really? What about your parents?'

Emily jumps off the bed and performs a twirl, 'I'm running away there when I'm eighteen. I get some of my trust fund and they won't be able to do a thing about it.'

'Can I come visit?' Issy asks, watching Emily prance around the creaking floorboards.

'Of course,' Emily squeals. 'We can spend the summer picking grapes and drinking wine. You can visit me all the time. It's super cheap on the Eurostar if you book in advance.'

Issy picks at a small hole in her sock, 'Mimi, do you think I'll ever be rich? You know, rich enough to buy a house like this with a garden? Mum says what with house prices going mad, not even nurses and doctors can afford it.'

Emily stops prancing to sit next to her friend. 'I'm sure of it. More than me. Artists are notoriously poor.'

'Unless you marry a rich man. Like Henry.'

'What? Who told you I wanted to marry Henry?'

'Sophie,' Issy's cheeks heat up as she remembers it was a secret.

'What did she tell you?'

'Nothing, just said you two have an on/off crush, that's all.'

'Anything else?'

'No,' Issy fibs, remembering the conversations well enough to understand Henry mucks Emily about and there's even been rumours of an engagement ring.

'Anyway,' Issy says, 'thanks, for not judging me on my grades.'

'That's fine. It's not fair to judge others based on things they cannot control, like the stuck up private school system or the rubbish state one. I really disagree with judging people. I really do. We're all different and come from different places. What matters is how we treat each other in the here and now. When I'm making art, I feel like I'm fed and watered and being my true self, I feel like I know who I am, anyone who tries to stop that, I need to fight off. You too, Issy, anyone. I mean it, even your mum or me. Anyone who tries to stop you being your true self needs to be stopped and if I have to run away, I will. I'll go and they won't stop me.' Emily looks at the clock and almost jumps out of her skin, 'Issy, you gotta go. Mum could be back any minute!'

'I don't mind seeing your mum.'

'I do. I'm supposed to be playing the piano. You know how strict they are.'

Issy pulls on her trainers and they both race down to the front door.

It's six o'clock on a Friday evening and Issy's mum is working until ten at the Co-op. Jerome is at a family thing in the church hall with his grandmother. Walking along the street, Issy feels lonely. There's no coursework because AS-Levels only just started. She could do some reading, but it's Friday night. It's moments like these, Issy realises how much she misses Hayley and her banter.

Issy heads to the lower park on Telegraph Hill and sits on a swing in the play area. She thinks about the times she spent having a laugh with Hayley. At least with Hayley, Issy never felt like she was faking it or had to put on any posh voice or internally monitor her actions all the time.

After her parents beat her up, social services intervened and took Hayley into emergency foster care, but because she's pregnant, her social worker pushed for Hayley to have her own room in a supported care home instead and start the process of living semi-independently after Hayley turned sixteen years old.

Issy lights a cigarette – stopping smoking, another thing she's failed at – and ponders on what Emily said about judging people. She takes out her phone and texts Hayley.

The walls are dirty with trainer marks and there are burn holes in all the carpets. Each door is scuffed or dented. Door handles bent or not there at all. As Issy waits for Hayley to get permission to let them both go through to her bedroom, a fight breaks out between two girls. One girl in a stripy top punches another girl in a blue top. They lock arms over each other's heads then girl in the blue top tries to ram the other girl into a table. Realising they are not play fighting, a staff member calls for assistance. The social worker puts down Issy's school ID card and leaps from her desk to help break up the fight. As she runs, her cigarettes fall out her pocket unnoticed. Hayley grabs the box and stuffs them into her own tracksuit bottoms.

'Let's get out of here.' Hayley signs herself back out and they head to a nearby wall.

As she jumps the wall, Hayley lets out a whimper.

Issy sees Hayley wince, 'You alright? Is it the baby?'

'It's nothing,' Hayley blushes.

Hayley takes one of the social worker's cigarettes and lights it. She sucks on the cigarette furiously, inhaling huge breaths of smoke.

'Ain't you supposed to quit, you know, now you're pregnant?'

Hayley looks at Issy. Issy looks back at Hayley.

'Dunno,' Hayley replies. There's a new coldness to Hayley. 'Want one?' Hayley holds open the box.

'No thanks.'

'So what you been up to?' Hayley asks, grabbing a nearby beer bottle from the wall and lobbing it.

'Just started AS-Levels,' Issy says, looking at the broken glass on the road. 'Mrs Salmon, you know her, the English teacher, she's helping me apply for uni.'

'Proper boffin.' Hayley squeezes her eyes shut as she smokes. The cigarette is a stronger brand, making her feel sick.

Issy watches Hayley flick the lit cigarette onto a parked car. 'Hayley!' She jumps from the wall to flick it on the floor.

'What? It's just some prick's car,' Hayley laughs. 'Since when do you care?'

'You know I never liked that stuff,' Issy protests. This was a mistake. Then Issy hears Emily's voice saying instead of judging people, get to know how they got to being that way.

'So you scared? About having a baby?'

'Nah, it's gonna be jokes. Me and Dwayne went and got baby stuff the other day. If that bitch hurried up and let you in, I could of showed ya. Got these proper small trainers and everything.' Hayley holds out her hand to illustrate how tiny the shoes are.

'So is things going good with youse two?' Issy hears her grammar going wrong. It feels as if her tongue is slipping to the back of her throat, reverting to South London speak. De-Emilying.

'Why,' Hayley looks startled. 'What's Jerome said?'

'Nothing,' Issy replies, searching Hayley's eyes for the answer. 'Has he done something?'

Hayley turns away.

'You can tell me; I'm still your friend?'

'Everything's fine, for fuck's sake.' Hayley lights another cigarette. This time she'll take it slow.

The girls sit in silence.

'Fuck it, I will have one.'

Hayley passes the pinched cigarettes to Issy.

'I'll probably have to go another women's only place soon. Won't get a flat until I'm eighteen.'

Issy doesn't know how to reply. The thought of being handed her own council flat fills her with dread.

'It's gonna be proper jokes. Gonna have house parties and nice sofas and we'll be able to cotch and smoke weed.'

'What? With the baby?'

'Obviously when the baby's sleeping.'

Issy looks at her phone. A text from Jerome: luv u babes. Wish u were here and I culd kiss u, Jxxx.

'Hays, I gotta go. Mum needs me to help with something.'

'I'll come. I ain't seen Carol for time.'

Issy looks at Hayley, 'You can't.'

Hayley feels a shooting feeling of abandonment up her spine, 'Please. I hate being by myself all the time.'

'It's family stuff,' Issy lies. 'About my dad. Besides, you're on curfew and I'd feel bad if you got tagged, being pregnant and all. Look, the 53 is coming. Better go.'

Issy gives Hayley a quick hug then runs up the road to catch the bus.

'See you tomorrow?' Hayley calls out, but Issy doesn't look back.

Hayley watches as Issy gets on the bus at the end of the street. She thinks about texting her own mum but realises she's got no phone credit. She counts out the cigarettes in the box: eleven.

50p each clocks up a fiver, she thinks, jumping off the wall, the pain hitting her back. About to flick the second disgusting cigarette at another parked car, Hayley stops, drops it on the floor. She takes the rest of the cigarettes out, kicks the box over a wall, and carefully places them into her left sock. Just in case she gets searched.

The reggae sound system is booming. Jerome and Dwayne are having a good time. For Jerome, this is one party that feels safe to be at, completely separated from the madness of the streets. The brothers have eaten plates of jerk chicken and curried goat with rice and peas. And drunk enough fruit punch to send them both tipsy. There's no weed on either of them, so as not to shame their grandmother, and the feeling in the air is calm. Jerome asks Dwayne if he wants to sneak out for a smoke.

Out the back of the church hall, Jerome looks up at his older brother, 'Nice party, innit?'

'Yeah, it's alright,' Dwayne replies, taking out a cigarette then lighting Jerome's.

'We should do this more often, you know, get away from the madness?' The soft reggae love songs the old folks have been playing have Jerome in a sentimental place. 'I love you, D. You know that, right?'

Dwayne screws up his face, 'Why you getting all batty man and shit?'

Jerome laughs, 'What? Can't say I love my brother? I'm proper looking forward to being an uncle, too. It's gonna be so cute.'

'Yeah, I'm gonna have me a mini-mafia boss.'

'Boy or girl?'

'Gotta feeling it's a little man,' Dwayne says, taking a piece of paper from his wallet and handing it to Jerome. 'Soon Hays will get her flat.'

Jerome looks down at the notes and calculations. Dwayne factoring in this new found flat as a resource for his drug deals. Jerome can't believe Dwayne would put his new family at risk.

'You can't use Hayley's.'

'It's perfect, bruv. Police ain't gonna raid a baby's room, get me.'

'Baby's bedroom?' Jerome squeezes his rum-blurred eyes to focus, 'That's raw, bruv.'

'Raw how? The baby ain't gonna reach up in a wardrobe and take it. It's the perfect hiding place.'

Why does Dwayne have to be like this? Even at a nice party, with good vibes, his brother has a way of bringing everything back down. Jerome turns, pretending to blow his smoke out in the opposite direction to Dwayne's face and spots Leeroy Simms walking past.

'Oh my days, Leeroy!' Jerome lights up with surprise, jogging over to hug the big dreadlocked man. Leeroy smiles and his gold teeth shine from the church hall light.

Leeroy notices Dwayne behind Jerome. He holds out his fist for a nudge, 'Me haven't seen you since you were lickkle pickney!'

'Come out my face before...' Dwayne looks at Leeroy like he wants to kill him there and then.

'Don't watch him,' Jerome says, shaking his head as Dwayne storms into the men's toilets by the door.

Jerome thinks for a few moments about asking, and then decides not to.

'Me nah know,' Leeroy says, guessing.

Jerome looks up at Leeroy. 'So you ain't seen him lately, nah?' Jerome nods like it's nothing.

Leeroy shakes his head.

Jerome looks down at the grass.

'Last I hear, him in Jamaica but you know what him like.'

Leeroy squeezes Jerome's shoulder, 'Keep up the schoolwork and look pon yuh grandmother.'

Jerome nods.

Then Leeroy takes out a twenty pound note.

'Nah, that's cool,' Jerome says. 'Thanks though. Appreciate it. We're all good.'

'Come check me, some time,' Leeroy adds, putting the money back in his wallet and handing over a business card for his record shop where down the back you can smoke weed and play dominos.

An exhausted Emily lies in bed staring at the ceiling. As her eyes wander around her room, she thinks about the afternoon with Isobel. How ashamed Issy feels about her GCSE results. They have been friends for just over a year now and it dawns on Emily that if they are to become genuine friends then she must tell Issy what her parents think. Taking a huge breath, Emily grabs her mobile and texts her cousin, Rosie.

Hayley is still waiting for a reply. She just sent her third text asking if she can come for Sunday lunch tomorrow: Not coking diner. Taking Kaya to cinima. Mum x

'FUCKING BITCH!' Hayley screams into her pillow.

Can I cum 2

Sandra doesn't reply.

The longer Hayley waits, the angrier she becomes. She punches into her pillow. Then gets up and kicks her bedroom door. She runs to the kitchen looking for the sharpest thing in the drawer: a blunt butter knife.

Back in her room, Hayley uses the knife on her arm, over and over and over until the tiny trickles of blood arrive. The knife isn't sharp enough for real damage, but the concentration of cutting calms her down. She eventually falls asleep, holding her phone in her hand, making sure vibrate is on, in case her mother texts back during the night.

The following morning, Emily meets Issy at New Cross train station. This is the first time Issy will have been inside art gallery without coercion from a school trip.

'There's Big Ben!' Issy shouts, as the train crosses the River Thames to Waterloo East. 'And the Houses of Parliament!'

Emily laughs.

'So we're going to the National Gallery on Trafalgar Square. Have you been before?'

'Nope. What's in it?'

'A gallery.'

'What sort?'

'Paintings, mainly. Do you know Turner?'

'Who?'

'Turner. He painted the sea. He's one of the most famous English painters.'

'Oh. I'll probably know the picture when I see it. I'm not good with names.'

The girls arrive at Trafalgar Square and Issy convinces Emily to jump up onto one of the black lion statues.

'Pretend we are on safari,' Issy whispers in Emily's ear.

The girls jump off the lion and run up the steps that lead to the National Gallery. As they enter the sliding doors, Issy takes in the atmosphere. Thousands of visitors from around the world squashed together. Two short plump men with tall slender women wearing designer sunglasses and bronze cheeks hand over their backpacks, while a group of tourists put on headphones to listen to the gallery speak to them about art in their own language.

'We don't need headphones,' Emily links arms with Issy. 'I can tell you everything.'

As they wander around Issy finds she's enjoying herself. But it isn't the paintings on the wall. The most fascinating thing is Emily. Issy watches as her friend's eyes light up and dance about, squint to read everything, then stop intrigued. Emily slowly walks the rooms, taking time with each painting, tiptoeing to see details in the larger pieces, bending down to notice others. She's like a ballerina. Issy's never seen someone her age so in love with something that wasn't sixteen years old and wearing a tracksuit and trainers.

What could move her as deeply...

'Isobel?' a voice calls out. 'Issy!'

'No way, Miss,' Issy turns in amazement. 'I was literally just thinking about you!'

'Really?' Mrs Salmon looks proud seeing her pupil in the National Gallery.

'Yeah! I forgot the word, Miss. Begins with E. About people watching.'

'People watching?' Mrs Salmon squeezes her husband's hand. 'Oh, ethnography.'

'That's it. That's kind of what I'm doing, Miss.' Issy smiles at the man holding her teacher's hand, 'Is this Jacob?'

'How do you know his name?'

'You told me, Miss. In the classroom, over the summer.'

'That's right, I did. Can't believe you remembered though.'

'When you said it I thought of the crackers. About the silver ring and I remember thinking Jacob's crackers.'

Mrs Salmon looks at her student in bemusement, then turns to her husband, smiling, 'This is Issy.'

Jacob holds out his hand and shakes hers warmly. 'I've heard about you, too,' he says.

Jacob is slightly taller than Mrs Salmon but not particularly tall. He has a kind face and a friendly smile and lots of big white teeth. Issy looks at his clothes. They are pretty smart for the weekend: a chequered jacket and a proper shirt beneath a blue V-neck jumper. He has jeans on though, but they are navy blue and look like trousers.

Emily comes over to join Issy.

'Mimi, this is my amazing teacher I told you about and her man.'

'You're doing a fantastic job,' Emily says, shaking hands. 'The whole of the United Kingdom needs more teachers like you.'

Mrs Salmon blushes.

Issy raises her eyebrows at Emily's forthrightness.

'Darling, we have to go,' Jacob says.

'Got a booking in Soho. Nice to see you, Issy and good to see you here, of all places.'

Issy watches Mrs Salmon and her husband hold hands and walk out of the room towards the main entrance. She wonders if she and Jerome will ever get up early on the weekend to go to a gallery before lunch in Soho.

'Hungry?' Emily asks Issy. 'My cousin just sent me a message to meet at the cafe. Shall we get something to eat?'

'I'm not a huge fan of this café,' Emily remarks, as they follow signs to the Getty Entrance. 'The one I like best is at the V&A. There's this courtyard and it's so nice in the summer. You can sit outside and look at all the beautiful doors. Though the Tate has a good one too, you can see the River Thames. I also like the Royal Festival Hall because...'

Emily is still listing favourite eateries, as they arrive. Issy watches Emily looking at cake slices from the open refrigerator.

Issy hangs back while Emily asks how much a toasted sandwich and a hot chocolate is. The woman at the till tells Emily, 'eight pounds and ten pence.'

Issy's eyes widen. She digs in her own pockets and counts out two pounds something in change. She knew the museum was free and was hoping to buy chips from the kebab shop on the way home.

'I'll just get some chips later,' Issy says.

'You don't do chips?' Emily asks, taking a ten pound note from her beaded purse.

'Too late for hot food,' the till attendant says.

'I don't know what to get.' A fear grips Issy as she realises she doesn't even have enough to buy a hot chocolate. Her belly is rumbling. For two pounds, she can get chicken and chips from her local kebab shop.

'Me neither,' Emily replies, unaware Issy hasn't got enough money. 'Chicken salad or BLT?'

'Are you going to pay or not?' an old couple ask almost simultaneously, while the man goes to poke Issy.

'Oi, don't touch me!' Issy snaps.

'We would like to drink some tea before they close,' the elderly woman growls.

A pretty young woman places her hands over Emily's eyes and whispers,

'Guess who?' into her ear.

Emily turns around to hug her cousin.

The old couple huff and puff as Rosie's hellos create further delays to their snack time.

'Excuse me? Are you looking after these two?' the man growls.

Rosie immediately sizes up the mood, 'Yes Sir. Is there something I can help you with?'

'We would like to have some tea and these children are holding up the entire queue.'

Rosie peers over the couple's shoulders towards a slight man in a black turtle neck who shrugs his shoulders, 'No rush,' he mouths to Rosie. He hardly has a chin and what he has disappears into his top as the old man shoots a glare his way.

'I can serve you first if you're ready?' the lady at the counter tells Issy with a smile. Rosie sees Issy counting out coins sweating in the palm of her hand.

'What would you like for lunch? My treat.'

'Oh no, no. It's alright,' Issy replies. 'I'm not really hungry.'

'Can I at least get you a drink?' Rosie asks, as Issy's belly rumbles again.

'If you're not hungry, why are you in a café?' the old woman mutters under her breath.

'You're pushing in now, are you?' the old man asks Rose.

'Terribly sorry. Please do go ahead,' Rosie sidesteps out the way.

She rolls her eyes behind his back, 'Tell you what ladies, go and find a seat and I will bring some stuff over. Got any allergies? Dairy? Gluten? Veggie?'

Issy shakes her head.

Rosie arrives with three chicken salad wraps, three different styles of cake, two hot chocolates and a bottle of fizzy water. 'Ignore the grumps.'

'He poked Isobel in the ribs!' Emily exclaims.

'Gosh, did he? Are you okay?'

Issy nods, feeling muted. She peers at the rolled up receipt on the tray. Total £25.10.

Emily unrolls her ten pounds and hands it to Rosie. Issy digs into her pocket knowing she doesn't have enough. Her back feels stiff in the hardback chair and she struggles to take a breath.

'My treat. I insist.' Rosie tosses Emily back the tenner. 'You too, Issy.'

Issy mumbles her thanks into her lap.

'Shall we do the phone thing now,' Rosie asks Emily. 'With the lunch?'

Emily takes out her phone. 'Issy, can you take a photo of Rosie and me?'

'Sure.'

'No, wait! Then they'll ask who else was there.'

'Mimi, we can say we asked somebody.'

'Asked somebody what?' asks Issy.

Rosie looks at Emily. Emily's face goes red.

'I haven't told Issy yet,' Emily whispers.

'Ah, I see.' Rosie puts her arm around Emily's shoulder, 'Not to worry. Issy will understand.'

Emily starts to cry. She slumps onto the table burying her head in her arms. Rosie whispers something in Emily's ear. Issy is totally confused so just admires Rosie's makeup; her lips look like the ones you see in chocolate adverts, soft and red and plump. Emily nods, gets up and walks to the toilets. Rosie leans across the sandwiches and takes Issy's hand.

'Hey Issy. Firstly, I just want you to know Emily thinks the world of you. She feels like you are one of the most genuine people she has ever met and she feels bad to have kept this from you. Really, it is about protecting you rather than anything else.'

Issy's confused. There's loads of really expensive food on the table and nobody eating it. It's freaking her out.

Rosie continues: 'Emily's mum and dad – my uncle and aunt – are a bit, well, bonkers. You met them, right?'

'I met Emily's mum once. She was nice. Baked me cupcakes,' Issy tells Rosie, eyes fixed on the chocolate fudge cake sitting between the carrot cake and strawberry cheesecake.

'But you've not met her since?'

'Nope.'

'That's because...' Rosie fiddles with her ring, then takes a packet of rolling tobacco from her bag and rolls a cigarette.

'You smoke, right?' Rosie asks.

Issy looks at the floor.

'Hey Issy, it's cool. I'm not here to judge you. Fuck knows you have enough people doing that.' Rosie glances at the old couple across the seating area, then winks at Issy before leaning in. 'Here, take this, I'll make another.'

'Do you think Emily is alright?' Issy asks.

'Will you promise me something?' Rosie says, licking the second rollup.

Issy imagines a black and white film with Rosie's lips remaining red throughout. She nods.

'Look after Emily. She's a delicate one.' Rosie gets up and heads to the ladies. 'Back in a bit.'

Issy sits looking at the food. She wants to take a bite of the wrap in front of her, but she feels she needs permission. None of it seems like hers, despite Rosie saying it was. In fact, as Issy looks round the room at the people sitting down, none of them look like her. They're like aliens. Making her frustrated in her skin. She knows all these people are posh. Rosie and Emily are posh and she isn't. Even the grumpy man and woman. Even them. They shout differently. Not as loudly, and Issy knows they'd never get arrested for poking her or even told off.

Eventually Rosie and Emily return from the ladies. Emily looks pale and flushed.

'Issy,' Rosie smiles. 'Emily has something to own up to.'

'I don't know how to say this but,' Emily looks at her cousin, who smiles and nods her encouragement. 'My parents don't–' Emily stops.

'They don't like me, do they?' Issy says. 'I kinda knew that.'

'It's not you, babes,' Rosie interjects, taking Issy's hand. 'It's their own issues.'

'My dad hasn't even met you and that's what gets me the most.'

'Why doesn't your mum like me?' Issy asks, hurt. 'Did I say something bad?'

Emily takes a moment. 'They think you graffiti and Mum has seen you in the park smoking weed a couple of times while she's been playing tennis.'

Issy pulls her hand away from Rosie's.

'Mimi got dealt ultra-conservative parents, it's not really about you at all.' Rosie is smiling, trying to reassure. 'Hey ladies, shall we eat?' she says. 'I've got to shoot off shortly.'

'I've lost my appetite now,' Emily sighs.

'Rubbish! Come on. What about you, Issy? Hungry?'

Issy nods slightly.

'Then let's eat!' Rosie pushes a chicken wrap all the way to Issy.

Issy looks at Emily and smiles. Emily smiles back and picks up her lunch. Issy copies. Rosie leaves red lipstick around the tortilla. As Issy puts the food to her mouth, she's conscious of the bloodied scabs where she bites the skin around her nails. One day. One day she'll have perfect fingernails like Rosie and Emily.

'You see, Mimi? Issy understands,' Rosie says. 'You can't change some people. Like those grumps over there.' Rosie gestures to the elderly couple. 'They forget they were young once.'

CHAPTER 15
STOP

'You alright Jay? Ain't seen you in ages.'

'Teena, what you doing here?'

'Fucking Mum kicked me out.' Teena stretches her chewing gum from her mouth until it snaps, then puts it back in.

Her hair is scraped back into a tight ponytail, with her afro curls in a ball above her head. Her tracksuit bottoms are baggy but her top is tight. She isn't wearing much and the weather has started to turn. September was mild but now it's October, come four o'clock its cold. Issy notices the little hairs on Teena's pale thin arms stand up. She needs a jacket.

'What you'se doing here?' Teena asks.

'Seeing Hayley,' Jerome replies, accepting a piece of gum.

'You seen anyone lately?' Teena asks, stretching out her gum again.

The conversation carries on with Jerome and Teena talking about who they saw, where they saw them, on what bus; what fights are going on, what fights Teena had, what madness Jerome and Dwayne have been getting caught up in; how police are inna their business, how much they hate police, who is still in prison for the riots, and then, to Issy's disgust, Teena starts going on about how "jokes" the riots were...

Issy stands there silent. At one point in time, she would be heavily into this conversation. In fact, she would have been loving it. A year ago, she was so into Graff, she thought up its name. Fights happened, here and there, and were never really violent: a slap, a push, cusses. Now? Now she doesn't even listen. She acts as though she's following the conversation, but instead, she's noticing little things about them both. Like Teena's blackened earlobes where she's put in cheap earrings. Like Jerome's baseball cap still having its label in; she used to find it cool but it suddenly looks ridiculous, even though it's still the fashion.

Teena offers Jerome a twos on her cigarette. Jerome hesitates, noticing Teena's cold sore. 'Have one to yourself, then.' Teena gives him a cigarette.

Jerome takes it, as if that's super generous. Why? Is he flirting?

Issy remembers when Hayley was being bullied by Teena and Teena got three girls to corner Hayley in school and squeeze prick stick into her hair.

Teena spits out her gum with force. 'Who you seen, Issy?'

Issy watches the gum hit the pavement, roll a bit then stop in the middle of the road. She remembers the time she was in a playground and got gum on her brand new dress. How she cried heavily into her father's arms when it wouldn't come out. How happy she was when he, not her mum, drove her in his big white van to get a new one. Her shoes, red and shiny, couldn't touch the floor of his van. How her dad would turn to her at the traffic lights and give her a smile and tell her she was special.

'Babe?' Jerome nudges Issy.

'Huh?'

'Who you seen lately?' Teena asks again.

'Oh, no-one. Keeping myself to myself.'

'Best way. All yutes either in pen or on some shit.'

'So what's it like? Living here?' Issy asks, nodding over at the care home.

'Propa nuts, blood. Every day there's drama. Some mad mixup; some girl fucked someone else's man. It's proper nuts. Feds are here every day, trust.' Teena laughs. 'It's wicked. I love it. You don't need TV.'

Jerome laughs along. Issy doesn't.

Issy used to be jealous of Teena in Year 7 and 8. She thought Jerome and Teena would get together because Teena had a crush on him. Teena would write 'I luv JC' on all her school books. She acted like JC wasn't Jerome Campbell, told everyone it meant Jesus Christ. It's how Tameika got nicknamed Crazy Christian Tameika. When Tameika heard Teena laughing about how she would fuck Jesus, she got up from her desk, picked up her chair and chucked it at Teena, then grabbed Teena's hair and smashed her head against the table before the History teacher ran in to grab her. The R.E. teacher was crying hysterically and shaking for the rest of the lesson. Looking back, it didn't help that Issy and Hayley and the rest of the bad ones in the class laughed at the teacher and would mimic the sound of her crying whenever they saw her. Apparently she got depression and left teaching altogether...

Now Issy looks at Teena and sees a car crash waiting to happen. She listens to how much everyone in the care home gets high: glue, pills, poppers, LSD, even crack, and one girl does heroin. The girls hang out with the dealers and go to mansion parties and get free drink for lineups.

'Let's go see Hayley,' Issy says, stubbing her cigarette on the wall and putting it in the bin, annoyed that she still smokes, annoyed to be back in this dump.

'Check you out!' Teena laughs, spitting a large ball of phlegm onto the concrete in front of them.

Jerome looks at Issy's unhappy face and frowns. Today, Issy can't pretend to laugh or find the conversation interesting. She just finds the whole situation a huge waste of her life. Something she doesn't want anymore.

'Coming in?' Jerome asks Teena.

'Nah, my boyfriend's coming to—' Teena stops as a car pulls up with blacked out windows. 'Just as I was saying!'

Teena watches the car turn in the cul-de-sac. The electric window on the driver's side winds down, releasing double the volume of bass; rappers shouting about how many guns they own, "fuck your pussy, bitch, I own it."

Even though it's getting dark, and there's no sun to be seen anywhere, the man in the car is wearing huge Gucci sunglasses. It's hard to know how old he is. He points a huge gold-ringed forefinger and signals Teena to get in.

Teena turns to Issy and Jerome, 'He's a producer, you know.' They watch Teena run around the front of the car. 'Laters!'

Jerome walks over to the car, takes a CD out of his small backpack and puts it into the jewelled hand. The man looks at the CD for a brief moment before chucking it out onto the road, winds up the window, and drives off at speed.

Jerome looks down at the CD. His cheeks burn with shame. His body stiff knowing Issy has seen the whole thing. He can't bring himself to face her.

Issy walks over, shaking her head, 'That ain't no producer, picking up a sixteen year old crackhead to fuck her. He's a fucking pimp, babe. And he was playing shit music. You produce better—'

'Alright, babe!' Jerome snaps.

Issy jerks back as if the words were flames in her face. Mrs Salmon has been discussing masculinity and status this week in Sociology. Issy didn't get all of the lesson but often boys need status to feel powerful because in patriarchy men are at the top and when they don't get status they can feel powerless and this leads to anger because anger is a way of getting power back, even if it's not the best way. It often happens like that with gang kids. To Issy's surprise, Mrs Salmon backs the kids that rioted in August. Society pushed them there, kind of like what Jerome says. So instead of calling him a prick and walking off, like she wants to, she goes and sits on the wall where she and Hayley smoked last time she was here, and waits for Jerome to come over and apologise. And, within a minute, he walks over, says sorry, and they go in to see Hayley.

On the bus home, Jerome is listening to his own music on his phone while making pencil notes in his notebook. He offers an earbud to Issy but she refuses.

'You all right?' he asks.

'Yeah,' she replies. But she's not.

Staring at the 'bus stopping' sign lighting up every time someone wants to get off, Issy becomes transfixed by the words illuminating in orange. That's what she wants to do. Press STOP with her life and step out of it to get perspective. She is too inside everything to have a clear head.

Hayley asked them to be godparents. Jerome's eyes welled up and he hugged Hayley for ages. Issy froze when Hayley pulled her in for a hug. Then Jerome put his arms around both of them and instead of feeling the joy of new beginnings, Issy felt trapped. She didn't even say yes she would be godmother. She didn't have time to even think about it. It was assumed she said yes because Jerome was so happy about being the godfather. He's the uncle anyway.

Then Hayley got out some drink from under her bed and toasted 'to the godparents.' Issy watched Hayley glug the blue alcohol, and all she could think about was what Emily says about food colouring, and how she would never put anything bright blue into her body.

Issy spent the rest of the visit trying to find a space to say that it wasn't a definite yes from her, that she would have to think about being godmother and get back to Hayley. But the drinks led to a presentation of all the baby clothes Dwayne's bought the little man, and how all the clothes are for a boy because she found out it was a boy, and how at the scan Dwayne got so happy he spent four hundred pounds on all this stuff.

Issy looked for nappies and baby wipes, but all she saw were baby trainers and matching tracksuits and caps. Caps for a baby. The clock ticked so fucking slowly, Issy opened the window just to breathe air that wasn't from the room; air that had travelled to places other than London, and would scoop up this congested air, thick with stupidity, and take it far out from her lungs.

She focusses on the streets outside, trying to capture every detail, not missing a thing. As the bus speeds up, when nobody presses STOP, Issy's eyes work harder to seize life, not to miss a moment: people getting takeaways, people walking. Which direction. What bags are they carrying? How old are they? The bus slows. A little girl crying. An old man drinking. Two females with headscarves chatting, wearing flip-flops even though it's October. Three men shaking hands. Two teenagers kissing. The cars next to the bus lane. The girl smoking. A couple arguing. A baby sleeping. A dog barking. Alcoholics begging. The shopkeeper closing. The pubs bulging. An African preaching. The kids riding bicycles. From the houses in Charlton, to the larger houses on Blackheath, to the dirty terraces of Deptford, and soon to New Cross where they live on Telegraph Hill.

The bus stops in traffic outside Goldsmiths College. Issy watches a small group of university students laughing together, smoking rollups from their pink lips with 1950s haircuts, wearing skinny jeans that stop above the ankles and weird-looking shoes that nobody her age would wear. One girl has amazing makeup – like Cleopatra. Issy sees them with their books and dirty linen bags printed with political slogans that might mean something deep. The girl with the Cleopatra makeup catches Issy staring. The group turn. Two guys in tweed jackets and thick oversized black framed glasses. Like twins. One girl with rollers and rags in her hair. Cleopatra blows a kiss and Issy blushes, realising she's been smiling at them. Issy feels the warmth from the group as they wave and smile. She imagines herself standing with them, her university mates.

Finally it's her turn to press STOP, 'I can STOP anytime I like, can't I?'

Fumbling to pack his headphones and notebook into his jacket pocket, Jerome doesn't reply.

The bus calls out: "New Cross Gate Station."

'Yep,' Issy says, getting up. 'I can.'

CHAPTER 16
A BABY

Issy has been at the hospital with Dwayne and Jerome for three hours. Hayley is in labour. Dwayne, frustrated this is happening on a weekend, tries to find out how long it will take.

'I've got things to do!'

'Bruv...' Jerome pulls Dwayne to one side. 'Now you know I respect you, but this is the birth of your son.'

'Bruv, with all respect yeah, I've been here for time. I might just sort my shit out and come back.'

'But what if you miss the baby?'

'I don't wanna be in there. I've done told them that.' Dwayne turns to walk out of the reception doors.

'Fine, go!' Jerome screws his face up, 'I'll be the first man the baby sees when he opens his eyes then.'

Dwayne stops. He turns to Jerome. Jerome looks at him, face screwed up. Dwayne walks over to the vending machine, as though that was where he was always headed. First he punches it, then puts some change in and buys two chocolate bars and some crisps. Jerome sees this and, as Dwayne comes back to sit with them, puts out his hand with a smile.

'What man? They're for me.'

'Fucking hell, Dwayne,' Issy snaps. 'D'you have to always be such a prick?!'

Issy walks over to the machine.

Dwayne looks at Jerome, 'Please tell your bitch best not chat to me like that.'

'Don't call her that, D.'

Dwayne takes a large bite of his Snickers, 'So she can call me a prick, yeah?' he says, displaying the contents of his mouth to his brother.

Jerome walks over to Issy, 'Babe–'

'I know! I shouldn't have called him that.'

Issy sighs, she doesn't want to be here either.

Jerome puts his arm around his girl and kisses her cheek.

Dwayne snorts from across the waiting room. Several people twitch but nobody says a word.

Sandra walks in with Hayley's little sister Kaya and Hayley's half-brother Ronnie. She notices Dwayne and walks straight up to him. Jerome stands tall. It's the first time Dwayne and Sandra have come face-to-face since Sandra beat Hayley up. Everyone, including Issy, has successfully avoided Sandra for the past six months.

'Didn't think I'd see you here,' Sandra says to Dwayne.

'Well boy, that's what happens when you judge people by your own standards,' Dwayne replies, opening the packet of crisps.

Sandra stares at him, but says nothing. She doesn't seem to be in an argumentative mood.

Jerome walks over to defuse things.

'Hi Kaya!' he says, offering her the Skittles Issy just bought him. 'Alright, Ronnie.'

Ronnie hunches his shoulders and keeps his head down. He's just finished seven months in prison for robbery. He looks fucked. Not the stocky hard nut that went around with his bulldog. Because he's nearly twenty, he went to adult prison this time.

Sandra smiles falsely at Jerome in thanks for Kaya's sweets, then finds a nurse to ask what's happening. For some reason, Hayley put Sandra down as birthing partner when Dwayne refused. Social services rang saying Hayley is in labour and what with Kaya on a child protection list, Sandra's keen to look interested in mother duties, even turning up to mediation sessions paid for by Lewisham Council. When Sandra goes off with the nurse, Ronnie and Kaya remain seated in the reception area next to Jerome, Dwayne, and Issy. It's an awkward reunion.

'Alright, Ronnie?' Issy asks. She too notices the change in him.

'Yeah, fine,' Ronnie mumbles, flicking through a magazine.

'Been raped, bruv,' Dwayne whispers in Jerome's ear. Jerome kisses his teeth.

'Excited you're going to be an aunty?' Issy turns to Kaya, who must be eight or nine now.

'If it's a girl,' Kaya says, 'she can play with my old dolls.'

'It's a boy,' Dwayne says bluntly. He can't stand Kaya. Spoilt brat.

Kaya looks up at Dwayne and studies his face before saying anything else. She peers down at her doll, then at Jerome holding Issy's hand. They both smile back at her.

'He can play with my cars then,' she replies.

Hayley's pain rises from the bottom of her back through her pelvis. She darts her hips to do something to shift the pain away, but it shoots up, like someone stabbing her with a blunt instrument and digging out her guts.

'Breathe.' The midwife is giving her gas and air. 'That's it. Looong breaths.'

'I can't fucking breathe,' Hayley pants. 'I'm dying, I'm dying!'

'You're doing fantastically well. It will drop, just breathe through it. The long golden thread.'

Hayley tries to remember what the long golden fucking thread is. She can't do it.

'Breathe.'

She breathes in, tears in her eyes, out again until the pain eases.

'Just checking your cervix.'

The midwife opens Hayley's legs, feeling inside her. 'Okay, you're ready to push.'

Hayley holds out her hand for her mother. Sandra appears to be in shock.

'When you feel the next contraction,' the midwife continues, 'push from the muscles in your lower back, like you're squeezing out a poo.'

Hayley feels her mother take hold of her hand and squeeze it. The pain comes in thick and fast, like a fairground ride taking off. Hayley screams.

'Push!' the midwife tells her.

Hayley pushes her feet into the stirrups, her bum lifting from the bed.

'Jesus Christ!' Sandra yells, freeing her hand from Hayley's grip, and shaking it.

'It ain't working!' Hayley screams, pressure pulsing up her neck to her temples.

'It is, I promise you,' calls the midwife.

'It ain't working! I need more gas and air.'

'Gas and air won't help now, push until the contraction is over.'

'Owwwww! I can't. I can't. I can't. I can't. I can't.'

'The baby can't stay in there,' the midwife says, 'You can do it.'

Sandra looks on, a helpless look over her face.

'How much longer?' she asks the midwife.

'Could be one more push, could be more. We never know. Baby decides.'

'This is stressing me out, I need a fag,' Sandra strokes Hayley's forehead. 'You can do it, if you're anything like me.'

Sandra turns to the second midwife, 'I had three, all natural.'

The midwife sees the fear in Hayley's eyes as her mother exits the room.

'Your mother is right. You will do it.'

The pain floods in again. Hayley screams, tears streaming down her face. 'I can't, I can't.'

'Push, from your bottom. Push.'

With no hand to hold, Hayley grabs both sides of the hospital bed. Her head feels like it's going to explode. She rams her feet against the foot of the bed and pushes with her entire body.

When the contraction ends, the midwife is smiling, 'Feel this.'

She guides Hayley's hand between her legs, 'That's baby's head. You're nearly there.'

Hayley looks around the empty room, 'Can you get my mum back?' she asks the second midwife. 'Or Dwayne, he's the dad.'

The second midwife nods, 'We'll ask someone to find them.'

Hayley feels again, the skull feels warm and slimy.

'Get ready to push. Bigger the push, the faster he'll be out.'

Hayley waits for the next contraction, her body exhausted, 'Oh fuck, oh fuck, it's coming! Get my mum! Get Dwayne! PLEASE?'

'No time, push now. Push. Pu-uuuu-shhh.'

A baby boy gushes out onto the hospital bed. The midwife wraps him in a blanket, sticky as he is with gunk, then puts him onto Hayley's breast.

His eyes are squinty, looking more hamster than human. Hayley winches as the midwife injects painkillers into her labia. The second midwife takes out a large needle but Hayley is so transfixed by the real life baby in her arms, she barely notices them stitching up the tears in her vagina.

Dwayne appears at the door. Seeing the small man he made sucking on his woman's breasts, tears unexpectedly fill his eyes. So this is what life's all about.

'Oh my days,' he says.

'Congratulations,' says the midwife.

'So is it a boy?'

'Yeah,' Hayley mumbles, transfixed with the precious bundle in her arms.

'Do you have a name?' the midwife asks.

'Jack,' Hayley says.

'Jamal,' Dwayne says.

'Jack, after my granddad.'

'Jamal, man.'

'You have time to think about that later,' the midwife says diplomatically.

'It's Jamal, trust.' Dwayne smiles at Hayley, 'You did good, babes.'

CHAPTER 17
CHRISTENING

This is the first time Issy has been to a church since her father was buried. No weddings. No funerals. Definitely no christenings. Being inside the church is nice. The beautiful stained glass images of love and forgiveness. She peers around with a feeling of peace. She holds out her hand. Carol's face lights up as she takes it.

As the wooden benches fill, there's a clear divide. Hayley's Aunty Sharon walks up to Issy and Carol. She leans in and whispers, 'Why you'se on the black side?'

Embarrassed, Issy turns around to see if anyone heard. Barry's mum pinches her lips, and looks down at the programme.

Carol stares at Sharon, 'We're all people, ain't we?'

Sharon joins her husband on the opposite pew. Issy notices Barry's mother looking at the length of Sharon's skirt and the height of Sharon's heels.

Hayley rushes over to Issy, 'Where's Dwayne? Priest needs to start.'

'Dunno. Text Jerome?'

'Thank fuck for that,' Hayley looks up in relief.

'You're in church!' whispers Issy.

'Leave it out.' Hayley storms off.

Jerome brings Mabel down the aisle to sit with Carol.

The priest opens the Bible. The organ plays Amazing Grace, startling baby Jamal from his sleep.

After the service, guests go to the community room annexed next door.

Hayley's side of the family look shocked by the celebration's extravagance. Hayley's father, Ray, paid for sandwiches, sausage rolls and cupcakes, which Sandra spread out on a foldup table in the far corner of the hall. On the opposite side, three women in bright-coloured headscarves are tending to huge silver trays of hot jerk chicken, fried fish and dumplings. The modest church hall tables are decorated with white cotton cloth and fresh flowers. There is a head table where Hayley is to sit with Dwayne, Jerome and Mabel, plus two seats for Hayley's parents. Ray looks at Sandra as Dwayne offers them seats then at the sound system is being set up by some men with dreadlocks and colourful shirts over their shiny suits.

Dwayne is looking sharp in his brand new suit. He also bought a new suit for Jerome. Barry has his own from church, so does Andre from going on trial for stealing during the riots. He's fresh out of prison after doing three of his six months. The boys stand together wearing matching corsages and ties. Anton's missing, still serving his riots prison sentence.

'Don't they look handsome?' Carol says to Mabel.

Mabel turns to see the young men posing for group photos with the baby. She is also shocked by the extravagance of this reception. Her eyes move slowly over her grandsons and their friends. Dwayne's recently acquired gold tooth keeps irritating her eyes, along with his thick gold chain and matching bracelet. His rings. The baby's outfit. The food. Hayley's dress. Her ridiculous hair curled into ringlets and overdone make-up. Andre's afro with a marijuana leaf razored across the back of his head. Mabel feels faint

'Help me sit?' she asks Carol.

'What's wrong?' Carol asks, as she helps her elderly neighbour into a plastic chair covered in a stretchy white cloth. Carol looks into Mabel's worried eyes, 'Mabel?'

But Mabel can't bring herself to say her thoughts aloud. Not in a place of God. She's also embarrassed to admit the truth. Her grandsons are criminals.

Six bottles of champagne are in ice buckets. Issy doesn't know the young females opening packets of plastic champagne flutes. Jerome assures her they're church girls.

Ronnie finds Hayley smoking round the back with Aunty Sharon. 'Did Dad pay for all this?' he demands. 'How much did he give you?'

'Dwayne paid,' Hayley says, proud that her baby father is a good provider.

Hayley's aunt pulls her aside once Ronnie goes and asks, 'Are they gangsters?'

'Musicians.'

'The Caribbean buffet is ready,' the DJ announces 'and please, white people, don't be shy; come taste a lickle treat – seasoned whole food pon the table Fill Dem Belly catering from Deptford's finest'.

Hayley's relatives stick with the cheese sandwiches, but Ronnie loads his plate with barbecue chicken – he's been to enough youth clubs in Lewisham to know rice and peas is not to be missed. He gets in the queue behind Hayley's social worker who put his little sister on the child protection register – the reason his whole family rallied here in the first place.

With the sound system in place, Dwayne takes the microphone and welcomes everyone to the hall. The room falls silent as his deep rich voice booms from the speakers. Andre, filming the event, puts his thumb up to show he's ready to record.

'Well boy, lots to say, lots to say. Firstly, wanna thank my people, DJ Mighty Mike on set, the ladies at Fill Dem Belly for the delicious food... So after lots of success with music, started a record label with my bro and business partner, Jerome plus my crew, making bare Ps, ya get me. Graff man dem - best rappers in London, number one hits on the horizon, Graff under Double-G serving the best Caribbean food, playing the best tunes, one time, one love, one respect, yeah. Oh and our latest tracks available for download and free CDs are on your tables. Peace out.'

Dwayne drops the mic on the floor then sits at his spot on the head table.

The room is silent. Dwayne nods to the DJ who begins to play one of their tracks. Baby Jamal startled by the bass, screams. The horns and harsh sound effects make Jerome wince, embarrassed. He walks over to the DJ, 'Maybe some soft reggae songs, since these don't really know our beats.'

I'm still in love with you boy...

Jerome walks over to his brother. 'You didn't mention Jamal once in your speech.'

Dwayne puts down his jerk chicken leg and wipes his fingers, 'Today ain't just a celebration for my baby boy. Today marks a new era. The start of my business. Our business. You think I don't know what I'm doing? I'm gonna show all mans, including all these white pricks, you don't mess with Double-G.' Dwayne points his finger at Jerome: 'They sit at my table. Eat my food. Listen to my music' – he looks across at Hayley, still carrying some baby fat, but all done up and pretty in her new dress – 'and I fuck their precious little white bitch.'

Jerome looks at his brother in disbelief, he starts to protest, then changes his mind. What's the point?

'Well boy, you mind if I say a few words? As his uncle?'

'Be my guest,' Dwayne chuckles, drunk on rum and power. Dwayne points to the mic on the floor. Jerome looks around the room. People are already leaving. The atmosphere frosty. Jerome picks up the microphone and does his best to patch up the day.

'Just wanna thank everyone for being here. Hayley's family for their support. The priest for a great service. To those absent, we pray for you, and think of you in these times. And to Jamal, so small, coming into this world all fresh, giving us something to smile about...'

Sandra and her sister Sharon are re-covering the sandwiches and pork pies with cling film. Hayley's father Ray refuses when Jerome offers the mic, and Jerome convinces himself he didn't hear the N-word.

'Baby's not that ugly for a–' Aunty Sharon says walking past Jerome to the exit.

Carol spies Barry sitting with his mother and father. The two bottles of wine on their table untouched as both parents don't drink alcohol.

'Nice to see you here,' Carol greets his parents. 'And well done on your exam results, Barry. All As and Bs, Issy says.' Barry looks uncomfortable. He loosens his tie, makes some excuse and leaves.

'We hear Issy is doing her AS-Levels like Barry?' Barry's mother, Femi says. A contented smile spreads across her face.

'Education is the best way,' Barry's father, Samuel adds.

'Such a shame not all the boys are studying,' Femi continues.

'Let us know if any jobs come up at the store?' adds Samuel. 'We're keen to get Barry earning some money.'

'When we bought our house, it was a stretch at eighty thousand. Now, a one bedroom flat is more than double that price,' Samuel tells Carol. 'Barry will have to earn at least thirty thousand a year and be in a stable relationship with someone equally competent to qualify for a mortgage.'

'Yes and what's with the fees?' Femi adds.

'Fees?' Carol takes the full opened bottle from behind Barry's mother who politely sides out the way, and fills a plastic flute.

'University fees.'

'Jumping from three to nine thousand pounds per year when Barry and Isobel go.'

'You what?' Carol almost spits red wine over the table.

'We were hoping some universities would stick at three or even six but they all went for nine.'

Femi shakes her head. 'Twenty-four thousand for the three years plus the interest rates for the student loan on top of that.'

'It's criminal what these politicians are doing to young people's life chances,' Samuel says. 'How will you pay for it, Carol?'

Carol has no idea. 'Nine thousand pounds a year for three years?'

'Plus the campus room,' Samuel tells her. 'About four hundred a month.'

'And food and travel,' Femi adds. 'We want to see if we can re-mortgage, release some equity then rent Barry's room out while he's away to help pay for his expenses.'

'Most students will be around fifty thousand pounds in debt by the end of their degree.'

Carol is as impressed as she is shocked with Barry's parents. They go on to explain all about the system and how the points work.

'Let's meet one day,' Femi kindly offers, 'to talk through the particulars; there are grants and bursaries Issy might be eligible for, since you earn less than twenty thousand pounds a year.'

'That's kind but Issy has it all sorted.' Carol replies, filling her glass.

'Take the bottle,' Samuel says handing it over with no judgement. 'We won't drink it.'

Carol goes outside to smoke a cigarette. That conversation was too much. Issy going off and leaving the flat empty. She's got used to having Issy in her room studying, not wanting to go out. Sitting down to dinner together most nights. Her daughter changed so much in that last year at school. The bouncy teenager pinching cigarettes and playing her music too loud is now reading books of an evening, going to museums and libraries with posh kids. Yeah, they still argue. And Issy digs at Carol for drinking that wee bit much but they're a team. Carol wants her daughter to do well, and study hard, but there's a part of her who would have been delighted if this had been Issy and Jerome's baby, ashamed as she is to think it, but a grandchild would bring joy into the flat and keep Issy home.

Having Issy was the best thing Carol ever did. She would have loved more children. Children are tonic to any problem, she thinks, pouring herself another fizzy wine. Kids make life simple. About survival, routine, the small steps, and by and by, life develops a rhythm, and rituals bring meaning. Birthdays, Christmases, the Easter Egg hunts, the summer holidays, paddling pools in the park, picnics, feeding ducks, playing on the swings: it's all beautiful. Family is nature's greatest creation, her own dad would say.

Hayley looks on, downhearted as the majority of her family relocate to Ray and Sandra's flat once the social worker goes. Issy sits with Jerome, watching the catastrophe unfold. She feels sorry for Hayley and goes over to give her a big hug.

Hayley eyes fill with tears as soon as she feels the warmth of her friend's arms. Her mouth trembling, 'That's the first hug I've had all day. My whole family here and you're the only–' she hands Issy baby Jamal and rushes to the toilet.

Oblivious, Dwayne and the other boys are out the back smoking weed. Issy looks down at Hayley's baby. His eyes tightly shut. So tiny. So helpless. Born into chaos. Trapped, more like. Issy kisses his soft forehead, 'I hope you never have to suffer at the hands of racists,' she whispers.

Carol walks over, 'I'm taking Mabel home. I think today's been a wee bit much.' Carol sighs. 'How would you feel if your eighteen year old grandson got a sixteen year old pregnant? She's sitting here thinking where's his dad? Where's his mum, Mabel's daughter? She misses her husband. These family things ain't always happy.'

Issy nods.

'And also–' Carol stops. 'Oh, forget it.'

'Go on?' Issy says, knowing it's important.

'No. Never mind.' Carol checks her watch.

'No, Mum,' Issy persists, 'Tell me.'

Carol takes another sigh, then gives in, 'How would you feel if your grandson done all this, but you know he's not out working?' Carol takes a bottle from a nearby table and examines it. 'So it not real champagne but this plus food all adds up. So how's Dwayne paid for everything?'

Issy looks down at baby Jamal.

Carol lifts Issy's chin, 'Is Jerome a drug dealer? Is Dwayne?'

Issy searches for an opportunity to equivocate, knowing Carol deserves the truth from her daughter. 'I can't speak for Dwayne, Mum, but Jerome's in college. He's making money from the music he's selling. The kids download each track and they makes hundreds on YouTube ads and stuff.'

'You know I'm a soft touch.' Carol strokes baby Jamal's cheek. 'You know I love that wee lad and God knows I know what it's like not to have your mum and dad around at his age. But don't protect Jerome. Not if it's drugs. Or anything like that. I know I ain't said much about this university stuff. I just don't know enough about it. I feel stupid when I hear you talk points and campuses. But I'm proud. Proud you're going for it. You know? You got your dad's brains and you're not afraid to use them.'

Tears fall so rapidly Issy has no time to stop one landing on baby Jamal's chin.

Carol clears the emotion from her throat, 'Look what I made you do!' She takes a napkin from the table.

'It's okay, I can do it.' Issy takes the napkin.

'All I'm saying is, wherever all this comes from, if it's dodgy, have nothing to do with it. Like when they all went rioting, you stayed away. Promise me? You've got more to lose.'

CHAPTER 18
WHITE

Ronnie shows Dwayne the tiny paper package, 'See, one wrap like this, you buy for like fifteen quid. Cut it up with, I dunno, something else, painkillers. Sell it down the pub for forty quid; you're laughing...'

Sitting on the rank sofa in the Crofton Park flat, Jerome feels the blood draining from his head as he watches Ronnie rack up four lines of cocaine. The flat is so cold he can see Ronnie's breath as he talks all animated and twitchy. Dwayne snorts the white powder. Done.

Ronnie offers Jerome the rolled-up twenty pound note. Dealing hard drugs is not in the "getaway" plan scribbled in Jerome's notebook. Knowing this makes him look like a pussy, he holds up the palm of his hand, 'Here to make money, not lose it.'

'Try before you buy, bruv,' Ronnie jokes.

Thanks to Hayley's brother's stint in Big Man prison, Dwayne and his boys are being invited to sell coke for this rich white bloke who lives in some mansion in the countryside. Ronnie's got his samples spread out like a Tupperware party. Jerome knows they can't sell expensive drugs to schoolchildren. Weed is pretty common for kids to smoke, but nobody can afford coke. Parents will definitely notice their money missing at forty a wrap.

'Most bredders don't take this shit,' Andre points out, snorting a line.

'Yet,' Dwayne says.

'D, I don't think peeps we roll with are gonna buy this for forty Ps,' Barry adds, refusing a line. 'They're more Morley's than KFC, get me?'

Barry tries to put on a tough voice, but he's blatantly nervous. Jerome sees Barry doesn't want anything to do with cocaine either. He has his regulars in college and a few youngers shotting weed for him, keeping money coming to Dwayne. Barry never wanted to make bare money with drugs. His parents are suspicious. He already lies about clothes and trainers, saying friends swap them around. His parents are not too technical, so haven't got into social media like Anton's. But Anton's dad supplies them the weed. What is he gonna say when Graff switch to cocaine?

'You can't sell to kids no more,' Ronnie interjects. 'Start selling shit to adults. Like them crackheads in Deptford, yeah? The proper hit only lasts ten, twenty minutes. My dealer makes two grand a week, easy.' Ronnie offers the fourth line to Anton.

Anton takes the rolled up pound note. Hesitant, he looks at Jerome, then at Barry, Andre and Dwayne. 'I'm gonna try it but just to see what it's about, get me.'

Before Anton snorts the powder, he pauses and turns to Ronnie, 'One line ain't gonna make me into some crackhead?'

'Nah, mate,' Ronnie replies loudly in his thick South East London accent. His cocaine kicking in. The stocky hard nut the boys know him as, returned.

'Because, best know. I end up a crackhead. I've seen what dem manz do. Crazy motherfuckers. If I look in the mirror and see that's me, all picky hair'n'shit, I'm burning your house down. No joke! Killing up your family.'

Anton talks like a stand-up comedian. The boys start laughing. His voice squeaks in places, adding to the comedy. Jerome smiles but his body doesn't feel right. It feels like déjà vu; like the day Dwayne texted to everybody that Peckham mans were gonna get it. He feels less and less in control of things. Except this time, Andre isn't there to back him up. Andre is on it. Sitting with Dwayne.

Dwayne notices the rush in his body. He feels stronger, more powerful. His eyes sharp and focused. He looks at Ronnie wearing his usual outfit, his favourite white tracksuit, with a white football shirt and a hoodie. Always ironed and smelling of the same washing powder as Hayley's clothes. Ronnie takes off his hoodie and Dwayne can see the definition in Ronnie's arms. Men get hench in prison. Except Anton. Since Anton, Andre and Ronnie got back back, the three of them exchange cell stories all the time and Dwayne feels left out when they compare their meals and screws, and how it all works, how the drugs get in, the porn, the bashing off. Through the banter, Dwayne wonders if Ronnie got fucked inside. Or if he found someone to fuck. Dwayne imagines all of them at it. No sex for months. When he wonders how big Ronnie is, he shakes his head. This stuff is fucked up. He turns to Ronnie, 'So what else this dealer sell?'

'Everything, mate. Got it all. Like I said, my man's clearing two large a week, easy.'

'I'm feeling that, still. That's a nice, nice amount of change.' Dwayne smiles, sitting up, rubbing his hands together, 'So, you can link man up?'

Ronnie takes out his phone, 'Text him now, mate.'

Sitting up on the edge of the shabby sofa, Dwayne starts telling Graff what he'd do if he made that much money. He lights a joint and inhales deeply. Others join in the daydreaming, but Jerome remains distant. He watches the rap songs playing on the television. Each music video almost identical, half-naked women bouncing their breasts and rubbing their bodies down men in baggy t-shirts and thick platinum gold chains. The men barely glance at the women; rapping to the camera lens. Even the solo female artists provocatively dance to camera. Jerome thinks back to this time last year, inside a billionaire's house. He imagines what George Addy would say about this set up: of the music videos and how they degrade the black community, especially women. How, far from being a belief system for Rastafarian religion, that weed, or the drugs trade is a form of social control, a way of keeping black people in check. How governments flood poor areas with chemically-produced substances. Trap them in poverty. Able to keep black people down. And we fall for it. We make choices. By smoking weed in a land that is Christian and eighty per cent white…

Jerome watches uneasily as the room changes in mood. Andre asks for another line.

'You gotta pay now,' Ronnie says.

Dwayne pulls out twenty pounds and hands it to Ronnie, 'Family rates, yeah?'

Jerome watches Ronnie pull out a wrap of cocaine while on the phone to some girl. He flips it to Dwayne, stuffing Dwayne's twenty pounds back into Dwayne's hoodie – the fastest way to Dwayne's heart. Jerome watches Dwayne sit up and start marking out the white powder on a video game cover. He sees Andre's eyes fixated on the process, already hungry for a next hit.

Ronnie's phone beeps. The main drug dealer from this white bloke with the mansion will meet Dwayne in a Deptford pub on Wednesday.

Ronnie shows Dwayne the text: **Better not waste my time.**

'One of dem ones, yeah?' Dwayne snorts the second line of cocaine. He lets out a chuckle, 'Tell him I'm on dis.'

A fear grips Jerome. As if in slow motion, the world is changing around him. The watch his father gave him ticks with precision. Each stroke definite. No going back. That moment gone, vanished like a pickpocket in the crowd. New moments take form. Choosing fate. Changing direction. Jerome wants to jump up and leave. He wants out but each friend acts like a prison wall trapping him in his life. His brother, the padlock. He knows

166

what it means now, to have someone on lockdown. They can't move, can't get away, despite no physical chains. He thinks about Issy and understands more and more why she wants out. Life for most people in Telegraph Hill is like Emily's. Families use the park on the weekends; they help children onto slides and swings, they feed the ducks. They use the café for actual coffee. Can afford the five pound sandwiches and three pound hot chocolates. The twelve pound yoga hour in the community hall. Life is easy for his neighbours. Who wouldn't want to be them? And Issy can slip into that world. She can change her hair and clothes. She can read books and just slip inside. White and unnoticed. What about him?

'Oi,' Dwayne pokes Jerome, 'Dem rich kids up West.'

'Get a car,' Ronnie says. 'Jay, these fat mansion parties make bare cash.'

CHAPTER 19
AND...

Dwayne struck a deal with Ronnie's contact, but is frustrated he's not making what he was promised. Dwayne and his boys have stood around the green behind New Cross Road and the corners of Deptford most nights selling to junkies. But the faster, richer lifestyle, selling crack isn't what they imagined. Relying on junkies to turn up for deals at the agreed time and place, with the correct money – real not counterfeit – is like relying on British weather.

Jerome, so far, refuses to take part, making it clear he'll only be shotting weed from his pockets. Like Barry, he's not happy the client group has switched from kids to adults, especially adults who rob houses to make the notes they put in his hand. What happened to private mansion parties with security? The drugs mean longer, tougher prison sentences. He's not Dwayne, dreaming of prison. Worst though, Jerome knows Issy would dump him if she found out.

The rain is belting it. A deal has been arranged for one hundred pounds worth of crack but the junkies are so wasted and drunk they can't remember where the meeting spot is.

'What the fuck, man! I'm not about to start looking for you in this weather!' Dwayne shouts at them over the phone. 'Where are you now? We're in the park? What can you see? Yeah you can see a fucking tree, you're in the fucking park! What else?'

Halfway through the conversation, the junkie runs out of credit. Dwayne calls back and it seems their battery died. The five boys discuss heading home, having made just twenty pounds between them.

'I make more money working in the butcher,' mumbles Barry. His mother applied on his behalf to a meat market on Rye Lane in Peckham and Barry now does Saturdays there, washing animal blood from surfaces and sweeping up cuts of fat, skin and bones.

'Shut up, man!' Dwayne shouts.

The rain falls harder, preventing them from leaving the shelter of the tree.

Barry quietens down, seeing Dwayne getting angrier by the second. He regrets leaving the house, he should be studying instead of this shit.

Jerome seizes this moment as an opportunity to tell Dwayne he wants Graff to concentrate on music, 'We ain't put a track out for time and the yutes are gonna move on.'

This frustrates Dwayne further. 'What's your problem?' Dwayne kicks the tree. Lightning and thunder rumble and flash – only adding to the drama.

'Maybe I don't wanna shot no more.' Jerome pulls his jacket up close, 'This's shit, fam.'

Jerome looks to his brother, searching for some sense. 'Issy ain't happy with me selling weed as it is. If she finds out I'm even connected to this shit, she'll go mad, trust.'

Dwayne doesn't even let Jerome finish his sentence, 'FUCK WHAT YOUR BITCH SAYS, BRUV!'

Jerome pulls his head back. Dwayne's insult rages through his veins. He stares at Dwayne and then looks at Andre, Barry, and Anton. He won't accept anyone calling Issy a bitch, but he won't undermine his brother in front of Graff. So he storms off into the rain.

Dwayne orders the boys to wait for the junkies, then chases after his brother's silhouette across the dark wet grass. He hears a feeble attempt of a wolf whistle. Over by a street lamp, Dwayne can see the outline of three slender bodies. The curved spines suggest the lost junkies. Looking at the increasingly small dot that is Jerome, Dwayne decides to make the deal and then head home. He doesn't have to tell the others and can pocket the hundred for himself. Done.

As Dwayne walks into the bedroom, Jerome stands up, 'Never, ever, ever, call Issy a bitch in front of the man dem, EVER again! You wanna treat Hayley like shit, that's your choice but don't see Issy like that. She ain't like that.'

Dwayne, not feeling in an argumentative mood, takes off his soaking jacket and hangs in on the radiator, 'Bro, you and me talked about this–'

'No Dwayne, we talked about getting rich, helping Gran have a better life. She put hers on hold, sacrificed it for me and you. But all I'm hearing from you is hype and madness, get me? I'm done. Sitting in the rain for some fucked up bredders ain't what it's about, bruv–' Jerome looks at his brother with pleading eyes, 'I wanna make it, the legit way.'

Dwayne waits for Jerome to quieten down.

'Tell me, seriously, how we gonna get rich? Is Mr White Man gonna give us a nicely paid job?' Dwayne marches out of the bedroom and grabs the newspaper from the living room, 'How many bredders in this photo? Yeah?'

Front page of The Mirror shows a sea of white faces from the city; how bankers here get millions in bonuses instead of being arrested like the bankers did in Iceland.

'This is real life, bro,' Dwayne says, his spit landing on the page. 'Media says we're nothing but violent niggers, so what then?'

'Shotting ain't the only way,' Jerome protests, 'I've seen rich black people, with my own eyes. House fatter than any Cribs.'

'That's just one coconut in a billion, bruv. You knock on every other door, you'll find white people, and don't tell me them white men are legit. Dodging taxes. Hiding money. MPs don't care when black kids sell weed, when my man can expense for his duck house. College kicks me out, yeah? Don't tell me, manz think I'm thick. Well, I ain't, bruv. I've got it all up here.' He knocks his head with his fist.

Jerome flicks through the pages of the paper. A teenager they know has been arrested for rape. He let a twelve year old suck him off, she's as tall as Jerome and lied about her age, plus the guy's got learning difficulties. None of that is mentioned. Just a black face. His age: nineteen. Her age: twelve. The Endz.

'Out of all the bredders you know, you can't name one who ain't poor,' Dwayne continues, his voice strong and unrelenting. 'That's a fucking tragedy. That's the massacre. Just because us black people ain't lying on the streets dead, don't mean this ain't no social genocide ting gwaaning.'

Dwayne spits his words as he points violently up at the ceiling. 'We're rotting in these little cages the council borrows us. Fuck that, bro. I'm getting out. Your' – and Dwayne pauses –'"girlfriend" has got one thing right. Only problem she's going off to white people's school, away from here, away from you...' Dwayne puts his hand on Jerome's shoulder, 'I ain't going anywhere, bruv. I ain't leavin' you. I got you.'

Jerome flings Dwayne's arm from his shoulder: 'Well maybe I don't want you backing it for me no more. I'll go with her. Get a job. Save some money.'

Dwayne lowers his voice and his tone becomes hard and spiteful: 'I swear down on my life she's goes without you.'

Jerome shakes his head.

'You won't stay together.'

'SHUT THE FUCK UP!' Jerome sizes up to Dwayne.

170

'Why shout at me, bruv?' Dwayne sizes up to Jerome. 'I'm your older, you get me?' Dwayne points firmly into Jerome's chest. 'I'm here for you. When your mother left you in dirty nappies, crying, I was there, hugging you. When your father is licking me for shit you did, I took it. You don't know the half of it. And you never will,' Dwayne turns and lifts his jumper revealing the scars across his back.

Jerome's seen the scars. That his father did to Dwayne. He collapses onto his bed, holding his head.

Dwayne's mobile rings, breaking the tension. 'It's Hayley. My yutes want five bags of weed. Teena and dem.'

'Tell them I ain't on it tonight,' Jerome mumbles.

Dwayne locks off the phone and looks at his brother. Not wanting to lose this moment, he softens his tone. 'Guaranteed, the day Issy packs and goes uni, you might as well be watching her walking down the aisle with some white man on her arm.'

'SHUT YOUR MOUTH, BRUV!' Jerome leaps up and pins Dwayne against the wall. 'I DONE TOLD YOU!'

Dwayne smiles. 'But me, we're blood. I make money means we make money.'

'How can you say that?' Jerome lets go. 'How can you be in love and say that?'

Dwayne screws up his face. 'I ain't in love.'

'What about Hayley?'

'What about her?'

'You've got Jamal—'

'Yeah. I got Jamal. That's blood. But Hayley? I've got bigger plans. Come we go?'

Jerome lies back on his bed.

'What?' Dwayne looks down at his brother, slumped. 'You said it yourself. You seen her fam.'

Jerome shakes his head. Making money is his only way out. Weed and downloads. Teena's got fifty pounds. Fifty pounds is a lot of money. Barry has to work eight hours in the shop on a Saturday to get close to that. Still, that's money Barry can't get seized or raided for. He might get ripped for being named Barry, but at the end of the day, his parents want the best for him. They've got his back. If Jerome thinks about things, Issy has his back and so has his grandmother. Dwayne thinks he does, but does he now? Who pressures their little brother into gang wars and selling crack?

Mabel looks out of her bedroom window, at the two silhouettes disappearing into the rainy night. She kneels down before the Bible on her bed, 'Jesus, please save my boys.'

She thinks about searching their bedroom, but, afraid of what she'll find, decides against it. If they have drugs in there then she would be forced to keep a lie. Or tell the police. Ever since Jamal's christening, Mabel's been having disturbed sleep, worried sick Dwayne lied to her about who paid for the reception. She knows Hayley's family would never have booked Caribbean food, or a reggae DJ.

Jerome changes his mind seeing Issy's bedroom light still on. He leaves Dwayne to check Hayley and knocks on Issy's door.

'Where's your mum?'

'Out drinking.'

She's pleased to see him. They keep the lights on because Jerome wants to see Issy's face. He strokes her hair, kisses her neck. It shouldn't be a loaded thing, for black hands to touch white, his hair against her hair but it's bugging him more and more lately.

Jerome hates how shit he didn't ask for keeps finding a way into his head, in his heart, fucking with his peace of mind. What if Jerome knows being with a white girl means something more than just thinking she's fit? Why is she fit? Who taught him that? Why hasn't he got a black girl? He tries to think back to what Toby told him and Max at the party, that racism doesn't exist, it's all about resourcism. Like happiness is the end game, 'resourcism' is the root of all race hate in the world. But it's easy to say that when you're dripping in money and your skin ain't dark.

Issy unbuttons his belt.

'Babe?' Jerome sits up. 'Can we just hang? I'm feeling kinda messed up right about now.'

Issy stops, surprised. She probably thinks he knocked so late for sex.

Without wanting to, Jerome starts to cry. He tries to hold himself together, as a man should, but once it starts he can't stop crying, uncontrollably, collapsing in her arms.

Issy holds him tightly, kissing the back of his neck while rubbing his shoulders. He wishes he had a mum like Carol. A dad like Barry's. He wishes he had a life like George. A music studio and friends who weren't fucked up. He feels trapped by Dwayne's view of the world but he knows there is truth in what Dwayne says. His dad's family told him white people marry white people. Don't get involved with them.

Jerome dries his face with the sleeves of his hoodie.

'What's happened?' Issy says it slowly, like she's scared for what he's about to say.

'Dwayne...'

'Yeah?'

'...said...'

'What'd he say? Babe.'

'When you go uni, it's over. With us.'

'No babe, we won't,' Issy looks Jerome directly into his eyes. 'I promise, on my mum's life. On my dad's grave.'

Jerome wipes the snot falling from his nose with the back of his hand. Embarrassed, he apologises.

'Means you love me.'

She's smiling, with her pretty freckles and no makeup and her green eyes. She is fit.

'I do, man. I proper love you. Wherever you wanna go, I'm there. I feel bad leaving Gran, but it'll only be a few years, right? I've thought about it. I'm gonna save for a deposit while you're studying. Then when you're finished, you can get a job and we'll buy a house with two extra rooms: one for your mum and one for Gran.'

'Well d'ya wanna hear some bad news?' Issy's smile drops. 'I looked at how much it costs to stay in uni flats and there's no way I'm gonna afford it. My sixth form year got that Education Maintenance Allowance cut, and from next year, university fees are nine grand. Nine thousand pounds, per year!'

Issy pauses, 'I can't afford that. I couldn't afford three grand a year, but I figured if I get a good job and everything. Miss Salmon says now a student's debt by the end of the degree is £42,000. It's either I stay here and go uni in London, or I don't go at all.'

Jerome cannot help but show his disappointment; he was hoping Issy would be a way out for him. Start fresh in a fresh place. Leave it all here on these streets.

'You're right,' he says, 'about selling weed.' Jerome omits the crack dealing. 'I wanna stop everything.'

'Babe, you can still stop. You can stop now.'

'I know.' Jerome takes Issy's hand and kisses it. 'I know I can. Just easier if I got away.'

CHAPTER 20
A FIVER

Walking down the street, Hayley has that familiar feeling. A group her age are behind, following her. She looks down at baby Jack-Jamal; his little innocent face smiling up at her. It's getting dark and she should have left Lewisham earlier.

She picks up speed, just two more roads and she'll be back at the care home.

'Oi Hayley, come here!' Teena shouts from behind.

Hayley pretends not to hear. She looks into the houses she passes and wishes she could knock on one of them, beg to be let in, pretend as if they were expecting her.

'Hayley!' Teena shouts again.

This time Hayley turns. Regrets it.

'Told you it was her!'

The gang start after her. Hayley runs with the buggy, hitting a pavement curb but Jack-Jamal doesn't cry.

Hayley feels a lump form in her throat. Not again. Not now she's a mum.

Teena's fast. She grabs Hayley by her hair and pulls her away from the buggy. One of the boys, wearing a grey and white tracksuit, takes it. Jack-Jamal smiles at him, and he smiles back.

'Why you ignoring us?' Teena shouts.

'I wasn't.'

'You was.'

'I was on my phone.' Hayley immediately regrets that.

'Take her phone,' Teena orders the only other girl.

The girl, wearing thick gold hoops and fake eye lashes, digs it out from

Hayley's pocket.

Teena pulls her hair tighter, 'Walk.'

The boy pushes the buggy away. They have her boy, she has to obey.

They go to the nearest house that looks empty.

Teena tries to force Hayley into the front garden but she resists, looking back at Jack-Jamal. She wishes she could fight her way out but she knows she's outnumbered. Two girls and four boys.

Teena tells the biggest boy to hit Hayley. 'And make her get in the garden!'

He shrugs, walks over and belts Hayley so hard that her right ear rings. Hayley starts to cry. She can't see the buggy.

'Don't start,' Teena shouts. She orders Gold Hoops to go in the garden, pulling Hayley with her. They are blocked from sight by a large hedge.

'You first,' says Teena, pointing to a scrawny fifteen year old.

He walks over to Gold Hoops, smiling nervously.

'You go with her,' Teena tells the big one that slapped Hayley, handing Hayley's ponytail across like a lead.

Pushing her onto the grass, he pulls down his tracksuit bottoms and takes out a condom. 'Take them off,' he says.

Hayley can't speak for sobbing. She can hear Jack-Jamal on the other side of the bushes. Finally some words come out, 'Please, let me see my baby?'

'Shut up, man. See him after,' he says, still gripping her hair. The teenager hands Hayley the condom: 'Open it. I ain't catching nuttin.'

Hayley looks over at the other girl, it's dark but she can guess from the way the street lamp reflects on her earrings, she's sucking dick.

Teena picks up Jack-Jamal. She lifts his head over the bushes, 'Don't worry, you'll get him back.'

The teenager that was pushing the buggy screws his face at Teena. Hayley prays he's got a baby sister or niece and it crosses his mind he wouldn't want this to happen to them. Teena hands him back the baby. Jack-Jamal stops crying briefly then starts again. Hayley can only hear her son. Her head is pressed into the dark wet earth of the flower bed. She feels him force his way inside her. The pain sears up from her crotch, and she wants to scream. The first time since having a baby. Tears stream down her face, but not for herself or the burning pain. The sound of her baby crying and being trapped from holding him is worse. She peers up at the purple-grey clouds and prays someone up there keeps her baby safe. That she'll get to be with him soon.

The longest minutes of Hayley's life. He moves up and down, crushing her rib cage; his body odour and the smell of weed releasing from his puffer jacket with each thrust.

Teena sends the next boy to the girl with the gold hoops.

Hayley pleads with her rapist, trying to make eye contact, 'I'm not like that anymore. Let me go see my baby.'

'SHUT UP, MAN!'

He continues to ride her, speeding up, pushing hard into her pelvis. The pain makes Hayley yelp then he cums.

The forth teenager, the one holding Jack-Jamal, is next. Teena tries to take the baby but he swerves, 'Let her see her baby first, what the fuck?'

Teena goes to shout at him, but stops as he hands her the five pound note from his grey and white jogging bottoms. Gold Hoops and her last client exit the garden. The garden is dark but he can see her camel-coloured tracksuit. He hands the baby over. Hayley sobs into Jack-Jamal's coat, ashamed to be touching his purity. The smell of his innocent skin all mixed up with baby lotion. She doesn't want a bit of anyone else's smell to pollute him.

Teena tries to open the gate.

'Oi come out, man,' the male teenager yells.

'I'm getting the baby,' Teena shouts.

'Baby don't know wah gwaan. Move yourself.'

The teenager whispers to Hayley, 'Just pretend we're doing stuff, yeah?' He strokes Hayley's face.

She knows he means well, but his touch makes her feel sick.

CHAPTER 21
DONE

Dwayne is done waiting for drunk, drugged people to turn up in parks. Although the deals are never less than fifty or a hundred, he's making less money than when all the Graff boys were in school selling CDs and blunts.

Dwayne also hates the lack of fear from these junkies. They're at rock bottom; nothing scares them. His threats or anger for not showing up on time simply fall on deaf ears. 'Ah, sorry mate, won't 'appen again, geezer.'

When Dwayne beat one junkie bloody and unconscious, Andre dragged him away before police showed up, but nothing gets investigated with junkies. The hospitals notify the police. The police seen it all before. Nobody so much as whispers Dwayne's gang name, Double-G. He got such a rush from the violence, Dwayne swore he could have killed the next man who walked past.

Jerome found himself that night rocking in the kitchen, like his grandmother. Racking his brain for a way out: the dull thud when that junkie's skull hit the pavement, the gurgle of blood, the cracking of Dwayne's fist breaking the man's jaw.

Dwayne's done. Ronnie warned that the supplier can be "a complete nutcase" and wouldn't appreciate disloyalty. The supplier has been happy to have five black boys working for him, raising his standing in Deptford, enjoying the cut from hard-working Dwayne. He pats Dwayne on the back and calls him "a good lad". Dwayne hates it, but he appreciates the free wraps snuck into his hand when he shakes it goodbye, promising big deals in clubs once Dwayne and the boys earn their stripes and a trip to meet the big boss in Hampshire when the time's right.

Dwayne and Jerome are in Deptford, dropping off this week's cash but they arrive to find the flat boarded up.

A neighbour leans over the main balcony and hulks a huge phlegm from his throat, spitting it onto the communal grass below. 'He got shopped in,' he says. 'Arrested. Refused bail.' He takes a gulp of super strength beer. His clothes are filthy and every so often, Jerome and Dwayne get a waft of cat piss from the inside of his flat. 'He ain't coming back.'

Jerome looks up to the sky and thanks whoever did this. Dwayne looks at the police-bashed door, then casts around the balcony: dog shit and broken toys and dead plants.

'He's looking at a minimum five years,' the neighbour continues. 'Plus, police bagged up a gun. He's fucked. You two better stay away. Probably on hidden camera already.'

They pull their hoods up instinctively and jog down the stairwell.

'What grown man, clearing two grand a week is living in a one-bedroom council flat in Deptford?' Jerome starts.

'This is what I'm saying, bruv. It's all bullshit.' Dwayne carries on, talking about going back to selling singular joints. How this was a good business model and compares it to the success of pound shops. 'Just need to put some real effort into getting youngers on it.'

'Shall we go check Hayley and Jamal?' Jerome asks. 'I ain't seen Jamal in time.'

Dwayne lights a cigarette. 'She's sucking next man's tings for money.'

Jerome looks at Dwayne, 'Who told you that?'

'I've got people inna that care place done told me the yute's not mine.'

Jerome scratches his head. 'Hays wouldn't cheat. She's on you, bruv. Nah, that's some mixup madness.'

'Trust, she's lucky I'm not on a hype ting at the moment. Otherwise, I won't feel a way to slap her up. Some next level disrespect.'

Jerome pats Dwayne on the back, 'If that's the case, get a test. Make sure Jamal's yours. Don't believe the hype.'

'Yeah, you done know,' Dwayne replies, holding out his fist for Jerome to knock in acknowledgement. 'So boy, I'm feeling West End. This cash is burning a hole in man's pocket. I say we go Trocs and rinse up the place.'

Jerome smiles at the idea. It's been a long time since the brothers were at the gaming arcade in Piccadilly Circus. 'I'm feeling that, still.'

When Dwayne is calm and happy, it's like the whole world is at peace. Life is good. Smooth. Chill. Jerome feels settled. He's happier when his day isn't focused on making Dwayne money or status. Issy's been talking to him about her sociology work. Mrs Salmon is teaching about the bell curve of delinquency and how this is all an age ting and it's gonna be over when Dwayne hits twenty-one. Jerome hopes Dwayne's coming through it. Not that Jerome can see his brother working in a supermarket or wearing a suit up London, but he'd be happy when his Dwayne's grown out of fighting other people. Issy says, one factor is having a baby, apparently it helps teenagers take life more seriously, like they want more for their kids so stop the madness. Sooner a paternity test is done, the better. Jerome knows that.

CHAPTER 22
PATHWAYS

Steve at the youth club has organised a jobs fair for 15 to 19 year olds, inviting everyone who hasn't been to the club for a while. The numbers at the club have dropped, and with deeper Government cuts, the youth centre is at risk of closure.

Dwayne refuses to go because he's 'a bigger man than that, still' so Jerome swings by Issy's house. 'There will be a UCAS expert for those worried about the tripling of university fees,' Jerome says, reading the flyer out. 'Plus lots of local companies looking to employ young people.'

'Shall we invite Hayley?'

Hit by a sense of nostalgia, Issy texts Hayley and adds a smiley face and kisses but Hayley doesn't reply.

'Perhaps she ain't got credit?' Jerome offers, dialling her number.

'Who dis?' a screechy voice demands.

'Hays?'

'Dis ain't Hayley.' The phone hangs up.

Puzzled, Issy tries again, but the call is rejected. Issy thinks about Emily, who may be interested in seeing how it is. Issy and Emily haven't seen each other for weeks. Emily is busy with new tap dancing classes, plus Maths tuition, and has also taken up tennis on a Friday afternoon; Janie Sutton making sure her daughter has no time to get involved with local teenagers. Emily texts back, 'Love to. Can I bring Merle?'

Issy waits outside for Jerome to pop home for a jacket. She notices some of the buds on the tree blossoming, and from some of the blossom fresh leaves are shooting. Things are changing.

'Hello everyone!' Steve calls out in his friendly Bristolian accent to a small crowd of around a dozen teenagers. 'Firstly, thank you so much for being here today. It's good to see some old faces. The reason I contacted you all is because you are at the age now where you will be looking for jobs or thinking about further education. Please make use of the experts who have given up their time to speak with you about the kinds of opportunities they have for young people, in their schools, colleges, companies and universities. A conversation you have today might change the course of your life. No joke. So please make use of this opportunity. And, hey, stick around; we've got pizza coming!'

Jerome, Anton and Barry continue playing pool. Issy is showing Emily and Merle around. The youth club still has photos up from a trip she went on when she was thirteen years old.

'Shame, look at my hair, man!' Issy exclaims, before turning red, realising she is speaking 'street' in front of Emily and Merle.

Emily laughs out loud. 'You look so different. Look at all those ribbons.'

'That was the fashion in those days,' Issy replies, trying to curb her South East London accent.

Looking at the photos, she realises that Hayley is next to her in all of them. She smiles as she remembers them wearing each other's trainers and swapping tracksuit bottoms and tops. She looks down at her outfit today, skinny jeans and flat shoes with a printed t-shirt and matching cardigan – a far cry from the tracksuits and braided hair full of coloured rubber bands and ribbons. Issy hasn't put gel into her hair for ages and, although she straightened it today, she mostly ties it up and rushes out the door. She looks at her companions: Merle's wearing the latest boots and spring coat. Issy saw them both in the TopShop window in Bromley. She even tried the coat on, but then looked at the price tag: pure wool and a hundred pounds. Carol could only budget for thirty.

'Shall we go see the UCAS stall?' Issy says, feeling low. The coat looks so good on Merle.

'Issy, do you have a cigarette?' Emily asks. 'For her?'

Merle is silent. She smiles briefly before looking at the floor.

'You don't have to be scared, you know. I don't bite,' Issy says with a hint of sarcasm. 'Mimi, I've got good news. I quit, like three days ago.'

'Oh, well done!' Emily hugs Issy excitedly. 'That's amazing news! I've got some news, too.' Emily's cheeks blush and she takes a moment.

'Don't tell me, Henry finally asked you out?'

Emily nods and the two girls shriek and giggle and hug. 'That's why I haven't seen you for ages. Friday afternoon is still my only parent free time and Henry's been coming most weeks now. We play tennis. Apparently!'

'No way! So he finally stepped up!' Issy hugs Emily again pretending not to care the girls snubbed all the jobs on offer. 'I'm so happy for you, babe. So how long? Did he ask you out, like properly? What did he say? When did it all happen? Tell me everything!'

'Okay!' Emily takes Issy and Merle over to a nearby bench.

Steve comes over to the pool players, 'The stalls will be packing up if nobody visits them. Come and make use of the experts and employers while they're here!'

Jerome starts talking to a man from a bank, 'But why did they get bonuses and tax payer bailouts for fucking the economy but marijuana, proven to be medicinal, is illegal in the UK but could bring in taxes?' The banker, looking confused, replies, 'Well drug legalisation is not really my field.'

'Basically, I ain't gonna lie. I'm in a family business,' Anton tells a lady from a Southwark college, 'We sell plant-based produce. Home grown, organic, get me.'

Steve shakes his head.

So Henry started at my school. There was all this confusion about him starting there or not and then he walks in one day. He's taking English and RE like me so we started hanging out. At first I ignored him, having decided, like ages ago, that my little obsession with Henry Sparling had to end. I visited his house in Bath and he wasn't there. His parents were awful; nothing like how I remembered them growing up. Anyway, Henry texted me to apologise for his absence. He said he missed me. I ignored all of his messages.'

'I remember!' Merle exclaims.

'Me too,' Issy replies, guarded, jealous even. Not wanting to be a bitch, Issy smiles at Merle.

'So I tried to not like him anymore.' Emily dramatically frowns and pokes out her bottom lip. 'But when he arrived at the school and sat next to me, it was pretty tricky not to speak to him. He blew kisses at me, like every day, and I did try to ignore him, but he kept doing it and eventually...' Emily hugs her arms around her body. 'One afternoon he grabbed my arm in the corridor and demanded to know why I was being so cold; "Where's the Emily Sutton I know?" I replied, "She's had enough chasing timewasters," and walked off.'

'Wow, go Mimi!' Issy high fives Emily.

'I basically took your advice. If he wanted me, he should make it clear, and if I had any respect for myself, then I wouldn't let someone use me like that.'

'So how did it go from there to now?' Issy asks, eager to hear the happy ending despite coming to see the UCAS woman.

Emily grins, 'Well this is the good bit. He calls his father to speak to my father to ask if he can formally ask me to dinner. My father knocks on my bedroom door with a smile on his face, a rare sight. He told me I am to have dinner with Henry the following evening. My father drove me to Mayfair. And there Henry was, wearing an amazing suit and carrying the biggest bunch of flowers I've ever seen. It was sooooooooooo romantic!' Emily squeals delightedly. Merle and Issy squeal in reply.

'Girls,' Steve calls out, 'Stalls packing up in five.'

'Yeah, coming!' Issy calls back. She feels knotted with anxiety. 'Shall we go see the stalls?'

'There's nothing really appealing,' Emily says.

'Agreed,' says Merle.

Issy nods though inside she knows she's letting herself down by not speaking with the professionals come to share opportunities with them.

'So did your dad eat with you?' Issy asks, trying to hide her disappointment. She wants to get up and speak to the lady at the University of Greenwich stall who keeps smiling her way.

'That's the best bit,' Emily says, 'Dad kind of handed me over after shaking Henry's hand. It was so embarrassing. People going in were smiling at us, women were squeezing their husbands' arms, saying "ahh".'

'That's so cool!' Merle beams.

Issy looks at Emily and wonders if she's finally had sex. She looks more grownup, and saying "like" a lot too, and generally more outgoing and confident since she last saw her.

'So like my dad gave Henry some money and said, "Ensure Emily is home safely and put her in a taxi." No time limit. Nothing. Henry said it was a test and so made sure I was back before midnight. Anyway, he told me how he'd always liked me and that he was sorry for acting like a buffoon–'

'Then he told you that his moodiness was really that he was intimidated by you,' Merle added.

Issy looks at Merle. 'You heard this already?'

'Mum and her dad do yoga classes together,' Emily says, maybe implying their friendship is not a hundred per cent her own choice.

'You live round here?' Issy asks.

Merle nods shyly at Issy, still apparently intimidated.

Issy works things out in her head. She knows Emily's mum is a snob and doesn't want Emily hanging with the local kids, but Merle's local too...

'Anyway, it's been like amazing,' Emily carries on. 'Henry posted that we're in a relationship on his Facebook. He's puts loads of photos of us up on his Insta, he's inviting me everywhere and comes round on the weekends; which has made Dad like so happy you won't believe...'

Later on, Steve calls everyone for the pizza as advertised. The younger kids come in from football to make up numbers after a poor, post-sixteen turnout for the event. The children and teenagers gather round the pizza boxes frantically trying to grab a slice before it runs out. Issy smirks at the twelve or thirteen year old girls pretending not to want to eat anything around the boys. She notices the younger boys looking at the food then up at Jerome, with Anton telling them, 'Oi, move man! Bigger manz eat first! And wash your dutty hands!'

Issy wants to laugh but she promised herself she won't talk to Anton after what he did to the woman at the riots. Issy is conscious again that, like the tree, she is changing. Growing up. Or that she has grown up. She remembers when she first came to the club Hayley took her under her wing, made sure she was accepted with no fuss or bullying. Back then, Hayley's brother Ronnie and his friends were the bigger boys.

Steve jumps onto the sideboard and shouts: 'I've got some really good news. Now I know some of you may have forgotten this but about two years ago we began plans for a music studio. We did a questionnaire with some of you and your number one suggestion was studio space to make beats. I took those comments to the youth service but, as you know, we've been hit by a string of funding cuts. Well, I kept your comments and put in a few more applications and I'm more than pleased to announce we've been given external funding to develop our music studio and will start offering courses on music production in the summer holidays!'

'Braaaap!' Anton shouts. 'Yes G!'

'So come June, we'll be kitting the club out with the latest music technology.'

'Steve, you are a don,' Jerome shouts. 'Trust.'

After the announcement, Steve approaches Jerome and shakes his hand warmly, 'I'm gonna need some help with picking what to buy.'

'I am on that, trust.'

'We've been given about six thousand pounds.'

'Six large!' Jerome licks his lips and claps his hands. 'Oh my days, Steve, that is some nice, nice chunk of change.'

'Happy you're happy. It took longer than I'd hoped. I know you lot asked for this a while back.'

'Better late than never,' Jerome knocks fists with Steve then changes tone: 'Studio's free entry though, yeah? Gold member discount, get me.'

Steve laughs and pats Jerome on the shoulder, 'We've missed you here, you know that, Jerome?'

Jerome smiles, awkwardly. The man dem used to be in club every week without fail. They started attending as children; pizza, pool and table tennis tournaments, trips to the seaside, film nights making popcorn and turning the lights off - that's when he first put his arm around Issy. Jerome blinks back into the present, 'Yeah, I know. Good times, still.'

'It's okay. I know you young people grow up and move on. So, what you up to these days?'

'At college, innit. Doing music.'

'Great stuff! Listen, part of the funding application asks how we are involving the young people in our work. We explained that we want to invite some of the older members to train to be mentors.'

Jerome looks at Steve nervously, not sure what he is hearing.

'I've always admired how you hold yourself,' Steve continues. 'You've got great listening skills. You're mature. You keep the younger people here in check and they all respect you. So I'm asking you to apply. If you can. If his application is successful, Jerome can start at the end of the month.'

Jerome's heart tightens in his chest as Steve continues to praise him. 'I would like to train you up to eventually become a youth worker.'

'Wow!' Jerome exhales in shock, 'Yes, fam. That is some nice, nice news.'

'Great!' Steve smiles, 'Part of the reason we won the money is because I've attached this apprenticeship programme to it. I want to train up future youth workers who can get the kids making music and away from crime, fights, skipping school... You know what I mean, right?'

'Yeah, I do,' Jerome bites his bottom lip, thinking of the weed currently stuffed down his left sock.

'I think you would make a fantastic youth worker. Always have. So you'll definitely apply, right?'

Jerome takes a moment. He has his own music to make, he's already skipped a few college classes himself, then there's the weed...

'You'll be paid,' Steve says. 'It's a paid apprenticeship.'

'Like real cash, not no vouchers or tuckshop credit; shit like that?'

Steve laughs. 'Paid as in cash, money; money in the bank.'

'Boy, where do I sign?'

CHAPTER 23
DON'T KNOW JACK

Issy sits in the kitchen, looking at the biscuit tin. It's never empty anymore. The creamy bits still between the biscuits. She chuckles to herself. She would get so mad with Hayley, who always denied putting the creamless custard creams back in, even though Issy saw her!

Stirring the teabag around the cup, she recalls how Hayley helped her when she first moved to the estate. How Hayley made her laugh and would shoplift presents for her. Back then, Issy hadn't known they were stolen; she thought Hayley was rich, and loved her for being so nice. Then Hayley told her one time when they were mashed that she stole each and every one of them from WH Smith and Savers.

She thinks about how it's all gone wrong. Dwayne stopped seeing the baby because rumours say Jamal isn't really his - that Hayley's been giving boys lineups for money. Issy shouldn't have, but she told Jerome what Hayley said about Dwayne wanting to do anal sex so she can't get pregnant again. That was the last time Issy saw Hayley. Hayley told her it's so painful down she cries but he doesn't stop. Issy told Hayley it's rape. When she confronted Jerome, Jerome said it can't be true - Dwayne hates all things 'batty', then he got upset Issy would even repeat it. Then Issy got upset that Hayley would make up lies to cover up her own behaviour. Issy squeezes the teabag with frustration. It bursts in the cup. As she puts the teabag in the bin, she notices a glass bottle. Vodka. Issy sighs. Carol's drinking heavy again.

Issy sits back down at the kitchen table with a fresh brew. Why do people do the things that they do? She knows her mum drinks to stop herself feeling lonely, goes through bad patches around her husband's death or birthday or their anniversary. Hayley fights because she's spent her childhood being beaten up. She's had to shoplift in the past to get new clothes and dinner when there's nothing in the house. Issy thinks about how she judges Hayley, but really, she herself has similar problems. Everyone does. Even Emily, who hardly gets any time to herself with all the expectations put on her, is often sick with colds and feeling run down and can't eat for feeling stressed.

Issy looks in on her mother as she grabs a fresh towel from the cupboard in the landing. Carol is fast asleep, still in her dress from the night before, hair stuck to her forehead, mascara all over her cheeks. She's been crying. Probably cried herself to sleep. Issy puts a blanket over Carol, before closing the door and stepping into the shower.

On the bus towards the hostel Issy is again watching people. She remembers the same journey months ago when she had the feeling she's in control of life; she can press STOP whenever she likes and change the journey. She should tell Hayley about this. She remembers how she used to spend every day with Hayley before they drifted apart. How meeting Emily made Hayley look so cheap, so rude; nothing Issy wanted to be. But at the youth club, Issy felt discriminated against. Why is Merle allowed to be Emily's friend? Because Emily's mother judges Issy, just as Issy judges Hayley.

She arrives to find that Hayley has been moved to a secure unit for young mothers. The staff won't give Issy the address as they're not allowed to give out private information. Teena walks past and starts chipping in, distracting the support worker from her job.

'I know where Hayley's gone!'

'Teena, please go back to the common room.'

'She's at Francis Street. It's like five minutes from here.'

'Teena, enough! Or you'll lose behaviour points.'

'So fucking what?'

'You'll miss your Happy Healthy Chart targets and you won't go–'

'Why you fucking threatening me? Do you think I give a shit?'

'Stop swearing!' the exasperated support worker demands.

Teena walks off, 'Stupid Nigerian bitch!'

'I heard that.'

'Goo-od!' screeches Teena, 'Issy-busy!! I'll text ya the address. And code to get in.'

Issy's back at the bus stop when she receives a text message, but this time it's from Hayley who has sent her the address.

A woman with kind eyes buzzes Issy in. She takes a seat. A few moments later, a plump, heavy-footed Hayley waddles down the corridor with baby Jamal.

'Hayley!' Issy smiles, as she gets up from the waiting room chair.

Hayley looks at Issy blankly. 'Yeah? What?'

'I got your text.'

'I didn't text no-one.'

Issy looks down at her mobile phone, perplexed, 'But I got—'

'Teena robbed my fucking phone.' Hayley looks over to the kind-looking woman. 'Excuse my French, Irene.'

'You're okay, my lovely. Do you want keys to the chillout area?'

Issy smiles. It sounds funny hearing the words "chill out" coming from such an old person.

Hayley shrugs and takes the keys.

'I'll make you both a pot of tea if you like?'

'Don't bother yourself—' Hayley begins.

'No, no, it's fine, my lovely.' Irene heads towards a small kitchenette.

Inside the chillout area, Issy gets a shiver from the coolness of the faux-leather couch. She watches Hayley rock baby Jamal.

'How's Jamal?' Issy asks.

'Jack.'

'What?'

'I've changed his name to Jack.'

'Does Dwayne-'

'Fuck Dwayne. He's seen his son once this year. Still, that's more than you, ain't it?'

Issy searches for words to defend herself but knows she can't.

'What's the matter? Cat got your tongue?'

Hayley looks so different. She's aged. Her breasts are bigger. Her hips are wider. She has grown about two dress sizes since the christening. Her hair is tied up in a high ponytail. It looks greasy and un-brushed.

'I'm sorry, Hays. I've been a shit friend lately.'

'Lately? Lately? Try fucking forever. What did I do to you? Three weeks ago I got my head kicked in by Teena and her fucking slag bitches. They robbed my chains, my gold clown Dwayne got me, my rings, my earrings, my new phone, everything. They even got one dickhead to piss on Jack's toys in my room. And where were you, eh? Where was Graff? My peeps, yeah?'

'I didn't know.'

'Of course you didn't know. You don't call, come round, nothing!' Hayley rocks Jack as he begins to whimper in her arms. She wipes away her tears, 'No-one came to help. No-one—' her voice cracks with pain. 'Not even my own fucking mother.'

Irene comes in with a tray of tea and biscuits, 'Here you go, my lovelies.' Sensing the atmosphere, Irene strokes the baby's cheek, 'An old friend come to visit?'

'Yep, you could say that.' Hayley stares at Issy, hurt bleeds back to anger.

'Should I stay?'

'No, you're all right, Irene, thanks though.'

'Well, I'll leave you to it. Call if you need anything, alright, love?'

'She seems nice–' Issy begins.

'Yeah because she is!' Hayley snaps. 'Irene's the safest person I know. She don't even get paid for it.'

Issy begins to well up, 'I came because I missed you, Hays. I was thinking about all our fun times, and I wanted to see–'

'Funny, cos I've been thinking about all the fucking shit times. How I've spent two years practically by myself, trapped in a shithole bedroom next to bitches who'd steal your soul if they could get it out of ya. How my baby's doubled in size and no cunt cares. How every time I texted you, you ignored me, or gave me some shit excuse, like you got coursework.'

'I have coursework. I've been doing mocks–'

But Hayley continues her tirade, 'Yeah, but you still find time to go parties with that posh bitch. Don't think I don't know. Dwayne telling me Jerome's shotting coke to mini millionaires… Yeah, I know. Jerome slipped up a few times when I asked about you and I pretended to your mum I knew when she told me how you go every Friday to that slag's house.'

Issy finds herself angry inside. Why should she be attacked for wanting other friends, having a different life, doing things that don't include Hayley? If Hayley was a true friend, she would want the best for her. 'I didn't come here to take this,' she blurts out, and begins to get up.

'Well take it. You call yourself a godmother?'

'I never asked to be!'

'You sat in church, yeah? Holding him, yeah!'

'You forced me! I can say STOP if I want. I can spend my time with other people, I can. YOU.' Issy points down at Hayley. 'You've got a good memory, ain't ya? How many times I would say, don't shoplift. Don't pick fights. Don't start madnesses. Don't slag people off online. Don't fuck without a condom. Stop bunking school.'

Issy feels every bit of sympathy for Hayley disappear as she remembers all the things she hated about being tied to this girl, the imprisonment of their friendship. 'Maybe you get what you deserve. Maybe no-one wants to be around you because they want a better life. Because you're gonna end up sucking everyone's cock while taking it out on him.' Issy points at the baby.

Hayley moves Jack aside and leaps up, pushing Issy into the sideboard behind her, knocking over the white Ikea lamp. Issy pushes Hayley off but Hayley grabs Issy's hair, pulling it down towards the floor, forcing Issy to bend her neck back. Issy struggles desperately to claw Hayley's hands off her ponytail, but feels a knee dig into her left thigh. They both collapse to the floor as Issy curls up protecting her face from Hayley who starts kicking her in the back ribs. Baby Jack rolls off the sofa and lands with a thump on the carpet, and starts crying hysterically.

Irene rushes in. She blows her whistle loudly next to Hayley's red-flushed face. Hayley immediately places both hands over her ears. Irene picks up the baby and presses the emergency button on her keyring. Two staff members arrive to restrain Hayley, spitting fury at her former friend, 'Fucking bitch. SELFISH FUCKING BITCH!'

As soon as Hayley is safely cordoned on the opposite side of the room, Issy rushes out in tears. The staff call after her, but Issy buzzes herself out of a fire alarmed door and runs across the street, then down an alleyway into a nearby estate. She hides behind a bush for a few moments before a man opens his door to see if she's okay. She can't reply, just buries her head in her knees and sobs.

CHAPTER 24
HARD UP DAYS

'Friends often grow apart,' Mrs Salmon says. 'We change throughout life and need different things from people. Especially teenage years, there's so much change. Not many people remain best friends with the people they were best friends with in school. We keep changing and expect everyone close to us to move with us, but it's not the case. It's difficult to grow together.'

Issy looks at the teacher fiddling with her engagement ring.

'My dad, Miss... He met my mum at school. They got together from fifteen.'

Mrs Salmon looks up, 'Wow, and you hardly mention your dad.'

'He died. Cancer.'

Mrs Salmon nods, 'I'm sorry.'

'It's not your fault is it? He drank, Miss. Loads. I quit smoking you know. It's been ages now.'

'That's great news!' Mrs Salmon looks at the scratches on Issy's face, 'I'm sorry about what Hayley did to you. Hope you're not too angry about it.'

'I ain't. She's the real victim, if you think about it.'

Mrs Salmon wishes she could wave a magic wand to gift her a new life, a new home and a guaranteed place at university. These should be basic things a wealthy nation can offer people, and yet the fifth largest global economy has raised university fees to over nine thousand pounds a year and thinks this is acceptable policy. Countries like Germany, Netherlands, Scandanavia, even Scotland seem to be able to educate their teenagers. She thinks about the cutting of housing benefit for under twenty-fives, how people like Issy would thrive living independently. The talent and the ability that young people like Issy and Jerome have. Imagine if society catered for this, built youth accommodation where young people could live for peppercorn rent and have access to a shared hub with free workshops and seminars and be around other talented young people. The provision for people like Hayley is too little too late. Mrs Salmon puts her thoughts aside.

'Do you want some good news?' she says, with a smile, 'I've seen your mock results. We've been talking in the staff room about how well you're doing.'

Issy sits up.

'If you carry on dedicating yourself to school, as you have been, you could end up going to any university you choose, even Oxford.'

'Really?'

'Yep. Your mocks have all been Cs and Bs.'

'Is that all?' She slumps back in her chair.

'I've looked at the breakdown. The Cs are really high and the Bs are climbing. You could build on this. By the end of next year, you could end up with three to four As and Bs.'

Issy shakes her head in disbelief, 'Miss, it wasn't even two years ago I hated school. Me and Hayley would bunk off. I didn't even care what GCSEs I got.'

'I know. That's why the school is so proud of you. That's why I'm proud of you.' Her eyes prick with tears. She blinks the emotion away and clears her throat. 'So have you thought about where you'll go?'

'I'm probably not going, Miss. I can't afford it. It's so much debt, it makes me feel sick. I hate owing people a fiver.'

'But the Head spoke to you, right?'

'Yeah.'

'And I thought you wanted to get away from the gangs and the area?'

'I do, but I've looked at how much it's gonna cost and it's way too expensive.' Issy looks up at the clock. 'Oh shit! Sorry, Miss, gotta go meet Mum in Lewisham. We're going bowling tonight!'

Mrs Salmon watches Issy rush out the door.

As Issy arrives at her flat, she sees a note stuck to the fridge door, **Bowling canciled, sorry luv. Got 2 work. luv u mum xx.**

Deciding not to stay in and study, Issy takes a walk to the park. On her way out, she notices the leaves on the tree outside her flats have matured to a deep purple. She stands for a while and watches them holding strong against the wind.

Instead of the Upper Park, Issy decides to sit in the Lower Park near the bottom gate. Graff hardly went there because it's full of babies and toddlers on the swings and the slides. They once got reported by some parents and a PCSO came over and told them to leave.

Lying back into the sunshine, she thinks about how the trees live their lives. They outlive humans by hundreds of years. How some are deep in forests and have never been seen by human eyes. How others are cut to make cheap furniture, like her kitchen table and chairs. She thinks about Emily's kitchen table. How it's been hand-carved and how the man who made it is dead, but his great-grandchildren are somewhere still alive and probably don't know that it was their great-grandfather who made the table in Emily's house. Is that leaving a legacy?

She sits up, hugging her knees to her chest and glances around. The people in the park, they're so different to her and her mum. They look different. They talk different. They dress different. The mothers have this expression on their faces; they look happy and healthy. Whether black, white, Asian, they have this fashion, like hippy clothes, sensible shoes, carrying their babies in long bits of cloth zig-zagged across their bodies. None of them seem to wear much makeup or dye their grey hair.

Issy watches the families play. How the parents speak to their children; they never really shout or get angry. She sees fathers holding babies, one taking out slices of green apple from yellow coloured airtight containers.

Issy tries to hear what some of them are talking about. She pretends to look for a sunnier spot and sits near the group of parents. Eavesdropping on their talk of nurseries, house prices, food and wine…

They talk about growing herbs in the garden. About organic food and that buying organic onions or oranges is probably not worth the money. They discuss whether barbecuing is safe given the World Health Organisation talking carcinogens. About the health problems that their parents are encountering. One man brings up university fees trebling and how he thinks it is worth setting up trust funds for their babies like parents do in America, most graduates there have six-figure debts and buy insurance against the interest rates. His American cousin just bought options to ensure her student debt interest won't go above six per cent. 'It's shocking,' he says, 'absolutely shocking. My parents both got grants and got paid to go, as did I.'

Issy looks at the man. He is slender with large bags under light blue eyes. He drinks the red wine faster than everyone else and spills some on his faded navy-blue t-shirt. His wife looks at him with a worried expression, almost embarrassed by him. She gestures for him to slow down a bit. He's wearing clumpy walking shoes made out of grey fabric and his wife has the same ones in beige. He looks at his empty glass, then at his wife, then pours a fresh one anyway.

Issy looks on as one of the couples leaves to put their baby to bed. They all get up to say goodbye and kiss cheeks. The men shake hands then hug.

Issy imagines Graff all getting up to shake hands goodbye. She giggles at the image of Andre and Jerome pecking each other on the cheek. The couples look over at her, but she has one of her headphones in, pretending to be listening to something on her phone.

The four parents sit back down and start discussing the absent couple's choice not to 'demand feed' but to stick to a strict feeding regime. The technical details of bringing up babies loses Issy's attention. She daydreams about her own life. As she watches the leaves sway above her in the breeze, she imagines what it could be like going to university. She smiles at the idea of making new friends. The Head Teacher spoke to the sixth formers about their choices now fees have trebled. One girl cried her eyes out, said her parents can't afford it and told her not to take on such debt, better to get a job and work your way up. The Head told everyone that loans are available and students only start paying them back when they get a job above twenty-one thousand pounds. Her mum doesn't make that much, so Issy's wondering if it's a gamble worth taking. If she can't get a good job, she doesn't have to pay it back and if she does get a good job, she can afford to pay it back. The thing that really cheered her up is that whatever happens, the debt gets cancelled after thirty years.

How great it would be to study away from London, but then looking around this beautiful park, Issy sees how nice it could be to stay close to home. How nice it would be for Jerome and her to move into one of the big houses that line the park. Posh people are moving here all the time, so it can't be that much of a shithole. You just have to get through the teenage years and all that peer pressure shit then you're free. Apart from Anton's dad who sells weed, none of the parents are gangsters or in a gang. The thought of slipping back into C and D grades forces Issy to head home to revise.

Mrs Salmon nestles under her husband's arm, resting her head on his chest, and listens to his heart beating. Jacob feels something trickle down his rib cage, 'Hey, what's wrong?'

She sits up to compose herself. Wiping her eyes with a tissue.

'I just sometimes wish I could fix things for these kids, you know? They have it so tough.'

Jacob stokes his wife's hair, 'You mean, Issy?'

'Not just her, so many of them. Their problems just snowball. Poverty, violence, drugs, gangs, sexual abuse, mental abuse. For some, getting to school in clean clothes is the daily struggle.'

She blows her nose. 'Sometimes, I look at them all and just want to magic the bad stuff away.' Her voice breaks and despite her best efforts, she returns to tears.

'Oh darling, come here.' Jacob places his arms around his wife and rocks her gently.

'I can't cope with it all, Jake. Why do these children have to have it so tough?'

'Hey, there's nothing wrong with having it tough. We all have it tough.'

'We don't all have it tough, that's the problem. And they're too young to have it tough. They did nothing to deserve having it tough.'

'You had it tough when you were young... hey?' Jacob lifts her chin. 'Now look at you.'

'Yeah, but I look around and think, where are all my school friends? Still on housing estates in Salford, that's where. No jobs. No qualifications. Lifts broken, corridors stink of beer or piss, or both.' She blots her eyes furiously as her voice becomes angrier, 'We're supposed to be a developed nation, Jacob. What a joke. London – a global capital while half the boys in my class can't spell four-lettered words? How?' She throws the tissue at the bin and misses, then watches it tumble under the wardrobe. 'I can't work it out in my head. I can't. It's like society wants this. We want kids to fail. We want them to go to prison, to live in poverty. Don't we?'

Jacob rubs his forehead. It's been a long week for him, and the sheets are clean. He feels fresh in his cotton vest and boxers after a long soak in the bath and was looking forward to the end of his novel.

'I just want to help her.'

'Who?' he asks tiredly

'Issy. I want to pay for her to get away from her estate. She can do it. She just needs support.'

Jacob looks at his wife, unsure how to respond.

Mrs Salmon stares at the wardrobes opposite their bed, 'She'll need about three grand a year for accommodation. I could do that,' she nods. 'I could private tutor on the weekends or in the evenings.'

'She's not your responsibility.' Jacob forcefully rearranges his pillow, 'She has a mother. She has a father–'

'Her father's dead.'

'My father's dead.'

'Your father left you all a share of a house! I know what it's like to have a pisshead for a parent, how insecure it makes the future feel, how scared you get, wondering if they are passed out or...' She takes another tissue to blow her nose again. 'You know the other teachers in my department love to blame parents on the estates for poor grades. Because the parents lie, because they cheat or steal, because they're on benefits, they all say it. But Issy's mum works full-time. She comes to parents' evenings and I see how she struggles to grasp the education system.' Mrs Salmon turns to face her husband, 'Since the riots, Issy's really changed. She didn't get involved when her friends did so she cut them off. Now she's struggling to find herself. She was going to find a job as a receptionist at a dentist or doctor surgery. That was her highest ambition. She didn't even know she could go to university. The thought hadn't crossed her mother's mind.'

'Why are you saying all of this?' Jacob asks brusquely, trying to get to the root of his wife's issues.

'Can't you see?' she snaps back. 'Wasted opportunities. Wasted potential. These parents have low ambition. They unwittingly pass it onto their children. Even the ones that work and pay their way. Cycles. Circles. Poverty and low attainment, just keeps growing and growing with each new life.'

'Exactly!' Jacob says, frustrated. He sits up properly to face his wife. 'I understand everything you say. I get it. I do. But what happens next year when another Issy enters your classroom? Or two? Or three? There aren't enough evenings and weekends for you to pay for them all to go to university.'

He takes a deep breath and slows down, 'Then what happens to our children when we have them? Hey?' He kisses his wife's forehead, 'When they grow up and need their fees paid?' A thought hits him. 'You haven't promised to pay her accommodation already, have you?'

'No.' She looks at her husband and sighs. 'I just thought about it on the way home.'

Jacob breathes out in relief and wonders if he should hide the credit cards. He wraps her in his arms. 'I admire you so much for even thinking this way. You're already there, helping her, and that's enough, really it is. Just one afternoon spent writing the UCAS forms will change that girl's life forever.'

Jacob sees sadness still in her eyes. 'Maybe we could buy her a laptop,' he continues. 'Or look for scholarships. But, honey, you can't invest tens of thousands of pounds you haven't got into a girl you hardly know.'

She turns to her side, pulling herself out of his arms, and placing the damp tissues on her bedside table. 'Just wish I had the power to make things better.'

'Oh darling, this is her struggle, not yours. The journey is what counts. Think how proud she'll be when she realises she's done it all by herself. Don't take that away from her. It's a gift, really. Look at my cousins – never lifted a finger their entire lives and depressed as hell. Remember what my father used to say?' Jacob reaches over and turns out her bedside light.

'Yes,' Mrs Salmon whispers into the darkness. 'Your hard-up days are your happiest.'

CHAPTER 25

Issy hasn't seen or spoken to Hayley since their fight and now Emily is dating Henry, she only sees her when Henry is away doing something like his army cadets. Jerome started his youth worker training sessions three times a week, from six until nine in the evening. Issy really misses him, but if she's being honest, finds it much easier than last year to stay focused on schoolwork.

Back in March, Emily bought Issy a wall planner and has been giving her photocopied examples of perfect exam answers and essays. The thought of getting Cs and Ds again spurs Issy on, even on the days when Jerome sends text messages inviting her to his raves or to smoke weed in the park – she doesn't like being lean and mashed anymore.

She got the job working in her local pharmacy – her mum sorted it out: a Saturday position came up mid-May and Carol's friend rang to see if Issy still wanted it. The timing could not have been better. Emily had been depressing Issy about buying lots of books at university, with some costing thirty pounds each. The price of going to university is enormous, and Issy feels sick whenever she thinks about it. When it all mounts up she tries to stay calm, sitting on the stairwell feeling the cool of the concrete on her back and wishing she could chain smoke a box of cigarettes. Despite not being in Graff, she still sits in her same spot since the boys don't hang here anymore. Even though the steps are hard and uncomfortable, she feels safe there, protected somehow.

Folded inside her purse, a list of things not to buy unless she needs them: cigarettes being something she definitely does not need. Chocolate.

Alcohol. Clothes. The less she buys, the more money she can save.

The manager at the pharmacy offered Issy more shifts over the summer and this morning when Issy checked her bank balance, she's saved nearly three hundred pounds. It won't pay the uni room rent or the fees, but it's a start. Whenever she finds herself dreaming of being rich, she thinks of Emily.

She understands Emily's life a bit more now. It's funny, but the envy she felt about Emily having a large house and a big garden disappears with every secret visit there. She feels sorry for Emily, thankful that Carol isn't strict. Emily and Henry apparently haven't had sex yet because they are worried about being caught by her parents. Issy thinks that's a lie. When she suspects Emily is lying, Issy gets upset. Hayley would tell her everything, whereas she gets the impression Emily keeps secrets, or tells half-truths, calling it "privacy".

Issy finds herself in a trance-like rhythm. She gets up and revises; taking short breaks to pee or make a cup of tea, but otherwise she's consumed in books. It's like her brain has become this fast car on cruise control. Doing timed exams with Emily and Emily's friends helps loads. She likes Sophie and Helena, and when Hendrike is out the way, Issy feels more and more relaxed in herself. The girls understand Issy is on a budget and never make money a barrier. They bring hot chocolate and muffins to revision sessions and always share. Helena made it really clear: this is our parents' money. They don't deserve to be rich as much as Issy never deserved to have her dad die and be thrown into poverty. When the last AS-Level exam ends, Issy feels as though she's walking on air, as if she's leapt a whole lot closer towards her dream life. Just one more school year and then she's eighteen; an adult about to go to university.

It's the end of July, and for Jerome the school year seems to have flown by without Issy. Now they're both working and their hours are so different, he feels another distance between them. A distance that he worries will get worse if she does study away from home.

When Issy put their "couple time" on hold while she revised, Dwayne began putting pressure on Jerome to start recording new tracks with Graff in the youth club's new studio. The boys have been spending the warmer evenings rolling joints for the send-outs to sell to the children outside Telegraph Hill Park. In some ways, it feels good for Jerome to be back in the Endz, doing things he enjoys – smoking weed and making music. Though, since taking the job as a trainee youth worker, he knows he should stop dealing weed. Whether weed should be legal, as it's just a plant, is irrelevant. The law makes it illegal and one of the sessions Steve at the youth club ran was on illegal substances. Steve told him there is zero tolerance on any illegal substances on the youth club site; that Steve can't stop Jerome smoking in his home but when it comes to bringing any into work, Jerome is putting his job at risk.

The new job has also got Jerome thinking about the future. After initially being put off by Issy's attitude towards their lyrics, his passion for making tracks has rekindled. Back in June, Steve sent Jerome on paid training about providing music programmes for young people at risk of crime and school exclusion. It was run by this huge, muscly American artist who had a tough life in Los Angeles and rapped his way out of it. He had been to prison, lost his home, and all his drug money. Jerome and the rest of the workshop were captivated by his life story. The man decided to set up his own recording business and offer free studio time to young people. 'Music can be a way out.'

When it was time for questions, Jerome asked, 'What do you do if yutes rapping use swearwords or talk violence?' The guy looked at Jerome for a long time before speaking. Then he replied with his deep American accent, his words slow and rhythmic: 'Censorship is not an option. We got to let the youth have a voice and if that voice is a violent voice, then it's a violent voice. If you tell these kids to shut up, you're gonna shut them down. I would recommend you listen to what they gotta say, before we put a judgement on the way they gotta say it. We need to analyse the system that creates these words, not shoot down the messenger. You know what I'm saying?'

CHAPTER 26
ONE YEAR SINCE THE RIOTS

Looking out of his kitchen window, tired and puffy-eyed, Jerome watches the August sunshine sparkle off the red leaves of the plum tree opposite his block as a light shower of rain comes in from the west. Yesterday, the main gang member from Brockley got out of Y.O.I. and he's written bare rhymes. He messaged Dwayne and Jerome about starting a new battle. This time, Jerome never got to ask Issy's approval. Dwayne said yes on behalf of Graff then started sending the news out via social media. Within minutes the hype was back on with everyone asking if the new downloads will be out before Notting Hill Carnival at the end of the month.

Dwayne was so hyped, Jerome was so nervous, especially when they saw that in two hours over eight hundred people liked Dwayne's status saying Graff are warring again.

'What the fuck is going on?' Before Jerome could wake up, Issy shouts, 'I'm coming over now!'

Jerome rubs his eyes, still not awake as he opens the front door and looks out onto the street. He takes a gulp of water, rinses his mouth out then spits it into a plant pot. He notices Issy's flowing hair coming around the corner of the flats and ducks so that she doesn't see him. Wiping the water from his chin, he scuttles inside to put a fresh top on. Dwayne moans at him to close the curtains as Jerome searches his wardrobe for something clean to wear. Pulling a cleanish T-shirt over his head, he rushes to the bathroom to brush his teeth.

Mabel, always up and about early, opens the door to greet Issy smiling warmly. 'I haven't seen you in time. Working hard like a good girl. Come,

200

let me kiss you pon di cheek.'

Mabel gives Issy a warm hug, somewhat diffusing her temper.

'Hey babe.' Jerome moves in to kiss Issy on the cheek, knowing she'll be nicer in front of his grandmother.

'Morning Gran.' He hugs and kisses his grandmother too, as Issy watches beady-eyed.

'You want me put the kettle on?' Mabel asks. 'Can cook up something nice fe breakfast?'

'No, Granny Mabel,' Issy says. 'I have to go work.' Issy acts awkward like this is the first time she's been in the flat. 'Thanks though.'

Issy looks at Jerome. He is gorgeous. So handsome in his white top and jeans, trimmed hair and two thin shaved lines down one eyebrow. Nothing nicer than watching him help Mabel take the frying pan out and clutching her favourite mug from the cupboard. She blinks it away. Must remain strong. 'Jay, can we talk? Outside?'

As soon as they get out of the door, Issy sears, 'Starting battles, again?'

Jerome searches for words to explain that won't make her angry.

'Well? Come on? I've gotta go work,' Issy snaps.

'Hey, my gran's just there, you know.' Jerome nods to the kitchen window.

Issy purses her lips, 'Come walk me bus stop then.'

Jerome goes back inside to grab his trainers while Issy walks down the stairwell towards the street.

'Oi?' He hops after her trying to put on the second trainer, 'Can't you wait?'

She stops and waits for Jerome to jog up to her. 'Tell me you won't do it'

'Do what?'

'Make these tracks. Promise me, Jay.'

Jerome looks up at the blue sky. The morning sun beaming down on them both. The rain making the road look like it's made of gold.

Issy watches his lips remain shut.

'You've got a job now. You don't have to get on this.'

'Issy...' Looking at her scowling back at him, he loses his words. She doesn't wear much makeup anymore and her highlights have nearly all grown out. 'Nothing's gonna happen. It's legit.' He offers.

'You said that last time, and those Peckham boys tried it. What if it happens again? Or Brixton or Woolwich or Tottenham or anywhere.'

'They won't.'

'How do you know?' Issy waits for an answer, but he can't give her a solid reason why any violence won't start up again. She looks at her watch and stomps down the hill.

Jerome follows. 'Look, I know you're worried, but I went on this training Steve put me on, yeah, and this man told me it's okay for yutes to express themselves. It's what we do at this age. He's making money running workshops.'

'Yeah, did you tell him it was violent lyrics?'

'I did. Swear down.' Jerome tries to hold Issy's hand but she pulls away, 'Babe?'

'He doesn't know how things are on road. How it can turn real.'

'He does. He's from America.' Jerome finally catches her hand and holds on. 'He even went to prison.'

'Great! He went prison!' Issy pulls her hand away. 'You see what's happening already? You're listening to people who went prison? Why can't you listen to me?'

Issy continues walking. Jerome jogs after. She's forced to a stop by the traffic lights opposite her bus stop. Jerome tries to put his arm around her. She stiffens.

'Babe?'

Issy keeps her eyes fixed on the lights. The red man lit. Buses and cars clogging up the road. The smell of petrol fumes.

'Issy, man!'

She turns her head abruptly. 'What?'

They cross the lights. At the bus stop, Jerome looks into Issy's eyes, then down at her uniform top. 'You look sexy in that shit, you know?' He licks his lips and tries a cheeky wink. That usually cheers her up. But it doesn't work. She's imagining him going back to all the raves, making the music videos with fingers pointed into gun shapes, getting threats from other gangs on YouTube comments.

She shakes her head. Her bus approaches. 'Getting this.'

Jerome watches as Issy gets on the bus, 'Babe, I'll pick you up after work, okay?'

Issy says nothing and walks to the back of the lower deck. He bangs on the window startling an old man, then mouths, 'Sorry, mate.'

Issy gets up from her seat, 'What you doing?'

The old man sitting by the window keeps his head down.

Jerome mouths back, 'I'll pick you up after work. Okay? Okay?'

Issy rolls her eyes and nods, 'Okay.'

The day at work gave Issy time to reflect on their situation. She had the job of reorganising the stock cupboard ready for the new delivery of patient prescriptions. The cool dim room was quiet and as Issy sorted through the use-by dates of all the drugs, labelling and sorting the returns, she thought about how things could end up for her. She felt bad about snapping at Jerome. She was never like that at the beginning. She is changing, for the worse. She doesn't want to be in a relationship where she's always rude to her boyfriend.

Jerome is standing outside with a bunch of flowers. Issy smiles. He wraps his arms around her and whispers in her ear, 'I missed you so much today.'

She smells him, that blend of cocoa butter and Calvin Klein. The day's still warm and the sun high in the sky. Jerome buys some donuts and asks if she wants to walk up to Blackheath.

'No, let's go back to mine,' she whispers in his ear. 'We haven't in a while. And I'm sorry. For being rude to you this morning. I just panicked. I saw all these messages on Dwayne's wall and then looked on yours, saw the same and got angry. Why didn't you tell me about it?'

'Babe, it wasn't planned this time, get me? Man like me didn't see it coming. It was like, boy, Brockley man got out of pen holding all these lyrics and just called up Dwayne asking if Graff are on it. You know what D's like, he's restless. It's been time since he stopped the coke–' Jerome stops.

'Cocaine?' Issy looks at Jerome, 'Jay? Tell me. Did you say coke?'

Jerome bites his bottom lip.

'Tell me?'

'Alright.' Jerome sighs. This is going to escalate. He knows it. His brother is ruining his sex life. 'Hayley's brother was trying to hook Dwayne up with some bredder from Deptford ways, saying how this man clears two large a week selling crack and shit–'

'What!' Issy gasps, before looking around to see who else is at the bus stop. She pulls her face closer to Jerome's. 'And?'

'Bredder got raided by feds. Now he's in pen. So that squashed that one.'

She walks to the bin to chuck her donut wrapper. Dwayne is a liability. She wishes he would disappear. That somebody kills him. She shouldn't think like that but that's how she feels. A rush of fear flows up her spine as she imagines Jerome getting stabbed defending his brother.

'You know what he's like,' Jerome continues as Issy walks back to him. 'He craves madness. It's been calm 'til now.' He takes her by the arm, 'Babe, trust me, this ting can work. It's just music at the end of the day. It's better for him to be sitting there writing lyrics. Stops him thinking 'bout other shit.'

'Why can't he just get a proper job like everyone else?' Issy rests her head into Jerome's chest, glad he is still alive, still close to her. She takes a few deep breaths and breathes him in.

'I know, babe,' Jerome rubs Issy's back, kissing her forehead softly. 'You know I spend bare time analysing this shit. Thinking, do I have to have such a mad life?' He lifts her chin and kisses her cheek, deciding not to tell her Dwayne wet the bed until about two years ago and still has panic attacks about his childhood and isn't the big man everyone thinks he is. His gran told Jerome she thinks the devil got in, strange men answering the phone at the yard, his mother nowhere to be seen. Dwayne wasn't protected like he was, because everyone was scared of Jerome's dad and his best friend Leeroy Simms, and Jerome's dad didn't give a shit about Dwayne and always made fun of Dwayne's Nigerian dad, still nowhere to be seen after they done scared the bredder off. Jerome sighs. 'He's my brother at the end of the day, yeah? My one and only. So, what can I do?' Jerome looks up at the bus approaching, 'Come, we get this one.'

As they take their seats upstairs, Issy whispers, 'Set an example, Jay. Do it differently. Start making non-violent tracks. Start playing the conscious stuff that boy George sent you.'

'I tried playing it, but the little yutes are on this hype ting. Three things people don't get bored of: money, sex, violence. The youngers believe it, whisper when we walk past like we're the mafia or some shit.' He chuckles then.

'It's not funny. To them you are, Jay! And Dwayne ain't gonna do nothing to stop that.' Issy scratches her head, and pulls out her phone to look at the latest posts. 'Look, he loves it.'

Issy opens the door to the flat. 'Mum?' she calls out.

'I'm in here,' Carol calls back.

They walk into the living room to find Carol in her blue towelling dressing gown.

'Hello, you two!' Carol smiles. 'How's my favourite lovebirds?' She gets up to give them both kisses.

'You been drinking?' Issy asks.

'Been where, love?'

'Drinking.'

'Well I've got my teapot here.' Carol waves a mug of tea in the air, accidently spilling a few drops onto the carpet. She looks down at the floor, 'Oh, bum.'

Issy stares at her mother, 'Booze, Mum! Have you?'

Jerome nudges Issy.

'Please don't shout at me, not today.' Mug in hand, Carol heads to the kitchen to get a cloth.

Jerome gives Issy a sympathetic smile. 'We're just gonna go upstairs, is that alright, Carol?' Jerome calls to the kitchen.

'Do what you like,' Carol calls back. She takes a gulp of tea walking past them and back into the living room. 'Free country ain't it?'

'She's pissed.' Issy whispers in the hallway.

'How you know?' Jerome asks, 'Maybe she's tired.'

'Jay, I know my mum, so stop defending her,' Issy snaps. 'She's watching the soaps. Who gets pissed watching telly?'

'Don't worry. Come,' he kisses her neck, 'let's go upstairs.'

'I don't want to while she's here. It's not the same.'

Jerome's phone beeps. 'It's Andre. He wants to link in the park. Wanna get out of here?' Silence. 'He got punished. Can't you just forgive? It's literally one year yesterday since the riots. It's done now.'

Issy rolls her eyes and goes to the kitchen. He follows her.

'It's not about the fucking riots. I just wanna be alone, Jerome. Just us, so we can sort this out.'

'Sort what out?' Jerome puts his phone back in his pocket. 'We're calm, babes.'

Issy stares at Jerome in disbelief. 'The music. The battle. How you're gonna tell them lot it's over.'

Carol comes into the kitchen, 'Do you two want a ham and cheese sandwich?'

'No thanks, Carol,' Jerome replies. 'I'm off.'

'You just got here!'

'I will,' replies Issy, eyes fixed on Jerome. 'I'm starving.'

Jerome sighs. 'Babe, I'll be up the park, yeah?' He kisses Issy's cheek and then Carol's, catching the scent of booze as Carol says goodbye.

'So you're gonna go, yeah?' Issy fumes.

Jerome looks at Issy and then at Carol taking out the white bread and watery ham pumped with sugar and salt. 'I'll check you later. Once you've had a shower and ting, yeah?'

'"And ting and ting" I love that wee talk,' Carol laughs.

Issy pushes past Jerome and runs up to her room.

Carol looks quizzically at Jerome.

'Sorry Carol. We're–' he doesn't want to say bad patch, it's not a bad patch, 'having a disagreement.'

'I'd leave her to it,' Carol mutters. 'She's a miserable b.i.t.c.h these days.'

As Jerome approaches the park, his phone beeps with a text from Issy.

So u can stay when u think ur getting sex. But then as soon as da boyz ask, u go runnin. If u do this battle and trouble starts. Its over 4 us.

Jerome frowns. He looks up to see Dwayne silhouetted against the sun, throwing punches into the air. He lets out a sigh, and walks over.

'What you saying, what you saying?' Jerome nudges fists, first Dwayne then Andre, and sits downs on the summer warmed grass.

'Dem boys already trying it, bruv,' Dwayne shouts down at Jerome. He throws an uppercut then a left hook.

'What boys?'

'Ain't you seen?' Andre asks, lying back.

Jerome takes his brother's Lilt. 'Been with Issy.'

'Best sky my drink then,' Dwayne shouts, warning against Jerome's lips touching the can.

Jerome kisses his teeth.

Andre smirks, inhaling a lungful of weed, 'That Peckham yute: Cyber. Making out like he's on this lyrical flex, get me. Man posted a vid today, blood, saying how Graff Manz is all pussyholes.'

Jerome's face drops.

'Yes, fam,' Andre exhales the smoke into the radius of a nearby dog walker.

The elderly lady puts her dog on the lead and marches up to them. 'Excuse me, but could you possibly not smoke illegal substances in the park? There are children who play here.'

Andre looks up at the woman, 'Dis ain't the kids' park. Dat's the other one.'

The woman, annoyed, looks the three young men over, 'It is not appropriate to be smoking here. I shall call the police if you don't put it out at once.'

'Shut up,' Dwayne replies. 'And take yourself home.'

'At the end of the day yeah,' Andre adds, 'I don't go asking you to take off your Jesus ting? So don't ask me to stop smoking. This is my religion. Rastafari. You get me. Show some respect for my beliefs.'

'Nonsense,' the lady snorts, 'This is why adults dislike teenagers. You're rude. You have no respect!' The veins pop out from her wrinkled hands like worms. Floppy hat and glasses masking any expression on her face.

'Come out my personal space, man, cha.' Andre takes another puff on his joint, then deliberately blows smoke at the woman. She backs away.

'This park isn't just for you to intimidate others, you know?' With that, the woman turns and storms off.

Jerome turns to Andre: 'It ain't a good idea to be rude. What if she calls feds?'

'I don't care, fam!' Andre replies, passing the joint to Dwayne. 'These people grate man like me. I'm just sitting here, chilling. I ain't going up to her asking her dog to stop shitting everywhere, get me? These people piss me off, trust. She can go suck out her mum, fucking bitch.'

Jerome looks at the London skyline while Dwayne and Andre exchange cusses. How to contain this: 'We should make the battle official. Like, make a poster listing all individual MCs involved and state anyone else is a beg or fake. That way, they can't be in the battle and if they try, they look bate.'

Dwayne looks at Jerome, 'So what if they wanna bring it? I say come, then!'

'Yeah but D, I'm not inna their madness. I'm not about to get stabbed up for a one track.'

'Stop acting like a pussyhole,' Dwayne snorts.

'Dem boys is just trying it,' Andre adds. 'What's the most Cyber can do? He gets a little one slap and it's done.'

CHAPTER 27
HONEYTRAPS

Issy's second year at sixth form has begun. Already she's studying at home or in the library most evenings and working in the pharmacy at weekends to save money. Her mother watches on as her daughter sits at the kitchen table, making notes in a crisp new exercise book.

'Head'll explode with all that reading.'

Issy looks up with a smile.

Carol sits down, 'Can we talk?'

'Yeah, sure.'

Carol looks down at her mug of tea, wishing it were full of the right words to explain things.

'Issy, love,' she starts, looking at her daughter. 'I'm proud of all this you're doing. I couldn't do it. You got your dad's brains,' Carol looks away, feeling the old hurt rising up. She swallows it back down: not now. 'You know that anyway.'

'You alright, Mum?' Issy asks, gently placing a hand on Carol's arm.

'Sort of… Look, Issy, love? You've asked a few times, I've been cagey. You know, about the wee drink.'

Realising this is a serious chat, Issy takes the earphone out and puts down her pen.

'I promised when he died. No more. No more drink in the day, not like we did. We weren't alcoholics but looking back at it, we weren't far off.'

'What, you and Dad?'

'You remind me of him so much. You got his eyes. His chin. His wee smile. You even got his stubbornness and determination. I never had none of that...' Tears well in her eyes, her heart tightens with grief. 'So many years ago and then it's like he died yesterday.'

Issy wished she knew him more. They would have been best friends. Everyone says how he adored Issy, took her places every weekend: crab fishing, funfairs, fireworks. Always said yes to an ice lolly; the kind of dad kids dream about.

Despite Carol's efforts the tears fall, 'I'm ashamed I started again. Sorry... I...' Her voice fails her as she tries to get the words out. 'I miss your dad. I miss him so much. He was everything to me. To us—' Carol chokes up and her body starts shivering. She buries her head into her arms.

Issy puts her arm around her mother, holding back her own grief to comfort the best she can. After a minute or so, Carol's face emerges sweaty and red, snot dripping from her nose. Issy grabs some kitchen towel from the side and hands it across the table.

'Sorry, love.'

'That's okay,' Issy replies, giving her mum another hug.

'It's just that you're all I got. And I see you growing up. It's all happening so fast,' Carol says, 'The thought of being alone scares me. It's brought it all back. It wasn't so bad before, when you was younger, I had to be strong. I'd be there to take you to school, put your frilly lace socks on, make your packed lunch, pick you up, take ya to the park. We'd go everywhere. Watch telly every night...' Carol sighs, 'I know you have to grow up. I know I did. At your age I was near enough married.' She lights a cigarette, then holds the packet out to her daughter.

'Nah, thanks. I've given up.' Issy says, weirdly ashamed, as if it's one more thing that separates them.

'You see? I don't know nothing about you, these days.' Carol exhales the smoke, turning her head so that her daughter doesn't have to breathe it in, 'Since when?'

Issy looks at the biscuit tin on the table, 'Just before the stuff with Hayley kicked off.'

'You two not made up then.'

'Probably won't, Mum. We're like strangers now. Don't even know who she is.'

Carol takes Issy's hand and looks her in the eye, 'I know I ain't perfect. I know I can't give you everything. But I'm gonna give you what I can.'

Her mother's hands look suddenly so old and wrinkled. They're shaking but there's the familiar warmth and kindness in her touch.

Carol holds her stare, 'Just promise me one thing.'

Issy nods.

'I've been doing extra shifts. I've been saving. I know I don't have enough, but by the end of next year, I'll have a grand extra saved. Plus I spoke to Nanna in Glasgow. Your Dad's money's still there. She's promised you could have it before your twenty-first birthday for your studies. Only on the condition that you spend some time with her.'

Issy looks up, 'Dad left me money?'

'Not much. About two thousand. Maybe three. We never had much. He mostly did cash-in-hand and a lot of that went on bills.'

'What happened to the money you got from selling the house?'

'What house?'

'Our old house.'

'We rented. We always rented.'

'I thought we owned it.'

'I've never owned nothing in my life.' She looks back down into her empty cup, finding the words she wanted, 'Just promise me, you won't forget me, when you go.'

Issy looks confused, 'Go where?'

'Off to uni.'

'But I'm staying here.'

'Not because you wanna, right?' Carol gently brushes the hair from her daughter's face. 'You're such a good girl. Why didn't you tell me how much money you need to go uni?'

Issy drops her head. 'I didn't wanna stress you out,' she blushes. 'Did Jerome tell?'

'I got a call from that young teacher, the Northern one.'

'Mrs Salmon?'

'She wanted to ask me about your UKIP form.'

'UCAS.'

'UCAS form. I didn't know what to say. She told me you want to study out of London. Get away from the problems on the estate, with Hayley and all that.'

'She said that?' Issy replies, with betrayal in her voice. 'What else did she say?'

'That you weren't gonna go 'cause of the fees.'

'She shouldn't have said nothing.'

'She wasn't doing nothing bad. I'm your Mum–'

'It's my business!' Issy snaps. She looks at her mother's hands, fingers still shaking as she flicks cigarette ash into her sapphire-blue ashtray.

'Sorry I spoke.' Carol gets up from the table.

Issy turns in her chair, 'No, Mum, wait.' But Carol leaves the kitchen before she can reach out to take her arm.

She finds her in the living room. 'I'm sorry. I dunno what's wrong with me these days. I get stressed easily. I'm snapping at everyone. Falling out with everyone. I'm sorry.'

Issy picks up the photograph of her with her parents as a baby. She doesn't know who she is anymore. She feels out of place everywhere. When she is studying, she is switched off. Real life on pause. Lost in the facts and lives of other, more important people.

'Why don't you take a break? Watch some telly? Go grab the biscuit tin and we can cuddle up like old days.'

Issy wants to say no but she knows it would mean a lot to Carol. She heads back into the kitchen for the biscuits, closing her notebook after putting a light pencil mark where she stopped reading about the American Civil War.

'So what is UCAS then?' Carol mutes the television as Issy sits on the sofa.

'It's the people you apply to uni through. They do all the admin and stuff.'

'So how do you get chosen for somewhere? No, you choose don't ya?'

'Well kind of. I get to choose where I wanna go. Then they read my application and what the teachers say I'll get in the end, like exam grades, I mean. Then the uni says to the school yes or no... Well it's called conditional or unconditional, which basically means definitely or maybe, based on what points I'll have earned by the end of the year. So it's like not worth someone getting low grades to apply to somewhere like Oxford or Cambridge because they ain't brainy enough to get the points needed and won't get in.'

Carol dips a biscuit into her tea, a bit confused, 'So what's points for if you got grades then?'

'Well the grades become points, like an A or no, an A-star is like the highest, so you get most points then it goes down for a B, C, D, etc. Then it also depends on what subjects you do and wanna do at which uni. Some courses want bare points and others are less. Like obviously studying English at Oxford is harder than doing it somewhere like Greenwich.'

'What's in Greenwich?'

'The uni.'

'Oh,' Carol shakes her head, 'I'm too thick for all this talk.' She unmutes telly and that's the end of that conversation.

Issy feels a hopelessness inside as the room fills with the theme tune to Eastenders.

The soap drags on and on. Every word spoken by the actors represents her cage tightening, reinforcing her class position. Does she really want to stay in London for university? Living away means an extra twelve thousand pounds in rent, plus food and bills. It's such a lot of money. Sophie, Helena and Emily's parents already pay that for private school, always have. It's more an annoyance for them, rather than a hindrance; 'an affordable inconvenience.' Sophie's dad told them explicitly to move away as that is ninety per cent of the experience. Sophie's dad got so angry about the new fees stunting the development of teenagers into adults. He said unless they're rich, Issy's generation will be worse off than their parents were.

Half-way through EastEnders Issy gets up to draw the curtains. She looks out of the bar-clad window and sees Jerome and the boys laughing and joking, trying to pull each other's jeans down. Anton and Andre start jeering at two teenage girls walking past.

Issy kisses her mum and decides to go back to her books but her concentration is broken. If she's honest, she wants go to a university outside of London. But money aside now, what about her mother? And can she really leave Jerome? They've been together over two years. She decides to ring Emily.

'Issy! How are you?'

'You got a minute? I need advice?'

'I'm at a barbecue with Henry. Bit random, I know. Are you okay? You sound sad. What's wrong?'

'Mum just told me my dad left me money that I can have for uni. She said I can use it to live away.'

'What?! But that's amazing! Hang on a sec...'

Issy picks at the paint flaking from the kitchen door. She can hear Emily on the other end, 'Richie, Issy's just received exciting news about some inheritance. Can she come and tell me about it?'

'Hey Issy, wanna come to this thing? It's at Henry's friend's house. You met him at George's party ages ago, Richie. I just spoke to him and he said you should absolutely come join us.'

'Where is it?'

'Knightsbridge. I'll text the postcode. We're already here; otherwise I'd have picked you up on the way. It'll take you about an hour, but you can come back with us. Henry's dad just bought him a red sports car. I know, before you say it, très cliché. But I can't help it. I love it!'

Issy smiles at the image of Emily in a sports car, such a far cry from the scruffy knobbly-kneed artist living in a poky Parisian apartment scraping coins together for a freshly baked croissant.

'Up for it?' Emily asks again.

Peering from the bedroom window, she sees the gang talking to the two girls, Jerome included. 'Yep, I'll be there as soon as.'

'So what you saying, fam?'

Jerome, leaning against the wall, looks up at his older brother, 'Bout what?'

'Going Peckham, man.'

'For what?'

'Dis boy's kidding me!' Andre exclaims.

Jerome takes the other headphone out his ear.

'Take these nice ladies back to their yard.' Anton smiles at Jerome cheekily; lifting his eyebrows up and down.

Jerome looks at the two girls then back at Andre and Anton, then at Dwayne. 'To do what?'

'To do what?' Anton mimics, laughing.

Jerome kisses his teeth and mutters, 'Lickkle pickney dem.'

'I'm eighteen, actually,' says one of the girls wearing more makeup than clothes.

The other looks at Anton licking his lips, then nudges her friend.

'We ain't gonna do nothing like that, ya get me?' the girl insists. 'Just chill.'

'Yeah, I know, I know,' Anton replies.

As Anton, Dwayne, Barry, Andre and Jerome walk down the hill towards the bus stop, Jerome grabs Andre's arm and hangs back a few steps.

'Bruv, these girls are like twelve or some shit.'

Andre chuckles.

'Nah man, I'm serious,' Jerome says. 'I eat fried eggs bigger than her tits.'

'Oh my days!' Andre laughs out loud. 'That's raw. That's deep, fam.'

The girls turn around, paranoid.

Jerome looks at the girls, then turns back to Andre, 'Where you know these ones?'

'I dunno, Anton moved to them.'

'Anton!' Jerome calls out, 'Come?'

'What, man?' Anton replies, walking closely next to the girls.

'Oi, come here, fam!' Jerome shouts.

Anton swaggers up the hill, 'What's your problem?'

'Who these youngers?'

'Some chicks I met, innit.'

Jerome looks suspicious, 'Met where?'

'Don't start this shit, fam,' Anton riles up. 'You wanna be batty and get possessive with man, but at the end of the day I ain't got that type of love for you.'

Jerome clips a giggling Anton round the head. 'Chatting pure rubbish!'

Anton runs back down to the girls, shouting up to Jerome, 'I'm your bro and ting, but that's where it stops!'

Issy knocks on the front door in Knightsbridge. She waits patiently, admiring the thick white Ancient Greek-style columns either side of her.

She steps back and looks up at the impressive four-story house for signs of life. Realising they probably can't hear. She tries Emily's phone again. The door swings noiselessly open to reveal those piercing sky blue eyes.

'Issy, darling!' Richie opens his arms as if he were greeting an old friend. He wraps one over Issy's shoulders and pulls her in. 'Great to see you again. It feels like forever!'

Issy blushes as she feels the warmth of Richie's body. Those butterflies reappear alongside the aroma of Richie's body spray.

'It was at George's party, that time,' Issy replies, thinking of something to say.

'Indeed. I remember well...' He leans in. 'I never forget a pretty face.'

Now Issy really blushes. Cheesy as that was, she can't help but smile.

'We're on the roof. Such a cracking autumn day.'

Richie walks Issy through an ornately tiled entrance, up a polished oak staircase, 'Actually, can I get you a drink, babe? There's beers up there, though I think now's a good time to start cracking open something more sophisticated.'

'Urm, okay. I didn't know what to expect, sorry. I've come empty-handed.'

'No, that's absolutely fine,' Richie smiles, each time looking into Issy's eyes just that little bit longer. 'We have plenty.'

'I feel rude, now.'

'Really, there's no need,' Richie places both hands on Issy's shoulders. 'I feel honoured you made your way here. That's enough. Your presence is my present.'

'Issy!' Emily squeals as Richie opens the door to the roof garden.

Issy can't quite take it in. The rooftop is full of people around her age. It looks like a swanky hotel bar you see on holiday programmes. There are outdoor sofas and coffee tables covered in tea lights and cocktails. There's a bar in one corner covered with flowers and colourful paper lanterns with people shaking their own drinks. Someone, who looks like Max from George's party, is mixing electro on his laptop.

Emily pushes through the crowd to reach her friend.

'Wow, Mimi. I feel like I'm in Ibiza!'

'I know, great isn't it?' Emily giggles, giving Issy a huge hug and kiss, 'I love an Indian summer!'

'So are you nervous about your UCAS form?' Issy asks. Emily still hasn't yet told her parents that she is going to Paris whether they like it or not.

Emily pokes her tongue out, 'I've not thought about it.'

'Aren't you back at school?'

'Not yet. It's private school: loads of money, half the time! Look Issy. There's someone I want you to meet.'

'Henry?'

'Yes, Henry!' Emily squeals, linking arms and heading towards a large group of boys, holding beer bottles with slices of lime wedged in.

'Henry darling, I'd like to finally introduce you to Issy.'

Henry leaves the group to join Emily and Issy. He holds out his hand and with a stiff and somewhat cold voice, says, 'Isabelle, I've heard a lot about you. I'm Henry.'

'I've heard loads about you, too. Nice to finally say hello. I think we were both at George's party, but never actually met.'

'In Nice?'

'No, the year before,' Emily chips in, 'George's sixteenth.'

Henry eyes up Issy's outfit. Clearly unimpressed, he asks, 'Would you like a drink?' holding out one of the beer bottles between his fingers.

'I think Richie is sorting me out. Thanks anyway, though.'

'Well have a nice night.' Henry smiles professionally then pats Emily on the bum before returning to his friends.

Issy turns to Emily. 'Well he's a bag of words.'

Emily looks a little distressed, but swallows her pride, 'It takes time for him to warm to people. God knows, I know that!' she giggles, to ensure Issy doesn't take it personally. 'Come and sit with us girls. Sophie and Helena are both here.'

Issy joins them on the sofa, the bitchy Hendrike also in tow. Richie appears with a champagne bottle.

'So ladies, hand-crafted and especially for you. Who cares for some fizz? Issy, you're in most need of a drink, may I?'

Issy can't help but blush. Richie has the most amazing skin, chiselled jawline, his pecs visible through the open buttons of his shirt. Issy feels her body temperature go up as Richie hands her a glass, brushing fingers with hers.

'She's got a boyfriend, you know!' Hendrike sneers with a sarcastic giggle. 'And he's a gangster.'

Issy smiles at her nemesis: huge gold loops and an empty glass, 'Hendrik-ah, good to see ya,' Issy says.

'You too. Where is that gorgeous man of yours?'

'Busy. Producing,' Issy replies awkwardly, wishing Richie was not there to hear; ashamed of Jerome's music production – or having a boyfriend at all?

'Good to see you, Issy.' Sophie gets up to give Issy a peck on both cheeks, 'and that's exciting. Producing, I mean. Is it a single or an album?'

Issy looks over at Emily, knowing how she disapproves of the lyrics, 'Not sure. Both. So how are you? Last time I saw you was at the V&A.'

'When did you two go to the V&A?' Hendrike pipes up. 'And where was my invite?' She folds her arms dramatically.

'Since when do you go to museums?' Sophie retorts.

'Exactly, you're a pisshead,' Helena laughs, reaching down to the prosecco bottle beside her and pouring herself another glass. 'Just like me!'

'Don't you want some champers, Hels?' Richie asks.

'No darling, waste of precious resources.'

Issy laughs as Helena lifts the prosecco bottle and shouts 'Six quid from Aldi!' her gold bangles falling down her arm.

Richie pours for Emily and Sophie.

'Well, more for you, Issy,' Richie smiles. 'I'll be back with an ice-bucket, okay?' He sets the bottle down on the marble top coffee table.

Issy sips her drink, aware that other girls are looking at her.

Hendrike downs the prosecco Helena just poured into her empty flute. She grabs the champagne bottle from the table and fills herself a glass. Hendrike leans in toward Issy as she returns the bottle to its spot. 'You better watch Rich-Richie, busy-Issy. He's a charmer. Dan-ger-ous.'

Issy wishes she could chuck Hendrike off the roof, or at least pull her extensions out. She looks around the party.

'She's right,' Sophie sighs. 'They say you have to kiss a few frogs before you find your prince; well, Richie's the opposite.'

'You can say that again, darling,' seconds Helena.

'Issy does have a boyfriend, you know!' Emily exclaims.

'Richie's all over her, Mimi,' replies Sophie.

'More of a challenge,' Hendrike says, licking her lips.

Emily shakes her head.

'I can handle it,' Issy replies. 'Besides, he's not done anything bad or anything.'

'Just make sure you wake up in your own bed tomorrow!' Hendrike laughs. Helena joins in.

Issy watches Hendirke high fiving Helena, giggling over something. Inside she feels a sadness. She is not them. They know they are not her. They say what they like. They have this voice that she can't seem to gather up. Then Issy wonders if the differences are really there or if she is making them up. Making up barriers that don't exist. But why would she do that? Probably the same reasons people self-harm. She starts to regret turning up. This constant internal questioning is draining.

Sophie jumps up to sit next to Issy, 'Don't mind them,' she whispers. 'They're drunken fools with no manners. How have you been?'

'I'm fine,' Issy replies, 'Still not sure which uni to go.'

'Oh I know. Total nightmare.'

Sophie takes out a cigarette holder from her purse. Issy notices that her clasp bag is Gucci and, as Sophie slips off one heel to bring her leg up onto the sofa, Issy reads Prada. Sophie takes out two super-skinny cigarettes and hands one across.

'No, thanks,' Issy says proudly. 'I quit.'

'Well done, you!' Sophie claps her hands to Issy's achievement. She pops one of the cigarettes back into its silver case, then lights the other one. Sophie's skin is like porcelain, her hair light blonde, and her style is like a modern take on the 1950s. She's wearing a leather skirt with a floral short-sleeve blouse that ruffles at the front.

'Issy?'

'George!' Issy jumps up.

'Great to see you again.' George hugs her tightly, before sitting on the arm of the leather chair opposite. 'Ladies,' George nods his hellos to the others, before turning back to Issy, 'So how are things?'

George looks so grown up. He has the beginnings of a moustache, his body is broader and taller.

'Oh my days, you look so different. You're like a proper man!'

'I could say the same about you. Something's changed. Your hair, perhaps?'

'Yep! Stopped bleaching it.'

'Looks much nicer... au naturel.'

'George, are you objectifying Issy?' Sophie jests, poking him gently in the ribs.

'Not at all,' George pokes her back. 'So Issy, how's Jerome?'

'You remembered his name!'

'Who could forget the man with the mic?'

'Oh no,' Issy theatrically buries her head in shame before peeking at George. 'He did take over your party!'

'No, not at all,' George says. 'We tried to stay in touch. Has he changed his number, actually?'

'He's got an iPhone now.'

'Everybody loved it,' Sophie says.

'Loved what?' Henry asks, landing on the sofa beside Emily. He strokes the back of her neck and shoulders.

'Issy's boyfriend's music... when he performed at George's party.'

Henry shrugs, 'If you like that kind of stuff.'

'As in...' Issy asks.

'Black music.'

George looks at Henry, 'It's not black per se.'

'Oh, don't start, George,' Henry groans.

'Urban is more appropriate,' Emily says.

Henry rolls his eyes. 'I mean Hip Hop, R'n'B, that stuff.'

George continues, 'I'm black and I don't much care for commercialised R'n'B, or Hip Hop as we have it today.'

'You're not exactly—' Henry stops himself by downing his bottle of beer.

Emily turns her head sharply to face her boyfriend wide-eyed. She turns back to Issy and George, embarrassed.

'I'm not what?' George asks with a knowing smile.

'You know... you're not like the black people in those music videos, are you? You're one of us, George.'

George's expression implies he couldn't be further away from who or what Henry represents. Issy places a hand on his thigh, in solidarity.

Henry gets up using Emily's back as a lever. 'You see,' Henry pats George heavily on the shoulders, 'Even she knows what I mean.' He nods to Issy then walks off.

'What's that supposed to mean?' Issy asks Emily.

Hendrike sniggers.

Emily searches for the right words, eventually opting for an unconvincing shrug.

'I think we all know what he means,' says George, mouthing the letters S.N.O.B. to Issy.

Hendrike laughs uncontrollably, 'This is... like... some crazy sketch show,' she shrieks.

Issy gets up, 'Where's the toilet?'

'Let me escort you.'

'Who ordered an escort?' Hendrike cackles at her own joke.

As soon as Issy and George are out of earshot, Hendrike chuckles, 'Well, that was awkward.'

Emily storms off to confront Henry. Helena shakes her head but can't help let out a disapproving grin.

'Come on, you two,' Sophie says, shaking her head. 'Give the poor girl a chance!'

'Poor Girl!' Hendrike shrieks, laughing harder, forcing Henry and Richie to turn.

'Don't be a dick,' Sophie protests, 'you know I didn't mean it like that.'

'You said it. Poor Girl,' Hendrike says, holding her belly with laughter. 'Please can we call her that from now on?'

'You're such a retard,' Sophie says, rolling her eyes. She kicks off her other heel to spread out on the sofa, drugs kicking in.

As they cut through the crowd to cross the roof garden. George reassures Issy, 'Please pardon Hendrike.'

'Why's everyone friends with her when she's such an arsehole?'

'Everyone has their backstory, right?' George gives her a knowing look.

Issy nods, 'Guess so.'

'So how is Jerome? I sent him a few playlists and stuff after my birthday.'

'I know. He tried playing them, but–' Issy stops, embarrassed.

'But his friends didn't appreciate?'

'It's complicated. Jerome gets into these' – Issy bends her fingers into quotation marks – '"lyrical battles" with this other gang near us.'

'A gang?'

'Well, it ain't really a gang. Like we don't go robbing old ladies. We just hang round where we live. Though not since...' Issy peters out, thinking back to the riots and how she's lost all her friends...

'Sorry, I interrupted you.'

'Oh, well, yeah, they make these fake wars, like, where they cuss each other. They set it all up, so it's proper fake and all that...' she pauses to gauge his reaction. 'Emily hates it. I do, too. We both think it's a bit dangerous.' She looks awkwardly at George, 'What do you think?'

He smiles thoughtfully, but says nothing. He opens the door for her.

Issy is now really feeling her bladder, 'Where's the toilet?'

'Richie's bedroom has one. That door. Shall I wait here?' George points to a velvet chaise-longue.

'No. Thanks. I'll find my way back. See you in a bit.'

It's literally the lushest bathroom she has ever been in. From top to bottom, there are emerald green marble tiles, like a Roman Emperor's palace. There are thick fluffy towels neatly folded and bathroom rugs to match. To one side, under a skylight, is an imposing cast iron bathtub with gold feet the shape of lion paws. Issy can't see a toilet. She opens one of the doors to reveal a cupboard of men's aftershaves, face products, body butters. Issy's jaw drops as she sees all the designer labels: Calvin Klein, Armani, Jean Paul Gaultier eau de toilette, pour Homme.

She shuts the cupboard, afraid someone might think she's being nosey or worse. Then she remembers that she is inside a locked bathroom and nobody can see. She opens the second door to reveal more fluffy towels arranged in size and colour order.

She wanders through a partition wall. Impressed by the patterns and colours, she fingers the swirls wondering where this stone comes from. She gasps as warm water sprays over her body from all directions. With no buttons in sight, Issy is trapped. She backs into the corner of the shower – because she sees now what this is – holding her hands in front of her. She huddles down. She knows she should just run through the spray back into the bathroom, but the thought of walking through the house soaking wet, dripping down the stairs with its nice purple carpet and posh rugs is paralysing. This could only happen to her. She starts to panic and wishes the ground would open and swallow her up. If only she could magic herself away. Make the water stop. But there's no taps or buttons in sight.

Issy hears a voice muffled through the sound of the water. What should she to do? She can't stay there but she's too embarrassed to move.

A few moments later, another door opens from behind the bathtub area to reveal Richie.

'So you fancied a shower, babe?' Richie says with a smirk.

'How do you stop this thing?' she asks, trying to play it cool.

'It works with sensors. While you're crouching there, it won't stop.'

Richie starts to chuckle.

'Oi, don't laugh!' Issy smiles. He is so fit.

'You're absolutely right. I should not find this at all funny,' he grins.

How this must look.

'You're going to have to run through it, babe.'

'But I'll get more wet.'

'Not sure that's possible, babe. Honestly it's fine. My bedroom's next door. I can lend you clothes.'

'I'll drip everywhere.'

'Don't mind that. It's only water.'

Issy looks at Richie. She can't help but find him attractive as he holds out his hand to her. She runs through the shower, slipping in her ballerina pumps, only to be caught by his strong arms. In a spontaneous moment, Richie takes Issy as if they are to ballroom dance, leading them both back into the shower.

'Oh my god, Richie, my mobile!' Issy shouts, trying to free her hand from his to pull out her phone from her pocket.

'Fuck your phone, babe. We're in a rainforest.' Richie takes the mobile phone from Issy and tosses it onto the soft bathroom rug. 'We're in a tropical storm, in the middle of a jungle.'

'You're mad!'

'Alive, babe,' Richie says, humming some melody into her ear.

Issy closes her eyes and feels the water's warmth find her scalp, her forehead, sink into her clothes. She relaxes into Richie's arms. Fully clothed, this is nothing, means nothing, just a bit of fun. Jerome might not be happy but it's just a dance in a fucking shower. Drinking champagne and dancing in the rain with a millionaire! Issy starts laughing. Nobody would have thought this could happen to her.

Richie twirls Issy around, until they are both soaking wet and full of giggles.

He leads her out the monsoon and towards the door from which he came from.

'This way,' Richie says, handing Issy a towel. He takes off his jeans and shirt. Issy turns away as his boxers come off and he puts on a towelling gown.

They enter what looks like the changing room in a clothes store. Glossy, full-length mirrors with gold trim line one side of the wall. Richie opens one of the floor-to-ceiling mirrored cupboards and takes out some fresh clothes.

Issy, again, cannot believe what she is seeing.

'Look what I'm doing to your floor,' she gasps, her hand covering her mouth.

'Nothing to fret over,' Richie says, grabbing a handful of clothes and opening another door... that leads to his bedroom. 'Only water.'

'So what you saying?' Anton licks his lips cheekily as he sits on the sofa next to Freya.

'What you saying?' Freya replies.

'Nah, nah, nah. I said it first, get me. What *you* saying?' Anton takes a puff of weed then exhales in Freya's face.

'Nuttin. What you saying?'

'Oh my days,' Jerome groans, putting on his headphones.

'Hey, yo!' Dwayne calls out from the other side of the cramped living room.

'Yeah?' replies Natalie.

'Ain't you got some next chicks to call?' Dwayne asks. 'It's like four of us manz and you two.'

Natalie winks at Freya. Freya winks back.

'Jerome lifts one side of his headphones up. 'DG's nearly twenty, so don't be dialling up illegal pum-pum.'

'Shut up, man!' Dwayne shouts. 'Bating man up.'

Jerome looks at the girl, still holding one earbud between his fingers, 'Any girl under thirteen it's classed as rape, even if the girl wears batty riders and makeup like a dance hall queen and says she's legal, and only sucks your dick, it's still rape. Prison. Bang.' Jerome's sexual health training left quite the impression.

Freya laughs as she taps her phone.

The sky is turning a deep purple. The tall houses becoming blackened silhouettes as the sun lowers.

Richie joins her at the rooftop edge. 'Probably the last barbecue of the year.'

'Yeah, probably.'

'Getting nippy now, though.'

She watches Richie put on the navy blue jumper around his shoulders. Even the way he does that has style.

'Thank you, for coming here. I know I shouldn't say this but I've been thinking about you all evening. You look great in my clothes by the way.'

She blushes, looking down at Richie's designer jumper and his sister's leggings and shoes.

Richie looks around to check who is nearby. 'After George's party I asked and asked about you but everyone told me you had a boyfriend. I saw you kiss him and I must say I felt a twang of jealousy.' He puts a fist to his chest. Dramatic.

'Really? As I remember, you only said a few words to me.'

He sips his drink and looks out across the skyline. 'I love it up here. It's a real escape.'

'It's like something out of a film with all them chimneys.'

'Sometimes, when I'm up here, I'm half expecting a dance sequence.'

They both chuckle; Mary Poppins uniting the classes.

'Hey Issy,' he looks straight at her, placing a hand on her shoulder, 'we're probably going to see more of each other, you know, since my best friend has hooked up with your best friend.'

Issy turns her head to see Emily sitting on Henry's lap.

'I know,' she replies. 'It's weird seeing Mimi with him. Makes her look older, more mature. She's changed so much since we met.'

'We all have,' Richie adds. 'We're supposed to, right? We'll be fully-fledged adults this academic year.'

'Off to university the next.'

'You too?'

'Hope so. Where do you think you'll study?'

'Nottingham or Durham. Not sure yet. Maybe Saint Andrew's. You?'

Issy looks into her glass. 'Well I was thinking about staying in London.'

'Really?' He puts the bottle to his lips and downs the last of his beer.

'Where's St Andrew's?' Issy asks, trying to mentally note the universities Richie will be applying to. She feels bad about it, but the idea of hanging with him over the next three years excites her.

'Scotland,' Richie replies with a smirk.

'Is it religious?'

'What about your boyfriend?' he asks, ignoring her question.

She blinks. 'What about him?'

'Where will he study? Do you think you'll pick the same place?'

Issy looks away, 'Oh, Jerome isn't going. He wants to be a music producer.'

'Doesn't everyone?' Richie snorts. He shifts his feet. 'Sorry. That must have sounded really rude.'

'No. It's fine.' Issy feels her cheeks burning with embarrassment.

'It's a sore subject in our family, that's all. My sister's boyfriend, he's been on the edge of stardom these past seven years. My parents tire of hearing about it. He plays a few bars and clubs, but that's the extent of his career. My sister isn't getting any younger and he is nowhere near settling down. If you ask me, he needs to grow a pair. Nothing worse than a beautiful, talented woman wasting her time with someone who doesn't want to man up.'

He amazes her. Someone her own age who has it all: good looks, charm, morals, great sense of style, kind, generous and polite.

'Shall we herd this party inside?' Richie asks, filling the silence, 'I think it's getting a bit chilly.'

Issy as a reflex checks her phone once Richie turns away. Several missed calls from her mum. This can only be bad news. Finding a quiet corner, she listens to a voicemail from Mabel. Jerome's been attacked.

Richie watches Issy from the corner of his eye, stuffing her phone in his sister's leggings, rushing over to Emily, whispering something in her ear, then leaving. The thought that there's somewhere more important than his party burns his pride, but at the same time he respects her for it; his imagination going wild as to where could be more enticing for Issy than in his own company.

CHAPTER 28
SENDOUTS

She patrols the playground. Her eyes focus in on boys playing football; he's not there. A group sitting talking, tapping on phones; he's not there. Finally she spots him in a huddled group.

Issy grabs the rolled up joint making the boys jump. 'Where'd you get this?'

They look on in shock as Tameika's brother stays silent. He knows she is Jerome's girl, but he Dwayne is the boss.

'Was it Double-G, was it? Are you a Graff sendout now?'

Issy shouts louder at Emmanuel. 'You know, if your sister finds out, what will happen?'

Fear flashes across Emmanuel's face.

'Tell me who's making you sell these or I'm gonna tell your whole family.'

Tears start to form in the poor boy's eyes. Some of the others smirk. 'Move!' Issy shouts, lunging at the Year 7s who back away. She grabs Emmanuel's arm, dragging him to the other end of the playground.

'What you playing at? You've got your whole life ahead of you and you're shotting weed in school?'

Emmanuel can't speak, muted by the terror of both Dwayne and his family. He's in a lose-lose situation.

Issy takes a few breaths. She pats Emmanuel's shoulder and lowers the volume: 'Look, I promise I won't say a word about it to your family. I just need to know. Did Dwayne give you these?'

Emmanuel mumbles 'Jerome.'

She grabs Emmanuel's school bag and starts rummaging through it. A pool of schoolchildren stop and stare. 'GO AWAY!' Issy shouts but they don't. She opens the bag to reveal scores of copied CDs with Graff graffiti over a group shot of Andre, Anton, Barry, Dwayne and Jerome.

Shaking with anger, she opens Emmanuel's pencil case to discover more spliffs. The crowd has attracted the attention of some teachers. Emmanuel starts crying now. Issy stuffs the spliffs into her fabric tote bag. The Head of Year 9 blows his whistle and the crowd part like the Red Sea story in the Bible.

'Keep your mouth shut,' Issy tells Emmanuel firmly. 'If the teachers ask, you're only selling CDs. You hear?'

After Issy gets out of a meeting with the Head of Year 7 and Head of Sixth Form, she is so angry with Jerome that she decides to visit the studio. Steve at the youth club made it clear Jerome can't record or sell his tracks on site. Youth club policy clearly states: no lyrics which incite violence or hatred of any kind are to be recorded inside. But Steve doesn't work Mondays and the other youth worker in charge is 'a safe chick' giving Graff access to equipment and time to organise after-school sales of the CDs. Mostly Year 7s and some 8s buy them, with older teens choosing to download singles or watch videos for free on YouTube. The weekly single releases has schoolkids rushing up to sendouts to buy them. Dwayne announced anyone who collects all CDs and takes a photo of them and shares it on social media, gets a chance to win tickets to a secret end-of-year party.

From the mixing desk, Jerome sees Issy peering into the studio. He's taken aback as she stomps in like one of the man dem. She listens as Andre spits rhymes about Cyber X.

'You don't know how nutz I be. You think honey gonna trap me, fam, watch when I sting like a killer bee. You best sleep one eye open, I creep in like chemical poison. Slit man's throat, no joke...'

Issy yanks open the soundproof door and slides up to Dwayne, 'Ain't you bored of this? You're nearly: Twenty. Years. Old.'

'Best sort your chick out,' Dwayne tells Jerome, taking off his headphones. She doesn't hear Dwayne finish his sentence with, 'before I slap her up.'

'What's your problem?' Jerome takes Issy's arm and pulls her into the recording room as Andre exits it for them.

'My problem? What's my problem?!' Issy shouts, 'I've just been in the Head of Sixth Form's office with Emmanuel trying to cover up your fucking weed dealing operation.'

Issy looks on, disgusted, finding his bowed head pathetic. 'Every day you smoke weed and make music. This isn't a life. Can't you see how dangerous this is? Fight after fight, this will end up with someone getting killed and what if it's you, Jerome? What if they decide to kill the music maker?' Issy fights her tears. 'You and Mum are all I got and I can't lose you, not to this. Not for this.'

Jerome tries to put his arms around her. 'I've saved almost three large, yeah, by the time you go uni, I'll have more than six grand.'

'Don't say that!' she shrugs him off. 'Don't say you're doing this for me.'

'Issy, you don't have to work for minimum wage on the weekends, on your days off. You can study, get good grades, go any uni you want.'

'Jay, what I want is for us to be legit. Not on money made from selling weed to kids.'

'It's music,' Jerome protests.

'It's violence, Jerome! Real violence,' Issy's anger rises. 'Look at your face? That scar is for life.'

Jerome touches his face.

'Not one song is about love,' Issy chokes on her words. 'This ain't love, what you're doing this for. It's all about money and ratings. This is all bullshit, Jerome. Two stabbings, five fights, rape threats - where's it gonna end?'

Jerome sees the boys sitting round the mixing desk.

She holds out her hand. 'Leave with me?'

'Issy, please.'

'I mean it. Leave here with me now, or it's over.'

'Is, you know I can't.'

'Why? Because of them?'

Jerome sits on the floor and puts his head in his hands.

'So that's it, is it?' Issy points to the gang watching them through soundproof glass. 'This is more important than me? Than us? Thanks for making my decision easier.' She boots the door and slaps the glass, shouting, 'Fucking dickheads,' giving Dwayne the middle finger.

Dwayne tries to go after Issy, his fist clenched. Andre uses his body to block Dwayne from getting close.

Issy sees Dwayne fighting to open the studio door, 'Come then?' she shouts. 'Punch me, then? See what happens. I'm not scared of you, Dwayne. I won't think twice before feds are called.'

'CALL THEM!' Dwayne shouts back.

'You're to blame for this!' she continues over his insults. 'You're the problem. Always have been.'

'Come out my fucking face, man.'

'You drop out of school and drag him down with you.'

Dwayne tries to push past Andre but Anton grabs him.

'GET OFF ME, BRUV!'

'You think you're big trying to attack a female, yeah?' Issy shouts. 'Go make your little songs, then. I'm done with all of you.' She slams the club hall door behind her so hard the frame shakes.

Issy runs up Jerningham Road in floods of tears. She opens her front door to find music blasting from the living room. 'Mum?' she says, opening the living room door.

Carol takes her hand out of her tracksuit bottoms hoping Issy didn't see her.

'Why are you sitting in the dark?' Issy turns on the light and sees her mum is drinking.

'Are you drunk?'

'No,' Carol slurs.

'Yes, you are.'

Carol wipes her fingers down her tracksuit bottoms then takes a sip from her mug, 'Your dad loved this song. Billy Fury.' She puts down her mug and stumbles to her feet, 'He'd take me in his arms and dance with me like this,' Carol tries to dance with Issy.

'No, Mum. Look at you,' Issy turns down the volume.

Carol's arms flop to her side. 'What harm is it to drink to the dead?' She throws a salute into the air.

She stops swaying. 'You look just like your dad did when he was angry at me. He adored you, his little princess.'

'STOP!' Issy yells.

Carol grabs the framed photograph of her husband from the arm chair and dances with it. 'Some women wish their husbands to die, but you,' Carol croaks. She takes another gulp, this time from the quarter bottle of vodka inside her pale blue dressing gown.

'Mum! Stop!' Issy tries to grab the bottle from her mum's hands but Carol swerves out of Issy's way. Issy tries to grab the bottle again. Carol swerves again but this time, she drops the photo on the floor. The glass shatters. Carol drops to pick it up, cutting a finger. She begins to sob.

Issy looks down at her mother then kneels next to her. 'Mum?'

'I'm fine.'

'Do you need a plaster?'

'A plaster?' Carol snorts. 'I need a drink,' she says, letting the vodka bottle empty out onto the floor.

'Mum.'

'Stop judging me!' Carol snaps. Taking the broken photo frame, Carol kisses her husband's smiling face, blood from her finger dripping down her dressing gown.

'You'll cut your lips!' Issy tries to grab the photo frame from her mother.

'Get off, alright. GO AWAY!' Carol screams, before running out of steam. A more desperate Carol looks into Issy's eyes, 'You're leaving me anyway, aren't you?'

Issy runs out of the flat. She runs past Hayley's mum's block, past Jerome and Dwayne's flat, along Ommaney Road. Not welcome at Emily's house, Issy runs up Pepys Road to Telegraph Hill Park. She collapses on top of the hill and sees Karen is there with the dog she walks for her elderly neighbour.

'Issy, love,' she says softly. 'What's wrong?'

'I'm fine,' Issy says, wiping her eyes.

'Not sure you are, love.'

'I want my dad back,' Issy whispers. Then anger rises, 'If my dad was here we wouldn't be on this estate. I wouldn't have met Jerome and his stupid fucking brother. We wouldn't be this poor. She wouldn't be drinking all day.'

'I know,' Karen says gently.

'I hate my life.'

'Now Issy Richards, what if your dad could see you now? He would say stop this talk. If you want rid of this estate and this life, you will. He was a grafter. Whatever he wanted, he earned it. If you want something, work for it. Thinking like this won't get you far.'

'I didn't choose this life, Karen.'

'You think you've had it tough? Think of your mum. She lost her husband and her home. If it wasn't for the council giving you your flat, you'd be homeless. Can you imagine that? Yes, it's a shithole in your eyes, but it's more than most kids around the world have. You got a warm bed and your mum works hard to keep the bills paid and food on your table. Sometimes we have to be grateful with what we have.'

'People don't think like that,' Issy snaps. 'They sell drugs and go rioting. Politicians steal expenses then make teenagers like me pay nine grand a year just to read books.' Issy's head fills with everything bad in the world. The pain in her chest tightens as she thinks about Jerome, throwing away his relationship with her. They supposed to be lovebirds like Mum and Dad were.

'Being a teenager is tough,' Karen says through the silence. 'Especially today. You're going into adulthood now. Let it make you, not break you. Your life is nothing to be ashamed of. Neither is wanting more. Being honest and living a good life means you can sleep at night with a clear conscience. How do those MPs really feel about themselves, eh? They can have all the money in the world but they know deep down they're worthless scum making the poor pay all the time. But you Issy, you just have to learn to do things with a good heart. Don't be bitter about things.' Karen takes a deep breath and sighs. 'It's complicated.' She puts the dog on the leash. 'Come on, let's get you home.'

CHAPTER 29
GO

Issy sits in English watching her peers like they're in a wildlife documentary. Her body feels tired and heavy from the load that's not hers to carry. All the students look odd. With their weird faces and necks tilting to read the whiteboard. Some with glasses and wonky fingers scribbling notes.

Mrs Salmon walks over to speak to one of the students. Noticing Issy distracted as she passes, she picks up her workbook. Nothing written except the date.

'Everything okay?' she asks.

'Huh?' Issy blinks up. Mrs Salmon in a bright yellow top with that worried, sympathetic look on her face. Eyebrows raised with concern.

'Should I call the school nurse?'

Issy shakes her head, 'Nah Miss, I'm cool, I'm cool.'

When the lesson ends, Mrs Salmon asks Issy to stay behind. She reluctantly sits on the table nearest the door.

'Want one?' asks Mrs Salmon pouring a sachet of instant cappuccino into a red VOTE LABOUR mug.

Issy nods.

She takes the little kettle she keeps in her desk and pours bottled water into it.

'What's happened?'

'Really wanna know?'

'I do.'

They watch the steam rise and the kettle switch off.

Mrs Salmon pours hot water into a blue mug before handing it to Issy. 'Careful. Don't burn yourself.'

'Everything's fucked,' Issy replies, taking the coffee Emily once flatly refused at her flat, calling it chemically produced coffee-flavoured fluff.

'My whole life. One fucking mess. Thanks for the coffee.'

'Issy, I've not seen you like this.'

Issy puts down the mug, 'Yeah, well, having dreams is bullshit. Year 10, I was happy. I played stupid games with my stupid friends. Had a best friend I cared about. Had a boyfriend I loved. A mother who wasn't alcoholic. All because of my dreaming, things are changing. I thought for the better but it's getting worse.'

'You're not responsible for other people's actions.'

'Yeah but my decisions are making them do stuff. If I didn't ignore Hayley, maybe she wouldn't have got pregnant. If I didn't hang out with Jerome more than my mum, she wouldn't have got all lonely and start hiding vodka in her tea. If I didn't wanna go uni, then I wouldn't have cared if Jerome is making violent shitty music – I never even thought about it before Emily told me. And if I never met her, I wouldn't want another life. I wouldn't have seen her big house, her friends' designer clothes and their swimming pools and roof gardens. I wouldn't know no better.'

The teacher gently lifts up Issy's chin so their eyes meet. 'You listen here.' Her tone shifts. 'I won't have moping about in my classroom while kids in this school haven't got a hope of getting a job, let alone a flat or house. But you,' she says softly, 'you've got it. You've got potential. Do you know what a gift that is? Potential is a precious, precious gift. Hayley got pregnant because she didn't protect herself, and allowed the man not to wear a condom. Your mum chooses to buy that vodka, not you. You can't blame yourself for not being there, although I know you feel you should. My father, same story. I spent years looking after him, but in the end, the drink was more important. That's your mum's fight, not yours, you hear?'

Issy nods, surprised by her teacher's sternness.

'And Emily? You were going to change irrespective of meeting Emily. We all change. We all mature and become different people. You're growing up, plain and simple. It's not rocket science. It would be weird if you didn't change between fourteen and eighteen. It wasn't Emily who sat your exams, or writes your coursework. That's your hard work, Isobel Richards...' She pokes her gently in the ribs. 'I hope...'

'I'm not a cheat, Miss.'

'So you are the person making the changes, improving your life. You are in the driving seat.'

Issy feels some weight lifting from her shoulders.

Seeing Issy smile, Mrs Salmon goes to her desk and takes out an A4 plastic wallet. She looks up at the clock, 'Issy, I have to get going now, but this is for you.'

Issy takes the plastic wallet from her teacher.

'It's your UCAS pack. Along with photocopies of universities that I recommend you consider. I've included your UCAS forms and added a filled out one as an example. You should start thinking about where you want to study. The application process begins now. All you have to do is choose your universities, fill out this form and hand it to the Sixth Form office for proof-reading. There are bursaries you are eligible for, which means the government will subsidise your fees. You can get a loan to cover your living costs. You have to pay most of it back, sadly, but as a Northerner I take no responsibility for voting in the Tories, not that Labour didn't start this mess but anyway, I'll help you with that. You should also see if you can transfer to a pharmacy near university so you can keep earning money while you study.'

Issy looks at the list of universities, 'You think I should go.'

'Yes, I do. Going to a London university was the best thing for me. I never saw a life for me living in my father's cramped flat in Salford. You want more Issy, so take it. It's obvious to me. To your mum. To your boyfriend. To everyone. Don't feel guilty. They live the life that's right for them. But it doesn't feel like your life, does it?'

Issy looks at her teacher. It doesn't feel like the life she wants, but to say it out loud makes her nervous. Before Issy can bring herself to admit it, Mrs Salmon acknowledges the unspoken answer and continues.

'So go Issy. Make your life happen. Yourself.' Mrs Salmon's lips quiver with emotion. Issy can see a tear in her teacher's eye.

'What about Jerome? Do you think we should get back together?'

Mrs Salmon takes a moment before saying. 'That's why we call it our First Love, Issy.'

Mrs Salmon unplugs her phone from the charger and picks up her bag.

'Miss? Why do you care so much about me?'

'Ah, that's an easy one,' Mrs Salmon smiles. 'Because I'm a teacher.'

Issy sits on the desk staring down at the UCAS form. She's still reading through the pack when the cleaning man comes and tells her it's time to leave.

CHAPTER 30
SISTERHOOD

Dwayne is at the kitchen table, tapping the calculator app on his phone. He adds a zero, then another, then another. Imagine being that rich, he wonders. Mansion, Ferrari, trainers for every day of the year. Right now he's saving for a diamond encrusted cross on a forty-two inch platinum chain. He makes projections based on his current earnings. If he reduced the amount of people he has to share the cut with, he would get his things faster: Andre. Andre is the best rapper, so Andre needs to stay. Anton. Anton is good-looking and attracts the females plus his dad deals Graff their weed. Jerome. Brother and producer. Vital. That leaves Barry. What's he good for? He studies and does legit work and the only one who won't hide things in his yard. He doesn't sell the most CDs or weed. Barry has to go.

Dwayne goes to the fridge and pours a glass of milk. Downing it in one, he takes a spliff from his room and grabs his coat. Heading down the stairwell by Hayley's mum's flat, Dwayne puts his hood up so the icy wind doesn't hit the back of his neck. He thinks about Hayley, how she would follow him everywhere, be jealous of anyone talking to him. He chuckles as he remembers Hayley fighting with her brother about going out with him. Ronnie eventually gave in and said yes, though he'd been fucking her for time by then.

Dwayne thinks about Issy and Jerome, back together again after their madness. At the end of the day, Dwayne can see why Issy got vex. He knows getting Emmanuel to sell weed is raw, but that's business. Youngers rarely get stopped by police. It's risk management. All entrepreneurs need a team and the younger they are, the cheaper the labour, the better for profits. He's just a businessman at the end of the day and Dwayne knows Jerome and Issy's relationship is on a timer. Once she goes university, it's done.

A man scrambles past up the stairwell holding Pound Shop bags full of baby wipes. Dwayne thinks about Jamal. Inhaling the blue-grey smoke deep into his lungs, he wonders what Hayley is doing now. He recalls the christening and how his grandmother keeps asking to see Baby Jamal. He has to admit that chances of Jamal not being his are small. Hayley may be a thief and a liar, but unlike Dwayne – who never really cared too much about her – she rated him.

Issy's phone beeps. **Babes, u'll neva gess who's ere. Cum my yard, Jx.**

She rings him immediately, 'Who?'

'It's a surprise, man. Just come!'

'This better be good, cos it's freezing outside!' Issy drags herself from the textbooks and layers up.

Jerome opens the door eyes bright and happy. He kisses her warmly on the lips.

'What's got into you?' Issy laughs. 'Santa here early?'

'You could say that, the amount of presents here,' Jerome chuckles. Holding Issy's hand, he pulls her into the living room.

'Surprise!' Jerome pushes her through the door where she's stunned to discover Hayley, Granny Mabel and Dwayne. On the floor baby Jack-Jamal lies on top of a colourful alphabet and numbers play mat. Mabel is holding up two black baby dolls with afro-style hair, saying she can't believe what she is seeing.

Issy feels her stomach flip as she makes eye contact with Hayley. She never told Jerome what happened at the young women's refuge centre. She didn't think it was worth it.

Jerome notices the awkward greeting between Hayley and Issy. 'Shall we get a drink?'

Still holding Issy's hand, he guides her into the kitchen. 'You okay?'

'Yeah. No. Sort of.'

Issy looks at the floor.

'You look shook when you see her. Did something happen?'

'Jerome!' Mabel calls from the living room. 'Take the milk and cocoa and make some hot chocolate.'

'Okay.'

'Jay, I didn't wanna say nothing... I still don't but–'

Just at that moment, Hayley walks in. 'Jerome, can I speak to Issy, alone?'

Jerome faces Issy, 'You cool with that?'

Issy nods. 'I'll warm the milk.'

He kisses her on the cheek, and whispers, 'Love you, babe,' in her ear.

'Still as sweet as ever!' Hayley remarks with a smile, but the smile soon fades as Issy turns her back to take milk from the fridge.

'Look, I just wanna say sorry, for what happened with us. I was in a bad state. I just lost it.'

Issy, her body stiff with self-protection, back facing her former best friend, pours milk into a pan and lights the cooker. She can't think of a reply.

'I know there's no taking back what I done, but last year was the hardest year I think I've ever been through. I had a baby, lost my family, my boyfriend, my best friend — you....' Hayley's voice trails off into a mumble.

Issy turns to face Hayley. She's even fatter than the last time they met, wearing a camel-coloured velour tracksuit that's too tight around her hips and thighs. She looks different, too. Her face is plumper but brighter; her hair thick and healthy looking.

'You look well,' Issy lies.

'You do. Skinny or what,' Hayley replies. 'Not like me, I'm a lump now I've had JJ.'

'JJ?'

'Jack-Jamal.'

'So you two back together?' Issy asks after some silence.

'Nah. I need space.'

Issy watches Hayley swallow her emotions. Perhaps she's grown up for real this time.

'I've been on a programme,' Hayley continues. 'After our fight, Irene put me on anger management training. And I've had counselling. I needed to sort my head out. Anyway, you don't have to forgive me. I just wanna say I worked it out with my therapist. You was changing and I hated being left behind. I thought you was choosing Emily over me. I know I was a little cow back then, but I was always loyal. I got a proper shock when no-one cared my phone and gold got jacked. I had no-one to back it for me. No-one even noticed.' Hayley bites her bottom lip, forcing any tears to retreat.

Issy turns again to check the milk, testing the temperature with the back of her little finger.

'Anyway, so that's all I gotta say,' Hayley says, before walking out the kitchen.

'Do you want a hot chocolate?' Issy calls after her.

Hayley returns with a smile: 'Got custard creams in my bag. Your favourite.'

'They're not my favourite anymore.'

'Oh,' Hayley replies.

Issy hates how ungrateful that just sounded. 'But I still eat them,' she adds.

'Hays?' Issy's voice cracks, 'I'm sorry too. I know I neglected you.'

A tear of shame falls down Issy's cheek. Hayley walks over and wraps her arms around her – and Issy lets her. The two girls hold on to each other, more than ever needing something in their lives to feel real.

CHAPTER 31

'I was Jack-the-lad, like you when I was young. But you have to do some things proper. You don't want the Old Bill on your case twenty-four-seven. Let me tell you, my son, life's a headache the best of times. I know, I got kids. Indicate. Mirror, mirror, signal. That's it, my son. Turn left there.'

Bob is a forty-seven-year-old ex-cab driver. He runs his own small business and has been offering reduced cost lessons to young fathers as part of a scheme called "Get Dads Driving". Part of Hayley's support worker's job is to engage the fathers of teenage mothers to play a more active role. Once the young fathers bond with their babies, they're more likely to support their babies financially and emotionally into childhood. Dwayne refused to take part in the working with fathers group, until Hayley told him he can get a driving licence for free.

The first week, Dwayne found the "my son" uncomfortable. The last bloke to do that was the drug dealer in Deptford, promising sweet cocaine dealing spots in West End nightclubs once Dwayne earned his stripes.

'Go on, my son, that's it. You're a natural. Right, back up now. And stop. I'm proud. You're doing great. Be driving in no time. Smart brain there. Wished I'd had them brains...'

Bob was born in Peckham and went to school in Lewisham. He met his wife on holiday in Jamaica and they now live in a semi-detached house in Bromley. Dwayne finds Bob fascinating. He's never met a white man married to a black woman before. He finds himself looking forward to the driving. After each lesson ends, Dwayne gets out the car feeling like a different sort of Dwayne. He started daydreaming the other day about how it would be if Bob turned out to be his dad, if Bob's wife from Jamaica was his biological mum in real life and Bob was actually his stepdad. Could happen. He doesn't know where his mum is. He thought he'd just pay cash for a car with blacked-out windows and teach himself how to drive, but Bob told him it doesn't work like that:

'When I started boxing, right, that's when I got things straight in my head. I went in thinking I need to know how to knock people out, but soon realised my body is a machine controlled by this'–Bob taps his head. 'Pieces of the puzzle was getting put together, know what I mean? That's when I got it. It clicked. Curbing my temper was the key to success, not fighting every Tom, Dick or Harry. Right, my son. See you next Wednesday. Same time. Don't be late. I may be some things, but patient ain't one of 'em.'

Dwayne lies on his bed after another lesson. Unaware it's Bob's job to get Dwayne into a headspace that sees family and relationships as things you need to nurture, Dwayne finds himself dreaming again about Bob being his stepdad. About how they would take Jack-Jamal to the park, and teach him football. How Hayley would be there and Bob's Jamaican wife. In his head, if she isn't his mum, then she looks like an actress.

Dwayne looks over at his phone charging. He thinks about checking his ratings, then realises he hasn't checked them all day. He didn't go online much yesterday because he was spending time with his baby, and he doesn't want Jack-Jamal to be around him when he's on some madness. Bob told him, 'One thing, we never ever fight in front of the kids. That's their innocence. They only get that once. Once you break a kid's innocence, that's it. It can't be unheard or unseen.' Dwayne knows that shit the hard way. 'Put the phones away,' said Bob.

Hayley reckons the council are finding her a small flat to live in, down in Catford. Dwayne thinks about how nice it's gonna be to have his own flat and his own space. He can decorate the baby's room. Jack-Jamal can have a car-shaped bed. Maybe getting back with her is the right thing to do. He could tell Bob next week he's gonna sort things out and one day get a house with enough space for Bob and his wife to visit. What Dwayne doesn't know is that Bob has funding for ten driving lessons per teenager and the high demand for "Get Dads Driving" means that after Christmas, that's it. Dwayne won't be seeing Stepdad Bob ever again.

Issy knows Henry Sparling doesn't like her. It's been five weeks since she spent any time with Emily and she's starting to think their friendship might be changing.

Hey Mimi, I'm free tonight, what you up to? Issy texts, sitting on the sofa opposite her mum.

'Why don't you stay in with me tonight?' Carol asks.

'I ain't seen Emily in ages, Mum.'

Carol lights a cigarette. She offers Issy one.

'I told you, I quit.'

'Still?' Carol asks, surprised.

'Yes.'

Issy stares at the muted adverts on the television, annoyed at her mother's lack of support. 'You should be proud of me.'

'Well I am proud,' Carol replies.

'Would be easier if I didn't have to smell it all the time,' Issy adds.

They sit in silence. Carol rolls the tip of the newly lit cigarette around the ashtray to have something to do.

Issy studies her mother's face. Her skin looks pale and tired. Her eyes are puffy and sore looking. The pinks under her eyes are faded like a washed out sock. Carol looks depressed.

'Mum? Have you ever thought about, like, marrying again? You know, meeting someone new.'

Carol's eyes flare up. Issy drops her head into her arms to protect her face. 'Don't' slap 'You' slap 'Ever' slap 'Ever' slap 'Ask' slap 'Me' slap 'That' slap 'Again!'

'Mum! Stop! Mum!' The ashtray falls from the arm onto the seat, 'Stop, Mum, your fag!'

Carol continues to hit her daughter, each strike weak, feeble; doesn't hurt her. Issy pushes her mum away grabbing the fallen cigarette, dusting off the burning embers.

'Look what you've done!' Issy cries. 'And you wonder why I don't wanna be here anymore? I don't deserve this shit!'

'You?' Carol spits out in disgust. 'You think you're something special now, don't ya? You think you can tell me what I need? You don't know the half of it. You think life out there is wee smiles and roses. It ain't.'

'Life's what you make it, Mum. You can't just accept living in a shithole your whole life, smoking cancer sticks. Dad's dead, okay, and sitting in this flat drinking all day won't bring him back.'

Carol snatches her wedding photograph from the shelf and runs upstairs.

'You stink of booze,' Issy shouts after her.

Issy slumps back on the sofa, staring at the remaining pictures of her father lined up along the plastic shelf. She's too shocked to cry. Too angry to scream. Ruined. The sofa's ruined. Now she has to look at that every day.

Issy, come to Richie's. Bring pyjamas. We're just having a pillow fight! It's fun!

Bring lacy underw¬

Sorry, that was Ritchie being naughty!

Her mood switches with a little flutter inside. She decides to phone Emily.

'Yah, hallo?' Henry answers.

'Oh hi, Henry.'

'Yes, Isabella.'

'Emily around?'

'I can't see her.'

'She just texted me to come join you guys.'

'Not sure about that,' comes Henry's painfully plummy voice. 'I'll let her know you called. Have a good one.' The phone clicks dead.

Issy's cheeks burn with embarrassment. Knowing she would have left her mum upset to go meet rich and pretentious arses like Henry stings. Angry with herself and feeling guilty, she tiptoes upstairs and gently knocks on Carol's bedroom door.

'GO AWAY!'

Issy tentatively pushes the door open.

There's a scurry, then thuds across the carpet and Carol's slams the door shut, pushing Issy back into the hallway.

'I mean it. Leave me alone!'

Issy goes to her own room and lies on the single bed, feeling the springs dig at her ribs. She stares at her pink bedroom curtains, then the photos on her dresser. She focuses on the one with her and Emily when they were sixteen, then the passport photo of Jerome hiding the corner crack in her dressing table mirror. She sits up and gazes out of the window, the days now are short and the dark relentless. Summer feels so far away. The orange glow of the street lamp over the tree outside. The branches have been cut by tree surgeons so it looks spooky.

Her phone beeps again. **Hey it's Richie, Please come, it's been ages, too long. Here's plenty of room and everyone staying gets bacon and eggs in the morning.** Richie was really nice during her break with Jerome, sending kind thoughtful messages and liking all her statuses and Insta photos.

Issy thinks about taking her Primark pyjamas to Richie's house, how he will charm her, how Henry won't. Emily will be there but not really engage like she used to when Emily liked radical feminist artists. Issy thinks about how she didn't even know what art was three years ago and now she actually enjoys museums and galleries, and doesn't feel like an alien landing as she walks through huge museum doors. She thinks about her life here in this flat and how far away it is from Richie's in his massive townhouse: From Emily's. From Henry's. From George's. Hendrike's, Helena's, Sophie's.

She doesn't answer the text. Instead, she sits at her desk and takes out a pen and paper.

Dear Dad,

I've upset Mum. Big time. I asked if she would get married again and she just flipped. I think she thought I meant forget you, but I didn't. More, move on. I don't know how that makes you feel. I wasn't meaning it in a bad way. Truth is, I think she needs to. Drink ain't the answer, you know that. I wish you were here to tell me it's okay to go uni. Mum has, but things ain't the same since I told her I've applied outside London. She's already started with the silent treatment.

Dad, I know you're in Heaven now, so maybe there's Jesus to give everyone advice. Can you ask if it's okay to be different? I mean, the more I change, the more I don't fit nowhere. Maybe this life here is who I am. Why change? This is where I live. Even if you was alive, we wouldn't be in a massive mansion, so why am I trying to be someone I'm not?

The bedroom lights flicker, then a lightbulb short circuits and the whole room goes black. Issy jumps from her desk and runs to the hallway. She flicks the lights in the landing but they're not going on either, 'Mum? Mum? MUM!'

Carol emerges with her lighter on. 'What's happened?'

'Mum? I'm scared. I think it's a ghost. I think it's Dad.'

'Come here, silly.' Carol walks slowly towards her daughter trying to keep the lighter flame going.

Carol guides Issy downstairs to the fuse box.

'It's just the switch popped out,' Carol says, rubbing her daughter's back to soothe the shaking. 'Don't be scared.' Carol flicks the switch and the flat lights up. 'I'm sorry for being a nutter, just then,' she adds.

'I'm sorry. If I'd known–'

'No love,' Carol interrupts, kissing Issy's forehead. 'Sometimes it's us parents who get it wrong. I know what you was trying to do. You're looking out for me and I love you for that.' Carol wraps her arms around her daughter – who suddenly bursts into tears.

'Hey?'

'I miss him. I miss him so, so much.' Issy wipes her tears away. 'Do you think he'd be proud of me?'

'Of course he would.'

'No, I mean it. Would he think I was trying to be something I ain't?'

Carol doesn't answer.

'Am I Mum? Am I? Am I trying to be someone I ain't?'

Issy wipes her dripping nose with her sleeve, then looks at the wet patch, 'See? See what I'm like? I don't fit nowhere. Nowhere.'

Carol laughs softly, 'Now you're the wee nutter.'

Standing in the hallway under the light from the orange lampshade, Issy laughs along.

'Sorry I hit you,' Carol says. 'Really am.'

'It's okay, Mum. It didn't hurt.' Issy smirks, 'You couldn't hit if your life depended on it.'

That weekend, Issy visits Hayley as she promised she would. She's stunned by the amount of baby clothes in Hayley's laundry basket.

'Hays, who got you these?' Issy picks up a designer cardigan.

'Dwayne. It's real you know,' Hayley says, not bothered how much of this could be stolen, or a waste of money.

'Don't you think you should be careful what JJ wears? You're on benefits.'

'I'll say the truth, innit. His father got it.'

'There might be a job coming up at the pharmacy, full time. They asked me but I can only do weekends until my A-Levels are done.'

'Nah, can't,' Hayley says, blowing smoke out of the living room window, cigarette in her hand, resting on the ledge. 'Got the baby to think of.'

Issy's thinks Hayley never intends on working, ever.

Hayley checks her phone as it beeps incessantly. 'Oh my days!'

Issy's phone goes off too.

'You got what I just got?' Hayley looks at Issy with wide-eyes and an involuntary grin, 'Dwayne's gonna go mad.'

Issy rushes to the bathroom thinking she might be sick. She looks in the mirror, checking to see if her face matches the feeling in her stomach, then sits on the toilet seat, head in hands. She sits bolt upright. With trembling fingers she calls Jerome.

'Babe—' Jerome's soothing voice that sounds like home.

'Jerome, what we gonna do? He's probably gonna wanna get everyone—'

'I know.'

There's silence on the other end of the phone, 'Jay, find him before he does something.'

'Babe, let me call you back.'

'Jay, just tell me, should I be worried about you?'

'Look, let me call you back, please?'

'Okay.' And the phone clicks dead.

Jerome watches Dwayne pacing. He watches Andre, Anton and Barry; they're staring at Dwayne, trying to see what the next move is. Each time a new track comes out, the ante is upped. But this track is different. This track is aimed solely at Double-G. Cyber X is calling for all surrounding soldiers to come together to take Dwayne down. Cyber X pays youngers more money because he's richer than Double-G. His weed is stronger; Dwayne's is cut up and fake. Cyber pours the champagne, while Double-G pours fake – even using footage from Jack-Jamal's christening showing the bottles of fake champagne in Dwayne's hand. The chorus goes, 'And if you don't like the truth, you can suck my dick.'

Jerome touches the scar on his own cheek as he listens to Dwayne.

'I know what dem manz is thinking,' Dwayne says. 'They're expecting me to come tooled up with my bredders, but no, I ain't falling for little tricks... Just wait and see... I need my army to make money, not getting stabbed up the place... Yeah, I've got my little boy now... Exactly, how's he gonna take over the empire, if Daddy ain't built it yet? Man in pen? Not for this.'

Andre looks at Dwayne and chuckles, 'Oh my days, bruv. I was not expecting all that to come from your lips!'

'Wow that's really cool of you!' Jerome says, impressed.

'Bro, did you just say "cool"?' Anton shrugs his body as if shaking off a spider.

'What's wrong with "cool"? You always use it.'

'Yeah,' Anton replies, 'but, tings like, "Cool-dat" or "Cool-cool". What's with the "that is cool" flex?'

'Come out my face, man!'

Anton and Andre chuckle.

'You hanging with dem posh peeps too much,' Andre says.

'Whatever,' Jerome laughs it off. 'All I'm saying is I'm fine with allowing shit.'

'Don't get me wrong, fam,' Dwayne snorts. 'I'll be squashing this ting, but my own way, get me.'

Dwayne updates his status, **Bitches & mans, best beware Double-G flexing next level psychological warfare.**

Later that night, Dwayne makes a call, 'Ruby, babes, you on it?'

'Yes, sweetness.'

Dwayne tries to leave the bedroom quietly but wakes Jerome knocking his knee against the bedpost.

'What's up, where you going?'

'Hayley,' Dwayne lies. 'She needs some powder milk from that 24/7 pharmacy.'

'D,' Jerome says in the dark.

'Yeah?'

'Today I saw a side of you I thought I'd lost.'

'What you on, bruv?'

'With the reaction, to Cyber's track.' Jerome rests on one elbow and rubs his eyes, 'Not tooling up and ting, and now sorting your baby out... I'm proud, bro.'

'Yeah, yeah.'

'Nah, serious tings,' Jerome continues, grabbing Dwayne's wrist. 'You're my brother. You know I got your back, but it ain't always about fighting. Love you, D.'

'Yeah cool,' Dwayne says awkwardly and they knock fists. Dwayne waits for his brother to settle back down, then pokes his head back into the room, and shouts, 'BATTY MAN!' and leaves laughing.

On his way to Ruby's, the driving instructor – Stepdad Bob's – voice enters Dwayne's head: That's it my son! You passed first time! Nah, can't make personal connections. It's the rules. There to protect you and me. Once that dashboard camera stops filming, I'm open to all sorts of accusations. You too. Nothing personal, son. Don't you worry. You're going places. I can see that. You don't need old codgers like me hanging around…

He arrives at Ruby's house, parks up quietly, grabs his weed and rum and pushes open the unlocked door. She takes him straight to her bedroom. He pulls off her dressing gown, bends her over the bed and reaches into the jar of Vaseline on the bedside table, smearing it all over her batty and up inside her pussy.

Afterwards, Dwayne hands her some money. He hasn't even started his engine before Ruby picks up her phone to call Cyber X.

CHAPTER 32

'Thanks for having us, Issy,' Emily says, busy hacking into a French baguette for their lunch. Emily still feels bad Henry put Isobel off coming to Richie's pyjama party so in a bid to make peace, she's convinced that if Henry meets Issy and Jerome on their turf, he'll be less arrogant – out of his comfort zone and she'll be more comfy in hers.

'Yes, very kind of you.' Henry picks up a cherry tomato from the plate of meat, but decides to skip the breaded ham. With his heavyset, six-foot frame, Henry looks like a giant as he awkwardly sits down at the small kitchen table.

Her flat disgusts Henry. Issy can see it all over his face – even though she spent all weekend polishing and cleaning.

Henry and Jerome are not getting along either.

'How is the rapping going?' Henry asks.

'Yeah, cool,' Jerome says. He briefly looks at Issy then down at the baguette Emily plops on his plate.

'Well that's nice to hear,' Henry replies, rolling his eyes at Emily.

Emily and Issy exchange glances; it's the wrong subject for everyone.

'I hear George is still keen to get involved?' Henry ploughs on.

'Yeah? He sent some samples. Man's got bare ideas for beats.' Jerome butters the white French stick, wondering how he's going to shit it out.

'"Bare" means a lot,' Emily says.

'I know, Emily.' Henry shoots his girlfriend a look.

Inside, Issy's blood boils. She loves Jerome, but if he ever dared to look at her that way, she'd knock him out.

Their lunch lasts under an hour, though it feels like weeks for all of them.

There were more awkward silences in that one hour than in Issy's entire adolescence, she thinks. Her skull throbbing with what felt like a constant fight and battle for her identity – under constant insidious attack from Henry. Issy had been careful to make everything as perfect as possible. Best table cloth. Best plates, cups, and glasses, keeping the chipped and stained stuff for her and Jerome to use. Supermarket's finest range of food. Super expensive bread from the artisan bakery. Cherry tomatoes instead of the tasteless orange-coloured ones her mum buys. But none of it worked. She feels smaller and cheaper than ever in Henry's eyes and turns into Jerome's open arms the moment the door closes behind their guests.

Emily and Henry exit the stairwell, past an old man spitting phlegm onto the communal grass. Along Ommaney Road, the flats turn into three-story houses. Henry stops then and stares at his girlfriend.

'Emily, these people are not your friends.'

'They are my friends,' Emily says. 'And what's with all your prejudiced asides and snide remarks throughout lunch?'

'They're a liability. What can they do for you? This boy is clearly a criminal. Whatever made you think it was a good idea to spring a day in a council flat on me?'

'It was one hour and –' Emily stops, as someone approaches.

Once the woman walks past, Henry continues, 'I mean, did you see that tat on her walls? These people are puerile. No education. No economic stability. Sponging off the council while they eat like kings on taxpayers' money.'

Henry storms ahead.

'Her mother works in a supermarket,' Emily calls out, chasing after him.

'Which is where Isabella's heading.'

He stomps up the entrance stairs of 55 Pepys Road. 'Her boyfriend is clearly going to prison.'

Emily pushes the key into the lock with unnecessary force. 'You're starting to sound like my father.'

'Well, Emily, I'm afraid he's right.'

The lock eases as Mr Sutton opens the door from inside.

'Right about what?'

'Ah, well,' Henry goes red and holds out his hand to shake Mr Sutton's.

'I was just telling Emily'–he ignores Emily's dig in his side as they walk into the house.

'About my relocation model for bad housewives?'

Both men laugh.

'Daddy!'

'Oh come along, Emily.'

'What I was saying to Emily, Mr Sutton, is that–'

'For God sakes boy, call me Edward.'

'Pardon me, Edward. That sounds rather odd, and strangely wrong. Even Emily calls you Mr Sutton.'

'That's insolence,' comes the voice of Emily's mother, sat in the corner of the living room with her sewing project.

'Mother's side, of course,' Mr Sutton adds.

'Really, Butty?' Janie Sutton says, looking up from her needlework.

Both men laugh again. Emily cracks a smile. She knows her father got called Butty for misbehaviour at school, and that her mother is reminding him of it. She likes it when Janie uses her wit to gently remind everyone she's not insipid.

'I seem to have lost my point now,' Henry says.

'What Henry is trying to say, Daddy-dearest,' Emily emphasises with sarcasm, 'is that poor people deserve what they get in life. That, no matter what misfortune comes their way, everything is their own fault and doing.'

'You make me sound so harsh, Emily. That's not how I think. But had her mother worked harder or been more educated, Isabella wouldn't be living on such an estate.'

'Her husband died.'

'Are you still going about that Isobel girl?' Mr Sutton asks, keeping his cool in front of Henry, plus it sounds like Henry is steering his daughter to dry land. He's in a rather good mood today having reviewed his judge's pension. He just scraped in being given a final salary pension by one year being born in 1956. Any judge born after 1957 is set to lose thousands, unlucky buggers.

'Only theoretically, Daddy.' Emily shoots Henry a 'keep our lunch today private' look. She hates Henry's put on serious voice and mannerisms in front of her dad.

Henry takes in the new information, and continues, 'Of course it's a tragedy that she lost her husband, but not every widow sucks up the government's housing stock. Had she and her husband worked harder or smarter, they would have investments, insurances, and such. It's not hard, is it? These people deserve what they get because they cease to take the vast opportunities this country has to offer...' Henry pauses, wary of sounding overbearing inside the home of his father's best friend. 'Apologies if that came across abrupt, Mr– Edward.'

'Not at all. Couldn't have put it better myself.'

'Thank you Sir, I mean, Edward.'

Emily can't take any more. She throws up her arms. 'To me it all sounds horribly divisive and against any principles I was taught as a child – by my parents – to share my stuff and treat people equally. I mean why send me to Sunday School to learn all that, if you don't believe in it yourself?'

'On the contrary Emily, this country does share resources.' Mr Sutton sits in his favourite armchair. 'We have free healthcare, free education, free housing; access to free libraries and books and the internet; affordable food, clean tap water. What more does one need to succeed?'

Emily turns to her mother, who has taken to the rocking chair over by the far bay window, keeping her head down sewing a circle-shaped tapestry from this month's Home Improvements magazine. God, she is so boring. This image alone makes Emily want to throw up.

'Laziness,' Henry suddenly says.

'Yes, you are quite right,' Mr Sutton agree. 'Look at what my great-grandfather made from the pennies in his pocket? This house was never an inexpensive investment. Or Henry's grandfather?'

'Indeed,' Henry agrees. 'I'm not moneyed England. We Sparlings are what you call, nouveau riche.'

'Footballers are nouveau riche!' Emily remarks. Feeling like a sailor trapped in mist inside the Bermuda triangle, she leaves the living room.

Henry follows her to the kitchen. He cuddles up next to her at the marble worktop. 'You must see why your father disapproves of Isabella,' he whispers.

'Is-o-bel.'

'Take that awful boyfriend of hers. What's he doing with himself?'

Emily rubs her forehead. 'Studying music.'

'He doesn't engage in political debate,' Henry talks over her answer. 'He doesn't read decent newspapers. He certainly doesn't follow the arts, the classics, anything. All these black boys want is to be rappers. I can't bear to listen to it. Those music videos with all their monopoly money and fake gold everywhere, and idiots like him think that's real life.'

'He's not like that.' Emily moves away from Henry to the sink. She pours water into her glass, then watches as the water turns a pastel yellow from the lemon squash. She holds the glass to the window, imagining herself beginning her great watercolour masterpiece: a pale daffodil meadow in morning haze.

Mr Sutton enters. Ignoring the dishwasher, he puts his cup on the side, takes his slippers from under the table and leaves without a word.

'Nobody's putting a gun to their heads, forcing them to sell drugs to all our friends. They do it simply because they don't want to do an honest day's work. They want the most expensive trainers, the most expensive – and in my opinion – cheap-looking clothes. You make it sound as if having a few knocks in life immediately justifies you to become a thief. I mean, come on, we're nearly eighteen. An adult in the eyes of the law. They need to grow up, Isobel too. Being party to such behaviour is a recipe for disaster. You must see this?'

Emily sighs. She feels herself retreat into silence, disconcerted that

Henry seems to see something she doesn't in Issy and Jerome.

'It just makes me so sad to hear all this.' she eventually says, sipping her squash. 'I know,' Henry puts his arms around Emily, 'You're so sweet and your nature is kind by default. That's why I love you, always have.'

Emily looks up from her drink in surprise. He's being so nice to her and in some ways, talking cold hard truths. And then he drops the L-word. 'Did you, just say, you know, what I thought you just said?'

Henry's plump cheeks, grow plumper from grinning. 'I did,' he whispers proudly. 'I've just been too much of a child to admit it to you, and myself. Do you love me back?'

'Well, I, I–' Emily finds herself put on the spot. She isn't sure. She's too conflicted right now. Does she love him? Or is it just that this particular talk has disgusted her?

Henry laughs, 'I know. It must be a bit of a shock. You don't have to say it back.'

'No I do. I do love you back,' Emily blurts, not wanting to disappoint him. Putting her discomfort down to the great problems of the world rather than the possibility that she just spoke aloud words her heart doesn't feel.

Henry takes the glass from Emily's hand. She watches it tumble clumsily into the sink, spilling all of that art down the drain as Henry kisses her firmly on the forehead.

CHAPTER 33
THE WOODS

It's late. Dwayne and Andre are at the flat in Crofton Park. They've snorted several lines of cocaine. Anton chose to meet some girl he has on the grind and Barry never showed up. Dwayne takes this opportunity to ask Andre what he thinks of Barry.

'Man told me he's getting a scholarship,' Andre says. 'Business school.'

'He can't spit bars, he ain't on the hype.'

'He's business minded,' Andre replies. 'You need a smart thinker in the crew.'

'That's what I'm doing, fam. I got spreadsheets looking at profit and costs. Barry ain't making us money.'

Andrew snorts the white powder from a small mirror he took from his parent's bathroom.

'Got plans, but I need a wingman to keep shit tight.' Dwayne pours out rum and juice into plastic throwaway cups. 'It's time to give some of dem youngers their MC names. Start getting new talent to battle for the title. We sell the downloads without wasting time in the studio. My yutes pay for studio time by shotting weed, so every hour yutes are in the studio, Graff are sitting raking in the cash, twice over.'

'Dem yutes get studio time for free though,' Andre says.

'Yeah, but when we're there we charge them. They ain't gonna snitch. We can make it like, 'you're paying to use our label,' innit?'

'Yeah, I was thinking, print t-shirts, jumpers and shit.'

'Yes, bruv.' Dwayne knocks fists with Andre.

'Get them online from China, pound a piece, sell them for like five or ten bar.'

Dwayne's phone vibrates. It's Ruby. He listens to the voice message, then gets up. 'I'm gone, yeah.'

'What?' Andre looks surprised Dwayne is off. 'And Barry? I can tell him.'

'Nah, I will.' He snorts the white line then leaves just as some Brockley Crew arrive.

'His parents will be happy, trust,' Andre says, lining up for the man dem passing through.

Dwayne stops, feeling a jab of something inside, jealousy, envy, hate? Yeah, he hates Barry now.

Fifteen minutes later he pulls up outside at a small terraced house in Streatham. Ruby, excited to be hanging out with Double-G again, is wearing fake eyelashes, too much makeup and not much else. She opens the door, smiling.

'Open the garage,' Dwayne demands. He reverses his car inside.

Ruby takes Dwayne into the living room. They sit down. She can't relax on the sofa, so fraught with anticipation. Does this make them boyfriend and girlfriend now? Can she add him on Facebook yet? Will he actually say the words, 'Will you be my girl?' She watches Dwayne take out his phone and then roll up a twenty pound note.

Her nipples can be seen, hard and erect, through the lacy tight top she's wearing. She slides a hand onto Dwayne's chest – running them across the muscles underneath his shirt. She can't help it. She's in love.

'Not now, man!'

She quickly takes her hand back like it's been scolded and smiles through her embarrassment.

He looks at her plump lips quivering with fear, then chuckles at what he's about to do. Cocaine massively kicking in. 'This is nuts.' Dwayne slaps his own face. 'This is so nuts!'

Her dark brown skin is shimmering from cocoa butter. Her long weave sewn in seamlessly with footballer's wife-style ringlets that fall around her cleavage. He licks his lips but then thinks about Barry going off to business school, wearing a suit, feet up on his desk at work in some shiny office block in Canary Wharf, and his mood switches.

'Go get your phone, man!'

Ruby leans over and picks her mobile off the living room table, 'It's here.'

Dwayne grabs it. Knowing her passcode, he dials Cyber's number, 'Remember what we said.'

Ruby nods, beads of sweat appear on her forehead. This wasn't how she expected it.

'So what you saying?' Ruby says at the phone.

'What you saying?' comes the voice on loud speaker.

250

'I'm here, innit.'

'At your yard, yeah?'

'Yeah.'

'Soon come, soon come.'

Dwayne types something on his phone, then holds it up for Ruby to repeat.

'I'm gonna send you some photos.'

'What you wearing?' Cyber asks.

Dwayne types: U an't redy 4 it.

'You ain't ready,' Ruby reads out from Dwayne's phone.

'Yeah, show me,' Cyber switches to video call.

Ruby mutes the phone, 'Should I accept?'

Dwayne locks the phone off. 'Send him photos.'

Ruby obeys, taking selfies of her lips with red lip-gloss on.

Cum tast it, Dwayne types for her and presses send.

Then they sit and wait.

'Maybe he won't come,' Ruby says after Cyber doesn't reply.

Dwayne elbows the sofa, 'Call the bredder, man?'

The tapping of her fake nails on the phone screen irritates him.

'Yo, where you at?' Ruby asks Cyber. 'You coming?'

Dwayne takes out the wrap and gently unfolds the paper. He pulls out his car key and dips it in the cocaine.

'He said he'll soon come,' Ruby says, after ending the call. She watches Dwayne rub cocaine over his gums. He doesn't offer her any.

'I ain't got all night, trust,' Dwayne snorts. 'Your parents ain't coming back, nah?'

'They're in Jamaica,' she mumbles, wishing they were here.

'No Aunts or nuttin' coming by?' Dwayne continues, looking at her false eyelashes. 'Answer, then?'

'Not now it's late,' Ruby says. She can feel the sweat gather under her weave and start to drip down her neck. She sits back from Dwayne and crosses her legs defensively. Dwayne follows her eyes to the front door.

'Don't worry, babes. I ain't vex with you,' he says, smiling and throws her phone back to her. 'Come?'

Ruby looks at him; this time with the caution she should have used the moment she decided to befriend him online – calling herself his number one fan.

'Come,' Dwayne says again, this time a little softer. He stretches out one hand and rests it on her thigh. He curls his forefinger in the hook of her jean shorts and pulls her closer, 'You didn't wear these for him, did you?'

Ruby shakes her head, eyes fixed on Dwayne, searching for danger.

'For me?'

Ruby nods up and down. The reality of her situation makes her breathing shallow. So many fantasies of her with Double-G, watching him in the camera making a gun sign, wearing his string vest. How she fingered herself over him, so many times, and now it feels dangerous but in a bad way. His sex is painful and she hates doing it. But she's in too deep to stop. She promised to honeytrap Cyber X to get to spend private time with Dwayne, but now she wants out.

'Then come,' Dwayne guides Ruby onto his lap. Kissing her cleavage, he tugs down on her top. 'You got big tits for your age. When you sixteen again?'

She doesn't answer. She only just turned fifteen.

Dwayne takes one of Ruby's breasts out from the lace bra and tugs on the nipple until it erects, 'That's better. How tings was before I got you shook.'

Ruby tries to relax. She goes to kiss his lips but Dwayne pulls his head away, 'Nah man, those red lips are turning me on. I don't wanna rub it off.'

Dwayne slips a hand inside her shorts and licks her nipples until he can feel her pussy wet. He starts to pull down her battyriders, 'Take a photo and send it to him,' he whispers 'that'll make him nuts, babe.'

'I don't wanna,' Ruby looks at Dwayne uneasily, 'What if he spreads it?'

'It's not your face, man.' Dwayne snaps. Then he takes a breath, smiles again and squeezes her breasts, 'Just these nice tings, then.'

He bounces Ruby on his knees to watch her breasts then leans over and slips the twenty pound note under Ruby's bra strap. Ruby's face drops. Her body flushes with shame while Dwayne presses SEND to Cyber X on her phone. His face lit up, as he takes pictures of her breasts. He tugs down her shorts and makes her spread her legs so he can picture close-ups of her. He spits on her pussy to wet it up and watches helplessly as Dwayne sends them to Cyber on her phone. She sits away from him after that.

Around midnight, there's a knock at the door. Ruby checks it's Cyber before opening it. Her heart is pounding. She is holding back tears. She doesn't want to honeytrap him. She doesn't want to honeytrap anyone! But it's happening. How she'd begged her parents to let her stay home alone. She's nearly sixteen, she'd shouted. She didn't want to go to Jamaica. Always going Jamaica to see family. Now look what she's done with their trust?

As soon as Cyber enters the living room, Dwayne jumps on him from behind the door. Gripping his arms around Cyber's neck in a firm headlock, Dwayne punches Cyber's face.

'What the fuck, blood!' Cyber splutters, trying desperately to free himself from Dwayne's hold.

Ruby gasps at the sound of Cyber's nose popping, spots of blood splattering across the real sheepskin rug her parents got for their wedding. Ruby watches in fear as a spookily calm Dwayne pushes Cyber down on the floor.

'Are you going to kill him?' she whispers.

'Shut your boat, man!' Dwayne shouts, struggling to prevent Cyber from escaping. 'Sit on his legs. SIT ON HIS LEGS!'

She drops down onto Cyber's kicking feet, receiving a couple of painful blows in the process while Dwayne ties Cyber's wrists together with a cable tie. Dwayne then binds his ankles. Cyber's eyes widen in alarm as he sees who it is attacking him. As Dwayne crosses the room for the flick knife in his rucksack. Ruby screams.

Dwayne points the knife at Ruby. 'Calm the fuck down!'

Ruby tries to leave the room but Dwayne grabs her by the arm. 'You done know dis is how I roll. So how you gonna roll wid me if you get all shook up, shook up?' He points to the chair by the computer desk. 'Sit there.'

Tears roll down Ruby's face; her body shaking uncontrollably as she sits on the chair.

'This is the problem with you yutes, man.' He turns to Cyber, 'You think this is all wasteman talk. You think words don't mean nuttin'? Like my man just pen a track cussing up Double-G and done.'

Cyber stares – eyes darting to and fro in search of an escape that isn't there.

'Please, don't kill him here,' Ruby mumbles, picturing blood covering the entire floor.

Dwayne tilts his head at Ruby, then turns to Cyber, 'Man like me knows exactly where dis one's going.'

Dwayne punches Cyber's arms to deaden them, then searches all pockets and socks for any phones, drugs or weapons. He grabs Cyber by the cable tie around his wrist and drags him towards the bathroom, ordering Ruby 'Come help!'

Inside, Dwayne locks the door. He pulls the shower curtain away from the bath. 'Pull his jeans down,' he tells Ruby. She can't do it what with her own shaking and long false nails and Cyber resisting.

'Piss in the bath!' Dwayne shouts. Cyber X tries to struggle away but Dwayne slaps his face.

'He's shaking like a prick.' Dwayne pulls Cyber towards him, 'Best piss now because you piss in my car, you're a dead man, trust.'

Dwayne watches Cyber struggle to breathe, his mouth taped up and his nose getting snotty. He's electric with power.

Cyber lets out a very small pee, which dribbles down his jeans. Dwayne orders Ruby, 'Pull up his jeans,' then they drag Cyber back through the house to the front door.

'Unlock the door and open the garage.'

Dwayne throws her his car keys – she misses her catch and scrabbles to pick them up from the concrete floor.

'Open the boot.'

Between them they haul Cyber over the bumper and into Dwayne's car boot. Dwayne slams it shut to thuds and bangs of protest from inside. Dwayne wrenches the boot open again and digs the flick knife into his leg.

'No mans gonna hear you once my music's on. So best save your energy.'

Ruby watches in terror. Aware of what she's doing, she creeps slowly backwards towards the garage door, then turns and runs into the house. Dwayne slams the boot and runs after her, bursting through the front door before she can lock it shut.

He grabs her tightly and reaches up with his fingers to wipe the snot from her nose and onto her shorts. 'After what I do to dis bredder, he'll be lucky if he can walk let alone chat shit, so I suggest you don't snake. I ain't Chilla. Your tits and pum pum don't mean shit to me. You wanna chat man's business, you get man's comeback. Get me?'

Ruby stares in numb horror.

'Get me!'

She nods.

Dwayne kisses her violently, his tongue filling her mouth. She wants to vomit.

She watches them drive off and locks the garage then runs inside the house, bolting it behind her. She doesn't know what to do or where to go. She paces the house, her entire home now tainted with violence – then stops at the blood stained rug. She can't tell police. She can't tell her friends. She wishes her mum and dad were here or she was there. Tears washing off the last of her makeup as she recalls arguing with them, refusing to go visit her grandmother only to be bored, demanding the house to herself for once. No parties or boys. No parties. No boys. Right now she could be in the Caribbean with fresh barbecued fish, relaxing on the beach, getting her hair braided, seeing her cousins. Ruby runs upstairs and slumps into a corner of her bedroom, trying to shake off the fact she's helped get someone kidnapped and killed.

Dwayne is heading for a woodlands car park about an hour from Streatham. Any kicks and muffled cries for help are drowned out by Graff raps about violence, money, prestige, power and bitches. The fat basslines pumping up Dwayne's super charged ego. Each time Leeroy appears, he turns the music up and thinks of Bob: Nah my son, I never went prison. Nah, can't say. Some of them things I've done in my past would give you nightmares. Why I never went down? Because I worked alone. No grasses.

254

When the only witness is the man opposite, you know he won't talk.

As Dwayne turns off the motorway onto smaller roads, he turns the volume down. The houses stop and the road thins out to become gravel. He switches his lights off and glides to a stop.

Reaching to the back seat for an empty sports bag, he stuffs the blanket, harnesses, and his knife inside. He picks up the collapsible stool and checks his torch for battery life. Everything in order, he opens the trunk to reveal a curled up, petrified Cyber with his hands and feet still bound and his mouth gagged. He can only watch as Dwayne polishes the knife with the sleeve of his jumper.

The night is pitch black and cold. Dwayne lifts Cyber out of the boot. Cyber struggles less, either believing he can't escape or already exhausted. Dwayne throws him on the floor like a sack of potatoes then straddles him. He places a leather studded collar around Cyber's neck, it's the one they give dogs who pull too hard. Any sudden movements and the collar tightens and Cyber's neck will be gagged by sharp spikes. Cyber's eyes spin wildly as Dwayne takes off Cyber's brand new trainers and socks, then, picking up his knife, makes two slits along the bottom of his feet. Cyber yelps behind the gaffer tape but Dwayne doesn't look up. Dwayne then cuts the tape at Cyber's ankles, hauls him up on his bleeding feet, and forces him to walk painfully over the stones through the wood. Cyber must by now be convinced this is the end of his life.

Once they get to a thick enough part of the wood, Dwayne unfolds the camping stool and sits Cyber down, zip-tying his ankles together.

'You think you can outsmart me?' Dwayne rips the tape from Cyber's mouth. 'I've got bigga plans but you think you can try move to me?'

Cyber wants to say it's just a joke, a track, just lyrics, this song don't mean nothing but he can't speak. He knows he crossed a line and that he wanted to cross that line for the ratings. 'Look, Dwayne,' Cyber starts.

Dwayne slaps his face, 'Dats not my name to you, prick.'

'Yeah, Double-G...'

'Nah, I ain't got no time for your story. You don't know me. You took me for a little yute, thinking you can boy man up. Well, now you know, nigga. None of my soldiers being stabbed up, my bitches moved to, none of my clients taken, no more music. War ends now, get me? You're retired.'

Cyber X is silent.

'Get me?' Dwayne takes the knife to his prisoner's throat. Dwayne can feel the cocaine in his blood. He feels, strong, confident, immense.

He starts humming a beat.

'Spit the bars?'

Petrified, Cyber mumbles a few words, then chokes to a halt.

'Nah man! That's not how it goes,' Dwayne says sarcastically, loving every minute, 'You're angry. You're meaning it.'

The woodland has a stillness to it, a peacefulness so far removed from the panic inside Cyber's mind – racing with thoughts of how to escape, of whether he'll die here, that this is it: his life, over. He's thought about being killed, all road man do. Anyone who heads up a crew has to imagine it, but it's always in a battle on the Endz, bare mans and blades, like some medieval king's battle he was taught in primary school only played out in Brixton. He'd daydreamed this moment. He'd see the tower blocks and his friends' faces over him pumping at his chest to keep his heart beating, squeezing the stab wounds to stop his blood flowing all over the concrete, down the gutter.

'Don't worry, mate,' Dwayne continues in a Southeast London tone, 'Got it downloaded, specially.'

The more fearful Cyber becomes, the more powerful Dwayne feels. He glares at Cyber as he hits play on Cyber's track. The beat echoes tin-like around the trees that surround them. Dwayne looks up to see the sky briefly clear, stars against the black, but the clouds are thick, moving fast with the gusts of wind high above. This is a true gangster in control.

Cyber's lyrics rap about kidnapping Dwayne, fucking his girl, making her suck his dick, 'And if you don't like it you can suck my dick.' Dwayne starts to dance, repeating the lyrics like an echo: 'Don't chat to me about Double-G. You little prick. You don't know me. My tings grow bigger than the tallest tree, as I grab your chick, put her on her knees. I'll fuck your bitch and make her suck my dick, and if you like that, you can suck my dick. Yeah, if you don't like that you can suck my dick…'

Dwayne locks the phone and straightens his posture like he just had a new idea. The mix of adrenaline and cocaine fuelling his imagination. Cyber's eyes are wide with fear. He wants to cry. He wants his mum. He thinks about the recent times he's been rude to her, told her to fuck off and not come home until all hours in the morning. She only ever wants him safe and doing well. Always on his back about being black and a target for gangs, suspecting he's in one…

'Tell me what man was thinking when he penned this shit? You want your tings sucked? Because I ain't gonna lie, I don't want you to fuck my bitch. I wouldn't like that, you get me.'

Dwayne lunges down and grabs the spiked collar around Cyber's neck and yanks him painfully to his slit feet. He ties him to a tree with a harness he stole from the neighbour who tightropes in Telegraph Hill Park. Once the harness is in place, Dwayne unbuttons Cyber's jeans. Cyber tries frantically to move but he's firmly held in by the straps.

Dwayne digs out Cyber's limp penis with two fingers. He drops the blanket onto the floor and gets down on his knees. Sweat, snot, tears run down Cyber's terrified face, he tries to scream – Is man gonna bite his dick off? But no sound comes.

'What, nigga?' Dwayne gets back up. 'You don't want this now?' Holding his phone directly to Cyber's ear, he replays the track. He takes Cyber's flaccid penis firmly in his other hand squeezing it to the beat.

Don't chat to me about Double-G. You're a little prick. You don't know me. My tings grow bigger than the tallest tree, as I grab your chick, put her on her knees. I'll fuck your bitch and make her suck my dick, and if you like that, you can suck my dick. Yeah if you don't like that you can suck my dick...

Dwayne lets go of Cyber's dick. Then kneels back down on the blanket and begins to lick it. He looks up at the whimpering victim then opens his mouth and sucks. He runs his teeth up and down the shaft and Cyber starts to cry. Dwayne takes his gag off.

'Oi, Stop man, please...'

Dwayne gets to his feet. He puts his lips close to Cyber's left ear. 'You don't seem to be feeling it?'

Cyber swerves his head to try headbutt Dwayne.

Cyber's head explodes in pain as he feels the full force of Dwayne's fist, then stomach, ribs. Something cracks in his chest. He doesn't know what. Agony shoots up – Is he having a heart attack? He can't breathe. His body wants to crumple into a ball except the harness has him standing straight.

Dwayne loosens the harness around Cyber's chest. He's in too much pain to run. He collapses onto the stool. Dwayne readjusts the harness around Cyber's chest and the tree.

'Well boy, after all that hype, I ain't impressed,' Dwayne crows. He holds the crisp silver blade of the flick knife to Cyber's throat, 'Now let's see what I got.'

Dwayne's dick is pulsating and hard. He reaches down and strokes it, admiring his thick ten inches. Dwayne smirks, clearly enjoying every second. 'Man couldn't live up to his lyrics. If I ain't mistaken, you said you'll bust in my girl's face. That's some next disrespect.' Standing astride Cyber's torso, he begins to wank himself. 'Now be careful with your next move.'

With one hand holding the knife to Cyber's throat, he uses the other to guide Cyber's jaw to his erection. Cyber pulls his face away. 'Suck my dick, nigga! You wanna talk like a big prick, then don't be surprised when you meet a real one.'

His eyes shut tight, Cyber feels strong hard fingers pull open his jaw, then the disgusting object pushing past his lips. He wants to close his mouth but the steel blade at his neck says otherwise. It's over. It has to be done. He sucks like a bitch at the glistening head of Dwayne's penis, tears running down his cheeks

'Harder. HARDER!' Dwayne shouts. 'Do it faster!'

Cyber feels ringing slaps across his cheeks.

Dwayne presses the knife into Cyber's neck with one hand while wanking his shaft with the other. Cyber gags and tries to pull back for air but Dwayne keeps forcing himself deeper down his throat. Cyber's choking, almost suffocating as Dwayne's thrusts in. He can't breathe.

Then finally, thankfully, Dwayne erupts. He pulls back and laughs, rubbing his cum in Cyber's face and over his afro.

Cyber shakes his head violently, spitting cum out his mouth. His fear switches to anger, 'Fucking batty man!' he shouts. If he were free, he would kill Dwayne with his bare hands, burn his body here in the woods. He's gonna do it anyway. Now Dwayne has to kill him or be killed. The pain tuned out by adrenaline, 'FUCKING BATTY MAN!'

'Shut up!'

'DUTTY FREAK!'

'SHUT UP!' Dwayne yells, Leeroy there again. Dwayne, eight years old. Nine years old. Twelve years old: 'FUCKING BATTY MAN, FREAK!'

Dwayne presses his hand over Cyber's mouth. Cyber bites him. Dwayne tapes Cyber's mouth – winding it repeatedly round his head. Dwayne picks up his knife like he's gonna stab him, here and now, straight through his eyes into his brain, slice his skin off, peel his face away. He holds the blade in his fist, it shivers millimetres from Cyber's eye, then suddenly disappears and lands with a heavy thud deep into the tree above his head. Cyber's heart thuds in his chest. His pants feel wet and he realises it's piss. He's still alive.

An owl hoots. Then hoots again. Dwayne turns and looks up at the silhouette of the predator but he doesn't know what it is. Everything suddenly slows down. Becomes still. With Cyber's mouth taped up, the real world returns. Dwayne feels sick. What he's just done overcomes him, like it has a lifeform of its own, as if evil just found a new gateway to seep into the world. Dwayne shakes his head. He hears his grandmother's voice, talking of devils. The devil got into her kids, and now him. He breathes deeply to calm himself down. Get back in control. But everything's blurring around him. He walks away and rests on a tree.

'Best know I ain't turned on by nuttin but being sucked off by a pussyhole. I ain't no batty man.' He whispers to the darkness, struggling to hold onto the role. 'See man like me is darker than you'll know. Smarter than you'll ever know. I don't need no hype in a studio with cameras. See this now, I'm in your head. No witnesses. No nigga knows but you and me. Get me. You. And. Me.'

Dwayne lights a cigarette and goes back to Cyber. 'Your crew's done. No more shotting. No more tagging. No more making tracks. They're my customers. No messages, no Facebook, Insta, WhatsApp, nuttin. I'm making money, not you.' Dwayne looks at Cyber. 'Shake your head, then?'

He smashes Cyber's skull against the tree trunk. The dull thud appears to knock out his shred of resistance. Dazed, Cyber blinks. Dwayne starts packing the things into a bag, then polishes the flick knife, setting it down by Cyber's feet. Leaving his hands still tied, Dwayne takes off the spiked collar and lead and packs it away.

Dwayne walks back towards the car and puts the bag inside. The yellow-orange flashes of the car indicators dramatically light up the trees as the locks are disabled.

He returns with just a torch. He shines the torch away from Cyber's face and along the gravel path, 'Down there's the station but be careful, I hear its pure racist round here. Wouldn't want anything bad to happen.'

Cyber says nothing.

Dwayne takes off the handcuffs and puts the flick knife handle in one of Cyber's hands, his arms and body still harnessed firmly to the tree.

Dwayne walks back to the car, turns on his headlights but sits, watching Cyber go to work on the harness straps. Once he's seen enough, he starts up the engine and slowly crunches over the gravel bumps of the country lane. He turns up his music as he hits the main road. Between stabs of sickness, panic and shock, he convinces himself this ended things. He stops at a roadside McDonalds for an egg muffin. Now time to move on to bigger business, he thinks, sitting down to eat. Done and dealt with. Dwayne smiles, wiping his mouth with a napkin. He wasn't feeling sick about what he done. He was just hungry.

Cyber is plunged into darkness as Dwayne's car lights fade down the path. He takes a few minutes to cut through the harness, then slowly gets to his feet – using the ever present tree for support. He walks bolt upright, adrenaline pumping enough to take some pain away from his bare, wounded feet. He trips over one of his trainers, left on the ground where the car was parked. He feels around for the second one and puts them both on. The stony path leads onto a lane, but there are no clear signs of which way to turn. With no money or Oyster card, he stands at the crossroads and wonders which way to turn.

The wind chills his bones. His body trembles. He unzips his jeans and is hit with flashbacks and shooting sensations of fear and terror. He pisses against the bush. Tears form in his eyes. He looks up at the sky as if the stars could magic the experience away. He feels the warm tears down his cheeks. He finishes, but before he zips up his jeans, the seventeen-year-old folds in. Holding his stomach in agony he collapses to the gravel. Looking up to the sky, again, he clasps his hands and apologises to God, and to his mum. Everything, all his choices to be a road man, look ridiculous, wanting the fame and the girls and the ratings. He knows he brought this on himself. But he could never imagine this shit happening. Maybe being rushed in a party or on road, but this?

He apologises to his family members and friends for starting the gang in the first place. He promises God from now on he will go church with his aunties. He will study harder at college. He'll forget selling weed and start a new life. Not because Dwayne told him to done the beef, but because he wants to end it himself.

A pair of headlights appear in the dark. Cyber gets up, wiping his face. If he goes back the way he came, he's back in the woods. If he goes left the car is going that way. If he goes right, he's walking towards the car. Indecision turns to panic as he fears this could be more boys after him, or racists Dwayne set up to finish him off. He decides to run for it but finds his legs stiffen, his sliced feet stinging. Everything hurts. The car draws closer. It's a land rover. An old man looks out of his window, 'You alright, there?'

'Yeah.'

His swollen face tells a different story.

The man gets out of the car. 'What you doing out here all by yourself?'

Cyber is too stunned to speak, he feels for the flick knife in his pocket.

'Stag do or something?'

'Yeah, Stag do,' Cyber agrees, keeping distance.

'Got dropped as a joke?'

Cyber nods.

The man looks at the scared, broken face of the young man in front of him, noticing his split lip, wondering to question his wounds or not. 'Where do you need to get back to?'

'London. Peckham.'

'Peckham!' exclaims the man, 'As in Only Fools and Horses?'

Cyber stands shivering in the cold of the late November morning.

'Well I suppose I better get you to the station.'

'Nah man, I can walk,' Cyber mutters, but his voice shakily adds. 'Just tell man which way?'

'It's a fair old trek, and no offence but if you're about to get married, you need your rest.'

'What you doing here, anyway?' Cyber asks, suspicious of getting into the man's vehicle.

'My land, to your right. I'm a farmer.'

Cyber looks at the field in front of him.

'This is where your Brussels sprout comes from!' the farmer chuckles. 'But don't suppose you Londoners know that.'

Cyber stands in front of the car headlights.

'Well, I have to get to work... So good luck.' The farmer climbs back in to his car. 'It's that way.'

'Nah, man. I will. Thanks.'

They sit in silence for the journey, Cyber watching the charcoal sky turn purple then pink with a gold trim. His body throbbing with pain. Should he go home or hospital?

'Going to be a beautiful day,' the farmer says, turning into a small village. 'So when's your big day?' he asks, though they both know that's a lie.

Cyber remains silent. He sucks on his lip, tasting the blood from where Dwayne punched him. He thinks about the day he is about to have. How to hide the injuries.

The man pulls up towards the station. He looks at his watch. 'First train into London is at 6.02am.' The farmer points to platform one. 'Got about a forty-minute wait.'

The farmer looks at Cyber, 'Do you have a ticket?'

Cyber shakes his head.

He takes a battered leather wallet from his pocket and hands over a ten pound note. 'That should see you home.'

'Nah, man,' Cyber says. He knows he is being rude. But the man's kindness feels false, tainted like there's nothing good in the world.

The farmer places his hand on Cyber's shoulder, which flinches so hard he immediately withdraws. With a look of concern, he leans back into his driver's seat to give the boy some personal space. 'I don't know what's happened to you lad, but let me give you a word of advice. Whoever put you there are no friends of yours and I'd stay well away from them at all costs.'

He holds out the ten pound note again. Cyber takes the money.

'Good lad. Now look after yourself.'

CHAPTER 34

'Emily keeps inviting me to things I can't go to,' Issy moans to Jerome. 'Private tutoring, ballet, theatre, skiing; it all costs.'

'What about the Tameika, Emma, Chelsea?'

'They're alright but…they're not me. None of them have boyfriends. They go on about teenage pregnancy but these girls barely been fingered. That's basically it,' Issy sighs. 'All the fun people dropped out or didn't get good grades. I should have gone a bigger college.'

Jerome looks uneasy as he picks up Issy's UCAS pack. 'Is this the application?'

'Yeah, gotta be in after Christmas.'

'When will you know?'

'March.' Issy starts biting her nails.

'Nottingham, Sheffield, Goldsmiths, and Lincoln,' he reads aloud. 'You don't wanna be in London, do you?'

Issy shakes her head.

Jerome, wounded, asks gently, 'Am I enough for you?'

'What? Yes, you are.'

'I mean it.'

Issy takes a moment to understand the enormity of his question.

'Am I enough? I mean, you're basically unhappy with everything and everyone at the moment. I thought it was because of Emily, but now, you don't even like her.'

'I do like Emily, just not her idiot boyfriend.'

'Well, what about me? Am I next on your list of people to hate? Since "the break" it's like I'm just waiting for the call.'

'Jerome, I might hate some of the stuff you *do* but I'll never hate *you*.

Never. You've been there since day one. I love you with all my heart.' Even as Issy says the words, they feel false. She wants it to be real, but there's a sinking feeling inside she's lying to Jerome.

'Issy, I ain't gonna lie, sometimes I'm awake at night thinking 'bout you going off to uni, leaving me behind. You'll start meeting people better than me and won't come back. I think about losing you and I'm freaking out. I'm getting jealous of bredders I ain't even met yet. I get so scared that I get scared of how scared I get. Like my head's gonna go nutz.'

Jerome takes a moment to control his emotions. 'The thought of you leaving, of me not being good enough no more, of us not being tight, not kissing, sitting up Telegraph Hill... It's all gonna change and you'll be seeing new things and won't even notice and I'll just be sittin' here, waiting.'

'But I will come back as long as you're waiting; I'll come back, Jerome.'

'What if they're right? What if you go uni and that's it?'

'I can't live like this my whole life. I can't be my mum, working all hours in a supermarket and only just making Lewisham Council rent, only paying bills when they're FINAL DEMAND; iron bars, grey concrete, broken swings, dirty nappies everywhere. You can't trust no-one. No-one trusts you. Why should we get the shitty flats and other people get houses? Why can't we be other people? I want what we promised each other on the hill.'

Jerome's tears trickle down and Issy catches one with the tips of two fingers and kisses it. Her feelings for him resurface. Seeing him sad hurts. She kisses him and the feeling of his lips against hers feels like the old days, like when they first kissed under the tree with deep purple leaves.

Issy pulls away. 'Come with me. Leave London. Come live with me?'

Jerome pauses. 'What about Gran? I can't leave her.'

'We could look for somewhere and she could live with us.'

'Issy, do you know what you're asking,' he says, his voice so gentle. 'I mean, do you really want that?'

'I'd love that. It's not you I don't want. It's here.'

Jerome wipes his face with the back of his hand. He feels the gentle warmth of Issy's breath as she presses her lips to his. The ache of believing they're at the end of things brings a new energy to her touch. In that moment, he understands Carol. Issy told him how her parents would cuddle for hours on the sofa when her dad was dying, holding on to something you know is going to end. But they don't have cancer. Why can't this be a fresh start? The end of them as teenagers in love, and the beginning of a more adult-like relationship, with its ups and downs, like everyone.

'This might be the right move for me,' Jerome says pulling away from the kiss. 'I could move out. I've gotta do it at some point.' But even as he says it, he feels false. Could he leave his gran alone to live with Dwayne? Can he trust his brother to keep Gran safe?

'We could all move, eventually,' Issy suggests. 'Me, you, Mum and Gran. One big happy family.' Issy starts smiling. That feels better. A team.

Jerome smiles too, but the idea doesn't sit right. There's a fundamental problem with this picture of domestic bliss: it's called Dwayne.

Andre and Dwayne are standing outside the fried chicken shop, waiting for their food. Tameika's brother Emmanuel and five other boys around his age walk up to them. Emmanuel bumps fists with Dwayne then Andre. The younger boys want to do the same but they fear being rejected.

'What you saying, my yute?' Dwayne says.

'They wanna buy the next track,' Emmanuel says. The boys stand admiring Dwayne and Andre in their brand new white trainers and tracksuits. Nothing faded. Labels with big shiny gold circle stickers still attached to their baseball caps

'Ain't ready yet,' Andre says.

'See I told you?' one boy pipes up.

Dwayne side-eyes the boy, who immediately looks at the empty chicken box on the pavement.

'Come,' demands Dwayne.

The boy shuffles nearer to Dwayne and Andre.

'Speak then!' Andre shouts.

'I'll say it?' Emmanuel says, backing it for his friend.

'Say it, then,' the boy mutters.

'His sister moves in Peckham, yeah,' Emmanuel starts. 'And she heard stuff, innit.'

Dwayne's mind flashes back to Cyber, licking his dick and him busting in Cyber's face.

'She said it's done between Graff and Peckham Manz.'

The boy, feeling braver says, 'Cyber killed it with his track about you and Graff backed down.'

Dwayne looks at Andre.

'Hey boss, you want chilli sauce?' shouts the Turkish man standing next to the block of rotating kebab meat.

Dwayne watches fat dripping from the heat of the grill. 'Put loads on,' Dwayne says, sticking his thumb up. 'No onion though, bruv.'

'What else?' Andre demands.

'That it's been time since the last Graff tune came out. Last one was before Suck My Dick. People on road chatting how Graff is moist.'

Andre nudges Dwayne, 'Come we go youth club.'

Dwayne thinks for a moment, then looks at Emmanuel. 'Manny, go Youth Club and text man if Tammy's in there with Jerome or that Steve bredder?'

The boys rush off to the youth club, happy to be on a mission.

'Fuck was that?' Andre asks, walking into the kebab shop.

Dwayne doesn't reply. Since kidnapping Cyber X, Dwayne's been up and down; sometimes he's buzzing remembering the night but he gets sick with flashbacks, regretting it, convincing himself that *that* didn't happen; just the drugs making him imagine shit. He bites into the salty fatty donner meat, spilling chilli sauce from his mouth down his brand new Nike hoodie, a piece of meat drops on his trainer. He kicks it off onto the dirty tiles of the shop floor.

Just Tammy, Emmanuel texts.

They stand at the top of the stairs leading from the table tennis area to the music studio. Dwayne, jumper off, flexes his biceps and clenches his fists as he shouts his lyrics into the camera hole on Andre's phone:

'Your Mum can suck my dick! Suck it hard, suck it long, I ain't cumming inside, I take her from behind, you can't even trust the mother by your side, as I hand her ten notes to give her dutty pum pum a ride.'

'That's deeeeeep, fam.' Andre chuckles. 'Deep!'

Dwayne glances through the glass door to Jerome, oblivious, organising a table tennis tournament in the hall with the under 12s.

Dwayne and Andre spend the evening laying the track over the video before putting it out. They shout *Your Mum* in unison and lay it over Dwayne's cusses to make it sound like an army are saying *Your Mum.*

The youth worker, Tammy, comes by again, 'Guys, you need to free the space for the younger kids. This session tonight is for eight to twelve-year-olds. You shouldn't even be here.'

'Yeah, soon done, soon done,' Andre says, licking his lips at Tammy.

Tammy knows exactly what's going on. 'Steve will go mad if he knew yous were all in here on his days off,' she adds, walking off.

The group of youngers who have been watching intently the entire evening, pluck up enough courage to ask, 'Can we be in the video?' Two eight year olds start doing dance moves. Andre laughs as he films their miniature bodies attempting breakdancing with their skinny ankles and sports socks up over their heads.

Andre looks at Dwayne. 'Done.'

Dwayne knocks fists with Andre. 'Now see what he wants to bring.'

'Ratings going nutz,' Andre says, watching Jerome run the tuckshop. 'Gonna be Christmas Number One, fam.'

Dwayne takes a third Freddo bar.

'20p each,' Jerome says.

Dwayne screws his face. 'Recession, bruv, recession.'

Jerome kisses his teeth as Dwayne passes Andre a can of Lilt. Neither of them digging in their pockets.

Andre starts filming close-ups of Tameika's little brother Emmanuel pretending to be gangster. Hidden inside Dwayne's balaclava, Emmanuel points his fingers like a gun and shoots to the camera phone.

'Dre,' Jerome signals to Andre, 'You can't film them. Child protection.'

'They asked.'

'Yeah, we wanna,' whine the boys.

'These yutes got minds of their own,' Dwayne adds.

'Don't matter. I need parents to sign photography consent.' Jerome hands each of the smaller boys a plastic cup of blackcurrant juice and two digestive biscuits. Jerome turns to Andre, 'You put that shit online I'm fucked. No more free studio time, get me.'

'Alright man, chill,' Andre says, annoyed with how Jerome's going on.

'Ohwaah,' the younger boys groan. 'We wanna be in it.'

'Don't look at me,' Andre says putting his phone away. 'I'm all about making you yutes famous. It's dis one here, Mr Health and Safety.'

Mr Sutton sits at his kitchen table, reading the newspaper. The doorway behind him is adorned with holly and ivy Christmas decorations, freshly foraged from the woodlands next to the Redbridge Golf Club. He slowly reads the front pages then lifts his head up to see his wife staring at him in disbelief. Mr Sutton's bushy eyebrows barely move. His eyes return to the pages.

Janie sits at the table. Her hands trembling. They've been trembling for thirty-six-hours. The veins, one by one, have popped up under her thin, pale skin. Though the kitchen is painfully cold, wisps of Janie Sutton's hair flat against her face, stuck with the perspiration caused by her nerves. Her blue eyes appear larger as stress sinks her eye sockets. She watches her husband, trying desperately to search for ways to let him know he is wrong. And he is wrong.

He folds the large sheets of news and collapses them to his side.

'Jane, put the kettle on, please,' he says in a commanding tone.

She gets to her feet and does as she's told. She asks politely, 'Do you want a sandwich or a snack of any sort?' Hoping that kindness will thaw his impenetrable stubbornness. He simply replies, 'No' then gets to his feet and heads to the living room. After a few moments, he returns with a crossword booklet.

Janie puts the teapot on the table. She pours some milk into a milk jug and places it in front of her husband, the whole time staring into his eyes, hoping he will look up and read the word 'desperation' in them. He continues to look down at the crossword. Janie puts her hand upon her husband's. She kisses his cheek. He looks at her, pitying her, it seems, yet irritated by her tactics.

'Might we rethink our decision?' Janie suggests.

'This is not our decision.' Mr Sutton slams down his crossword, 'You are fully aware whose decision this is.' He grabs his wife's arm, forcing her to take the seat next to him. 'This is my decision,' he growls. 'I go to work. I earn the income for this household. I pay its bills. And I will certainly be responsible for any tuition fees.'

He eases his grip, but retains Janie's arm. 'How can I be a responsible parent if I pay for my child to make senseless collages? No, no, no!' He shakes his head. Releasing his wife's arm, he reaches for the teapot, 'No, indeed!'

The pulse in Janie's temples pound and throb. She leans into her husband, quivering. Her body quivering as she whispers, 'She is starving herself, Edward. She hasn't emerged from her bed since Friday.'

Mr Sutton lifts his heavy frame from the kitchen chair. He walks towards the fridge, opens it and takes out cheese and ham, then opens cupboards looking for a side plate. Eventually he takes one out the dishwasher. Opening the bread bin, he cuts two slices of bread and furiously butters them. Tearing the first slice, he throws it at the food-bin and cuts another.

'Why have you put this in the fridge, woman?'

'The butter is where it always is,' Janie bites back. 'You just this moment took it from above the fridge.'

Mr Sutton tears another slice of bread. He throws down the knife, 'This is impossible! Look at this!'

'Perhaps if the bill payer were more generous with heating this house during the winter, your butter would spread!'

Mr Sutton sharply turns. He reaches back for the block of butter and aims it at his wife. Janie ducks. Neither of them watch as the butter hits the wall and thuds to the floor. Mr Sutton returns to his project, adding cheese and ham to the broken bread. He cuts the sandwich roughly into two uneven triangles, then stomps through the hall and up the stairs. Janie quickly follows.

He bangs Emily's door, 'Emily! Emily!'

No answer.

He bangs louder, 'Emily, open this door at once!'

Nothing.

He fiddles with the handle only to find the door locked.

'Emily, open this door immediately.'

Mr Sutton becomes furious. Seldom disobeyed, grown men cower in his presence in court as he decides their fate and yet here he is, fighting with his seventeen-year-old daughter. He hands Janie the sandwich, takes a step back and rams his shoulder against the door.

Janie screams and wills him to stop, 'Those doors are antique and no money in the world will pay to fix them,' she says.

Mr Sutton stomps into his study. Opening his desk drawer, he pulls out a jar and empties it on the holly green leather once designed for ink blotting paper.

Janie watches her husband return with a handful of keys.

'One of these works,' he tells Janie and begins to shove various keys into the lock, twisting them furiously.

Janie urges him to 'be gentle' but Mr Sutton gives her a firm look that tells her to mind her own business.

At last, one of the keys turns.

The door swings open to reveal their pale daughter lying on her bed staring at the ceiling. She is wrapped up in blankets.

Janie searches the room for signs that she has eaten, but all she sees is an empty glass. She rushes to the radiator to turn the knob and switch it on.

Mr Sutton marches straight to the bed. He is shocked by the state of his daughter; thinner than ever with dark disks below her eyes.

He decides to remain firm and in charge; he shakes his daughter's right shoulder, 'Emily!' Her eyes remain fixed on the ceiling. He follows her gaze to see the words **Art Sets You Free** written in the Chanel lipstick cousin Rosie bought her on the bedside table. Wondering how she got up there, Mr Sutton looks back at his prostrate daughter.

'You listen here, young lady. You may have spooked your mother, but you are certainly not spooking me. Now sit up and eat this sandwich – at once!'

He hears his wife sobbing quietly behind him and, without turning, yells at her to stop. He grabs Emily, forcing her to sit up. Her body remains limp. Her head lolling back over the headboard, eyes continuing to look above her: **Art Sets You Free**

'This is absolute nonsense.' Mr Sutton looks at his daughter and then helplessly back at his wife.

'Should we call Henry, perhaps?' she offers.

'Absolutely not. I'm not having him tell his father what a bunch of lunatics I have running loose.' Imagining Charles Sparling giving yet another sympathetic pat on the back, Mr Sutton's thick fingers pick up half a sandwich from the plate Janie is holding. He grabs his daughter's jaw and attempts to stuff it into her mouth, forcing Emily to gag.

'Stop, Edward. She's choking!' cries Janie.

'Let her choke, then!' Mr Sutton uses his thumb to stuff part of the broken sandwich back into Emily's mouth. She spits the contents out, infuriating him further. He grabs her cheeks, this time treating Emily like a stubborn cat who won't swallow medicine. Janie cries for him to stop but rage has taken over, 'Eat it!'

'Please, Edward. Enough!'

He rounds on his wife, 'Shut up, woman. Shut up! Do you think I had it this good in my day? She'd be black and blue by now.' Mr Sutton grabs Emily's arm and yanks her slouched spine upright. He opens her palm and puts the other half of the sandwich into it.

Emily looks at her father.

'Take it!' he demands, 'or I will force it down your throat!'

Emily takes the sandwich and bites into it.

'There,' he turns to his wife.

Emily chews the bread, cheese and ham three times then spits it into her lap the moment her father turns back to face her. He slaps her so hard across the face, that the sound echoes the room. Janie screams and rushes to comfort her daughter. Mr Sutton holds his arm out to block the way.

'Oh Emily, why? Why won't you eat?'

'Because she is a spoilt rotten brat, just like her brother. This is your fault, Jane.' He points his finger at his wife's face. 'Your fault entirely. I trust that my wife is capable of caring for her children while I go to work. I put in hours and hours and for what? This shoddy family? Really? The fruits of my labour?'

Janie shudders with every insult, as if each word is a strike to her own face. Mr Sutton drops his wife's arm and storms out, slamming the door behind him. Janie crumples into a heap on Emily's bed. Emily remains still, eyes fixed to the ceiling, thick finger marks reddening her ghostlike cheek.

Janie looks up to observe her still stony-faced daughter. Picking up the spat-out food, she wraps it in a handkerchief and sets it down by the lipstick. She takes her daughter's hand. 'Darling, please. Please just behave. It isn't so bad. You can paint when you're older, in your spare time.'

Emily's eyes finally move from the ceiling. She stares at her mother in disbelief at her subservience. 'How can you accept this?' she whispers.

Janie gulps. Her daughter has worked it all out, as children do. Parents are little more than flawed beings, stumbling through life. The last of the veils uncovered. Janie can accept that Emily's mummy is no longer the champion, a winner, the greatest or bestest, but this, this is painful. Mum is a fool. Mum knows nothing. Mum is a doormat. Mum is powerless. Janie's heart shatters into something unfixable and all she can do is remember to breathe.

Emily turns coldly away from her mother and stares back at her mantra: Art Sets You Free.

CHAPTER 35
SNITCH

'If someone ever cussed my mum, watch blood.'

'Get me, best strap up.'

'Done know. Next level madness.'

'I'm doing time for that, trust.'

'We need something proper raw,' Cyber shouts over the group, while wishing he could escape this life, but another part of him ready to do anything to fuck with Dwayne's head.

'We could tag up the entire estate,' a smaller boy suggests.

'Nah that's youngers shit. I'm talking something manz go pen for.'

One teen licks his lips, 'We could gang rape his girl, post it online.' A smile spreads across his face.

'That's fucked up,' someone else says.

'I ain't putting my tings in dem nasty bitches anyway,' backtracks the teen, pulling at his jeans.

'We could kidnap his baby and scar your name into its skin.'

'Come on man, that's a bit obvious for feds, Who did this to your baby? Man called Cyber – too many snakes out there.'

'Dat yute ain't his anyway,' says another.

'Firebomb his yard?'

'Nah man, he lives next to my mum's friend,' says another. 'If it was a house then I'd be on it, though.'

'Fuck up one of his boys, like proper merk him,' says Dwayne's informer.

'I'd love to fuck that Anton up, fucking punk,' someone says.

'Anton's dad's a proper Yardie bredder,' the informer says. 'How about Barry? He's working in some butchers on Rye Lane. I see him cleaning out the shop, last man with the hose.'

'Which one's Barry?' Cyber asks.

'Chilla,' says the informer. 'The fat one who can't spit. He wrote the lyrics.'

Dwayne increases security on the flat – never trusting a snake. He checks his phone, then smiles: **Barry's the target**. Dwayne picks up the power drill he borrowed from the neighbour who's gone from giving Dwayne sweets as a kid to being terrified of him. Mabel stares into the hot chocolate inside her Welcome to Jamaica sunset beach mug while Dwayne drills two new bolts to the front door without her permission. Mabel jolts with Jerome entering the kitchen. 'Me nah want no trouble pon me yard.'

'It's to protect you, Gran!' Dwayne shouts.

'What I done fi need protection?' She gets up, shuffles away, into her bedroom.

Seeing his brother is awake, Dwayne goes into the kitchen.

'Put this in Issy's yard,' he tells Jerome, giving him a box.

'What is it?'

'Don't watch what it is,' he whispers. 'Just hide it somewhere.'

Jerome knows exactly what it is.

'Dwayne, you're off your head, blood.'

'Look bro, I've got an informer. Cyber's plotting some next revenge ting as we speak.'

Jerome starts laughing, 'Dwayne, Cyber's seventeen. You're nearly twenty-one. My yute might have a blade, but strapping up?'

Dwayne looks at Jerome, 'Promise me, bro, you ain't telling no-one?'

'Yeah, I'll put it on Facebook.'

'I talking next-level shit.'

Dwayne takes Jerome into their bedroom and tells a very watered down version of the Cyber X kidnap.

'I did it to stop the beef, so dem manz never come back. But my nigga's stopped being shook.'

Jerome stares in disbelief at his brother's poor judgment.

Dwayne takes the gun out the box. 'So now you know why we need this.'

'You're crazy, blood. That won't protect us. Might as well put it to our heads and pull the trigger.'

'Shush, man. Do you want Gran to hear?' Dwayne whispers. 'Look, I'm doing what I gotta do to have our backs.'

'D, serious. Google how many people get shot with their own strap? We have to do gun and knife crime sessions at youth club, yeah. Feds showed us how easy it is to turn a gun on the owner.'

'Feds now? Oh my days...' Dwayne fake chuckles, rubbing his jaw.

'Quoting feds.'

'You done know I won't put Issy in danger. She'd get five years. No joke.'

'You don't tell her, fam. Just hide it without her knowing. Somewhere they don't go, like the fuse box or some shit.'

'Dwayne, do you get how hard this year's been? She's going nuts I'm still making music, let alone having a fucking strap in her yard. Even if she didn't get caught, if she found it, it's done between us.'

'Bro, I can't believe I am actually hearing this. These bredders have stepped up and now we need to: thick and thin.'

'I never signed up for this. Our crew was a family, spitting rhymes – was about having a laugh, bunning weed, sitting in the park, going cinema, Trocs, what happened to that?'

'That ain't sustainable when you got bills to pay.'

'What bills, blood? You don't give Gran no money.'

'I got a son. Who'd you think I'm building an empire for?'

'Well put the gun in his cot then? Wrap it in fur and call it his new teddy bear!' Jerome kisses his teeth. He sits on his bed, head in hands.

Dwayne says nothing. Jerome looks up and realises Dwayne took what he said seriously – 'Wait, nah, nah, nah. D?' Jerome jumps up and into his brother's face, 'You cannot, and I mean cannot, put a strap in Jack-Jamal's room.'

'Bro, it's the perfect hiding place.' He pats his brother on the back. 'It won't be loaded.'

Jerome goes to the kitchen for a glass of water. He crosses the narrow hall to Mabel's room. His grandmother is sat on the bed, rocking; her strong, wrinkled fingers counting the rosary.

'Gran, you okay?'

Jerome waits.

'You okay, Gran?'

Mabel mumbles, 'I'm praying.' But Jerome doesn't hear her.

'What the fuck is happening to my life,' he whispers, opening the new bolts on the front door to see Issy's block opposite.

Issy hasn't seen Emily, or heard from her, for ages, not since New Year's Eve when she called to wish Issy luck for this 'make-or-break year'. Despite Henry and studies and Emily's parents making her do a million classes and extra tuition, Emily has time for a text or email.

Issy calls Sophie to see if she knows anything.

'Hey Issy,' Sophie's soft posh voice answers. 'Emily's not been going to school since the holidays ended. Her parents aren't saying much. Even Henry doesn't know details; just that they are coping with a very private matter.'

'Have you spoken to her at all?' Issy asks.

'Her phone is off. Last time we spoke, she was in bits because her father refused to let her go to Paris.'

'I've got this bad feeling,' Issy says, glad to be sharing her worries with someone in the loop.

'Me too,' Sophie says softly. 'Thing is, her parents.... we've thought about knocking on the door spontaneously, but you know what they're like?'

'Yeah.'

'Painfully private,' Sophie sighs.

'Maybe I could pop round?'

'Maybe you're lucky and Mimi opens the door. Sorry I can't be of much help. Oh Issy, before you go, there is one other thing you should probably know…'

Issy texts Merle, **Go with me?** but Merle says she can't. Probably because she knows what they think of Issy and her friends on the estate. So it's just a nervous Issy knocking on the door of 55 Pepys Road. After a little too long for her nerves, footsteps sound in the hallway and the door swings open to reveal Emily's mum. Issy is shocked by how bad she looks. Her face is puffy and her eyes bloodshot. Issy has been staring too long. She musters some manners, 'Hello Mrs Sutton, is Emily there?'

'Afraid she's out. Good day.'

As the door begins to close, Issy blurts out, 'Why can't she study art?'

Janie Sutton freezes.

A moment passes. Then the door opens fully. Mrs Sutton looks at Isobel as though seeing her for the first time, a harsh wind blowing around her flimsy jacket. It has been nearly three years since Isobel first entered her house. She looks different. Her hair is natural. Her face wiser. Though she was always polite, there's something so rough about the girl.

'Please, Mrs Sutton, whatever you may think of me, or however you see me, I care a lot about your daughter and if I can help in any way, I want to. Please, tell me.'

'I shall, thank you,' she says eventually, then attempts, once more, to close the door.

'I'm not who you think I am,' Issy quickly adds.

Janie's voice cracks, struggling to keep up appearances. 'Emily is sick,' she whispers.

'She's starving herself, isn't she?' Isobel says, using what Sophie just told her.

'Who told you such a story?' Janie's eyes widen in horror. She checks either side for neighbours. Mr Porter is out with a pitchfork, braving the cold.

Issy sees Emily's mum is upset by what's happening, 'Mrs Sutton, if you don't mind, could I see Emily–'

'How can you say such things aloud?' Janie hisses back. She watches the old man digging the tough winter soil, daffodil bulbs in a pile on the lawn. She should tell the gardener to check on her bulbs. The squirrels can be pests to them. Mr Porter pulls up his collar to shelter his neck from a gust of wind. He looks over and waves. Janie raises a hand, then feeling the cold herself, blinks back to Isobel. 'I'm sorry, but Emily doesn't want any visitors.'

'But she won't ever believe you'd let me in. This could change something.'

'She has a very bad cold, nothing more. Now off you trot.'

One more attempt to close the door.

Issy lifts herself on tiptoes to be seen through the stained glass part, 'I know she loses her appetite when she's sad.'

The door clicks shut.

'I know she dreams of being an artist and living in a crooked flat in Paris,' comes Isobel's voice from outside.

Janie rests her head on the stained glass window, trying to breathe.

'I know she's with someone who doesn't appreciate her dreams,' Isobel continues louder this time. 'And I know her father won't indulge them either.'

Afraid Mr Porter will hear Isobel's rising voice, Janie hauls the door back open; he happens to be chairing the local society meetings at the moment. Janie leans forwards. 'This is a private family matter,' she sternly says in an icy voice.

'She's like a sister to me, honest. I'm so worried about her. Please, I'm begging you, just five minutes, please.' Issy searches Janie's eyes for a moment, just one fucking moment of acceptance that she can be a good person, a real friend to this woman's precious daughter.

'Emily didn't leave her camera on the wall,' Issy continues bravely. 'She was being mugged by three boys. Me and my boyfriend–'

'My boyfriend and I–'

'My boyfriend and I, we saved her. Since that day, that moment, we just clicked. Please, Mrs Sutton, I know it's serious because Henry spoke to me and he hates me more than you do.'

That word. She pulls the door wide open. 'Fine, Fine! Go to her room!'

Issy walks past then bounds up the stairs.

'Wait!' Mrs Sutton calls.

Issy turns on the stairs.

'Promise that you'll keep this visit confidential. This is a private matter. Do you understand? Nobody shall know.'

Issy nods.

'Right, follow me.'

Janie knocks gently at the bedroom door, like it too has feelings. 'Emily, there's someone here to see you,' she says softly, and pushes it open.

Emily is asleep.

Issy gasps in horror. Her friend looks like a corpse. Feeling her mother's soft fingers on her cheek, Emily opens her eyes. She blinks and opens them again, not believing what she sees. Isobel standing, wide eyed, at her mother's side. Her first thought is that she's dead. When she realises she's not, she just turns her head between her mother and her impossible friend. She hears Janie offering Isobel afternoon tea. The clock says two. Emily pauses at her mother, who smiles at her. Emily smiles back.

After delivering a tray of tea, sandwiches and cake, Janie Sutton returns to the kitchen. She takes the sapphire glass bottle stopper from the pinot noir and pours herself a large glass of red wine. Perching on the arm of her husband's favourite chair, Janie stares at the bushes being battered by the winter winds. She watches smaller twigs snap from the tree, too weak to withstand such force of nature. Then she gets up, gets out the box Emily wrapped in silver foil some six or seven years ago and takes down the Christmas decorations.

That evening, Barry hangs around outside the shop, waiting for Dwayne. He thinks about where Dwayne's going in life. How he is happy to have a job, a legit excuse not to play gangsta. Barry's felt for some time now that it's pointless. He's been reading about entrepreneurs. It's inspiring him to think about his future. His dad got him the book for Christmas. All about self-made people born with less than Barry's got. Secret is putting in the hours. Dwayne is actually a born entrepreneur, Barry thinks. He's made thousands of pounds over the years. He's pure business-minded. If Dwayne thought about doing a business course, he could really go far. Get an apprenticeship in a bank.

Using the streetlight to read his book, he doesn't see the boys approach, clad head-to-toe in black. By the time he hears them, they are too close. He runs across the road, but they're quick, and easily catch him, dragging him up against the shop opposite the butchers where he works. Cyber pulls out a blade, the same flick knife Dwayne left him with in the wood. Some students scream and an African man shouts 'Hey! Go away! Someone call da police!'

The gang surround Barry, and he crashes down in a flurry of punches and kicks. He feels the sole of a trainer smash into his face.

He hears the, for once, welcomed wail of sirens. Even though the police car flies past – as they often do through Peckham. The gang run off, disappearing down a dark alleyway as quickly as they came, leaving Barry on the floor, confused and shocked. Not yet feeling the stab wound, he asks for someone to call his parents. He wants his family. Everything in him wants to feel the kisses of his mum and dad, to hug his sisters. The street is blurred and people move in slow motion. Barry notices his small rucksack by the crates of rubbish he stacked ready for the bin men in the morning. His book lying face down on the pavement. People gather around him, crying and shouting, one woman pressing into his wound, holding his wrist, checking his pulse. He fades in and out, 'He's took some beating' he hears, 'That's not a pretty sight.'

Barry's family arrive at the hospital and are asked to wait patiently. The family hold hands and softly hum prayers while Barry is in the theatre having surgery.

No matter the outcome, Barry's parents are moving. Their house is the one thing that's gone right for them the last five years amid pay freezes in both their salaries, then redundancy and a long spell of unemployment. The stress has made his mother sick. The prospect of debt has slowly turned his father inward and quiet as if London's grind has finally defeated him; one more dejected loser to the relentless city.

Barry's father wipes his tired eyes. 'My son got As in his AS-Levels,' he says softly to the nurse handing out plastic cups of water. 'He's not a gang kid. He's going to university in September.'

The nurse nods, sad to see another fellow young black male stabbed senselessly by his peers.

By the time the eldest sister arrives, the doctors have completed the surgery. His parents hold each other's hands, as a doctor and a nurse step into the room.

'Barry has responded well. He's very weak. He lost a lot of blood and been kicked about a fair bit, but luckily the instrument didn't penetrate that deep. His has a wound on his arm which may have some lasting damage; he might lose some function but we need time to see how much movement there is once Barry gains some strength.'

His mother breaks down, falling to her knees. The relief. And the pain of that relief.

The doctor bites her lip to keep composure. It's been a long, hard shift. She already had to tell two parents this week they've lost their son to a senseless stabbing over a stolen mobile phone. Luckily for Barry the gang stopped at his arm.

'These kids haven't even lived their lives,' she rants to the nurse as they walk out the relatives section. 'They live in a developed country, in one of the best cities in the world, with access to schools, roads, food, shelter, jobs.

So many opportunities and the thing they decide to spend their time and energy on is loitering on the streets, worshipping their postcode, fighting with their neighbours. It's not why I became a medic,' she declares. 'Helping idiots live while rarely being at home myself, attending to my own children's needs. If I could throw in the towel right now, I would. It's not what the National Health Service was made for.'

CHAPTER 36

Springtime, and Mabel's eyes light up as she opens the door to Issy's bouquet of flowers.

'What?' Mabel sings, 'And fe what?'

'I felt like it.'

'I can't remember the last time I had fresh flowers.'

As Mabel makes the tea, Issy listens to the soft crackles that come from the radio playing old reggae love songs. The Trojan beat penetrates into Issy's system making her tingle like a huge inhalation of weed used to, though she's not smoked for months now. The music is setting off all kinds of nostalgia.

Issy notices Mabel's hands shake as she rests the teapot on the kitchen table. Mabel carefully takes the plastic wrap from the biscuits and places some on her best china plate.

Issy watches Mabel, wondering where Mabel would be if she were still in the Caribbean. If she had not moved here to give her children a better life. Without realising it, Issy is overcome with emotion.

Mabel looks at Issy in surprise. She places her hand on Issy's shoulder.

Issy wipes her face with her sleeve, 'I'm getting all emotional these days. Everything sets me off.'

'I only put a biscuit pon di plate,' Mabel chuckles to her own joke.

'Can I ask you something? But I don't want to upset you.'

Mabel sits down and takes the rosary hanging from her pocket and fiddles with the beads, 'Go on. I'm ready.'

'Do you ever wish you never came back, here I mean, to England?' Issy tries to catch any devastation in Mabel's eyes as a signal to change subject sharpish.

278

Mabel raises one eyebrow and nods her head as she does when thinking deeply. 'It were hard. You love someone so, so much. But the children got to come first.'

'Aren't you angry with them? Dwayne, so disrespectful to you.'

'Tell you the truth, I close my eyes to it because it burn too much. But what can I do?' Mabel shrugs as if to gently shake the worry from her shoulders, 'He's just a hurting boy who never had his mother. Sometimes I think I shouldn't have left. I failed my children by leaving them to go back. There was riots in Brixton and all the police hate. Neighbours calling us names, spitting pon me front doorstep...I thought we go back home, back to peace. But di children, they nah want it. They stayed. Me and my husband left. I made a big, big mistake.'

'But you can't control what other people do,' Issy says, thinking of what her head teacher says about personal responsibility: that people make their own choices.

'But you can guide them,' Mabel takes a sip of tea. 'To make di right choices.'

Issy looks into her cup, 'I can't guide Jerome.'

'You be surprise,' Mabel exclaims, breaking her biscuit in two, 'He's not so wild. Him think fe you before listening to his brother. I hear everything. These walls thin.'

Issy gulps, knowing in her heart she's not fully there for him, but for herself.

The radio plays one of Mabel's favourites. 'Like an old dusty road, Emmhmm...movin' on, movin' on...'

'Do you ever want to go back?' Issy asks. 'To Jamaica?'

'Fe what? Him dead, the other children grown up. I got to be here for these two. They got no-one. Dwayne may be following the Devil's path, but him no devil. Him a scared child, scared to be hugged, scared to be loved.'

'Was he always like that?'

'Truth be told, no. He was a sweet boy. He got angry and stubborn when his father left. Then me daughter took in Jerome's father. Less than two months pass, she pregnant with Jerome. I see how him treat the two boys differently. So who knows what him went through. One minute his father pon di table; now a next man come and beat him for stupidness. Dat daughter of mine got corrupted, corrupted by the Devil. By bad men. Lawd, a shame.'

'Why aren't you angry with this country? With the white people? With the racism you got? Why you so forgiving?'

Mabel clasps her fingers around one of her beads.

'My people are a strong people. Not all white people corrupt. Not all black people innocent. Riches and power do things. Made white people put di shackles on black wrists and feet and done more sin than this world can take. I tell you some truth. When I cut I bleed. My heart beat like yours. I wouldn't wish black history pon anyone. The world would be no better had things been the other way round. And fe what? A big house? A new car? Kids rioting fe trainers and music equipment. Now dat boy in the paper, who stole a bag a rice, dat not his fault. Him take RICE! That's real NEED! When dat boy take the rice, dat's a crime fe politicians!'

'Exactly, the system is corrupt. It sets people apart. Divide and conquer! And it's not fair. That's why people get angry.'

'Angry nah work! Love and hate is like water and oil, it can't mix, it can't mix.' Mabel clenches a fist and gently knocks her chest, 'Here. When you full of love, truly loving the Lawd, no matter what the Lawd is, me nah care, Allah, Jah. Me? I believe in Jesus Chrsit. Jesus help me through tough times, long times of hardship, and I'm here now. I'm still alive. When I pass, nuttin' I bring but my soul. That's why it important to follow di Lawd's path. Clean shirt fe church, clean soul fe heaven.'

Issy thinks about how much she wants out; how many hours spent thinking about having a house with a garden, stretched out on the grass under her own tree, looking up at the sky. She feels bad for being angry with what she's got. For being angry with her mother for accepting their stake in life.

'Lawd have mercy!'

Jerome comes crashing through the front door slamming it shut with such force that both Issy and Mabel jump.

Issy briefly catches Jerome's eye. 'Jay?'

He storms through the hallway and slams his bedroom door.

Issy looks at Mabel. Eyes wide with worry.

Issy looks at her watch, 'He shouldn't be back yet.'

Mabel takes a deep breath. She dips the other half of the biscuit into her tea. 'You know, I always thought it bad taste to dunk, but after I reach sixty-two, I tried it. I can't believe I was eating some dry biscuit my whole life because I heard it's not the proper thing fe do.'

'I'm gonna go and see him. Is that okay?'

Mabel nods, humming to the radio, 'hmmm hummm, And before my life is done, Got to find me a place in the sun.'

'Babe?' Issy feels a flutter inside her tummy standing outside Dwayne and Jerome's bedroom door. 'Can I come in?'

Issy slowly draws open the door. Jerome is sitting on Dwayne's bed. His head in his hands.

Issy watches to see if he'll burst with anger. Instead he looks up at Issy and, anger turning to pain, Jerome bites his bottom lip, willing himself not to crumble again in front of his girlfriend.

She places her arm around his shoulders.

Jerome, unable to find the words, takes a few short breaths. He hopes they would be deeper but his lungs are too closely linked to his heart and he can only muster some gasps of air before letting out the painful words, 'Got sacked.'

Issy gasps. She tries to force Jerome to draw closer to her so their chests can meet and embrace, but his body remains tense, facing the wall opposite.

'For dealing weed to the yutes.' Jerome shrugs Issy's shoulder off him, 'So don't feel sorry for me. I fucked it myself. Just like you said.'

The room is silent. A number of things race through Issy's mind. She cans her anger, knowing now's not the time.

'I'm sorry babe, I know how much that job means to you.' Issy gently places her hand on Jerome's knee then reaches over and kisses his cheek. The soft approach only adds to the disaster. Jerome looks around him. He stands up and kicks the cheap office chair into the desk, he rips all the rappers faces from the walls, then picks up the computer monitor and tries to fling it out the window.

'Don't Jerome! Kids could be down there!' Issy screams, 'STOP!'

Jerome chucks it back on the desk, and in hopelessness, he cries, 'I hate my life.'

Issy tries to console him but he turns and shouts louder, 'I hate my fucking life. I hate it. Get out. Get out. GET OUT! Please.'

Issy leaves the room. Mabel stands in the hallway clutching her rosary.

'He got sacked,' she whispers.

Mabel walks back into the kitchen. Issy follows her. She puts the kettle on the stove, 'I'm making barbecue chicken, rice and peas tonight. Want me to teach you?'

Issy nods.

'Come. Bring me that pan.'

Jerome lies on his bed staring at the ceiling. The events that just took place run over and over and in his mind. Every time he gets to the point where Steve says: 'I trusted you, Jerome. I told the team we need to invest in boys like you to keep young people away from drugs. Well thanks a lot. You made me look like a prick and you let yourself down.' 'I'm sorry. I won't do it again.' 'Doesn't matter mate. Does it? I didn't catch you. Rachel did. And now we're both fucked. I told them it was a one off. You told me it was a one-off. Now we got kids saying you've been dealing to them since they were nine years old, filming them for music videos holding spliffs inside the club?' Jerome flinched when Steve kicked the bin over, 'Jesus Jerome! This was a pilot mentoring programme. You were supposed to be a role model. Now I've got parents asking me how long this has been going on and Rachel calling for the Youth Service to investigate...'

Tears appear in Jerome eyes as he recalls Steve saying: 'They'll call the police. You're eighteen. You're an adult now. You're an adult youth worker selling drugs to kids. Don't you get that? Weed is illegal, for Christ's sake.' 'I'm sorry Steve.' 'Don't say sorry to me mate. Say sorry to them. The programme will get shut down. No more recording. No more DJ nights. No more funding. Nothing. Do you realise how much work goes into setting up a youth project? Do you? I spend months and months writing funding applications that nine times out of ten gets rejected. We're struggling to keep our costs down and no staff member has taken a pay rise in four years. This was a pilot project that could have seen us get a reputation for being a leading music production centre and you fucked it, mate.'

Jerome's guts churned as Steve ripped his training certificate from the wall, 'I'll say it was all me. I'll say no one else knew.' Steve tore the certificate in two. 'Doesn't matter, mate. That's why managers are in place. I've got kids telling my team you've been doing it since the first week at work. Is that true?' Jerome put his head down in shame. 'Jesus Jerome! What's wrong with you? At least in your own home, smoking a few spliffs, I can say it's personal or hearsay but dealing? On council property? The Head of Children and Young People's Services is going to come down on me like a ton of bricks. And what then? You gonna pay my rent? My bills? I've got two small kids at home.'

Jerome stares into space until the walls suffocate him. Everything he looks at is cheap and unwanted. The trainers, the tracksuits, the designer labels look unnecessary, worthless; representing hundreds of bags of weed sold to local children and teenagers. He pulls on the wool jumper his grandmother knitted him and the coat she bought him last Christmas and walks past Issy and Mabel, out the front door, down the steps, into the cold dark night.

CHAPTER 37
TRUE LOVE

Cyber X has waited for today. A normal day when nobody suspects a thing. When people think ball is in Graff court for some madness. But Cyber's not been right since Dwayne raped him. And a one jab in Barry's arms doesn't equal that out. He wants to get to Dwayne's heart, inside his head, fuck with his whole system. Give Dwayne nightmares. Make Dwayne have panic attacks. Cyber has been keeping the information to a minimum, suspecting an informer, bringing just his closest man dem.

Mabel Clarke crosses the road, wearing her best dress. She walks up the hill, towards the church humming Joy to the World.

Cyber X approaches the old lady crossing the road, 'Is your grandson called Dwayne?'

Mabel Clarke, looks up at the slender face. He's holding a bunch of flowers. 'Yes, darling,' she says looking at the tulips. 'Dwayne's my grandson.'

'Tell him, this is for the woods.' Cyber hesitates, but the gang are behind the parked van, watching.

'What fe what?' Mabel asks.

'THE WOODS!' Cyber shouts in her face but the flick knife behind the flowers is jammed. It won't open. Cyber thinks for a split second then clenches a fist and rams it in her face. Mabel gasps, dropping her bag to hold up her hands to protect herself. Cyber punches her again: in her arms, claps her around the side of her head. Images of Dwayne forcing his mouth open Mabel hunches over as he hits her. Soon Mabel's legs collapse. She falls to the frosted pavement.

Cyber doesn't know what to do once she falls. He shouts out to his boys to come. They know this is crossing some next line of morality. Adrenaline pumping through their veins, the peer pressure of not doing anything, of looking like a pussyhole. Shutting out any second thoughts, one boy runs over, then another, and then four boys are surrounding her, kicking an old lady who was just on her way to church. A man nearby yells at them to stop. Another lady starts shouting 'Get off her! GET OFF HER!'

Carol comes out on the balcony to see what all the commotion is about. Issy joins Carol and sees some boys kicking a body on the floor, 'Oh my god!'
    'Issy, Don't go!'

Jerome peers out from the kitchen window. Still in his boxer shorts, with Dwayne still in bed, he shouts 'Peckham yutes! PECKHAM YUTES!' banging on the bedroom door.

As Jerome rushes out the flat, Dwayne takes the gun from above his wardrobe. He looks at himself in the wardrobe mirror, a split second, just enough to see the gangster, not long enough to see the fear. He fires from the balcony. The bullet hits a nearby car, shattering the glass. Neighbours scream and rush behind walls.

Jerome is almost down the stairs when he hears the shot slamming into the car, shattering the windscreen. The gang flee revealing Mabel bloodied and beaten. Jerome runs after them, not knowing it's his grandmother lying on the floor.

Issy is halfway across the courtyards when she realises it's Mabel lying in the middle of the road. Those boys came in broad daylight kicking and punching an old lady. She gently strokes Mabel's bloodied hair, 'It's okay, it's okay. I'm here. I'm here.'
    'Call an ambulance!' Issy screams as Carol approaches. 'Call the fucking ambulance!'
    She scrambles for her own phone to dial Jerome's number. 'It's your nan. It's your nan. They've killed her!'

Dwayne runs down from the flat to the street just as Jerome arrives. Seeing the gun in his brother's hand, Jerome flips. 'PUT IT AWAY, FAM!'
    Dwayne points the gun at Issy, 'This is your fault.'
    Jerome goes for Dwayne, 'What you wanna pull a strap on my lady, yeah?' Jerome tries to take the gun away. Dwayne fires a shot into the air.

'Stop it, Dwayne,' Carol pleads. 'This ain't the time for that. Your nanna is dying on the floor.'

'You turned him into a pussyhole.'

Jerome pushes Issy out of the way, 'Shoot me, then. Yeah. Blood thicker, yeah. Shoot your blood then, bruv?'

Issy stares at Jerome and then at Dwayne.

'Dwayne!' Carol says firmly. 'Police will be here any moment. Put the gun away. She needs the hospital.'

'Bro, don't you get it?' Dwayne says in a trance. 'This is war now.' Dwayne snorts, looking over at his grandmother. Sirens can be heard in the distance. He quickly stuffs the gun in his jeans.

'Where you going?' Jerome stands up. Dwayne runs off.

'Fuck him, Jerome!' Issy screams. 'She needs you right now.'

The police turn into Ommaney Road. Some neighbours retreat into their flats, steering clear of the feds; others come out and gather around Mabel's body, feeling safe now police have arrived.

Jerome touches the blood soaked corners of his grandmother's blouse. Paramedics arrive. Shaking his head, violently, Jerome wraps his arms around his head. 'This is nuts,' Jerome whispers, 'This is nuts.'

'This is your fault,' Issy tells Jerome.

Jerome stands back. His heart thumping, watching his grandmother being given oxygen.

Issy watches Mabel being lifted onto a stretcher by three paramedics, then at her mum's puffy eyes fixed on Mabel, then at the police officers hanging back with eyes focussed on Jerome, one officer inspecting the car where the bullet was shot shattering its window. Issy stares at the neighbours on the estate that have fallen to the edges like beads inside a wonky glass. The paramedics placing Mabel into the ambulance. Everything scrambles up in her mind, making no sense.

Issy stands up and screams. She stamps her feet, 'I hate you. I fucking hate you all!' She walks her body in circles: 'None of you care. None of you.'

One policewoman steps over to Issy and tries to restrain her arm. Issy moves out the way as the policewoman again asks her to remain calm. 'That's my nan in there. Can't you see?'

Another female officer comes over. 'That's my nan in there!' Issy sobs into the policewoman's arms, 'I can't do this, anymore.'

Jerome tries to walk towards Issy. Issy wipes her face, 'No, Jay. Stop where you are.'

The policewomen use their bodies as a block, outstretching their shoulders in protection.

Issy looks at Jerome. The torn feeling between wanting to comfort him and kiss him, but knowing what's happened is a direct cause of his actions.

The anger slips in too easily to allow her to forgive him this time, 'I can't do this anymore.' Issy clutches her stomach, falling to the ground.

The ambulance door closes. Carol goes over to Jerome also walking round in circles holding his head.

Jerome meets Carol's pale eyes, 'Pull your wee self together and focus on your nanna. She needs you now.'

Jerome stares at Carol's blue eyeliner then up at her pencilled-in eyebrows pointed with concern.

'You can be upset,' Carol continues softly, 'but not now, okay?'

Jerome nods, collecting himself.

Carol takes Jerome by the hand and leads him to the ambulance and knocks on the back door.

'Excuse me ambulance man, this is her grandson. Can he go with her?' The paramedic looks at Carol and suggests she takes him, in case the team need to deal with a cardiac arrest or coma.

'I don't drive,' Carol replies.

The policeman offers to drive Jerome to the hospital.

Jerome looks into the ambulance, 'Please, can I go with her?'

The other paramedic nods and allows space for Jerome.

Issy is shaking violently. The ambulance takes Mabel away, its sirens loud and piercing, become faint as they drive down the hill to King's College Hospital.

Dwayne's forehead is sweating. The cool beads look unfamiliar against the cold March air. People in the street stare at him; his jeans and tight-fitting black wool jumper are not exactly jogging attire. Finding a corner down by Sainsbury's, Dwayne calls Hayley.

'Babes, can I come check you and Jamal? Cool. Just gotta get something from the shop, then I'm there.'

Dwayne jumps into a cab to Hayley's flat. He tries not to think about his grandmother. If he thinks about it, he'll blame himself. He thought it was done. How can Cyber think he can attack an old woman? For this, he's a dead man.

While she makes him a sandwich, Dwayne goes to Jack-Jamal. He sits in his cot, completely asleep. Dwayne strokes his son's face. Hayley opens the door. Dwayne jumps.

'Want mayonnaise?' Hayley asks, completely unaware of what's just happened.

'Nah, thanks.'

Hayley comes in to see the baby, 'Getting big now ain't he?'

'Proper.'

'You alright? You seem out of sorts.'

Dwayne strokes his son's ringlet curls, 'Give me a minute, with him? Alone. My little man and me.'

'Yeah course,' Hayley smiles. 'I'm next door.'

Dwayne shuts the door, and switches the baby monitor off. He looks around for a safe place to store the gun. Taking the duct tape from his back pocket, Dwayne puts the safety catch on then straps the gun to the bottom slat of the crib.

He kisses his son's cheek. To Dwayne's surprise, Jamal opens his eyes. He wiggles his legs up and down and smiles. Dwayne feels a jolt in his heart. He picks up his son and takes him to the living room.

Hayley comes in from the balcony, blowing the last of her cigarette out, 'Cold out there. Hello little man. Hello little man. You awake? You awake now?'

Hayley smells Jack-Jamal's nappy while Dwayne holds him.

'Mummy change your nappy?' Hayley goes into the baby's room and brings out the changing mat and a fresh nappy and wipes.

Watching Hayley so womanlike, so mumlike, it stirs something inside him. 'Hays. Do you wanna have another go at things? You know. Like start it again. This time, I'm gonna be here. Be around more.'

At first she doesn't speak. Looking only at the baby.

'You know, I ain't really looking for a man right now,' Hayley says, looking away. 'Even if I wanted one, my head's messed up from my childhood and shit. Now's time for me and JJ.'

Dwayne clenches his fists then releases them.

Since Jack-Jamal came into Hayley's life, the world is a better place. She's happy. So happy. He smiles at her every day. He plays with her. If he cries, it's for a reason. She can't understand how anyone can beat their children the way she got beat. He's so innocent. Can't do a thing wrong. Watching him get bigger and learn things and taste new food is making Hayley see things differently. Her support worker has been amazing. She gets free stuff for the baby, and vouchers to go to soft play and meet other single mums. A local artist came in and decorated the baby's room and made it so magical, like a fairy tale. Complete opposite to the world of her, Dwayne and Ronnie. That life is no place for children. She's understanding more and more. Her parents decided to abuse her. Her little sister Kaya is still on a Child Protection Order. For her own safety. Ronnie's back in prison for robbery. Her mum is better kept at a distance. Her dad prefers the pub and that suits Hayley. Her life is with the baby and that's it.

'Besides,' Hayley looks at Dwayne with her baby in his arms.

'Yeah?'

'Doesn't matter.'

'Nah, tell me,' Dwayne says.

'Well I... I just don't think, you know, that I'm your type, that's all,' Hayley says, fully aware he is holding the most precious thing in the world to her.

Dwayne sits down. He puts the baby on one knee and rubs his own face with his free hand. Images of Cyber sucking his penis morph into his grandmother being beaten up.

Hayley sits on the sofa, 'At the end of the day you're my baby's father, so you can stay here as long as you want.'

'What a day, man,' Dwayne looks at his phone. It's been on silent. Jerome and several others been calling. Text message after text message demanding to know where he is. If he's coming hospital. Whether it was his gun. Where's the gun now. That his gran might die. Did Cyber attack her?

'Anyway,' Hayley says switching on the television, 'your sandwich is in the kitchen.'

She takes Jack-Jamal and undoes his full nappy. She tickles his feet and blows raspberries on his belly.

When Dwayne returns from the kitchen, he notices his son. 'What the fuck, blood?'

Hayley laughs, 'I know, nuts innit? Boys get hard-ons from day one.'

'Why's he's turned on?'

'He ain't, Dwayne.' Hayley laughs, trying to calm Dwayne's nerves.

'What you done to him?'

Nothing. It ain't sexual.'

'He's got a boner!'

'Yeah, and? He's just a baby. All babies get boners.'

Then it comes again. The panic. The anxiety. Dwayne's flashback of himself, age six or seven, seeing his step-dad's boxing magazine. Glossy pictures of Mohamed Ali and thinking how strong the boxer's arms looked, how his erection showed through his pants and how Jerome's father beat the shit out of him after Leeroy snaked: 'What di ras? Check dis lickle batty boy here.' pulling up Dwayne's arm, exposing him to everyone in the kitchen. His mum disgusted. The men laughing. Then his step-father smashing into Dwayne with the back of his hand. Then the start of Leeroy touching him, confusing Dwayne's sense of sexuality. Always a bit of his mind wondering if he liked boys and if his love for fucking girls is just an act. His feelings forever messed up from that day. And Dwayne thought it was his fault because he saw Ali and... Flashback: Leeroy always opening the bedroom door, babysitting the boys so Dwayne's Mum and Jerome's dad could go dancehall. Leeroy whispering to Dwayne lying in bed pretending to sleep that if he doesn't do things then Leeroy will make Jerome do them instead. Dwayne rising from his bed, saying, 'Don't touch my brother,' crying tears, as he got forced to do stuff with Leeroy. Never forgetting the sick look of pleasure on Leeroy's face. Always wondering why when Leeroy touched him that he would go hard. He always went hard...

Hayley finishes Jack-Jamal's nappy and wipes her hands with a fresh baby wipe. She sees Dwayne's shocked and gives the baby back to him, putting her arms around Dwayne, thinking he's sad she just rejected him. She seen Dwayne's softer side more than anyone.

Dwayne nods, feeling the warmth of Hayley's embrace, wanting to run, wanting to stay, thinking he deserves none of it. He cries uncontrollably. He doesn't know where from and can't do anything to stop. Meanwhile, a corner of the silver tape securing the gun to the cot unpeels.

At the hospital, the beeping of the machines is a reminder to Jerome that he is in a living, breathing world. Mabel is on the hospital bed, her face swollen like bruised plums. The police have not moved far, waiting for a time to continue the questioning. Carol reminds them this is a critical time and to give Jerome some space as he tries to leave the room to smoke.

'He's a good kid caught up in a shit life,' Carol tells them.

Under the watch of the two officers, Jerome and Issy share a cigarette in the small smoking area outside. Jerome tries to hug Issy, but her body is like a corpse stung into rigor mortis. He steps back, searching his girlfriend's eyes for some comfort.

'My gran's in hospital and you're going on cold,' he says, offering her the lit cigarette.

Issy shoots Jerome a cool stare, 'I'm here for her, Jay, not you,' she inhales and exhales the smoke in equal fury. 'She wouldn't be here if it wasn't for your music. They couldn't have made it any clearer.' Issy feels her knees giving way, she collapses onto a nearby bench. It's been a while since she smoked and the nicotine hits her with some force. She returns the cigarette to Jerome.

Jerome remains standing. Issy remains sat down, eyes focused ahead of her, watching the mint green medic uniforms walking past the chrome plated windows.

'Babe,' Jerome begins.

'Don't babe me!' Issy's eyes fill with tears, 'Your nan is in hospital unconscious. They don't even know if she'll pull through. Don't, don't you dare, I can't.'

'I know. You were right all along. You said it from day-.'

'Doesn't matter anymore. What's done is done,' Issy croaks quietly, as if it were her last words to offer the world. 'Now is what counts.'

Issy peers up to see the sad eyes in front of her, wishing things to go back to the in-love days when Jerome had sparkly eyes and a cheeky smile.

When they both had them and were happy.

'What if she dies? What if they've killed her? Then it's like she came here for what?'

There is a photograph of Mabel and her husband smiling on the boat to England, dressed smartly in his suit and Mabel in her long dress and overcoat, her hat with a net clasped to it. Elegant, honest, deserving more. Mabel always talks about how they drank tea and watched the waves become sliced by the ship. How they played cards and joked about meeting the Queen, getting good jobs and becoming wealthy, sending their children to study at university. Issy wipes the tears from her eyes, it hurts as if they were her own broken promises.

Jerome sits there silently, her words burning through his soul like fire destroys houses. Only yesterday his gran was cooking up a big pot of chicken, how he noticed her swaying to the old reggae station on the radio, how her rackety hips would still move even when the reception faded in and out; she still hummed the tracks, whether the signal was there or not, 'Doesn't that piss you off? Sorry I mean get on your nerves?' 'What darling?' 'The radio, keeps cutting out.' 'The music can't cut when it's playing inna yuh soul.'

'Jerome,' Issy says, breaking the silence. This time a different tone, softer, how he knows Issy to be. 'I need a break. From us.' Issy begins to shake, 'I need to think about everything, okay?'

Jerome bites his bottom lip tightly so as not to let a single tear come.

'I can't be your girlfriend right now,' Issy's says, her eyes filled with tears. 'Please, just stay away for a bit, promise?'

Carol arrives, opening the glass door, 'Police want to talk to you now.'

Jerome nods.

CHAPTER 38

Issy arrives at the hospital with flowers. She sees Jerome sitting on the bench in the smoking area. He doesn't notice her, she could slip by. Since Mabel's attack, he's been true to her request and given her the space she asked for. At times, this felt like someone ripping out her vital organs, messing with her guts, stabbing her heart. Pain that nothing can stop except studying and sleeping and crying, lots of crying.

'How are things?' Issy asks, closing the door and sitting beside him.

Jerome turns to Issy. 'Really wanna know?'

She nods.

'Shit. Dwayne still missing. Gran is shook up like you can't believe. Keeps talking about her rosary beads. I'm looking everywhere.'

'I read on your profile, you quit Graff.'

Jerome looks over his shoulder to see who else is about. A patient hobbles with a Zimmer frame to finds a place to smoke. Inside, a doctor rushes past a couple with their new baby. He turns back to Issy, 'Well boy, when the two women you love most–' Jerome stops himself, emotions too thick. He clears his throat.

She holds out her hand, already knowing what he is trying to say.

'You here to see, Gran?'

Issy nods.

Jerome looks at Issy, 'I miss you.'

Issy nods.

'Can we talk?'

'What now?'

'Yeah.'

'Maybe when your nan is out of hospital.'

'I never made that track,' Jerome says, 'that cussed his mum. I didn't even hear it before they put it online.'

Issy nods, but isn't ready to go back to thinking about the battles and the weed and the warfare. She looks down at the flowers. Now she knows why people give them. They offer something beautiful to the eye and kind to the mind, 'When Mabel gets better we'll talk. But right now, I need space from all that.'

Emily, still painfully thin and frail, sits with Issy watching the YouTube videos put out by Double G and Cyber X.

'The lyrics are so violent,' Emily says.

'You predicted all of this. I warned him. But he still carried on. As if selling these tracks isn't like selling weed. So what? It should be illegal for people to say such things.'

Emily moves closer to Issy and gives her a hug. This time she takes it, and hugs back. Issy can feel every bone in Emily's back. She's tried to talk to Emily about her eating disorder but each attempt has Emily's eyes glaze over or go stern with Emily becoming frosty or dismissive.

'Issy, I am so sorry. I feel like I've not been there for you. I didn't realise things had gotten so bad.'

'Jerome and I were so tight the year we first got together. We'd hang out all the time. He used to sing me love songs and eat my mum's crappy white-bread ham and mayo sandwiches.' Issy bursts into tears.

Emily holds Issy; tears falling from her own eyes, 'I feel like I haven't been a true friend to you. After all the things you've done for me. If they only knew you like I do.'

'Who? Your parents?' Issy asks drying her eyes.

Emily looks embarrassed. Now she bursts into tears.

Issy looks puzzled, 'Mimi? What's wrong?'

'I haven't been completely honest with you. Henry...well....he's...'

'...a bit of a snob?' Issy offers.

'Yes,' Emily replies.

'I kind of worked that out.' They both laugh. 'You can't help who you love, Mimi. Henry may be a dick but he loves you and that's what counts.'

'You're not disappointed in me?' Emily asks, leaving out the part where Henry told Emily to keep clear of Issy, concentrate on her studies, and make life decisions after taking her exams.

'Why?'

'For falling for someone like him back. I mean, I was a bit ashamed of him last time we had lunch.'

'Mimi, look at Jerome. Come back to me when Henry produces a deadly album,' Issy says, pressing pause on Cyber X, his face in an ugly angry freeze-frame on the screen.

'You're not like that and that is what counts. You don't agree with him, do you?' Issy asks.

'Me, no, not at all. In fact, we debate and I clearly put my foot down on the matter.'

'What do you say?'

'One shouldn't judge people on their circumstances as one really doesn't know where come from and what's happened to get them there. He's just looking out for me. He's been great, he helped me get well again, you know, after what happened. He's also applied for Oxford, different college, but still, if we both get in, then he'll be close. The other day, he brought over new paintbrushes and a sketchpad.'

'Wow, I miss that in-love stage,' Issy sighs. 'I want to break up with Jerome but the thought of not being in his arms, but it doesn't feel the same. I want to hug him, but when we do, I'm like a block of ice.'

'Give it time,' Emily reassures. 'It's not like Jerome's a bad person.'

'That's why it's so hard. He's actually a good person. I know it. I believe it.' Issy leaves out the gun part, and the police questioning, and the flat searches.

'See. You'll forgive him. This just shows that you are a real person with honest feelings. You would be odd if you didn't need some time to reflect on what's happened. You just witnessed a terrible attack. You know, you've suffered an immense trauma. You need to mentally and emotionally process things. That's healthy, in my view.'

'Mimi,' Issy looks at Emily unsure and nervous. 'My teacher says the reason people say First Love is because it's never meant to last. Do you think that's true?'

Emily ponders Issy's question, considering the passport photograph of Jerome stuck in the corner of Issy's bedroom mirror.

'What about True Love?' she offers. 'True Love can be your First Love because no matter when it comes, it's True.'

'How am I supposed to know the difference?' Issy asks.

'I'm not sure. I think you just feel it.'

CHAPTER 39
FIRST LOVE

Jerome spies Issy exiting her block of flats. He looks away when he accidently catches her gaze.

Issy feels the pain rise up to choke her. Jerome kept to his word and has left her alone for over three weeks. Funny how two people can live so close and not cross paths. A shiver runs down her spine. She can't move. So much history stands between them.

Jerome stubs out his cigarette and walks towards her, his trainers soundless on the concrete. 'I know we're not together anymore, but I just thought I should let you know, Gran's home tomorrow.'

Mabel has been staying with her friend Lucille's daughter from church. She phoned Jerome yesterday and said she is ready to return. He's re-painted Mabel's bedroom in her favourite colour and bought her a new rosary, which he's left on her bed after asking the priest to bless it. The past weeks have been agonising. The empty flat has felt like prison.

'That's great.' Issy looks at Jerome. It's not just the scar that makes him look older, she knows he hasn't been online since the attack. She knows this has changed everything. That he now gets the true cost of his music and what it's done.

'I didn't break up with you; I just wanted space.'

He nods.

'I got my uni offers,' Issy says.

'And?'

'I've accepted a conditional offer from Lincoln.'

Jerome nods again. He's spent hours wanting to hold her, but now there's a part of him that's angry with how selfish she's being.

'You could move with me?' Issy offers, half-hearted. 'Like we said. Get away from here. We could start afresh?'

'I can't uproot Gran now she's been attacked.'

'She needs to be away from here, too.'

'She needs to be around the people from her church. They've proper stepped up, kept me sane. Pure kindness.'

Issy swallows her guilt, 'I still want you to come with me.'

'Issy, think about it. You're going in a few months. How am I gonna get a job, pay rent, support three people? You can just uproot and leave. We'd need to be re-housed by the council.'

'To Lincoln?'

'I've thought about it, now Gran's been attacked, we *could* get re-housed. But it takes time...'

Issy nods her head. Hearing it might be possible they get rehoused to Lincoln doesn't bring her joy. Why not? She's so exhausted by her feelings changing on her. It's like whenever her dreams step closer, they get poisoned by reality, as if real life, in itself, has to be shit.

'...and if she don't wanna go, how am I gonna leave her?'

'I know, Jerome. I'm sorry.'

'Can't you stay in London? Switch uni?'

Issy shakes her head.

'Why not?'

'Because I can't. I've picked Lincoln.'

'What about Goldsmiths? You can still move. Get a room in Brockley or somewhere and catch a bus. But at least we can see each other.'

Issy pauses, 'I didn't get an offer there.'

'I would have moved to Lincoln, I still would but I can't just up and leave. Now ain't a good time.'

'Jerome, I can't because—'

'You won't.'

'The process won't allow me.'

'Yes it will. They do cleaning, where you can change at the last minute.'

'Clearing's only if you don't get your grades.'

Jerome looks away, his eyes rest on the spot where Cyber attacked his grandmother. He wonders how Mabel will cope with that. Issy starts sobbing. 'I didn't apply to any in London, alright. I lied. I thought about it but when it came to it, something inside told me Lincoln is the place I need to be. It feels right. Do you know who Abraham Lincoln was?'

'Some American.'

'President. He fought for the emancipation of slaves. He inspires me. Don't you think this estate is like a slave fort? I mean who really gets out of here and into a fat house and a new car and an easy life?'

Jerome shakes his head in disbelief, 'You know what the last few weeks have been like for me? Dwayne's on the run. Gran's in hospital with a broken hip, cheekbone, ankle, fractured wrist, ribs... And you, supposed to be my girlfriend, yeah...' He wipes spit from his bottom lip, 'You know I defended you 'til the end. You're my lady. None of these boys could ever disrespect you. Now, I know I done wrong, yeah. I know the music ting was the wrong ting to do, I see that now and I know you done told me this shit time ago, and if I could turn back the clock I would, but where were you? You see me tell everyone I'm done with Graff. Done. Where was you knocking on my door?'

Now he has started, he can't stop – it all spills out, 'I needed you so much, needed you to just say "Babe it's okay, your gran's gonna be fine, we'll get through it together" but nah, you just kept on your same flex.'

'I'm sorry,' Issy whispers.

'I needed you. For the first time, I proper needed you to back it for me. Where was you?' He screws up his face in pain. 'You never thought about my feelings, just your own escape plan!'

Issy bows her head in shame. His words sound right.

'When you said to stay away, I respected that. I thought about ringing you, trust, over and over. Phone in hand. I ran everything through in my mind. I locked off everything. Told everyone, best stay away from me and I know you know that because Anton done told me he told you.'

Issy looks away. She told herself repeatedly that her exams are more important. Concentrate on them and ignore everyone. Her exam dates won't change. Her coursework can't wait. Deal with everything else afterwards.

'Issy, man? Why didn't you come check me?' Jerome's eyes well up. 'I proper needed you.'

'That day, my head was in another place. I needed to breathe. I felt like I couldn't breathe. That things had gone too far. That no matter what, you're always gonna do what you're doing and I know it's selfish, but if I don't watch my back, who's watching it for me?'

'I am. I do.'

'But you didn't, Jay. You didn't.'

'I was trying to get us out of here. Get us money so we could get a flat and pay for your uni.'

'Don't you get it? Making money took over everything. It's like money is the way out, but at the end of the day, what's money when you get banged up? When your nan's unconscious? When your brother pulls a fucking gun out on me? Am I supposed to feel safe enough to knock on your door?'

Jerome sits on a nearby wall. 'You could have called. I could've come over.'

'I just want a normal boyfriend, with a normal job. So what if it takes us our whole lives to buy a house or a car? So what?'

Jerome is silent for a moment.

'So, you definitely leaving London?'

She nods.

'Then it's over,' Jerome says. 'Dwayne was right.'

Issy sits motionless as her first love gets up from the wall and without a single glance back, walks away from her.

CHAPTER 40
TWO MINUTES

The hall is cold despite the June weather making her journey to school sticky. Issy looks down at the A4 piece of paper, questions facedown. In a couple of minutes, she will turn it over and her final exam will begin.

The students are told to start filling out their names and the exam title onto the top of the lined answer sheets.

'You have two minutes remaining,' calls out Mr Murray, the Geography teacher.

Mrs Salmon smiles over at Issy, putting both thumbs in the air.

Issy nods. The knot in her stomach turns. She sips some water.

'You may start.'

To celebrate, Emily takes Issy for drinks on the Southbank. Henry and Richie decide to join them.

'We did it, guys!' Richie says, raising his beer. 'And well done Issy, I hear that you are entering the summer holidays single.'

Issy is taken aback. Emily blushes. Henry rolls his eyes.

'I say we drink then hit a club. My parents are out of town, so we can pile back to mine, then grab breakfast. Lie in the park. Weather is going to be gorgeous again tomorrow.'

Issy feels the heat of the sun on her face. Summer is here and she hopes it'll be a good one. Richie is charming and sweet – it makes her happy that he wants to spend time with her.

He puts his arm around her shoulders as they walk to the river's edge and points out the building his father works in. 'I'll be working there one day; can you imagine the view?'

Issy looks across the river to an imposing white stone building.

'When the sky goes pink at sunset, let me tell you, the Thames is stunning. No place better in the world,' Richie says, then whispers in her ear, 'Apart from inside you.'

Issy straightens up. Did she hear that right?

Richie bites his bottom lip with a grin, 'Apologies, I speak truthfully when I take these bad boys.'

He presses a blue triangle-shaped pill into Issy's palm.

'Try one. You have my absolute word I'll look after you, all night.'

'What is it?' Issy asks, all night, all night, all night, Richie's voice echoes inside her head. The cava has already made her tipsy.

'Ecstasy. It brings out the inner love.'

Issy looks down at the pill.

'Be discreet,' Richie says, holding his hand over hers. 'Those two are not fans.'

Issy looks over at Henry and Emily, who seem to be in some unhappy conversation, their body language speaking volumes.

Richie puts his arm back around Issy. She feels the heat of his body, through his thin cotton shirt. His aftershave surrounds her as a swirl of breeze moves around them. He takes the pill and pops it into her mouth. Tastes like washing powder. Then raises his drink to her lips. Issy swallows.

Henry walks over, 'I'm taking Emily home. She's feeling unwell.'

Emily hangs back. She waves to Issy but doesn't smile.

'Yeah man, sure. Do what you need to.'

Henry rolls his eyes again, 'Enjoy.'

'See ya,' Issy says with added South Londoner, sad to see Emily go but glad the downer part of the afternoon is going with her.

They watch the couple walk up the steps towards Waterloo, then Ritchie turns to her and says, 'There's magic in the air tonight. Do you know how long I've waited to hang out with you? Just you and me. Alone. I didn't think it would ever happen. I'm so happy right now.'

Issy is as puzzled by Richie's words as she is flattered. She wasn't expecting this. A fizzing inside her belly begins. She grins.

'You are absolutely gorgeous when you do that. Keep doing that.'

'What.'

'That.' Richie touches her mouth, strokes her cheek.

They walk along the South Bank, sipping cava from plastic cups. Issy's skin tingles up and down her body. She lets out a sigh, each breath makes the tingling stronger.

'What's happening to me?'

'You're coming up, babe. I wish, I wish these were our first ones together. I love that feeling.'

Issy looks at the Thames, her eyes feel watery but there are no tears; she's content.

'I love my mum,' Issy says. 'She's been working so hard, to send me uni.'

'Where does she work?'

'Supermarket. I didn't want to say when we first met.'

'Why, babe? Why? You think we're all posh twats?'

'Opposite. That I'm scummy.' The hairs on Issy's arms stand on end. The people chattering around her, they are all so beautiful, like a flock of birds. People are amazing. Look at the bridges we build. The trains. The stations. The museums. The planes. The boats. Bicycles. Jewellery. Sandals…

'We're all equal, babe. When I first saw you, I knew me and you, we would–' Richie stops, his eyes dart back and forth. His hair is damp from sweat; he wipes it back. He looks like he's just come out of a perfume advert, the ones by the sea where everything's in black and white. He takes a chewing gum out. Then hands one to Issy.

She finds a tree and sits under its shade. Her heart is thumping; she's sweating too. 'Oh wow, I feel amazing.'

'Good eh?' Richie leans over. His fingers gently stroking her neck feels so intense, shivers run up and down her whole body…

Issy wakes up. She is lying next to Richie, naked. Her mouth feels like the inside of a bin. Richie is sleeping. She looks around and recognises his room. She strokes his hair. He doesn't stir.

Careful not to disturb him, she climbs out of his king-size bed and walks through the wardrobe area to the bathroom where they once danced like idiots. She chuckles to herself. She never thought she'd be back here. Not like this anyway. After relieving herself, she takes the toothbrush that's in a cup by the sink and runs the tap. As she runs it across her teeth, she thinks about how they'll see each other, being at different universities. How she'll tell Emily that Richie's got together with her. Will the other girls will be happy for her? How will Henry react to his best friend seeing a commoner? She thinks about Jerome; a puncture to her daydream. Her heart tightens. She splashes cold water on her face.

A lot of the previous night is a blur. She remembers taking at least two more pills. They spent most of the evening outside. London was dazzling. They smoked a lot. Soho square. There was a club. At some point they kissed. Her stomach churns. The taste of mint toothpaste. The feeling of the brush on her tongue makes her gag. Nothing comes up. She doesn't remember eating much, a sandwich at lunchtime. Her stomach churns again. She looks in the mirror. Her pupils are massive, like some creature, a cat.

Richie remains fast asleep. Issy smells his shirt from the night before. Feelings of being high return. She chuckles aloud. Of all the people to feed her hard drugs, after living next to people like Ronnie and dating Jerome.

Jerome. Her heart pangs. Three years. Nearly together for three whole years. She takes one of the neatly stacked fluffy white towels and this time purposely walks into the shower sensors. The welcomed jets of spray hit her body. She smiles, remembering Richie taking her hand and singing in her ear. Running shampoo through her hair, there's this happiness that she's got together with Richie mixed with a sadness it's over with Jerome.

Richie wakes up to find Issy wearing one of his shirts, sitting on the sofa at the foot of his bed, reading one of the books from his shelf.

'Morning.'

'Morning,' he says, rubbing his head. 'You still here?'

Issy's smile drops. What does he mean by that? She doesn't know what to say. She must have got that wrong.

Richie gets out of bed, his body, also naked, walks past her to the bathroom.

Issy, unsure really as to what's going on, wonders if she should follow him. But she waits. Perhaps he's hungover.

Richie takes ages before he returns to the bedroom and when he does he is wearing cotton trousers, still topless, showing off his six pack, holding a pot in one hand, two mugs in the other with a newspaper under his arm.

'Coffee?' he asks, pouring himself a drink.

'I prefer tea.'

'Suit yourself.'

He sits on his bed and looks at the headlines.

Issy wants to join him, but she senses he wants his space. The touchy-feely, loving person from last night has evaporated like rain in a desert. Her stomach churns.

As Richie continues to read, she deflates further. She's an outsider again. Belonging nowhere. Stuck between borders. She doesn't want to be friends with her old friends and she doesn't feel like her new ones are real.

'Do you want me to go?' Issy croaks. Her mouth is dry but the thought of black coffee hitting her stomach makes her want to gag.

Richie ignores the question and flips the pages of the newspaper.

In the silence, Issy starts to laugh. 'This is a prank, innit? Richie, it's not funny. You got me for a minute.'

Richie looks up. He squints his eyes, 'God, I feel like shit. Why are you laughing, babe?'

CHAPTER 41
2 YEARS SINCE THE RIOTS – 15 AUGUST 2013

Thudding footsteps down the hallway. Issy looks outside, the weather is cloudy and looks like it might rain. Her stomach flips. It's like this day was never gonna come. Waiting and waiting and now Thursday's here. Issy feels paralysed by the sudden stark reality.

A cobweb dangles from the lampshade. She stares at it. Inside a mix of excitement and dread. She needs two A-Levels to be graded C or above to secure her place at Lincoln. She needs the loo.

Carol, hearing the toilet flush, yells out, 'Today's the day!'

'Yep,' Issy says walking into the kitchen. Carol has put party rings biscuits, sandwiches and drinks out on the table.

'What time is it?' Issy asks.

'Midday,' Carol replies, lighting a cigarette. 'You slept in.'

Issy gets a rush of nerves. She can go to Sixth Form now; the results are there, waiting. There's comfort in knowing that her exams have been read and marked and that those marks are decided. No going back. She wonders how parachuters jump out of planes for the first time, imagining them staring out the open door - all up to the mind to tell the body to leap.

She looks inside her wardrobe, her heart racing as she puts on jeans and a jumper. On the bottom shelf are Richie's clothes from the shower incident at his barbecue. Sophie's invited her along to a pre-uni party, to celebrate everyone's results. Issy puts Richie's stuff on her bed so this time she'll remember to bring it with her. Awkward as it will be to see him again.

Jerome sends Issy a text message wishing her luck, hoping she gets the results she needs. She knows he's been feeling bad since he broke it off with her, and blames himself that she's been avoiding him. What he doesn't know is that Issy's been hiding from him, unable to look him in the eye after fucking someone like Richie. No matter how much Issy could tell him he's a million times the man Richie isn't, Jerome will only see a rich, successful white boy who's got more going for him and can give everything Issy needs. None of which is true. But there's no avoiding it, at some point she needs to say goodbye to Jerome, face-to-face, assuming she's going somewhere that is. She can't face any of the food on the table, and bolts out of the door.

Mrs Salmon hands over a brown sealed envelope with a smile. It hits her that today's the last time she'll see Mrs Salmon. Who has taught her so much more, in the last three years, than English and Sociology.

Issy sits down on her usual blue cube chair in the students' common room. She looks around for a friendly face, but few students remain, most have been and gone already.

She takes a deep breath, and with trembling fingers, rips open the envelope: CCC.

A lump forms in her throat. She wasn't expecting A-stars but at least a B or two. This is shit. She's average, so average, in every single way. All that study, hours spent reading, making notes and for what, CCC?

'You know, you're eighteen now, so we can go for a proper drink.' Mrs Salmon as followed her into the common room, glancing at the results over her shoulder.

Carol is waiting back at the flat with a spread that was supposed to be a picnic but the weather keeps changing. Issy ponders either letting down her mum or refusing Mrs Salmon's invite. This might be the last time Issy gets to speak to her beloved teacher. She's the only one she can talk openly to about fucking Richie, trying drugs, avoiding Jerome, about anything. Stuff is rising up. Stuff she's been putting a lid on. The shame of doing so rubbish. The anti-climax of her results. Finally getting the guts to jump out of the plane only to be told there's no pilot, the engine's failed, it's too windy…

They sit under a canopy out the back of a pub a short walk from school. Mrs Salmon pours the last of the wine into Issy's glass, having herself drunk most of the bottle.

'You know Issy, my husband's a snob. He's a posh conservative. I know there's more Tories down South, but where I come from it's like Original Sin, you know, after what Thatcher did to us. I guess I thought because he's black, he'd be a leftie like me. Well frankly, that's not the case. He believes people get where they are in life on *merit* alone. That inheritance is justified. I'm rambling, what was the question again?'

'What should I do, you know, if I see Richie at the party?'

'Nothing. Hold your head up. Keep your cool. Give him nothing of you.'

'And what should I tell Jerome?'

'That's your choice. You were single when it happened. You're still single, and all I can say is be careful who you fall for. You can end up trapped on a path you didn't ask for, or want. We all make these judgments, these stereotypes, but more often than not, they just mask what's really there. There's no such thing as class really, Issy. It's all in the mind. There are good people who listen to their moral compass, and bad people who only care about what's good for them and their circle. The first lot keep the world from collapsing. The latter keep us remembering why we do it. Of course it all gets messy as most of us move between the two camps, depending on how many of these we've had.'

She plonks the bottle nose down into the ice bucket.

'If you want a prince, don't kiss a frog, a wise woman once told me that.'

Issy looks at her phone, Carol is waiting at the flat; the sandwiches are drying up, curling at the corners. Still she wants to stay with her teacher, sink another bottle of wine.

'You need to go?' Mrs Salmon asks, gulping too much wine in one go.

Issy nods. 'Miss, thank you so much. You've changed my life. You don't know how much.'

'You changed your life. You did it,' her teacher says, wiping the spilt wine from her chin.

'Nah, Miss, you have to take some of the credit.'

'Thank you, Issy. It's been such a pleasure, honestly. If I have a child even half as amazing as you, I'll be the happiest human alive.'

Outside the pub they hug, holding on tightly to each other. Then Issy watches her teacher stumbles up the road. Time to go and thank Mum.

Someone Issy doesn't recognise opens the door to Sophie's party. The weather is still unsettled with most people in the kitchen and conservatory. Sophie notices Issy's arrival and greets her with a vodka and tonic.

'I thought this day would never come,' Sophie smiles. 'Mum and Dad bankrolling my booze, legitimately!'

Sophie's parents shake hug Issy and welcome her back to the house. They are the nicest people as they mingle with the crowd.

'And this is my uncle and aunt,' she says, introducing Issy.

'Oh, great to finally meet you, Soph says so many nice things…'

Issy makes her way to Emily. Henry is nowhere to be seen, and neither is Richie, thankfully.

Issy pulls out the bottle of vodka she pinched from Carol's cleaning cupboard and hands it to Sophie.

'Thanks darl,' Sophie kisses Issy's cheek. 'And nice bag.'

'Thanks,' Issy replies, looking at the Monet Water Lillies tote bag Emily bought her from the National Gallery.

'So, all good? Resultswise?' Sophie asks.

'Got what I needed,' Issy says, sheepishly.

'Amazing!' Sophie cries.

'Fucking brilliant,' Helena says, giving Issy a high five.

Emily gives Issy a hug, but it's not her usual 'prolonged hug' as Helena calls them.

'Well done,' Hendrike says, and for once she looks like she means it.

Mixing with the crowd, most people are talking about how much of an anti-climax it is, after all the pressure and anticipation. The fact that everyone in the room is moaning that they have to pay triple the university fees, putting all of them in the same 'financially fucked over' boat as her. Suddenly she fits in fine, and is actually enjoying herself.

At some point in the evening, the parents go out for supper, letting Sophie know they booked a table for eight and might be home around one.

'That's code for get every fucker out this house by midnight,' Helena shouts to Sophie over the music.

'I've already asked Aunty Viv to have them sleep over.'

'Tenner says they come back at eleven?' Helen pulls out her purse.

Sophie laughs. She's as captivating as ever. Her hair has been curled like Marilyn and her red belt pulls in tightly at the waist, separating a white top with red polka dots and a hip-grabbing skirt.

Henry turns up with Richie around nine. Henry's already pretty drunk, Richie is off his head, Issy recognises those darting eyes. She looks at her drink and wonders if it's been spiked as the ecstasy feelings return.

Emily tries to greet Henry with a kiss, but he blanks her, moving through the kitchen to some boys Issy doesn't recognise: his hand shaking hands and hugs all round.

When Henry does decide to join the females, he boasts about his grades, and makes a big thing about getting into Durham. Though it seems most of this crowd are going to Oxbridge. Issy doesn't care; she's happy with Lincoln. When the conversation moves to wine, Henry slurs on Issy's ignorance. Emily says nothing in Issy's defence. Neither does anyone else.

Bored with them all apparently, Henry starts flirting with a girl in a long green dress and a headscarf. He ignores Emily trying to catch his eye, then pushes her out of the way when she attempts to go in for a proprietary peck on the cheek. Issy watches her friend leave the room and head upstairs.

Issy turns to George, 'Where's Emily gone? Two years ago she was this feisty artist, rebelling from all this bullshit. Now she accepts being a doormat? What does she see in him?'

George agrees, 'He's a bully. An exceedingly charming one, apparently.'

'But you're not scared of Henry are you? You tell him what for and he shuts up.'

George stands in his usual way, straight back with his shoulders relaxed.

'You know that saying, keep your friends close–'

Issy nods, 'and your enemies closer.'

'Precisely. Let's just say I am one of Henry's enemies.'

'Why?'

'I know things about Henry's family history that, perhaps, I shouldn't. But my father being the man that he is, equipped me with some choice information. He did so after much thought, so as to prevent me suffering the kinds of bullying that goes on at my school. My father also informed Henry's father of my knowledge, and one can only assume Charles Sparling passed this on to his son.'

Issy stares at George, 'Wow, must be serious.'

George clears his throat. 'Indeed, so let us leave this conversation for now, Issy. I hope you will treat this with discretion.'

'Your secret is safe with me,' Issy says.

'Not a secret, privacy,' George replies seriously. 'Secrets are things that should not be held by someone against someone else, whereas privacy is a right of all. Not every conversation between two people needs bleeding out to others,' he adds, looking over at Richie, and now Issy knows for sure (not that she didn't already) that he's told everyone he fucked a council estate dweller. 'Richard Saunders – man of the people.'

George places his hand on Issy's shoulder, 'My purpose in telling you, is to reassure you that Henry Sparling is no giant. None of us are. We are all mere bones and flesh on an egg timer to rot. It's what we do with our time whilst the sand falls that counts.' He smiles kindly, then picks up his jacket and starts saying his goodbyes.

Issy watches George leave the party. She wonders how it must be for someone like him. She has times like this where she feels out of place, but to feel it throughout school, with all your friends, all the time? Jerome comes into her thoughts (he's never far away). It was ignorant to say Jerningham Court is like a slave fort. And Sociology helped her think about riots differently. She owes Jerome a conversation.

Watching Henry with the girl in the green dress sickens her. Makes her ashamed of herself. Lust is an ugly thing. She decides to find Emily.

'Hey, babe,' Richie approaches Issy after coming out of the toilet. 'I wouldn't go in there if I were you. I've done a bad, bad thing.'

'Have you seen Emily?'

Richie shakes his head. 'Want one of these?' Richie asks, this time a rose-coloured pill with a line through it.

'No thanks.'

'Remember, I'm here when you change your mind. You're the prettiest girl here, you know.'

Issy looks at Richie biting his bottom lip and grinning. He believes his own shit. His pupils look like frogspawn about to hatch.

'I will Richie, don't you worry,' Issy says, watching him bumble down the stairs. 'I've got your jumper in my bag!' Issy calls down after him.

Richie doesn't turn to face her but puts a thumb up in the air.

She finds Emily sitting on Sophie's bed with her friends clustered around her. Emily looks like an orphan child found by the roadside. Helena has an arm across her shoulders and Sophie is sitting on the floor holding her hand. Issy stands at the door of the scene and feels unable to enter. Instead, she storms back down to the party and grabs Henry's arm, pulling him aside like a naughty schoolboy.

'Stop being a dickhead.'

'Excuse me?'

'Your girlfriend's up there crying because you've ignored her all night.'

The girl in the green dress excuses herself.

'Issy, I would suggest you take your attitude somewhere else.'

'That's funny, because you seem to be the one acting like a fuckwit.'

'That language again.'

'Your actions, again.'

'Look, I get you might be jealous, but–'

'Don't flatter yourself.'

'To be honest, you're right. You're not exactly a medal worth modelling.'

'What's that supposed to mean?'

'Work it out, you've got C Levels.' Henry crunches his beer can, chucks it in the sink and crashes out of the kitchen into the living room, then out of the living room and on up the stairs.

A few moments later, Emily and Henry are together in the hall: Emily crying and Henry looking fierce. The girls are on the stairs when Issy approaches. He grabs Emily's arm and pulls her outside to the front of the house. Worried for Emily's safety, Issy goes after them. In the streetlight, Issy sees Henry put his hand up to Emily as if to slap her.

'HENRY!' Issy yells, running at him. 'You hit her and I swear I'll kill you with my bare hands.'

Henry turns his raised hand to her. 'Fuck off.' He pushes her away and she stumbles to the ground. Emily tries to stop him and he snarls her away. 'Nobody wants her here.'

'Are you going to let him treat you like this? ' Issy shouts from the floor.

'Please don't shout,' Emily whispers. 'You're cause a scene.'

'I'm causing a scene!' Issy jumps to her feet. 'What about wife beater here?'

'Those are strong accusations,' Henry spits. 'Why don't you go back to the poverty pit where you belong?'

Issy grabs Emily's drink and throws it in his face. She watches the red wine leave the cup and is immediately disappointed with herself – he's right; she can't behave. She wants to go home. She runs back into the house to grab her bag.

'That little bitch is the epitome of everything wrong with this country.' Henry says, looking at the stains splatted across his baby pink shirt. 'I won't get into the club like this.'

Emily stares at him. Like she's seeing right through him. 'Be sure to let your dry cleaner know it's a Côte de Nuits and not a Côte d'Or, won't you?' And follows Isobel back into the party.

Issy enters the party with tears in her eyes. She searches for her bag under a pile of jackets and cardigans. She pulls out Richie's jumper, spying him with his hand on someone's thigh.

'Here's your jumper.'

Richie looks up, 'Oh, thanks babe. Amazing.'

'Watch out,' Issy tells the female, 'He drugs people. Then fucks them. Then treats them like shit.'

Richie smiles, his ecstasy-laden eyes darting back and forth, trying to catch the compliment.

CHAPTER 42
TRAGIC

Feeling bad about the night before, Emily decides to bring cupcakes to Issy. Walking up the concrete steps, she feels sad that things have come to this. Henry has made it clear there is no room for Isabella in his life. While Emily understands some of this, she's been here before with her parents, Once again, Issy is in the firing line for protecting her.

A subdued Issy invites her in. Emily places the cupcakes on the small kitchen table. After a briefing, it seems the two have very different opinions of what went on last night. 'Henry was drunk, he admits that, but the girl was a friend of his cousin and you embarrassed him in front of her,' Emily says. 'There was no flirting, I had got that wrong.'

'He hit you.'

'Henry didn't hit me,' Emily assures.

'I saw it, Mimi. He had his hand up. You were scared. One thing I never was, was scared of Jerome. You have to break up with him.'

'Don't be silly. I wasn't. I can't end it for something he hasn't done.'

'He grabbed your arm, remember? He pushed me.'

'He apologises for that. He was off balance, with alcohol.'

'Really?' Issy looks away to control her anger. 'You can't allow yourself to be submissive.'

'I won't.'

'He'll grind you down.'

'He won't!'

'Do you want to end up like your mum?'

Emily looks startled. 'She knows when to stick up for herself,' Emily snaps.

'Come on Mimi, you've seen the downers in her cupboards stuffed in vitamin bottles – you told me.'

'Please stop using things I've confided in you against me. Besides, your mother's no different and the way you acted last night should send a warning signal–'

'Me? What did I do? You're heading in the same direction. Do you think if you wear pearls and floral blouses and talk in polite words, nobody will notice the unhappiness?'

'How dare you. To think all I do is defend you.'

'Defend me from what? From their snobbery? Their judgments? People who avoid inheritance tax and vote in education cuts to girls like me who barely have a running chance while you lot–'

'You lot?'

'Yes, you lot, with a lot, loads in fact, too much. Every house I've ever been in, full of everything anyone could want and more, while people like Jerome's grandmother, invited to this country to work on a British passport, from a good Jamaican family, end up living their lives on council estates where the soil is so shit the roses can't bloom.'

'So this is how you really feel about me? The whole time, seeing everything with hate. Issy Richards, consider our friendship over.'

'No Emily, it was over the moment you chose to have a violent chauvinistic bigot *racist* boyfriend over your friend.'

'Big words, Issy. Without me, you wouldn't even know what they mean.'

'Get out!'

'Issy,' Emily steps back, immediately feeling awful for saying such a thing. That was a wrong move.

Issy hands back the plate of cupcakes. 'Enjoy living life with your rose-coloured glasses.'

Issy opens the door. Emily steps out.

'I hope you're not wearing them when Henry smashes your face in!' Issy calls down the corridor after her.

Emily stops for a moment, shudders, before marching the cupcakes home.

People like us can't be friends, Issy thinks, watching the dog walkers in Telegraph Hill Park. We're different. More different than skin colour. More different than religion. We're so, so different. From day one, set apart. Money. Manners. Life chances. Debt. Living space. Travel. Jobs. Holidays. Clothes. Food...

All the same, she can't help but be affected by Emily's words. She knows her mum drinks too much, drinking herself lonely. There's a humming pressure inside Issy's head, worrying what will happen when she goes to study in Lincoln. Karen's no help; she's Carol's drinking buddy.

Sitting on the grassy bank she looks over London's skyline. Seven million people out there. The amount of chaos in her teenage life, in the few streets surrounding her; how is there not constant riots around her?

Issy looks up at the thin wisps of cloud. The aeroplanes look like boats, making white waves, slicing through the sea. There's one person who she owes an apology to. The one person she knows always cared for her.

'Thanks for coming,' she says.

'You alright?' Jerome asks, sitting down by her side.

She shrugs. 'How's things? How's your nan?'

'You wanna know?'

'Yeah.'

'Dwayne's in custody.'

Issy nods, not surprised that day has come.

'Police found the gun,' Jerome says. He omits where.

'I'm sorry.'

'No chance he'll be let off. Lawyer's done told Gran it's gonna be hard to defend him. Possession of an illegal weapon. If he didn't pull the trigger at the car, if he didn't shoot it from the flat – meaning he had the gun, he didn't find it somewhere, tings might be different. Then they found all this shit when they raided his car. Weed, coke, cash. Five years. Maybe more.'

'And you?'

'Gonna find it tough finding a job, after the Youth Service's investigation. Even after all the mess, Steve's been backing it for me, arguing: How can anyone expect the world to change if we don't engage with young people like Jerome and give them more than one chance?'

People like Jereome. Jerome swallows the acidic taste in his mouth. He watches a train snake through the tower blocks. Three years ago, things were easy, uncomplicated. Now the two of them sit here, riddled with life.

A flock of geese fly over in a V-shape. They honk like antique cars before landing in the lower park, by the pond.

'When you off?'

'End of September. But might be going Scotland first to see family.'

Jerome nods his head. He can't look at her but he wants to. Instead he fixes his eyes on the red, white and blue cranes building new tower blocks in the distance. 'I just wanna say I love you. I know we can't go back to how things were and shit. I know you gotta love someone, set them free, I know all that. I know you're not coming back. I know I'm not going there.'

'Stop, Jerome,' Issy's eyes fill with tears. She wants to tell him she fucked someone else, just to stain her in his eyes, stop him thinking all the time that he's not good enough but she can't bear breaking his heart further. He won't take it the way she means it.

Jerome wipes his face, 'You got man crying in public.'

Then he smiles that smile. That smile that should have taken him away.

To better places.

FINAL CHAPTER
OUT OF MANY, ONE

Issy looks out her window. It feels like life is playing out in slow motion, like it's not real, like she's stepped into a film or storybook. Tomorrow she leaves for university. Hayley's asked her to visit, say her goodbyes. Issy catches the bus to Hayley's flat. She walks down the corridor, the wallpaper peeled off from one corner of the communal hall. Hayley opens the door. She looks terrible.

'I found the gun. Loaded. And where did the cunt hide it?' Hayley shouts.

'Where?' Issy asks, realising there is to be no hello or welcome hug. 'Don't tell me Mabel's room.'

'Jack's room. Under his cot.'

'No,' Issy gasps, walking on into the flat, there is to be no 'come in' either. Who needs formalities, anyway?

'His own fucking baby. Anything could have happened now Jack's moving about. I could have set it off with the hoover. That's how I found it. Never shit myself so much in all my life.'

'So what did you do?'

'I called the police and told them to get it out of here. And that he won't see his son. Ever.'

They sit at the table. Issy takes a custard cream and pours herself a tea to dunk it into but the milk's off.

'I don't wanna tell you this, but since you're going anyway… Jerome told him to… It was his idea.'

The biscuit stops mid-air to her mouth. Issy puts it down, feeling sick. Calling Jerome, she puts him on speaker phone. 'It's not like that, get me...' he stutters. 'I meant it as a joke... He wanted me to–'

Issy hangs up on him.

'Joint enterprise,' Hayley says. 'Joint enterprise.'

Issy takes the bus home feeling like absolutely everything in her life is now dirty, poisoned, corrupted. When she arrives at the flat, she starts sorting through her stuff. She goes to her windowsill where she keeps a row of photographs – one of her and Emily, one of her and Jerome... She chucked the one of Graff after the riots. She picks up the one of Hayley and Mabel Clarke – the last good person in the world – holding baby Jack at his christening; Carol is in the background, sat down with her drink, smiling up.

The phone rings. It's Jerome's number again. She ignores it. It's not until late evening that Issy decides to listen to the voicemail. Mabel's soft Jamaican accent sings in her ear: 'Issy, I hear yuh gone soon; come say goodbye.'

She leaves tomorrow afternoon. The last person she wants to see is Jerome, but the first person she wants to hug and say goodbye to is Mabel.

The next morning, Issy showers early and has a cup of tea. She knows Mabel will be up and hopes Jerome will still be in bed.

When she gets to the front door, she can see the old lady in the kitchen, cooking porridge. Issy gently taps the window so as not to frighten her. Mabel still jumps. She's aged a lot since the attack and she's not so fast on her feet opening the door. Issy feels worst about leaving Mabel than all the others. As if somehow, Issy wanting more is a rejection of her adopted nanna and everything she stands for.

'It's a big, big day.' Mabel gives Issy a glorious smile. 'Why yuh nah look happy?'

'I feel sad to leave. I didn't think I would, but now... I don't know... I don't know why I'm not happy.'

'Let me tell yuh, leaving Daddy for England, I cried like you can't believe. But I had a husband and future to think 'bout. Once that ship pass the docks and the thought gone I can still jump off, mi tears dem dry up. You still in the ending. Yuh nah yet pass di docks.'

'Are you gonna be okay?'

'Mi? Yeah man. Always.'

Issy thinks about Dwayne being in prison and Jerome grieving and heartbroken. She looks down at the mug of hot chocolate Mabel puts on the table in front of her. Always the same cup, sand coloured with a sketch of a palm tree, the beach, an orange sun and the word, Jamaica. She can't stop her tears and Mabel lets Issy cry it out.

'I know, I know.' Mabel pats Issy's back. A tear of her own appears but she catches it.

'You're like my family.'

Issy stands up and wraps her arms around Mabel, holding on tighter than she should. But that little woman is tough. She squeezes right back with a grip strong.

'You go. Go become a brilliant woman. Shine like the stars. Make the Lawd God proud.'

It's time to leave. Mabel opens the front door for Issy. She holds on to Issy's hands as this may be the last time they speak face-to-face. Issy bends down to receive a kiss from the legendary Mabel Clarke, who pulls a small envelope out from her cooking apron, 'Open it when yuh reach.'

Karen and her mum are waiting by Karen's car. Issy finally gets into the back seat after a series of panics about forgetting stuff and needing a wee. She puts on the seatbelt with that feeling she's still missing something.

Emotions come thick as they pull slowly out of the estate, down Jerningham Road, past New Cross Gate station, past Goldsmiths College, through Deptford and over Blackheath where they join the A2 out of London. It's over now, she thinks. She doesn't have to come back.

Her tears dry once they hit the motorway. The ending bleeds into a fresh start. Karen puts on the stereo and demands everyone stop looking so sad and celebrate this day as a joyous occasion.

'And we can't do it without the help of the best West End musical hits 2013!' she shrieks, putting on her playlist.

Driving into Lincoln, Issy fills with excitement and happiness. She winds down her window. The air smells good. The scenery, beautiful. The town is like something out of a children's bedtime story, with cobbled stones and old Tudor pubs.

They pull up outside the halls of residence, to find a bunch of older students waiting to welcome families to the university. A particularly pleasing looking young man shows them to her room.

'Smaller than your room at home,' Carol says, looking around. 'And you still got a single bed, that's a shame,' There's a chair at the foot of the bed and a small window opposite. Issy looks at her mum holding the curtains her father picked for her as a child. 'You only need one. Maybe I can make a cushion with the other?'

Issy smiles. 'Okay.' Everything is more than okay! She gets to live in an apartment with a brand new kitchen and bathroom.

'Fully fitted kitchen, laundry facilities, 24-hour on-campus security, free internet, bicycle storage, if you got one,' he says.

Carol has also noticed his shiny hair and sparkling white teeth. 'Are you sure you're not a wee model hired to make this place look good?'

'Mum!' Issy cringes but the student showing her around is absolutely gorgeous.

He laughs, a little embarrassed then looks at Issy blushing.

'There's some good nightlife too,' he says, making eye contact with Issy. 'We'll be out on Friday, if you fancy joining.'

Once all the boxes are unpacked, or stored away, Karen treats the two ladies to pizza at a local restaurant. There's a sign in the pub opposite that says 'Karaoke every Thursday 'til 3am.'

'Shame it's not today, you'd've had us here all night!' Karen says tearing off a piece of cheesy garlic bread.

'I'm gonna save for your driving lessons, and I can send you bus tickets so you can come home on weekends,' Carol insists. 'Probably not this weekend but one after?'

Issy looks down at her pizza, 'I'm not sure. Probably Christmas break.'

Carol swallows her disappointment, she is determined not to make a scene and ruin Issy's special day. 'Well you know you've always got a bed,' she continues, bravely. 'Come home whenever you like.'

Carol isn't the only parent with that look of pending loss. Around them in the restaurant sit other such families, mums and dads sending dearly loved children off to start their journey of independence. No more looking out for them, calling to see if they need a lift home. Peeking in their rooms at two in the morning, after needing a pee, not being able to get back to sleep wondering where they are, if they're safe or drunk and throwing up somewhere. No more getting upset when they haven't cleaned their room. When they miss lunch with the grandparents. When they come home and eat the whole punnet of strawberries. When they take out parts of the newspaper, never to be seen again. When dishes are found with congealed food under their beds, even in wardrobes. When the new box of wine is almost empty…and yet somehow, a part of them feels cheated; it's gone too fast. The ache of missing their children, the wish to return them to babies, just for a moment, so they can cuddle and kiss them and melt to the sound of giggles and that distinct fragrance of pure new life.

The small hand on the restaurant clock clicks across the picture of gondolas chiming to ten. Karen and Carol need to drive back to Telegraph Hill. Work in the morning. Soap operas tomorrow evening with a pot of tea and cigarettes. The sofa opposite Carol's armchair will be empty of an Issy Richards - wrapped up in her fluffy dressing gown and matching pink slippers.

'I'm so proud,' Carol says, through her tears (she was never going to hold them back all day). 'I wish, I wish your father could be here to see this, to kiss you. First ever Richards to go university.'

'I haven't passed yet,' Issy manages to say in reply.

'You will, you will, no doubt about it.' Carol holds on to her daughter.

'I'm gonna need to breathe, Mum,' Issy says eventually, gently pulling herself free.

Karen wells up. Not one for public emotion, she fetches the car to give them some space.

Carol strokes her child's cheek, 'I'm gonna miss you so much, Issy. You've been the best daughter.'

'Mum, don't,' Issy laughs. 'I've been a moody shit.'

'No, I mean it. It's you that's kept me going. I know I have to let you grow up...' Carol's voice trails off.

'You're gonna be fine, Mum,' Issy insists, the reality sinking in that her mum is now properly alone, her dad first, and now her. 'Promise, you'll be okay? You won't drink too much, will you?'

'I'll be fine.' Carol wipes her smudged mascara, composes herself.

Karen pulls up beside them and beeps the horn.

'Bye Issy, love,' Karen calls from the wound-down window. 'Show 'em what you're made of!'

Issy gives her mum one last hug and then helps her into the passenger seat.

'Thanks so much for bringing me.'

Tears stream down Carol's face. Her hands start to shake as she waves out of the window, thankful for Karen, because who can drive away from their only child?

Issy stares after the car until it turns the last corner in view. She doesn't move. She can't, knowing the moment she walks away, that's it. Inside feels like a looping fairground ride. Nothing settles. She takes a deep breath. This is happening. Her ship has docked. She's in Lincoln.

It's a fifteen-minute walk back to the campus. Issy sits on a bench by the canal watching other students slowly getting rid of their own parents. The light from the rooms reflects on the water. Tomorrow, she starts a new life. A new her. She can be anyone she wants to be.

She takes out her new door key and admires it. Where will the next three years take her? Who will she meet? What are her housemates like? What new things will she learn? Will she like it? The people, the place, the subject? It's as exciting as it is terrifying.

Putting the key into her bag, she feels the envelope Mabel gave her that morning. She takes it out and looks at it for a while, as if opening it does something further to the journey, closing the door on her old life that little bit more. She outlines the envelope with her little finger. The pain surfaces, threatening to pierce this new hope and excitement.

Issy gently opens the envelope. Inside is a note in the squiggly neat handwriting Mabel was taught back in Jamaicia along with a book voucher for fifteen pounds. She reads the note in the half light from the street lamp then stares out across the water, thinking about the water that old lady had crossed all those years ago.

You can shackle a Man and force Him your Will, but unless he is a slave in his Mind, then a slave He is not.

ABOUT THE AUTHOR

Melissa Jane Knight is originally from Plumstead, London. Born in 1982 to an East End father who she doesn't know, and a Maltese mother who raised Melissa and her siblings as a single parent, mostly on benefits.

Growing up, Melissa campaigned to stop school expulsions, would write to young offenders and perform as an MC to drum and base and two-step.

At 14, Melissa was elected as one of the first ever Greenwich Young People's Councillors where her youth workers "changed the course of my life forever". Passionate about community, Melissa won several awards for her inclusion work including Greenwich Woman of the Year Runner Up.

At university, Melissa graduated top of the class with a BA in sociology & politics from Goldsmiths, and holds an MSc in social policy & planning from the London School of Economics and Political Science (LSE).

Melissa now lives in Berlin with her husband and their two children where – between writing novels – she practices Traditional Chinese Medicine.

Printed in Great Britain
by Amazon

24552437R00189